Cornflowers
by the Roadside
by Dorothy Sherman

Third Printing: September, 2010.

1 2 3 4 5 6 7 8 9 10 11 12 * 16 15 14 13 12 11 10 9

Published in Freeport, Illinois, by Sumatran Press

Sumatran Press is a division of ShermanArt, Inc.

Sumatran Press book titles may be purchased in bulk for educational, business, fund-raising, or sales promotional use. For information, please email SpecialMarket@SumatranPress

Original Page design by James Mateika

Reformatted for Createspace by Eric Van Brocklin

Sherman, Dorothy

Cornflowers by the Roadside / Dorothy Sherman

ISBN-978-1-45633-708-7

Library of Congress Control Number: 2010933866

Printed in the United States of America

For Merritt;

Who knew I was a writer and married me anyway.

Dorothy Sherman

PART ONE

Chapter 1

The cat was heavy and insisted upon struggling. My parents had said that we were not going to take Meetzer with us but I had refused to listen. He was family; how could they say, just like that, that he must stay behind? It had taken me quite awhile to get up enough nerve to enter the woods to fetch him home.

You never knew what might be in those woods- hobos, maybe, taking shelter from the unseasonably hot early June sun; possibly bears. None of us had ever seen a bear around there nor even heard one but somebody must have or else why would they put out such a warning? "Once," it was whispered, "some gypsies had camped in the field just beyond the woods and everyone knew *they* stole little children." The trees were tall but with thick underbrush that could hide just about anything. Taking a deep breath, I had set my right foot onto the narrow path and with determination and crossed fingers taken the initial footsteps into the dank leafy darkness, gritting my teeth and continuing on calling, "Here, kitty, kitty, here Meetzer."

I had found him crouching under a tree, ready to spring on a small gopher. Angry that I had grabbed him up, he shut his eyes until they were mere slits in his head and held his ears back so he would not have to listen to me instructing him that he would be left- behind if we did not hurry. His twisting and squirming to be free, made my self-imposed task all the harder. I hardly had the breath to gasp out my words of assurance: "It's only… a little way now…kitty…you have to come … with us. We're… moving far away and… you won't know…where we are. Be nice…I'm not hurting you!" He was not about to listen to reason; the entire while he was hissing and his tail was beating against my legs as regular as my oldest sister, Vi's, metronome when she practiced her piano lessons. I had to squeeze him in the middle to keep hold of him. Full-grown and not very friendly, a tawny and white striped feline, he was a loner who had attached himself to our premises but barely tolerated our attention.

As I determinedly made our way back along the winding path through those scary trees, he let himself grow longer and longer until, by the time I saw my father's tin shop and our red brick house beyond it, his hind feet were touching my shoes.

Passing the tin shop's open doorway, I glanced inside at its unfamiliar emptiness then continued up the driveway leading to the house. My mother came down the steps of the side porch. Her green eyes,.usually large and friendly, were squinting and her hands were on her hips, too, which did not make me want to come any closer.

"So there you are, Jessie. We've been calling you. And put that cat down; we told you this morning that he's not coming with us."
My hold on Meetzer tightened more than ever.
"That cat stays here! Put him down, I said. This minute!"
"But Mama…"

"Down, Jessie." Her finger was pointing in that direction.
Tears rolled down my cheeks and fell onto Meetzer's fur and I added quite a few sniffles for good measure. No use. There was nothing for me to do but obey. Reluctantly, I watched as Meetzer scampered off in the direction of the cars and trucks lined up in the driveway in readiness for out imminent departure to the new house.

Mama's kiss on my straight blond hair did nothing to make me feel better but I did as she said and accompanied her into the house to eat something before we left.

There was quite a crowd of people in the kitchen. The last of the furniture had been loaded onto the large stake bed truck waiting first in line in the driveway, so some were standing while others sat on up-ended wooden soda pop or beer cases. Carefully washing my hands at the sink and drying them on my dress, since the towel was missing from its usual place, I leaned against the wall and observed, something I enjoyed doing.

My two uncles, Bill and Max, were making sandwiches and doling them out, joking, and stirring up laughter, as was usual when they got together. Uncle Max held a long roll of summer sausage against his chest, cut slices from it with his penknife and handed them to Uncle Bill, who placed them onto the rye bread slices lined up along his bent upper legs, from stomach to knee. Hands reached out to accept the open-faced sandwiches which were being washed down with swallows of soda pop or beer drunk straight from the bottles.

"Somebody packed the mustard and butter, but I guess we're all hungry enough to enjoy these anyway," Uncle Bill declared.

"Just keep them coming," somebody else advised.

Moving over to accept one for myself, I let Mrs. Malenka, our already-no-longer-housekeeper, as of yesterday; open my bottle of cream soda. Like all the others: my father's fore man, Otto; three of his work crew: Charley, Walter, and Gus; and the apprentice, Gilly, she had volunteered her services today, since my father was unable to get his money out of the bank to pay anybody.

This bright sunny room, with its many cupboards; the back stairs leading to our bedrooms; the swinging door to the dining room; the gray and white tall-legged gas stove with its four burners and oven from which so many wonderful meals had been delivered to our table; the walk-in pantry lined on both sides with shelves holding the accumulation of pots and pans; the white porcelain sink; the side hall with the stairway leading down to the basement and out to the porch: all had been her domain.

It had always been fun to sit at the center table and watch her roll out pie and cookie dough or help her wrap bacon around chucks of meat topped with slices of onion, all held together with toothpicks, these to become what she called "Roll-em-ups" that she served with buttered cabbage and boiled potatoes. Now, everything moveable had been removed, including her rocking chair, with its thick flowered cretonne pad, in which she would rest her feet and read a bit.

I could read the sadness in her hazel eyes and understood why she gave me an extra pat on the head as I left her to scrunch down against a wall to eat my sandwich.

It sure would not be the same without the rounded sections of Mrs. Malenka in her brightly flowered housedresses and flour sack aprons coming into view as she went about her duties. She wore shoes as big as Daddy's. When I was little, I used to sit under the table and watch them as they moved from here to there and back.

Once she had accidentally stepped on my fingers and I was immediately scooped up and rushed to the sink where cold water was run over them until they stopped hurting. To help matters more, I received a ginger snap fresh from the oven. Nobody could make ginger snaps as good as hers. She was family, as far as I was concerned, and I sure wished she did not have to leave. I wished none of us had to.

The large sheet of galvanized tin, I noted, where the long narrow black cast iron coal range had stood, was still bolted to the floor. On winter days when the hot air registers could not keep up with the bitter cold of the north wind, that stove would be filled with coal from a metal bucket and lighted. I loved to hear the hissing of the teakettle when the water inside came to a boil and its spout emitted steam. It was my ambition to someday insert the lifter into the slot in one of the two stove lids and lift them up, like Mama or Mrs. Malenka did, to check the burning coals to see if they needed replenishing. Those lids were sometimes so hot they glowed red. We kids knew better than to touch them.

My eyes moved to the drilled hole in the floor where the wooden icebox had stood. My father had inserted a tube of tin to carry the melted ice water down to the basement and into the floor drain so nobody would have to keep emptying pans, as most people did, whenever they threatened to overflow. Now, he or somebody had covered the hole with a round piece of tin. I tried to lift it to look down through the hole but it was wedged in too tightly. Instead, I sat there, chewing, sipping soda pop, and wondering if the kitchen in the new place would be as warm and friendly.
My father's bank had locked its doors after the Stock Market Crash and nobody

could get at their money. I really did not understand all that stuff. What was a stock market and how did one crash? In addition, why didn't somebody have extra keys for the banks? Mama, Daddy, and even Mrs. Malenka had keys for our house. Then, there was that word that was only whispered… "Bankruptcy!"

My questions were always answered with, "Never you mind now." I hated that! Maybe I was only seven but I had a brain, didn't I? Why did everyone always feel that kids were too stupid to talk to? There was so much to learn; so much catching up to do. You came into the world somewhere in the middle of it all, like not ever having met George Washington or Abraham Lincoln or not yet existing during the World War. You needed answers.

My attention fastened on Gilly, who had one haunch resting on the windowsill. He would never have done that when the nice, snowy white curtains hung there, with Meetzer sunning himself in his usual place outside on the sill, between the window and box of geraniums.

He kept looking out across the yard to the tin shop where he and Mrs. Malenka had rooms on the second floor that they reached by a railed wooden stairway attached to the outside of the building. Those rooms were cozy in winter because my father had installed a furnace in the shop, with asbestos-bound pipes sending heat upstairs, and cool in the summer because of the huge fan that drew the hot air out through vents in the roof. Now they could no longer live there.

I could tell it made Gilly sad. He had been so proud to have his own quarters and now he was going to have to move in with Otto and Otto's family. My father had taken on Gilly straight from the Catholic orphanage when Gilly wrote to him seeking employment. I guess they did not let orphans stay there once they reached eighteen. We helped him celebrate his twentieth birthday back in March. In a way, he was family, too.

Mostly, I liked Gilly. He could be really funny and he had nice curly black hair and long, thick eyelashes. Sometimes, though, I was afraid of him, he being Black Irish and having a real temper. Just the week before he had taken my little sister, Laura, and me over his knee and spanked us when he caught us pouring muriatic acid over our mud pies; acid that we had filched from the tin shop. His dark blue eyes had appeared to be sparking, he was so mad at us, and he had used Irish words on us that my mother would have washed right out of his mouth with Lifebuoy soap if she had heard. He never told on us, though, which we appreciated, because we would have received another spanking from our mother. How were we to know that muriatic acid could have done terrible things to our eyes and skin? Kids do not know everything, do they?

My sandwich eaten, I pushed through the swinging door leading to the dining room and followed family voices that led me through room after room devoid of familiar furniture and rugs until I reached the front porch. There, my older sisters, Vi and Maggie, and little Laura were sitting on the front steps.

Mama, leaning against the porch rail, was reminding Daddy of things he should do at the last minute, like checking out the basement and the tin shop. He had a habit of forgetting things, such as tools. Mama was forever sending Gilly, Charley, or one of the other men to fetch tools he had left behind on "one of the jobs." In between running a sheet metal and furnace business, my father invented things, so his mind was overly busy, I suppose.

Studying him for a bit, I wondered again why our Grandmother and Mama's sisters, my aunts, Rose, Arlene, and Mimsy, considered him not as good as Uncle Max and Uncle Bill. Well, maybe not Mimsy, since she hardly ever spoke her mind, probably because she was the youngest and not yet married, though she was " engaged."

I had once heard them remark that it was a pity that our mother had married Daddy. He was just as good looking as the uncles, with his thick grayish blond hair and heavy eyebrows that arbored kind blue eyes crinkled at the corners, and he had nice strong teeth and his ears weren't huge with hairs in them, like Otto's. His nose was rather big, but nice and straight, and it fit into his face just right. I liked the way he looked and how he treated Mama and us. To me, he was in every way just the kind of father to have, so why didn't they like him?

Quite often, I overheard conversations not meant for my tender young ears. When you live in a house with two parents, three sisters, and a housekeeper and share a bedroom with your kid sister, there isn't much privacy available. I found mine behind my father's black leather Morris chair or under the dining room table, except when Meetzer got inside the house and disdainfully messed the carpet there and made both Mama and Mrs. Malenka angry enough to chase him out with a broom. Twice Mama had to go to the Espanhain's and select another dining room rug to replace the one Daddy had to throw away because of "that darned cat."

To either of those privacy places I would take my favorite books and read. Sometimes I was so absorbed that I did not hear grownups enter the room until it was too late and then I would be very quiet, to escape notice, because most times their conversations interested me.

Should I be discovered, I was sent from the room with a scolding but if it were by any of Mama's sisters, I had to apologize and go to my room to "think about how naughty I was to eavesdrop."
My aunts would throw up their hands and complain: "Why is that one so different? Why can't she be more like Laura?" and scrutinize me from their tall heights.

'That one' was "too thin" or "too pale." She made people nervous with her fall-to-summer asthma cough and was nowhere near as cute as Laura, who had nice rosy cheeks and got tan from the sun instead of freckled. "That one's" eyes were blue, with short lashes, while Laura's had fringes of long dark lashes that rested on her cheeks when she closed her large green eyes, like our mother's. Clara Bow eyes, my aunts called them and, like that silent screen star, Laura used them to get her own way. Usually she succeeded. She still had her nice, evenly spaced baby teeth. I, on the other hand, was losing mine and the new ones coming in promised to be far too large for my thin face. My one redeeming feature was my nose, which gave me what Mama called "a sweet profile." Laura took after the Hohenfeldt's side, Hohenfeldt being Mama's maiden name. I supposed, then, that I must have more Renz in me. Maybe I should have despised Laura for being so much more acceptable to our aunts but I didn't. We were, in fact, the best of friends.

Daddy, as usual, was nodding his head at Mama's reminders and saying, "Ja, Lydia, ja, ja, I'll do it right now," as he and Mama left the porch and re-entered the house.

Spying me, Laura came to where I was standing and studied my face." What's the matter? How come you been crying?"

This made more tears form. "It's Meetzer. Mama says we can't take him with to the rooming house."

"Why not?"

"I don't know. Wish we could; he's our kitty. I went into the woods, and carried him all the way back here and then Mama made me let him go. He's under one of those cars in the driveway. Least he was."

"Shh. Let's go find him," she suggested.

"Why? We can't take him along."

"Well, we can at least tell him good-bye, can't we?"

The two of us slipped over the porch rail and away to the gravel driveway to peer under the various vehicles. Locating Meetzer under Daddy's old model T truck, we crawled in after him. Cheshire smile on his broad rust and white face, he waited until we almost had him and then backed away from us and took off. Out from under, we clambered up onto the running board of the truck to see if we could spot him but he seemed to have disappeared into thin air.

"Come back here, you darn old cat," I cried out to him, tired of his willfulness.

"Hey, you kids, get away from that truck! You want me to skin your hides?"

It was Gilly, holding up one end of the large, filled-to-capacity humpback steamer trunk with the picture of a pretty lady painted inside the lid, that Daddy used for a tool chest. , His legs, bowed from rickets, were even more bent. The words came out funny and his face was red from effort. That trunk was heavy. Gus was holding up the other end and his face was red, too.

We jumped down to watch as they set the thing down to wipe their brows with bandanna handkerchiefs they kept in their overall pockets for such use. Then, nodding to each other, they bent their knees and together they lifted the trunk up onto the truck bed and set it in place.
Fastening the tailgate, Gilly ordered, "Now you two go back in the house with your Ma, hear me? We don't need people getting hurt at the last minute. Now SCAT!"

We took off, and I knew that wherever Meetzer was, he was keeping out of sight, too. Gilly's voice carried.

Chapter 2

Not too long after, all of us poured out of the house and into our assigned vehicles, while Mama and Mrs. Malenka locked up the house and placed the key on the lintel above the side door, for the bank people.

Situated in North Milwaukee, on a frontage road running parallel to Green Bay Road, it was a nice, large, comfortable house; that red brick one, the only home Laura and I had ever known, with a big, big yard behind. The driveway ended at the side door of the tin shop, which is where out father went to look around for the last time and grimly lock up.

Charley and Walter climbed into the cab of the furniture truck, which belonged to Uncle Max, with Gus seated in an armchair in the back. This was the third load for them, the one with Mama's Steinway baby grand and the living room things. They led the parade out of the driveway: we four girls riding with Uncle Bill in his shiny black Packard with the metal covered tire set into the running board, like the one Daddy had to give up, followed by Mama and Uncle Max in our newly acquired second hand brown Essex. Behind them were Otto and Mrs. Malenka in Otto's Model-A Ford. Otto was going to take Mrs. Malenka to her sister's, where she would now be staying.

As soon as Gilly cranked enough to get it started, he and my father would be bringing the washing machine and tubs, the tool chest and whatever else did not fit onto the stake bed, in the old Model T that had once been my father's only truck, when he first started his business. The other two trucks that could carry big loads of furnace parts; pipes, gutters, elbows, register grids, and whatever else made up the heating system in a house, had been taken over by the bank, though not the one that had closed its doors with my father's money inside.

Turning left off the frontage road, at Kusick's Korner Grocery; we entered

Lawn Avenue and made a right onto Green Bay. Here Otto left us and turned north while the rest of us went south to Milwaukee proper. Both Vi and Maggie tearfully waved good-bye to our house for as long as it was in sight, which made Laura and me do the same. Uncle Bill's comforting words did not help much. We were too sad to listen to them. I had been kneeling on the rear seat, keeping my eyes on and waving to Uncle Max and my mother in the Essex. Later, when I thought about it, I realized that not once after we left the driveway, did Mama look back; it was not her way. She was white in the face and her lips were set tight, but she was being brave.

The night before, at the supper table, she had told us, "I know how much this is hurting all of us, but we have to move forward, each and every one of us, because that's how things are, now. Look at it as the beginning of a *NEW ADVENTURE*. Daddy and I have never ever run a rooming house before. It's wonderful that Mr. Rhineholt offered us the lease on it for the next year or so. He owed Daddy a great deal of money and his bank closed its doors, too, so this was his way of getting his dept paid. Mrs. Rhineholt had a nervous breakdown over everything and is too sick to manage the place right now so they're having to move in with some relatives. So… if you look at this in the right light, why, he's less fortunate than we are, wouldn't you agree?"

I decided to be brave, like her, and dried my eyes. It took several wipes with my sleeve, because once I start to cry it's hard to stop. Laura curled up against me. Only just turned six, she still sucked her thumb when she was upset. Usually, I would remind her to stop but I let her keep on sucking it this time. We were sisters and we had to stick together, like Mama always told us, and then we would never be lonely and would always have someone to talk to and share things with. That thought was comforting. However our *"new adventure"* turned out, at least she and I would be in it together. All of us would.

Green Bay Road turned into Green Bay Avenue and that became Third Street. Now we were driving through city traffic and having to stop while streetcars let off or took on passengers.

Eventually we reached Kilbourn, where Uncle Bill turned west to Fifteenth. A few blocks south on Fifteenth and we were at Wisconsin Avenue.

I always checked the sun to see in which direction I was heading. It's a good thing to know where you are. You started from the sun coming up over Lake Michigan, where was the east, even though you were too far away to see the water. East was east; that never changed. Gilly had explained that to me. You could also use the moon, which also rose in the east but we were not allowed out much at night, so that information did not help too much.

"Well, here we are," Uncle Bill exclaimed.
To our left was a magnificent castle-like lannon stone edifice that he said was the headquarters of the Knights of Columbus and, to our right, a White Tower hamburger place with a miniature golf course behind. Directly across Wisconsin Avenue, on the right, set far back from the street, with a black wrought iron fence all around it, stood a Victorian mansion complete with *porte-cochere to pr*otect alighting passengers.

"Is that it?" Maggie asked, hopefully.

"No, that's Marquette University's Conservatory of Music," Uncle Bill said and pointed to the grayish stucco building on the remaining corner that reached halfway down the block and had three identical small porches painted a darker gray. "That one's yours."

Our new home. It, too, had once been a mansion, the home of the Bellford family, he explained, but it had been divided into three sections, each one a separate rooming house. Ours was the corner one, facing Wisconsin Avenue, with Fifteenth running along the side. Right then and there, we decided to refer to it not as "the rooming house" but as "the mansion."

Crossing Wisconsin Avenue, Uncle Bill parked on the Conservatory side, leaving room for the Essex to pull up behind. Mama gave each of us a hug and together we stood in a little group while she looked back along Fifteenth and up and down Wisconsin Avenue to see if my father's truck was anywhere in sight. It was not.

"Oh, dear," she worried aloud to our uncles, "I hope he hasn't broken down somewhere. That truck is so old and the things on it are heavy."

I saw my uncles wink to each other as one of them remarked, "Probably he took a shortcut, Lydia. You know Paul."

She smiled. "Yes I do." My father's shortcuts sometimes took us several miles out of our way. "Well, shall we go home, girls?"
Together we crossed the street and turned the corner onto Wisconsin Avenue. The stake bed truck was parked in front of our section. A policeman, on foot, was watching as Gus, Charley, and Walter dropped the tailgate, put the boards into place and began to hand furniture down and set it onto the sidewalk.

We were just about to mount the steps of our porch when we heard the wail of a siren in the direction of Sixteenth Street.

"Lord in Heaven!" Charley cried out from his vantage point on the truck. We all followed his gaze and Mama's eyes got wide with surprise and worry. There was my father's truck, careening all over Wisconsin Avenue, pursued by a police car with a mounted-policeman cantering behind that!

With screeching brakes and tooting horn, the Model T rounded the corner on to Fifteenth, barely missing both the Packard and the Essex. Making a turn into the driveway behind the rooming house, it came to a jolting halt.

A parade of us: the foot patrolman, Mama, Charley, Walter, and Gus, Vi, Maggie, the two uncles, Laura and I rounded the corner in time to view this. There were others who poured out of the houses lining our side of Fifteenth and pedestrians and other motorists, all hurrying to observe this unusual event.

By this time, the police car had roared to a stop and the officer ran up to the truck and ordered, "Out of this vehicle, mister!"

The policeman astride the horse had clop-clopped to assist him. When my father and Gilly cautiously opened their doors and exited the Model T, each was wearing strange headgear.

Because most of those in the crowd were taller and blocked our view, Laura and I did not get to see what happened next but we heard about it afterwards from just about everybody who was there, all of them laughing and recounting that scene over and over again. Years later, they were still telling about it.

On top of our father's head was a hissing Meetzer, claws dug firmly into his scalp, tail waving back and forth in front of his squinting eyes that had blood running down into them from several places. Spitting out cat hairs, Daddy was letting out a stream of words in both German and English, ending with the plea, "Somebody get this *gol-danged* animal off of me!"

Several people, including the two policemen not on horseback, reached out but were hissed at and scratched for their trouble. Meetzer could be mean when he was in a bad mood.

Gilly, meanwhile, was trying to extricate himself from what had once been a beautiful lampshade; Mama's favorite. Unable to fit it into the stuff on the back seat of Essex, she had entrusted it to Gilly at the last minute with instructions to "Take good care of this; I'd never find another one like it." Now, even though the black silk fringe was still intact, many of the hundreds of tiny glass beads that had formed the gorgeous peacock design on one side were missing and the silk material of the shade was slashed.

Leaning down from his horse, the mounted policeman grasped the shade by both hands and twisted it so that the frame wire under Gilly's chin was moved on up and past Gilly's nose.

I guess Gilly had thought they were going to crash and maybe be injured or even killed because when his face appeared it was really white. He let out a long sigh of relief and then suddenly his color came back and he began to first giggle and than laugh until tears ran down his face. That's when Laura and I finally managed to get through the crowd. There was our father, looking as funny as could be, with Meetzer hissing and clawing at everybody from on top of his head. Neither Laura nor I noticed the blood on our father's face; all we saw with happy smiles was our very own kitty.

"Meetzer! Kitty, you're here! What are you doing on Daddy's head?"

Probably he recognized our voices and thought I was going to grab him around the middle again because he let go of Daddy, jumped onto somebody's shoulder and from there to the ground. Before we could stop him, he was off and away, over a tall wooden backyard fence and out of sight.

"*Mein Gott in Himmel*, look at us!" my father sputtered, lifting his scratched and bloodied hands and pointing to Gilly's. "Who put that cat in the truck? I gave strict orders that he wasn't coming along!" His voice had turned high- pitched and the words came out like he was choking.

Dodging Mama's handkerchief, with which she was trying to mop away the blood from his wounds, Daddy told the officers, "We were driving along and all at once that danged cat was there from out of nowhere, biting and scratching! I tried stopping but he was all claws and teeth, so I kept going the best I could. When Gilly, here, finally hid under the lampshade, that danged animal jumped up on my head and stayed there, swishing his doggone tail across my eyes so I could barely see to drive. Every few minutes he gave me another scratch. Man alive, look at us! SOMEBODY get the IODINE!"

A first aid kit was retrieved from the patrol car and Daddy and Gilly were led into the rooming house by Mama and two of the policemen. The one on the horse had placed Mama's poor, ragged lampshade on top of Uncle Bill's Packard and, with a few "*tsk,tsk's*," had ridden off, probably to wherever it was he had been when he first spotted the Model T swerving all over the street.

Under the circumstances, Daddy was not arrested for driving in an irresponsible manner. The two policemen were very nice, cleaning out his and Gilly's wounds and bandaging them in the long, narrow, window-less butler's-pantry-turned-kitchen. They offered to drive the two of them to the hospital, but Daddy shook his head, "No" and so did Gilly.

Mama offered everybody coffee. As if there were not any law against it, Prohibition still being on the books as the Volstead Act, she went to the cupboard and brought out the bottle of Canadian whiskey that her mother's cousin, Sedelia, and her husband, Jasper, had sneaked across the border when they attended the banker's convention in Toronto, the year before last.

"Kept on hand for medicinal purposes," Mama told the policemen as she poured a bit of it into Daddy's and Gilly's cups.
They did not arrest her, either.

Chapter 3

Having called out Meetzer's name all along the high board fence with no results, Laura and I pouted our way into "the mansion," and were told by the bandaged Gilly to "Light some place, you two, and stay out of the way until every piece of furniture is off that truck and don't get in our way, either." He and Daddy, in spite of their wounds, still had to unload the Model T, most of the stuff on that intended for the basement.

We decided to explore the second floor. I was enthralled with the beautiful crystal chandelier that hung down from the high ceiling above the red-carpeted stairway, its prisms catching the sunlight streaming through the open doorway and bathing the entire area in faceted glory. The upper hall had its own chandelier, but nothing that fancy.

L shaped, the hall was lined with mahogany doors with cut glass knobs. Most had transoms above them and six had brass numbers attached. The one at the head of the stairs had no number and turned out to be a utility closet with shelves for linens and a special area for mops, pail, brooms, and a vacuum cleaner.

Next to that was a large bathroom, its unnumbered door ajar. Here we found an old- fashioned toilet with water box high up, near the ceiling, complete with pull chain, like the one in our grandmother's bathroom. Next to that was a gray, marble-topped, free- standing sink with brass faucets above which hung a long oval mirror too high for us to see ourselves. Beyond those, a large claw foot bathtub reached to the far wall, which boasted a window with patterned glass panes.

Across from the sink was another mirror, tilted enough so we could prance about in front of it and make faces at ourselves. I alternately grinned and practiced my "mean" look. Because I did not have a Clara Bow face with which to get my way, if I wanted to win in a clash of temperament or ideas I had to use words, the more high-sounding the better. Since yelling, in our family, brought on scolding and punishment, these were delivered with eyes narrowed to slits and in a soft voice that caused the listener to cup an ear to catch the words.

I often wished I could be more like Laura; most people liked her better. More adventuresome than I, it was she who thought up most of what Mama called *dummheit*. Both Mama and Daddy spoke fluent German and English and often integrated German words and phrases into their sentences. Since Laura usually managed to involve me, the two of us would often receive identical spankings that might have taught us to not repeat *that* particular act but did not stop her from thinking up new and daring *dummheit* undertakings.

"I have an idea," she suddenly exclaimed. "Let's see if we can see Meetzer from here." In another moment, she was up on the bath stool beneath the window and trying to unlock the catch. "I think there's a porch out there. C'mere, you're bigger 'n me; look out and see."

"Hey, what're you kids doing there?" A strange man in striped pajamas was standing in the doorway.

"We live here. Who're you?" I demanded.

"What do you mean, you live here?"

"We're moving in. Look down the stairs and you'll see."

"Oh!" His grin made him look quite handsome. "So you're the new landlord's kids. Well, I'm Pete and I live here, too, in number 4, and if I'm to get to class on time I'll have to use this room."

"You go to school? You're too old to go to school- unless you're dumb and didn't pass!" At seven, kids don't realize how rude they can be. "I'll tell you all about it some other time. Right now, scoot!"

We scooted to the third floor via a stairway that did not have a fancy mahogany banister and was lighted only with a shaded fixture without prisms. There we were met with more closed doors, also transomed, numbered 7 through 10, but painted ivory, with white china doorknobs. Nothing fancy, not even the rug; nothing like the one on the second floor, which was red with peacock designs in the center. Things like that interested me and I had mentally recorded it as I walked across its oriental beauty.

As on the floor below, at the head of the stairs was a bathroom, this one smaller. Not one to be put off when she wanted to do something, Laura was again on a stool trying to open the window. This time she succeeded and was half-way out when I caught hold of her dress to keep her from falling.

"There's a porch out here," she announced. "C'mon, let's go out on it."

"I don't think we should."

"Well, I'm going" and she was up and out. Concerned for her safety, I climbed after her.

Now we were on what, we later learned, was a fire escape: black metal bars you could see between. Afraid of height, I stood there, hanging on tightly because down below, oh, so far down below, it seemed, were grass and partly bare earth and some trash barrels filled with bottles and stuff.

Laura had no such phobia. Leaning over the railing, she was calling out, "Here kitty, kitty. C'mon, Meetzer, where are you?"

Directly across from us was the side of a house facing Fifteenth, separated from our small back yard by a high board fence. The other two sections of 'the mansion' had their own yards with fences. We studied the entire area without catching even a glimpse of an orange and white striped tiger cat.

"We'd better go back in; Mama'll be looking for us," I worried, turning back to the window just as someone slammed it shut.

"Oh, no! How're we going to get back in?"

"Follow me. I see a ladder. We can go down it." Laura suggested.

"No! You know how ladders scare me. I… can't" I protested. I could remember the night we all had to go up a ladder to the bathroom in the red brick house because Daddy had varnished both stairways and neither had dried by bedtime. It had taken someone in front of me and someone behind me to get me up that ladder and this one was much higher than that. Besides, this one did not reach to the ground but stopped just about even with the top of the first floor windows. No way was I going down that ladder.

"Then let's see where this porch goes. I'm the leader. Follow me." How brave she was! I followed past more windows, all shut, to the very end of the building. There the porch stopped but not Laura. She had spied an open casement window set into the slanted roof of the building next door. Over the railing went her foot and leg, followed by the other. Then, reaching out and grasping the window, she used it to scramble up the roof. Bloomers showing, she dove headlong through the curtain- less opening, then appeared with a grin and swung the window out for me to grab.

How I did it, I will never know but I followed her and found we were in somebody's attic! There must have been nobody on the floor below to hear us as, with curiosity, we examined old garments hanging beneath white sheets and vainly tried the locks of several old trucks. Sitting in a peeling leather doll buggy with a fringed umbrella top was a beautiful doll with real hair and porcelain features. We each wished aloud that we could hold her but caution took over. Instead we tiptoed across the floor to the stairway.

A door at the bottom opened out onto a hall carpeted in blue as elegant as that of our second floor hall but thicker, softer. The only door standing ajar revealed a bathroom. Being aware of our now very soiled hands, we entered it, softly shut ourselves in and, turning the gold swan-shaped faucet handles of the reddish marble pedestal sink, carefully washed them with the bar of soap lying in a fancy dish. Just as carefully, we turned off the water, dried our hands on our dresses and, checking to make sure nobody was about, headed for the open stairway leading to the floor below.

Like ours, this one had a polished mahogany banister and beautifully turned posts. We could hear voices. They were coming from a room to the left of the stairway on the floor below. Peering down, our eyes took in an expanse of black and white mosaic tiles ending at a pair of partly open French doors flanked on either side by the thick fronds of potted ferns, giving us a view of the back of a man's head.

Very quietly, fingers to our lips to shush each other, we crept down the stairs, managed successfully to reach the heavy inner door with its frosted glass panels, opened it, carefully closed it behind us. We found ourselves in a vestibule with carpeted floor; turned the knob of the heavy outer door with its beveled-glass panes and stared up at the postman who was bending down to place the afternoon mail in its slot.

"Hello!" he greeted, stepping back to keep Laura from rushing headlong into him and helping to right her.

"Hello." I greeted, making my way around him to follow Laura down the stairs, out to the black wrought iron gate, and through it, lickety split. I am not sure about Laura's but my heart was racing. I was certain the police would be coming for us at any moment.

None did, so we sat on the grassy plot beside our porch stairs and watched as Walter, Gus, and Charley maneuvered Mama's piano up the steps and inside our new abode. They were used to juggling heavy cast iron furnace parts, so they did a good job of it, warning each other to avoid this and that along the way. Now the stake bed truck was empty.

"Guess we really live here now," I proclaimed.

"Guess so."

Inside of me, there was an empty feeling, as if somebody had pulled something out that belonged there. Adventure or not, I already missed our old house. Here there were no lilac bushes to play house under; no shouting back and forth by Daddy's men as they pounded out things from metal in his shop 'out back,' and Meetzer was probably gone for good this time.

Mama came out to look for us and smiled when she saw us sitting on the steps. "Well, we're all moved in and I have a nice supper for everybody. Now you be good girls and go up and wash your hands."
I looked down at mine. "We just did Mama. See?" holding them up for her inspection and using my narrowest-eyed frown on Laura so she would not suddenly gush out about our latest *dummheit.* I knew, only- too- well, that Mama would not approve and I could almost feel the spanking and talking to she would have doled out to each of us.

*** *** ***

Usually we all slept with our bedroom doors closed but that first night nobody shut theirs so I could hear conversations in undertones from my parents' and my sisters' rooms. Maggie was tired and crabby from having to help Mama and Vi make up the beds and arrange the closet and dresser drawers. She wanted only to sleep but Vi was in a talking mood.

"I wonder what the roomers are like? Mama said they're mostly students at Marquette. That's the university a few blocks down Wisconsin Avenue."

"I know that. How dumb do you think I am? Just go to sleep!"

"I'm too wide awake to sleep."

"Well, I'm not. We'll be living here for at least a year, so you can find out about the dumb roomers between now and then. I'm tired; I just want to close my eyes and go to sleep."

"Well, do that! I'm going to lie here and think things over. Daddy was sure a sight with Meetzer on his head, wasn't he? I felt sorry for him, with all those cuts and scratches, and for Gilly, too, but it was like those Keystone Kops comedies where everybody is chasing everybody. I mean, that policeman on the horse galloping along…" She had erupted into giggles.

"Girls," Mama called out," close your door and go to sleep. We have a busy day ahead of us tomorrow, including going to Sunday school and church."

Laura had curled up in a little knot and was already fast asleep but, like Vi, I was restless. One thing that kept coming into my mind was the space between our building and the one we had entered through that attic window. We could both have fallen and been badly hurt, probably even killed! Shivers kept running down my spine. For some reason I always had delayed reactions to things. Somehow, I would have to get rid of such thoughts.

With my sisters' door closed, I concentrated on our parents. Daddy was restless, too. His scratches and cuts and his sore muscles from lifting so many heavy things all day combined with his sadness at having to leave his beloved tin shop behind was giving him "the willies."

"Maybe a nice hot cup of Postum will help," Mama suggested.

"Maybe. But you've worked harder than you should, Lyd. I'll get to sleep, don't worry." He promised.

"Listen, do you hear something?"

"Like what?"

"Like… oh Paul, you're not going to like this but I think Meetzer is back." She, like Vi, was suddenly engulfed in giggles.

"Doggone! I'm too tired to get up and let him know he's not welcome," Daddy groaned but in a few moments he, too, was giggling. Shaking Laura, I told her the news, though in the morning I had to tell her again, since she sleeps so soundly nothing penetrates. Now I, too, could go to sleep. Meetzer was back, meowing his presence outside of my parents' window. Our surroundings might be strange and unfamiliar but we, as family, were once more complete.

Chapter 4

Back of all our financial troubles was a man name Martin Krieger. He had walked into my father's shop one day and introduced himself as a building contractor. Daddy had a small shop at the time, located miles from our house, with only Gus, Charley, and Gilly to help him to install furnaces on a one-at-a-time basis. Mr. Krieger explained that he had an option on a hundred acres of land north of Brown Deer, a well-to-do area adjacent to Milwaukee. He had plans to build two hundred homes there in assembly line fashion, the way Henry Ford built autos. The name he had chosen for his project was Lakewood.

There were two other sub-contractors already in the deal, he said, an electrician named Hans Schultz and a plumber, Joseph Reimer, both of whom my father knew slightly. Good men, well respected.

"How did I select you, Mr. Renz? I have friends in Madison and learned that you had helped to install the heating in the new capitol building. Checking you out, I found you to be honest, with a good reputation in your field as well as a decent family man. That makes you *A-number-1* in my book, just the sort of man I want to work with. Those houses are going to be my pride, good sellers that will last several lifetimes. I don't go for shoddiness, man; I have a reputation to consider, too, remember. It's my dream to be a millionaire someday and if I can help fill the pockets of you three as well, all the better, eh?"

At first Daddy was not convinced and neither was Mama; the shop was too small; he had no workspace for a large crew of men nor storage space for such a project. They discussed the pros and cons of the project. It would mean that each subcontractor would have to hire a large crew of men, order supplies by the carload to put up the proposed twenty-five homes a season.

Mr. Krieger cut through these arguments by offering to replace the too-small shop with a large one built according to my father's specifications. Daddy could pay him back out of his profits. There was plenty of room behind the red brick house to put it up and enough driveway room for the trucks. Eventually all four men shook hands and contracts were signed. Daddy's fine new shop was in no way an eyesore but blended in splendidly, though I do not suppose everyone in the area was happy with the noise that rang out from it as hammers met metal and trucks pulled in and out of the driveway every day but Sunday. Still, there were no complaints that I learned about. Had there been, I am sure my father would have handled them with kind consideration.

Furthermore, Gilly no longer had to sleep on a cot in the basement and Mrs. Malenka no longer had to stay at her sister's, several miles away, and ride the bus to our house each day.

Her nieces and nephews were getting on her nerves. She wasn't allowed to scold them into behaving like she could us. If we sassed her back, it was soap on our tongues from Mama. Lifebuoy soap; orange and tasting of carbolic acid! Phew! One session of that was enough to teach anybody to hold back naughty words.

Wisconsin winters are hard and mean, mostly, so Daddy could still keep his men at work repairing and cleaning furnaces, once the work was done at the project for the season, and stockpile pipes, gutters and whatever for the twenty-five houses to be built the following Spring. These were cut, according to pattern, from sheet steel, using large, heavy tin shears, or 'tin snips', as Daddy called them. Other pieces of equipment were the brake, which bent metal as if it were cardboard and the crimping and rolling machines. With the aid of muriatic acid and long, silvery bars of solder melted over the seam juncture via soldering irons heated in three-foot-tall round firepots, the men created whatever parts Daddy required. I had loved to watch these tasks being done from the doorway of the shop, since we kids were not allowed inside, and savored the acrid odors, the ringing out of hammers on metal, the grunting as muscles were brought into play, the laughter as jokes were told. Men hard at work, some with knees bent as they knelt on the sheets of galvanized metal, others lifting, carrying, consulting together over blueprints and templates.

The Lakewood Project soon became a builder's dream. The first twenty-five homes were built and sold. All four men made good money from them. New autos were purchased, new furniture installed in the three subcontractors' homes; my parents were talking about a proposed trip to Europe. Life was filled with happy, hope-filled days. Then came disaster. The second twenty-five were going up when the Stock Market crashed. Suddenly, there were no buyers and no funds to pay for materials. When Mr. Krieger's bank closed its doors *that was it*! He explained that he had no money to pay Daddy, Mr. Schultz, or Mr. Reimer, at least not for a while, and all three subcontractors were financially in the hole. Then, one day, the sheriff and another man came to my father with questions as to Mr. Krieger's whereabouts. He informed him that Krieger and his wife had cleared out, taking the earnest money that he had received from sales of the last ten homes. Eventually, it was rumored that he and his wife had gone to Germany, where she had relatives. The purchasers and the three subcontractors were all left "holding the bag."

To make matters worse, my father learned that Krieger had never paid the lumber company for any materials, including that used for the new shop, and was being sued. The lumber company wanted their money "or my father would have no shop" and his money was in a bank that had also "temporarily" closed its doors.

Reluctantly, to pay off his creditors and meet household expenses, Daddy sold our cottage at Pike Lake that had been our family's summer home for years before I ever arrived on the scene; the hunting lodge up north, near Rhinelander, and had to turn over to the bank the two-flat he was having built, as an investment, in South Milwaukee, since Krieger had supplied the lumber for that, also. In the end, all that Daddy had worked for was taken over by the banks, with no way to recover anything. Every furnace, gutter, , drainpipe, hot air register, and other materials in the now partially finished second twenty-five homes was lost, since none of the subcontractors had known enough about Wisconsin contract law to place liens against the properties and could not take them out at that late date. Paul Renz, Hans Schultz, and Joseph Reimer were financially ruined.

With deep shame, Daddy finally declared bankruptcy. He had hoped to salvage the red brick house and had gone to Mama's cousin, Sedelia, and her husband to secure a loan.

"Lend you money?" Cousin Jasper had sneered. "Any businessman in his right mind would have declared bankruptcy immediately but no, you had to be an 'honest John' and sell off your assets! With what would you pay me back, Paul; jelly beans? I am not about to throw good money after bad. It's fools like you who make men like me rich, Paul. *Gullible*, that's your second name; you so trusted that fellow, Krieger, that you didn't even take out a lien on the properties! And you call yourself a businessman?" Daddy had sworn than and there that he would never ever take a nickel from anybody in Mama's family.

Joseph Reimer did not declare bankruptcy but his widow did. He hanged himself from an attic rafter of one of the partially finished Lakewood homes, poor man. Hans Schultz was able to find work at the Johnson Cookie Factory, keeping the machines going. For some reason, people bought cookies all through the Depression years. Every time we bit into a chocolate, frosting-filled 'twilight' sandwich cookie, we thought of Mr. Schultz; in fact, we referred to them as "his" "Could I have just one of Mr. Schultz's cookies, Mama? I promise to eat every bite of my supper."

Chapter 5

Maggie and Violet were in their teens, a term not yet coined back then. Unlike today's youth, they had no idea that they were supposed to go through a stage of rebellion, so they obediently did as they were told. This meant helping whenever they were needed, and needed they were, for my mother had never before found herself having to strip beds and launder sheets for persons not of her own family. It had been years, in fact, since she had done this task at all.

A few months before my birth, she had begun to suffer from poor health. Her doctor gave her the terrible news that she had cancer of the stomach and would not live long enough to have her baby. He had given her a large box of morphine tablets, which she took whenever the pain was too great. He was out of town when she ran out of them and went into convulsions. Maggie had spied another doctor, complete with medicine bag, entering a house down along Lawn Avenue and Daddy ran down there to fetch him to ours.

He was on the teaching staff of Marquette and became our family physician after he rushed Mama to St. Joseph Hospital, treated her for morphine addiction and brought me into the world a month early. Then he gave her the wonderful news that she did not have cancer at all but needed kidney surgery. He was very angry and upset about the morphine.

Her Aunt Alice came to take care of Mama and make her strong enough for the operation. Daddy's oldest sister, Tante Kate, came to take care of me. Her husband and their eighteen year old son had recently died from consumption, so Tante Kate was lonely and cried many tears that fell onto my too-small face, though I do not remember that.

The two aunts did not like each other. Almost the same age, each one felt she was to be in charge of the kitchen, so there was a lot of banging of pots and pans and "hmphs" and "tsk tsks." There was even more of that when it was discovered that Mama was once more in 'the family way.'

It all had something to do with my father having "hung his pants on the bedpost one time too many." I used to ponder this but could never figure out how a man hanging his pants on a bedpost could bring about a new baby in the family. Great Aunt Alice, who looked upon all men as just this side of evil, began to treat Daddy as if he had leprosy or something equally as bad.

Somehow, Mama survived Laura's birth and finally had that bad kidney removed. Due to Aunt Alice's good care of Mama during her pregnancy, little Laura was a rosy, chubby baby.

My father had truly wanted a son because his and Mama's very first baby had been a boy, Baby Ralph, who had died when he was only six months old. When Dr. Becker warned him that Mama must never again have a baby, Daddy must have felt really bad because Gus had found him stretched out on the pile of long lengths of galvanized sheet steel in the old tin shop, crying bitter tears. He had claimed it was because he was so glad that Mama was fine but Gus did not believe him. Now, he finally confessed to his long-time employee, there would be no son to carry on the Renz name.

Gus, who was a simple, good-hearted soul concerned about Daddy's welfare, made the mistake of confiding this to Great Aunt Alice, who began to say things to Daddy that he did not like. In the end, he hired Mrs. Malenka to run the house. That plan almost went awry because Aunt Alice made friends with Mrs. Malenka. Mama eventually told Daddy that she was well enough to not need anyone's help.

At Daddy's insistence, Mrs. Malenka stayed on and from time to time Aunt Alice and Tante Kate came to visit but never together. Daddy even hired a part-time maid, Erma, who came to help whenever he and Mama entertained.

Now Mama had nobody except her two teenaged daughters and Daddy, who was not much help around the mansion because he was moping so much and getting more and more 'down in the dumps.' Laura and I ran small errands and dusted a bit but generally we were left to our own devices.

Our sisters were both pretty. Because there was no bathroom on our floor, it was necessary for the family to use the ones upstairs or the small one in the basement that we females avoided. This gave Vi and Maggie the opportunity to meet at least some of the roomers, something that cause Mama to worry. Since most of the roomers were young men, Mama felt that Daddy should somehow take more interest in his daughters so none of the 'hot-blooded young men' would feel free to 'socialize too much' and somehow 'compromise' them. I tried to look up the word "compromise" in the dictionary but was afraid to ask how to spell it lest Mama would know I had overheard that conversation. I also mused over how those men roomers achieved hot blood. So many unanswered questions! Hopefully, by the time I became a fully grown woman, I would know at least some of the answers.

Losing his business and having to move to the mansion-turned-rooming house made Daddy change from someone who laughed a lot to someone we hardly knew. It was as if he only drifted through the hours of the day, barely taking notice of them. He slept much of the time and did whatever chores Mama required of him but never volunteered to do anything.

He was never one to dandle us on his knee and play horsey with us; not one to go to with problems. Mama had always been the one to handle those. Most of his hours had been taken up in dealing with salesmen, going out to give estimates and supervising the actual work both in the shop and on the jobs. All of the designing of metalwork was done solely by him. The son of a merchant tailor who had designed men's garments, Daddy had worked with metal instead of cloth.

Now he had time to get to 'really know' his daughters and instead seemed, each day, to become more detached from us. Some men would have taken to drinking; many did, in fact. The Depression was well-named, for it caused a pall over the land that families lived under day after day, changing personalities, taking away dreams of the future, clouding even the best of minds in gloom.

I discovered Mama crying at the kitchen table and put my head against her back. It made me want to cry, too. She reached out to bring me to her side and put her head on mine and told me things would be all right, that she was just temporarily 'full of the blues.' Then she kissed my face and told me to check on my little sister to see that she wasn't 'into anything.'

Laura was sitting on the front porch, with her doll, watching traffic go by on Wisconsin Avenue. I joined her and in a few minutes we heard Mama playing something sad on the piano.

Whenever I hear Chopin's Elegy, I remember that time when Mama gave in to her feelings. By supper time she was her bright self once more. That was her way.

The Essex had been purchased from a used car dealer who had told Daddy that the previous owner had been a little old lady who scarcely drove it except maybe to church or to the cemetery to tend her departed husband's grave. She must have attended church way up north somewhere, according to Daddy's complaints, because it had far more wear and tear than what he had been told, and the cemetery was probably in Timbuktu, maybe even in Timbuk Three! She must never have changed the oil or attended to anything else it needed because it was a constant source of trouble, the radiator boiling over at times and the darned thing coming to complete stops at the most inconvenient places.

Daddy took to walking, walks that took him to the railroad freight station where he would brood about the days when it was his carloads of furnaces and sheet steel that were being unloaded from the boxcars, to be loaded onto his trucks by some of his crew of men.' He would return from these walks even more depressed.

At first Mama treated him like a small boy and tried to coax him out of his moods, but eventually she became angry and we would hear her voice scolding him from behind the bedroom door. These words were always in German, so we kids would not know what was being said, but the tones spoke volumes. Not that it did much good. He would go to bed and cover his head and sleep. It made all of us worried and frightened. Not once, however, did the word 'divorce' ever come up. That was as shameful as bankruptcy, maybe even more so.

Then came the Sunday when Daddy finally dressed in his best suit and meekly stood by while Mama and we girls seated ourselves in the Essex for the long drive to the north side to the Lutheran Church that the family had attended since way before my birth. Mama had wanted us to go there for several weeks but Daddy had not gotten out the car and obliged so we had walked up Wisconsin Avenue to Nineteenth without him and attended another Lutheran Church instead.

The route should have taken us up Fifteenth Street, but Daddy went down Wisconsin Avenue. He continued on, down past Marquette University buildings and all the businesses of the downtown section, across the bridge and on until we reached Juneau Park. Disregarding Mama's and our protests, he crossed Lake Drive, entered the park and, to our horror, drove right onto the sandy beach and headed toward the cold turbulent waters of Lake Michigan.

"Whatever it is you have in mind, Paul, remember that none of us, here in the car with you, is entertaining such cowardly thoughts. I know how bad you feel but your solution is one that is permanent and this situation is only temporary. Things change, you know that, and I have faith that God had better things in store for us." Mama's voice was calm. Inside she was praying.

"*God*!!" He cried out, "What sort of God takes a man's only son from him and gives him daughters in his place? What kind of God is He that He strips a man of everything he'd worked for? What's left for me? For any of us? Dear God in Heaven, I can't provide for my family and I can't see anything ahead for any of us. Lydia, I can't go on any more!" With that, he drove right into the water, but only a foot or so, because we girls were all screaming and trying to get out of the car.

Maybe God heard him, heard his cries. He had always fallen asleep during the church service and whomever was at his side had to poke him in the ribs to rouse him. Maybe this was God's way of getting his attention. Who can know? Suddenly, he stopped the car, sat very still for a long moment, and said, "You're danged right, Lyd! Let's go home."

We were all silent as we drove back along Wisconsin Avenue and when we entered the rooming house. If Miss Wentworth, who had room 3 and was a Seventh Day Adventist whose task it had been for years to 'tend the place' while the manager went to church on Sunday, wondered at our sudden reappearance, she didn't say so in words, only in her frown as she mounted the stairs to her room. I suspect she kept her door open a bit to see if she could catch any words. If so, she would have heard only good ones, for each of us hugged Daddy and told him we loved him and Mama made coffee and brought out more of the *schnecken* she had baked the night before. It was a meal of celebration and I'm sure God was smiling as we ate and drank, because under our breaths we were all thanking Him for turning Daddy back from driving us far out into Lake Michigan. Later, from sheer relief, we took to our beds and sobbed. The following Sunday, after church and dinner, we drove to forest Home Cemetery where little Ralphie was buried. There was a little lamb atop his stone. Laura and I petted it. I thought about the baby brother lying so still in his coffin under that stone. Once, Mama had allowed us to gaze at the picture of him in his casket. A photographer had been scheduled to come to the upper flat, where Mama and Daddy lived at the time, to photograph him in his Christening gown. Instead, he had found little Ralphie in his white velvet coffin surrounded by tall ferns. Mama, in her grief, had forgotten to cancel the appointment. She wasn't aware that he had taken the picture until weeks later, and then, grateful that she at least had that one photo to remind her and Daddy that there had once been a tiny son, had purchased it.

I guess that trip to the cemetery held closure for Daddy. He looked at each of us, his daughters, and told us that he was sorry. From now on he would be a better father to us; that it wasn't that he didn't want daughters, for he did and was glad he had us, but he had never had brothers; only three sisters, all older and bossy, and he had looked forward to a houseful of boys..

Vi took his hand as we strolled back to the Essex and promised that someday she would give him grandsons. Daddy stopped, looked down at her and told her, "Well, not until you're safely married, and if any of those roomers get foolish ideas, you let me know and I'll cool them off!" Mama smiled. Daddy had muscles that showed through shirtsleeves. No young man in his right mind would forget that. Her daughters were safe, at least for the present.

That night I had the willies. I dreamt that Daddy had not stopped the car but had caused us all to drown. People were crying because there was no money to put us into coffins and nobody to put lambs on our gravestones.

Mama must have heard me crying in my sleep, because she sat beside me on the bed and held my head against her warm, soft bosom. How nice and fresh she smelled. Her tears falling and mingling with mine, her words soft and musical as she told me over and over again that everything would be all right from now on. She would always be there, no matter what, she promised. Assured, I fell into a deep and restful sleep.

Chapter 6

It is usually quite easy for kids to meet other kids. You just stand there, shyly presenting yourself for their inspection or, if you're Laura, go right up to them and say 'Hi!' and get "Hi" back in return. There were plenty of kids in the neighborhood, although whose they were and even *who* they were I no longer recall. We were sized-up, accepted and even allowed to play hopscotch and jump rope with them.

An unlimited amount of chalk for the drawing of hopscotch outlines and numbers was available. Marquette Dental College was located on Sixteenth Street, between Wisconsin and Clybourne. Its cream brick back faced Fifteenth, neighboring the back fence of the Conservatory of Music, and there, in a large trash bin guarded by a fiercely-frowning- loud-voiced janitor, was a huge pile of chalk impressions of patients' teeth and gums that the students had used in their laboratory work.

Luckily, for us, that fearsome janitor went home to sleep at night and then we would raid the trash bin, the boys climbing into it and tossing down the imitation dentures that we girls caught in our outspread skirts. Division of the 'booty' was done without problem, the boys getting the larger share because their task had been filled with more danger and we younger kids grateful for anything received.

That chalk was wonderful, just right for drawing on the cement sidewalks. If anyone saw anything weird about kids using model dentures complete with blood-red gums to draw with, nobody let on. The bigger kids used the chalk in the game Run, Rabbit, Run, drawing arrows on trees and other places to lead us foxes on the chase.

Laura and I were not involved in that game very often because our orders from Mama and our sisters were to "keep in sight." One of the places we were warned to "*never* go" was Clybourne Street. The warning came from the other kids but nobody would answer our often-asked "Why?"

"It's just at the end of the block, down either Fifteenth or Fourteenth. Why shouldn't we go there?" adventuresome Laura would demand in my ear as we lay curled up in bed together.

I had no answer other than, "It's out of sight and the kids 'said.' They must have some reason."

"They just don't want to share something with us, I'll bet," was Laura's reasoning. "Besides, it's only just going around the block. We could run and skip and then we'd be back in no time, and at least we'd know."

"We..ll..." I had no desire to find out what was there, on Clybourne Street, that we should avoid but I also knew that it was my duty, as her older sister, to see to Laura's welfare. I wished she did not think up so darned much *dummheit*!

The day came when she would no longer be 'put off.' Our light household chores done, our sisters still assisting Mama with her tasks, we had received permission to go out and play. Daddy was washing the Essex in the driveway on Fifteenth so, to avoid his seeing us, Laura ran the length of the block along Wisconsin Avenue to Fourteenth.

"No, Laura, Mama won't know where you are!" I protested, remembering our expedition into the attic next-door, the house I always ran past in case someone inside had caught a glimpse of us as we left that day. "You don't have to come, if you're such a fraidy-cat!" she called as she turned the corner and hippity hopped down Fourteenth.

I caught up with her and grabbed the back of her dress but she continued on. Giving up, since we were halfway down the block already and past the tobacco, candy and sundries store on the other side of the street, I decided the best thing was to hurry both of us along so we would be home before it was discovered that we were 'out of sight.'

At the corner of Fourteenth and Clybourne, we stooped to stare down the length of the block to Fifteenth: nothing but houses on this side and a plumbing establishment halfway down the block across Clybourne; also a corner tavern directly across from us. Some boys around Vi's and Maggie's ages were sitting together on the porch steps of one of the houses.

Feeling safe, we started down the block. When we were almost up to the boys, Laura gave them a friendly hand wave and a "Hi, we're new kids. We live in the mansion on Fifteenth and Wisconsin."

Suddenly one of the boys left the group and jumped in our path. "Oh, yeah? We know where you live. Whatcha doin' in OUR TERRITORY?" He had hold of the fronts of both of our dresses and was shaking us, and I could see that he was nothing like the big boys we had known back in the red brick house, especially Melvin, whom I had wanted to marry some day when I grew up, even if he was ten years older than I. I wished Melvin were here now. He would save us!

The boy had slanted eyes and yellow buckteeth, very black greasy hair, and his fingernails were filthy. I hated filthy fingernails. Now his friends were forming a circle around us. Laura got free and began to run but was tripped and went down on her face on the sidewalk. When she began to get to her knees, a pair of one of the boys' hands suddenly bared her plump little bottom. I, meanwhile, had received such a hard shove that I, too, went down, skinning both knees and feeling the sidewalk meet my face with a sudden thud.

"We were j-just g-going ar-around the block!" Laura sobbed, reaching for me with eyes blinded by tears. I hugged her to me, wiping blood from my nose with the back of my hand, blood that would not stop running into my mouth and onto my dress. I wanted Mama and Daddy, too, but I needed to protect my little sister! Oh, why had I ever let her convince me to investigate Clybourne Street? How would I ever explain this to Mama and Daddy if we ever managed to get home to them? I felt a great big sob fill my chest. It hurt so badly but something was happening to me- my fear was leaving me and anger was taking its place.

"We live in the mansion!" mimicked one boy.

"Yeah, and she likes to show us her hinder." Another jeered, pulling Laura's hair.

"I never, never, you filthy pigs! You pulled them down! Mama told me never, never to show anybody my…my… oh, Jessie, I want to go home!"

"Home, huh?" our first tormenter grinned. "Tell you what. You want to ever see home and Mama again; you do exactly as I say. Get it? From now on you're our slaves, see?"

Slaves? How could we be slaves? I had read Uncle Tom's Cabin and slaves had black faces and hands and were sold by terrible men to rich people with plantations and mistreated except by little Eva's Papa. "What do you want us to do?" I was suddenly able to look each of those boys directly in their eyes. At that moment, I believe, I learned that I would always somehow come though in an emergency. It would not be until later that I would fall apart inside and give way to fear and anger.

The bucktoothed boy must have been the leader, because he did most of the talking. He stared back at me for a long moment, then gripping my arm so tightly I knew it would show a bruise, he said, "See that store down there, the one with the awning?"

"I see it." My eyes were as narrow slits as his now.

"You two go down there and tell the storekeeper that you both fell down and need help."

"And then what?"

His hold on my arm was so tight it burned. "And then you don't say one word about us, hear me? We know where you live and we know how to get into that place and you say one word and..." He drew his finger across his throat. The gesture was very graphic, well portrayed; though having never seen it before; I could not mistake its meaning. My ever-present imagination summoned up the feeling of my own warm blood flowing from his imaginary cut. "No more Mama or Daddy or ANY OF YOU, THAT'S WHAT!!!" he added for good measure, his voice spitting out the menacing words, one by one, each embedding itself into my mind like unwanted visitors bent on staying for a long visit.

Not waiting for what might occur to him next, I hustled Laura in the direction of the grocery store situated on the corner of Fifteenth and Clybourne followed by an admonition from one of the other boys, five in number I knew by now, "You slaves shouldn't never of invaded our territory. Now you belong to us, hear me, slaves?"

We ran the rest of the way. I was tempted to just keep running, up Fifteenth to Daddy, but that awful threat, the one with the finger across the throat, had been too strong.

Out in front of the store were trays of fruit on a tall stand. Inside, when we opened the screen door and entered, the shop was cool. Rows of cans lined the shelves and at one side was a meat case from behind which appeared a chubby, white haired man with an apron as bloodied as my dress.

"Heavens to Betsy, what in the world? You two look like you ran into a sidewalk! New around here, are you?"

Laura was still sobbing. He put her on his knee and wiped her tears with a big handkerchief. Both of her hands were bleeding as well as one knee. Turning to me, he sized up my injuries and asked where our parents lived.

"Up that way," I indicated Fifteenth and lied, "They're not home right now. We were running fast and fell down. I was supposed to buy something but I lost my money somewhere in the grass."

"Well, first-things-first. Let's get you here at the sink behind this meat counter and we'll wash the blood away. I'll fetch my kit. Got some bandages here, somewhere, and something to put on those sores. Don't worry, it's a salve and it won't hurt." Reaching into the meat case, he brought out two hot dogs for us to nibble on in the meantime.

How good he was, how kind and gentle; I wished I didn't have to lie to him, lying being something we had been taught was sinful. Still, I had to make sure I did nothing to make him know the truth lest those boys slip into our house and kill us all, or something.

Our wounds bandaged, he led me to the front of the store to see if I could remember what it was we were to have purchased. Laura said licorice sticks but I shook my head and said, "No, it was Campbell's tomato soup, remember?" and made narrow eyes at her.

That dear old man took two cans of soup from the shelf, placed them into a brown paper sack, added two licorice sticks and told us we could pay for the soup later. The candy was free because we were new customers. I had never had a grandfather and he seemed to meet all of my requirements for one save not being married to our one and only Grandmother. I felt so guilty accepting anything from him and even worse when he led us to the door and was suddenly aware that most of his fruit display had disappeared!

While we had been keeping him occupied, those boys had stolen his fruit! I knew it without being told. THAT was why they had told us to go to the storekeeper with our injuries!

"It's those Clybourne Streeters, those lazy good-for-nothings that cause trouble for everybody," he bemoaned his loss, first holding his head in both hands and moving it from side to side, then shaking his fist in the direction from which we had come, though now nobody was in sight. "I'll call the police! Those devils, they are nothing but useless punks!" He was muttering to himself; we had been forgotten as he hurried back into the shop to phone authorities.

Daddy was nowhere in sight when we reached the mansion. It was Mama who listened to my tale of having tripped on an uneven spot on the sidewalk and fallen down.

"Well, who bandaged you so nicely?"

"Oh, it was a nice lady in one of those houses on Fifteenth." I was vague about which house it was in which she lived.

"Well, when you see her again, you thank her. I hope you remember to do that."

"Oh, we did. She even gave us each a nice licorice stick." I had hidden the soup in the bushes. Inside I was feeling more and more sinful, piling lie upon lie and hoping that Laura would not give us away.
She, too, had been badly frightened by that threat. That night, and for many nights after, she wet our bed and even began to walk in her sleep. Mama was worried enough to take her to see Dr. Becker, who recommended a daily dose of cod liver oil, which we suffered without too much protest. Anything to keep our family safe from those awful boys.

I developed the habit of getting up in the night to check on the doors to see if any of the roomers had forgotten to lock them and to make sure the key was turned in the door leading to the basement.

One afternoon, Laura and I were pulled into the bushes and given orders to "go to the drugstore" on Seventeenth and Wisconsin and "accidentally knock some stuff off a shelf." We protested that we were not allowed to cross Wisconsin Avenue and the ugly boy with the funny eyes and yellow teeth made that awful finger across his throat gesture.

That night I could not sleep, remembering how the druggist had yelled at us for causing his display of hot water bottles to tumble onto the floor in a heap.

"You brats leave this place at once and don't show your faces around here again or I'll have the cops after you!"
Another time it was the plumbing place on Clybourne, where we asked for curtain rods and were patiently told how to get to a hardware store somewhere on Michigan Street, wherever that was. Each time, we knew, things were being stolen. It was not until we were sent to the candy, tobacco, and sundries store on Fourteenth that things ceased.

The beat patrolman, Officer Jim, who had helped to dress Daddy's and Gilly's wounds, was a friend to all of us kids and to our parents, also. He would watch us at our games and stop in and have coffee with Mama and Daddy to learn who was new in the rooming house and where that person had come from. Keeping tabs on things on his beat was his job. We would see him reporting in to the station from the red call box with the blue light on top that was for use by the police. This was mounted on a thick black metal pole located on the corner of Fourteenth and Wisconsin. He was making his call the day Laura and I were in the shop on Fourteenth, selecting penny candy and then discovering that we had "lost our money."

Out of the tail of his eye, the storekeeper had noted one of the boys stuffing something into his shirt. He had immediately grabbed hold of the boy and, spotting Officer Jim through the window, yelled for him to come. The boy managed to get away but Laura and I were still in the shop. Evidently word had gotten around that two little girls had always been there when things were stolen.

Officer Jim stooped down and looked into each of our eyes with his kind Irish blue ones. "Och, and what are the two Renz girls doing here, trying to buy candy without any money? I thought you were not to cross any streets and here you are, across Fourteenth. How did you lose your money in that short distance? Tell you what, we'll take you home and ask you Ma about it, hmmm?"

We were both in tears by now, pleading with him to "please, don't say anything to Mama or something terrible will happen to our whole family! Please!!! They… they'll do…DO…s…something ter…terrible to…to us if you go… go there and… and t-tell her!" I sobbed.

"Like what, Jessie?"

I ran my finger across my throat.

"So that's the way it is, is it? You've been setup by the Clybourne Street gang, have you? Well, you leave things to me. I'm not taking you to the station. We'll go home, now, and you just rest assured, this is the end of things. No more being decoys for those fellows. And don't you worry; nothing will happen to either of you OR your family!"

Leaning against his strong, uniformed chest, we cried with relief while the shopkeeper gave us each a bag of penny candy to take home to make us feel better.

"I don't think we should have this," I told him. "We don't deserve it!" but he gave it to us anyway.

"You're not bad girls," he told us," just scared little ones. You eat that and remember that I forgive you. Now go along with Officer Jim and don't worry, I won't press charges."

I didn't know what charges were or how they were 'pressed' but I was grateful.

Mama and Daddy were horrified at what had happened. They promised to appear at the police station to confront the parents of the boys involved and go to court, if necessary. It was the last we ever saw of that group of boys. It was also the last time we ventured down Clybourne Street.

News gets around fast and the kids in the neighborhood learned of our venture into the world of crime. Nobody held that against us because, at one time or another each of them had come under the thumb of the Clybourne Street gang themselves. They had been afraid to warn us, I suppose.

Laura was rather docile after that Clybourne Street scare but I was certain her spirit would eventually rally and I would find myself involved in more *dummheit*. Her bedwetting stopped, as did her sleepwalking, but I still got up and checked out the doors for a long time. We also continued to receive daily doses of Peterson's Cod Liver Oil from a brown bottle shaped like a fish complete with scales and an open mouth holding a cork stopper. I liked the bottles and saved them for a time but hated every drop of that oily liquid.

Officer Jim was a hero to all in the neighborhood over that incident. It made us all feel safe to see him strolling down the street, hands clasped behind him, billy club swinging from a strap at his wrist, his friendly smile always at the ready.
***** ***** *****

Often I thought about the difference between this life we were leading, here in the city, and our previous existence. Here we had to learn our boundaries and our world seemed so much more restricted, like in the story of the city mouse and the country mouse. I much preferred the life of the country mouse.

Back in the red brick house there had been no sidewalks for hopscotch but we had enjoyed other compensations such as brook where, in Springtime, we could catch polliwogs; stands of trees called "woods;" the lowing of cattle; meadows alive with grasses, flowers and, at early dawn sometimes, fragile spider webs hung with jewel-like drops of dew. I remember one morning when Vi gently shook me awake and motioned for me to follow her to the window. The field across the road was a fairyland of intricate spider webs spun onto the tall blades of grasses like a display of lollipops in a candy store window, each slender thread hung with drops of dew that sparkled like myriads and myriads of diamonds. We sat there, in our nightgowns, silently caught up in the breathless beauty of the scene until the morning sun finally turned the field back into its usual prosaic appearance.

I told Mama about it and she said she used to get up early to gaze at such sights and that her mother and grandmother had done the same, our Grandmother from the window of the log cabin in which she had been born! Later I tiptoed up to Vi and kissed her cheek and she stared into my eyes and said she knew I would appreciate sharing those moments with her. What a nice sister she was, at times.

Back there, on Green Bay Road, we knew our boundaries; fences and rules outlined them for us. For instance, you did not enter the property of Old Man Steiger because he and his wife kept goats. The big billy goat would butt you with his horns if you dared to enter his domain and that danger was constant because he was never tethered. Those Steigers were a somewhat strange couple. They actually washed their money and hung it on the line to dry! Germs, they claimed, abounded on paper money, as if none resided on those goats or on the old rusting machinery, bathtubs, broken-down davenports, and all the other junk left laying about their property. Nobody ever tried to steal the money as it dried; not with that watch-goat doing sentry duty.

Once Old Man Steiger's bull got away and dashed through Mama's freshly washed laundry, carrying off one of her best sheets on his horns. An ever-enlarging group of men armed with pitchforks finally cornered the animal along the railroad tracks almost a mile away.

The next morning Mr. Steiger was at our door with an envelope containing five freshly washed dollar bills for Mama, for the loss of her sheet and her having to purchase a new one. He didn't seem so bad after all. Still, there was that nasty billy goat that kept us at bay.

I wondered, wistfully, if we would ever again have the chance to live "out in the sticks." Darn that old Depression, anyway.

Chapter 7

One morning, after some discussion with Mama about a phone call she had received from Aunt Rose, Daddy took Laura and me by the hand and started off with us toward downtown. He and Mama had been speaking to each other in German, so it was an important conversation not meant for kid's ears. Their voices never rose to a crescendo but the tones held both anger and frustration. At last Daddy exclaimed "Mein Gott in Himmel, na, ja!" and, slapping his hand down on the kitchen table, strode off toward the front door.

It was Mama's somewhat fearful suggestion that we accompany him. Frowning, he nonetheless accepted our company and away we went, Daddy taking his usual long strides, the two of us running and hippety-hopping alongside to keep up. We had no idea where we were going and found ourselves passing important looking buildings which I managed to identify as the Schools of Law and Medicine; part of Marquette University. His mouth was set in a pained cement grimace. When he spoke, it was not to us but in German, as if Mama were still present. There was no conversation on our part; how could there be when we were gasping for breath? He did stop at each intersection to guide us across, but when we came to Red Arrow Park, which offered an inviting wading pool and children our ages having fun, he did not slow down. We tugged at his hands and tried digging our heels into the sidewalk to get his attention, to no avail. This left us moving forward with our heads turned backwards so our wistful eyes could take in the sight of other kids splashing in the water. I doubt that he was aware of any of it; the imposing façade and rose window of Gesu Catholic Church; the fact that Wisconsin Avenue had become a boulevard; that on the opposite side of the street were the Milwaukee Public Museum and the Milwaukee Public Library; or the people, mostly old men, sitting on benches enjoying the shade of the trees in Red Arrow Park. Did he even realize we were only little kids and were fast becoming tired and breathless?

On we hurried, into the business area. Now the boulevard was gone and streetcars and autos accompanied us past the Boston Store; Penney's; Espanhain's Dry Goods and Fine Furniture; Walgreens; shops selling candy, cigars, stockings, shoes; past the various restaurants and theaters, past the Plankington Arcade; City Hall, and Gimbel's Department store until we came to the Milwaukee River and the bridge spanning it. The sidewalks downtown held scores of other people but I doubt that Daddy was aware of any of them, although we had deftly maneuvered through without bumping into anyone along the way.

Now we came to a complete halt. Daddy leaned against the rail and looked down at the greenish-brown waters of the river with its bits of debris floating downstream: a Dentyne gum wrapper; a sales slip, bits of wood; each castaway, compelled by the river's flow, traveling to some unknown destination. I was worried, remembering that frightful morning when Daddy had almost driven us into Lake Michigan.

Silvery gulls were flying overhead, crying hoarsely to each other and dipping swiftly onto the water only long enough to catch and make off with unsuspecting fish. Atop a piling stood a crane on one leg, the other drawn up to his body to make him appear that he had only the one. The brown water of the river had a smell of its own, a mixture of fish and other things blended into an odor I disliked.

Laura began to whimper that she was hungry. I shushed her and stood quietly at Daddy's side, something telling me that this was best. Suddenly bells rang and up ahead, to our right, appeared a large boat. Our gaze followed the pointing fingers of other people to where the bridge tender sat or stood in his isolated little tower room. Within moments first yellow then red lights had traffic stopping as the middle of the bridge began to rise up, up, up until it was in two halves and the vessel, its black hull almost touching the pilings on our side, was granted passage.

I wondered what it was like aboard something like that. We could hear men's voices and I saw one fellow with red hair peering down at us. Laura and I waved to him and he returned out greeting with a wide grin. Eventually, the boat passed out of our sight.

When the bridge was once more a part of the roadway and traffic had started up again, Daddy took a deep breath and said, "Na, ja, then." and led us across Wisconsin Ave and up Water Street to and though the arches of City Hall to the next street. We crossed that and walked to the center of the block.

At an office-building doorway he paused, rubbed the back of his neck, let out a long sigh and, opening the door, led us inside to a small lobby with a mosaic titled floor, a stairway with fancy brass rail, and an elevator.

The uniformed elevator operator told us to "step back, please." Efficiently his gloved hand first closed the heavy brass outside door and then the brass folding gate of the car. Reaching for the wooden handle of a half-moon shaped brass control, he moved the indicator to the number 2 and up we went. A man carrying an armful of folders got on and up we traveled to the next floor. Eventually we reached the one Daddy had requested and we exited the car, being warned, of course, to "watch you step, please."

It had taken a few seconds of maneuvering of the control to get the cage even with the floor and another few moments for the brass gate and the outer doors to open. By this time Laura was complaining of her terrible hunger. She emoted in vain; Daddy had his mind solely on an office door down the hall, one with the name "J.L. Murray, Accounting" in black lettering on the crinkly glass pane.

A pretty lady seated behind a desk asked if she could help Daddy. He replied that he had been told to see Mr. Murray regarding a personal matter. Writing his name down, she smiled, pressed a button on a machine and spoke into it. A man's voice replied that she should "show him in."

"You two be good girls and behave yourselves; I'll be out in a little while." Daddy instructed, and followed the lady into another room. She returned to her desk and proceeded to flip pages in her steno pad.

"I'm so hungry I think I'll die!" complained Laura.

I stared her down with narrowed eyes that threatened silently all sorts of punishment. She made a "now you made me cry" face and squeezed out a few tears. The pretty lady opened her desk drawer and brought out two suckers.

We sat quietly enjoying them until we heard Daddy's voice raised in loud tones, though we could not hear his words. Then the door opened and a man somewhere behind Daddy's emerging figure remarked, "Lydia did herself no service in marrying you, Paul. I'd think it over before I turned the opportunity down. Kaufman can keep you well supplied with work, I promise. And remember to give my regards to Lydia. She's the one you have to think of right now, Paul."

Always aware of details, I noted that Daddy's adam's apple was moving up and down as he stood with his back to the now closed door and that his jaws were working so that a little muscle danced on the cheek turned our way. Taking several deep breaths, he came towards us, disregarding the pretty lady until he had taken each of our hands in his now sweaty ones and, giving a nod in her direction, hustled us out into the hall. We did not take the elevator but instead walked down five flights of stairs that to Laura and me seemed endless.

Outside once more, with people and traffic swirling about us, Daddy led us back to Wisconsin Avenue where we turned west toward home, past the Riverside Theater, restaurants, and many shops. When we came to the Karmel Korn shop, he purchased a nickel's worth for himself and the clerk gave Laura and me each a free small sample bag.

Laura contentedly walked along, popping the delicious confection into her mouth until her bag was empty, and then eyed mine. Always a slow eater who savored each bite, I had at least a half bag left. Her eyes pleaded with me to share. I tried to ignore her but at last I gave in, anxiously aware that my luscious confection was now disappearing at an alarming rate. Daddy must have noticed, because he poured some of his into my bag, and then shoved his into his suit coat pocket.

I sensed that he was still upset. We continued homeward until we came to the Library. By our shoulders, he guided us up the stone steps and through the lobby. "You two be good girls now and sit down and be quiet," he ordered in a loud whisper.

We were duly overwhelmed by the enormity of the place, at the stacks of books, the high ceilings, and the lady at the desk looking at us over her half lenses. She told Daddy where the newspapers were located and for an interminably long time he pored over the classified sections, heaved a loud sigh and shook his head. I noted that what had held his interest was something called 'Employees Wanted.'

"What's an employee, Daddy?" I asked as we were heading home once more.

"Someone who works for a lawyer named Kaufman," was his bitter reply.

Mama greeted us with relieved hugs and, leading Daddy into the bedroom, began questioning him about 'the interview.' I heard the name Murray and knew they were talking about the man in the office. Daddy came out red-faced, as though his anger had returned, yet he did not slam the cups or coffeepot when he poured some for himself and Mama. She had been crying but walked past us and into the kitchen where she and Daddy sipped their coffee laced with milk, his with the usual three teaspoons of sugar, and dunked the donuts she had made in our absence. We were offered one apiece and glasses of milk which we carried outside to the front porch to join Vi and Maggie who were sitting on the steps watching traffic and wishing that they could play "Goofy Golf" at the course up the street or gorge themselves with White Tower hamburgers. It was tacitly understood that this was a time when Mama and Daddy needed privacy since our parents were again conversing in German.

We had long ago learned that when they spoke German we were excess baggage. "*Gehen sie*" Daddy would say, indicating with a nod of his head that we should scamper off somewhere. His tones were not at all threatening, yet we dutifully obeyed. Mama was the one who usually meted out punishment, an over-the-knee spanking of three smart slaps for Laura and me or scoldings and maybe an ear-tweak for Vi and Maggie. Sometimes, when Mama was sewing, it was her thimble, rapped one or twice against our skulls, which was the tool that taught us to be sorry for our misdeeds; I was certain that if someone were to shave my head it would resemble one of our Cousin Rudy's golf balls.

Whatever had transpired that day, it resulted in Daddy becoming a "danged process server." The coin telephone in the hall would ring and it would be the secretary of Attorney Kaufman, J.L. Murray's friend, informing Daddy that she had "work for him." Heaving a loud sigh and with shoulders drooping, Daddy would drive off in the Essex, which had finally been overhauled and "purred like a kitten," and maybe not return for hours. Mama merely said that he was "serving papers," but never enlarged on the subject. Whatever sort of "papers" he served and to whom we didn't know but sometimes they put Daddy into jeopardy. One evening, he came home with a black eye and sat silently holding a piece of raw steak against it. Another time Mama had to take a taxi to the Emergency Hospital because he had to be stitched up.

Upon returning home from the hospital, they went into their bedroom and argued in German. I heard Daddy say, "No! Not one *red cent* do we ask from your family, Lydia, and that's that! I'll keep this damned job if it kills me! Then you can go back to that old flame of yours, Murray, and thank him for helping to make you a widow!"

For some reason this made both of them suddenly burst into laughter. Mama asked, giggling, "Is he really losing his hair? Oh, Paul, it was Mama wanted me to marry him, not me! I still remember how he would sit there making "goo goo eyes" at me and bore me absolutely silly! He wouldn't have the *grit* to go out and serve papers on anyone and we're not going to let him know about your stitches, either. Jack Murray can sit in his office and think whatever he does about you; to me you're my "dearly beloved" and don't you ever forget it!"

Those words were not meant for my ears; thirsty, I had come into the house for a drink of water and interested, as usual, in what grownups were doing, paused outside the bedroom door to see if everything was all right. Their door remained closed for maybe a half hour more and Daddy had a smile on his face when we girls asked to see his bandage, which was on his left forearm. Mama had gone upstairs to use the second floor bathroom but she, too, seemed in a good mood when she came back down. At any rate, Daddy stopped walking around with his shoulders down. At least for a while, anyway.

One question had been answered for me: the reason why Grandmother and our aunts disliked Daddy had something to do with Mama not marrying J.L. Murray. I wished I had seen the man, so I could compare him with Daddy. I was glad to know that Mama truly loved

Daddy and not that Murray fellow with the thinning hair. Maybe he even had a pot- belly, like Cousin Jasper. I hoped so.

Chapter 8

On a hot afternoon, after we had begged awhile and promised to obey our sisters, Mama consented to having Vi and Maggie accompany Laura and me to the wading pool at Red Arrow Park. Too old to be allowed to wade, our older sisters dangled their feet in the water while they read movie magazines acquired from one of the roomers.

Several big boys came over to flirt with them, then escorted us home and would have stayed but Mama came out on the porch and sent them on their way. Girls did not bring home strange boys, especially some they found in a park! For a time our sisters sulked in their room but later were their same old bossy selves.

I was into Cinderella and looked upon them as mean stepsisters. They certainly primped enough, dabbing their faces with white cream that hardened and had to be cracked off, the gift of Helen, one of the girls in room 6, upstairs. She and her roommate were waitresses at the Waffle House, downtown, and seemed to have quite a bit of money to spend. Mama did not approve of Vi and Maggie getting too friendly with them although she knew how lonely it must be for young women away from their families. Both, it seemed, had lost their fathers and were sending money home to their mothers to "help out." They lived up north, somewhere, around Wausau. Our sisters were not allowed to attend the movies with them or to go downtown, evenings, so their friendship was restricted to making up their faces and the borrowing of magazines and phonograph records that were played on our console Victrola machine.

After a time Laura and I were allowed to go to Red Arrow Park on our own but together, never alone. We had to wear our old swimming suits from the summer before when we still had the cottage at Pike Lake. They were a bit small but still usable after Mama added a strip of contrasting material to the waistline area to lengthen them. She let out sighs while doing so and we all recalled the good times we, as well as our relatives and friends, had enjoyed at the cottage in previous summers.

We could swim, having learned via Daddy's special contraption, which was a stout pole fastened to the pier, and a rope and pulley. He would slip the rope about our waists, toss us in, then reel us out and back, until we caught on to the various strokes in imitation of Vi and Maggie, who were accomplished swimmers. Vi specialized in high-diving. How we envied that achievement!

Since the shallow water of the pool at Red Arrow did not allow for swimming, the enjoyment it offered came from the splashing and chatter of the other children we met there. Some had water toys, such as rubber seals, and small ducks. This gave Laura a brilliant idea. "Next time we come, let's bring Amelia."

Amelia was a life-sized rag doll which she had stuffed with her own hands during kindergarten class shortly before the end of the semester. Miss Pluckhorn, her teacher, had laid butcher paper on the floor and drawn around each child, then taken the paper patterns home where she pinned them to white muslin. By the end of the week she had twenty two muslin dolls ready to be stuffed with cotton batting.

Faces and hair were drawn on them with wax crayon, each child doing this task with smiles and gusto, not knowing that their teacher had only a few more weeks to live, a victim of complications due to a burst appendix.

Laura loved Amelia. She had no idea that taking her swimming would be a catastrophe. Skipping gaily at my side, she talked to her and told her how much fun it would be in the wading pool.
Poor Amelia! That cotton batting soaked up water like a thirsty sponge. Shortly she was lying at the bottom of the pool. We hurriedly rescued her but she now weighed so much that the two of use found her too heavy to carry back home.

"We're going to have to get the coaster wagon," I advised. This posed a problem; we were not allowed to travel to or from the park alone, an order to not be disobeyed lest we forfeit the right to play there at all. We would both have to go after the wagon.
What to do with Amelia? We had reached the hedge surrounding the rectory where the priests of Gesu Church resided. This we did not know; all we saw

was a hiding place for Amelia that would keep her safe until we returned with transportation. Shoving her through the space between two of the bushes, we hurried home.

When we returned, Amelia was gone! Burrowing into the space where we had left her, we saw, to our dismay, that a man wearing a long black dress was carrying her into his house! Oh, no! We screamed to him to stop and give her back but just then the bells of the church began to ring out and he could not hear us. To our child-minds he was disregarding us. Laura wanted to dash up to that door and pound on it and make him give Amelia back but we had been told that we must stay away from Catholics. Mama and Daddy never told us that, but Grandmother's cousin, Sedelia, had sat us down and with wagging finger given us at least fifteen minutes of instruction of sinfulness of Catholicism. Staunch Wisconsin Synod Lutheran; she felt we, who were members of the more lenient United Synod, lacked instruction in such things. I doubt that she was ever taught that in her church anymore than we were taught it in ours but she had evidently been born with a biased eye for she always saw the bad and pitfalls of life before she saw the good.

Poor Laura! Heartbroken over the loss of her doll, she cried so hard that I sat her in the wagon and pulled her home. When I looked back at her, she was lying curled up with her thumb in her mouth, her forefinger hooked around her nose, something she had not done since the day we moved. I knew then how much she was grieving for Amelia.

We did not return to the pool for at least two weeks, but we did accompany Daddy downtown. Letting loose of his hand as we passed Gesu Church, I boldly stepped into the vestibule, opened the door to the chapel and yelled out, "Thief! Kidnapper! Catholic!" My voice echoed through the hushed interior. Satisfied, I dashed away to take Daddy's hand in time for him to guide us across the next intersection.

One afternoon, when we returned from somewhere, Laura and I were greeted with Amelia, water stained but almost as good as new, sitting in the big Morris chair in the living room! Mama, smiling, told us that officer Jim had delivered her. One of the priests at Gesu Church had informed him that he had found her, soaking wet, one afternoon. Surmising that she was the beloved toy of some child, he had done his best to line dry her, without success, and had finally removed her stuffing, handed her over to one of the nuns for re-stuffing and presented her to Officer Jim with the hope that he might know who owned her. He, of course, on his rounds, had noticed Laura playing with her on the front porch.

Cousin Sedelia was wrong! Catholics were *not* bad people, at least those connected with Gesu Church. I cried myself to sleep when I remembered what I had done in my self- righteous anger and frustration. But first I asked God in prayer to please forgive me. When Mama baked some of her delicious *apfel strudel* to deliver to the priests as a *thank-you* gesture, it was I who accompanied Vi on the errand. The housekeeper answered the door and I told her to tell the priests that I was very sorry.

"About what, little girl?" she asked kindly. I could not explain and merely turned and ran, tears of shame streaming down my face. Vi questioned me about the incident but I merely bit my lip with my remaining teeth and shook my head. Understanding that it was something I could not discuss, she let the matter drop and never told on me. It was the beginning of a bond between us that would grow stronger through the years.

Chapter 9

Life settled into the routine of summer days. Visitors began to
make their appearances. Since only one of the women in mama's family
knew how to drive and *definitely* none on Daddy's side, it was the bus
stopping in front of the rooming house that usually delivered them. Great
Aunt Alice, however, had her own chauffer-driven limousine in the form of
a taxicab.

For many years the same driver had been picking her up and taking
her places, then returning to deliver her home again. His name was Clyde.
He would pull up in front of our house, just behind the bus stop, jump out,
open the rear door of the yellow cab and hand her out as if she were some
royal queen. All five feet ten of her would emerge, like some Mammoth
butterfly leaving behind its cocoon, mid-calf skirts and redingote flapping
about her lanky frame, hand-made shoes of finest Italian suede, smooth
leather, or Parisian silk planting themselves firmly on the sidewalk, her
long slim fingers clasping tightly her ever-present black silk English
umbrella. It was claimed she carried a hatpin for protection as well.
She never came unannounced; her knowledge of social courtesy was
impeccable. A good thing, for Daddy was then given the opportunity to
"make other plans."

Vi and Maggie were glad to see her, for she always came bearing
gifts for them. To her, any child below the age of twelve was
inconsequential, so Laura and I did not receive gifts except at Christmas
and on birthdays. These, admittedly, were always selected with care and
gave us great pleasure.

Looking back, I feel that she was a loving, stifled woman who had
a great sensitivity to our needs and our desires. Why else would she have
presented to us the most extravagant objects one could imagine, such as the
French bed doll, with its exceedingly long, thin legs and arms, dressed in
exquisite garments including satin and lace chemise, that I received on my
seventh birthday? She had told me

its name was Mademoiselle Mimi Poppet and that she had purchased her for me while in Paris when she and her sister and brother-in-law, our Great Aunt Beatrice and Uncle George, were "touring the Continent." In the midst of our poverty, she brought to our lives something of elegance. I loved Mademoiselle Mimi. I wonder whatever happened to her? Did I leave her behind with my childhood in that land of *Was*?

One afternoon, when Clyde had delivered Aunt Alice to us, she informed Vi that she had made a dress for her which needed to be hemmed to the correct length. What a beautiful dress it was, of Alice blue silk with exquisite lace trim. Vi was Aunt Alice's 'god child,' and so was often the recipient of lovely garments which Maggie inherited as Vi outgrew them.

Mama sewed most of our clothes and was an excellent seamstress but these days she could in no way afford the expensive materials and accessories as those provided by Aunt Alice. I loved to watch Aunt Alice's tapering fingers as they moved, the beautiful jewels in her rings casting light refractions on the ceiling, especially the full carat diamond which she had received from her fiancé, who had died of a sudden illness only a few weeks before what would have been their wedding day. No man since then had ever held a place in her heart, not even distantly, including Daddy, whom she had the tendency to view as if he were some lab specimen carrying the Plague. Clyde, of course, being a valuable means of transport and therefore a servant, of sorts, was considered for his worth and not as a man, per se.

Secretly, I was scared stiff of her. Her eyes could bore holes through one as if she knew exactly what the object of her viewing had been up to. She would spank a naughty child and send one to its room. Deservedly, silently, the culprit suffered banishment; to disobey was to receive another three slaps on the "sitting down place." Yet, she never held the memory of the misdeed to be brought up time- and- again, as would Cousin Sedelia.

Mama had baked her 'special *butter horns'* and brought out her best china coffee set for the occasion. Vi and Maggie were allowed to sip coffee with them "because of their age." Laura and I, on the other hand, were to accompany Daddy to the museum.

We had never been there, so it was an adventure for us. Breathless, as usual, we ran beside him, glad when we reached the boulevard and crossed Wisconsin Avenue to enter what, for me, was to become a frequent ride on a magic carpet that whisked one into a wondrous world of enchantment where the everyday world was left behind; exchanged for bits and pieces of past history. The MILWAUKEE PUBLIC MUSEUM. I would read the carved stone letters with awe.

Daddy did not give us free rein and allow us to roam at will. We were ordered to stay by his side and examine each exhibit with critical eye. The very first thing that greeted us was the huge skeleton of a dinosaur. Under his guidance we noted its small head in comparison to its tall neck, its short arms, and the huge bones, discussing what amount of flesh and skin must have covered this gargantuan creature. Laura became itchy and wanted to move off to something else but I gratefully took in every detail. It set my imagination into motion so that I could almost hear, smell and certainly *feel the immensity* of what meeting such a gigantic reptile might be like.

There were dioramas of dinosaurs in their natural habitat along the one wall. These Laura liked and enjoyed but she had to use the bathroom and began hopping from one foot to the other. I was finally allowed to accompany her to the public washroom while Daddy sat and rested his back on one of the stone benches in the main hall.

Several years earlier he had suffered a severe back injury while unloading furnaces and was probably the best customer of the makers of Sloan's Liniment, which made him smell up a room with its pungent odor. Mama would pour some into her cupped hand and drip it here and there onto his bared back as he lay face down on their bed, then gently massage it in, working harder on those spots where he groaned the most. When this treatment did not suffice, he would visit a chiropractor. Sometimes he would even resort to a back brace, a thing made of canvas straps.

When we returned to the great hall, he decided that we had seen enough for one time and led us outside where we were off and running to the downtown area. This time we took a side street where there were restaurants and cafes, movie theaters, and various businesses. Stopping at a doorway between two stores, Daddy pressed the brass handle, opened the door and we went up a flight of stairs to an office.

"Be good girls," he instructed as we stepped inside. A woman greeted him by his first name, saying, "Well, Paul, we're very pleased with your work. I have an envelope for you. You'll note that you've received a ten cent raise."

Grinning, Daddy thanked her, deposited the envelope in his left inside suit coat pocket and we departed the building.

"Is that where you work, Daddy?" Laura asked.

"In a way, yes. Most of the work is off in all directions. What say we three go to the Waffle Shop and get something to eat?"

Neither Helen nor Betty were at work there, which seemed strange since they worked days. Daddy inquired and learned that *there were no Helen nor Betty working there at all!*

Having finished our delicious waffles and milk, Daddy's preference coffee, we strolled leisurely along the street. Then Daddy became aware that we were passing the Gaiety Theater, which featured live entertainment unsuitable for children of all ages. Hustling us past the pictures showing what was being featured, he suddenly stopped still, then told us to stay put while he walked back to the pictures and studied them. We edged toward him to see for ourselves what interested him and covered our mouths in shocked surprise. Red-faced, he tucked each of us under one of his arms and with his usual long strides hurried us homeward.

As was usual when Aunt Alice was there, Daddy did not want to return home too soon. Sending us in to see "if the coast was clear," he waited on the porch, watching traffic go by. Laura and I burst into the foyer, dashed down the hall and into the living room where Vi was standing on a stool, arms at her sides, modeling her new dress while Aunt Alice was busily marking the hem with straight pins.

"Mama! Mama! You know those two girls, Helen and Betty, up in room 6, who said they were waitresses at the Waffle Shop?" I cried, beating out Laura with the news, "WELL, Daddy and we saw their pictures in front of the Gaiety

Theater and they had only their HANDS keeping us from seeing their BARE BOSOOMS! Daddy recognized them right…away…the girls…not…their… bosooms…" my voice trailed away.

Aunt Alice did not faint nor did she swallow a single one of the straight pins held between her lips but I knew right away that I had said something wrong by the sudden silence in the room after Vi and Maggie let out their loud gasps of shocked dismay.

Hurrying out to the porch to Daddy, Mama said the three of us should go somewhere and not come back for at least an hour. I do not recall where we went, actually; somewhere via the Essex, maybe for a drive along the Lake Shore. When we returned Mama and Daddy spoke German for a while. Aunt Alice had departed.

Helen and Betty remained in residence in room 6 but Vi and Maggie no longer visited them nor did up their faces in that plaster stuff. They secured their movie magazines from the storeroom in the basement. Mama's sisters, Aunt Rose, Aunt Arlene, and Aunt Emilia (nick-named Mimsy), sometimes arrived either singly or together. We literally jumped for joy when they phoned ahead to let Mama know they were coming, because they would bring our cousins along. Aunt Rose had one daughter, Nancy, almost my age. She was taller than I and often her mother had with her one or more of Nancy's outgrown pretty dresses and slips that she thought might fit me. They usually did after Mama made major alterations. Nancy never rubbed it in about them being "her clothes," so we got along well together.

Much more fun, however, was Aunt Arlene's son, our cousin Lawrence. Later, he would be joined by two brothers but back then he was her only child. Three months older than Laura, he had a devilish little mind that got all of us into trouble, from time to time. One weekend he was allowed to stay with us so Aunt Arlene and her husband, Uncle Bill, could attend his relative's funeral "up north" somewhere.

Inside the walls of our butler's- pantry- turned- kitchen were speaking tubes leading to the former servants' quarters on the third floor. They were hollow pipes with flanged openings, once used to call the servants to their duties. Beside them was a dumb waiter leading to the basement laundry room, once the servants' kitchen. These intrigued Lawrence to no end. He talked us into rising from our beds at midnight and whistling and making eerie sounds into the flanged mouthpieces of the three tubes.

Two of the roomers must have been sound sleepers but the one in room 10, a very nervous type of older woman, dashed into the third floor hall and let out such a piercing screech that Daddy and Mama came dashing from their room and up the stairs. There was no hope of our returning to our bedroom, since Vi and Maggie were also awake now. Lawrence made a dash for the dumb waiter. Laura and I followed. In making our escape, I completely forgot my fear of spiders that I "just knew" must be inside that old thing from which Mama had sternly warned us to stay away.

I don't know how Lawrence knew how to operate it but he pulled one of the ropes and down we went. We were not aware that its door in the basement was padlocked. Suddenly the piercing screams were not coming from the third floor but from our prison.

After our rescue, we three culprits could not sit comfortably, due to the over-the- knees spanking each of us received from Daddy. Mama hurried me off to the second floor bathroom and bathed me from head to foot in nice warm water when I had suddenly decided that I was *covered with spider webs and their inhabitants* and became hysterical. Her tender hands calmed me as she whispered soothing words of comfort. I fell asleep on her lap in the wicker rocking chair in hers and Daddy's bedroom. It was the last time Lawrence was allowed to stay overnight at any of the places in which we lived.

Aunt Mimsy, the baby of Mama's family and at twenty-five unmarried, though engaged, was our favorite. With us she was at ease but around her sisters she was usually silent, as though her words carried no weight. Probably they did not, for Aunts Rose and Arlene always seemed to speak in tones dripping with authority while Aunt Mimsy's were soft and seemed to surround the listener with the feeling that here was femininity personified. She would never be looked upon as a matriarch, like Grandmother and Mama's sisters. Her finance, Edmond, would most certainly "rule the roost," that is, if they ever married. He was still taking courses at Marquette's School of Engineering. The other thing that held them back was that he was a Baptist. Aunt Mimsy had actually placed her hand on the family Bible and sworn that she would never become a Baptist nor would any of her offspring, so it was a waiting game until Edmond could bring himself to accept the precepts of the Wisconsin Synod Lutheran Church that had, by now, baptized three generations of Mama's family.

Having studied my aunts, as was my wont, I perceived them as good looking women. Aunts Rose and Arlene were tall, like Grandmother and Great Aunts Alice and Beatrice, whom I dubbed "The Three Graces" because of their regal bearing. Each had the straight nose, firm chin, and heavy hair as well as the large eyes that men find so attractive. Aunt Mimsy had her own form of beauty that included a turned up nose and rounded chin making her and Mama, fifteen years apart in age, look much like each other. They resembled our Great Grandmother, whose pictures always showed her lips to be set in the tiniest of smiles as if she secretly knew that something nice was about to happen.

Aunt Mimsy belonged to the modern generation. Edmond's transportation in good weather was a motorcycle. He supplied his "little girl," as he had dubbed his fiancé, with a leather helmet and goggles, like the aviators wore, and the two of them, clad in jodhpurs, leather boots, and heavy sweaters, would take off on trips to secret places, their picnic hamper strapped on behind. It was even hinted, with curled lips, that Mimsy had been guilty of smoking at least one sample cigarette.

Her dress lengths showed her knees and she marcelled her hair! Yet she attended church every Sunday and even sang in the choir so nobody accused her of being a flapper nor dubbed Edmond a "good-time Charley." Indeed, he was looked upon as almost too mature for his age and people like Cousin Sedelia and Aunts Rose and Arlene wondered if all that education he was pouring into his head would not, in the end, set him too apart from the rest of humanity so that he might never 'fit in,' especially with him being a Baptist.

Mama was the oldest of the four. Though she seldom raised her voice, she yet managed to be in command of situations. She would allow her two middle sisters to speak their pieces, promise to "think about it," then go her own way. It was the route of common sense. People looked to her for answers to their problems. She, in turn, read her Bible and prayed for answers to hers, though this was always done in private. She had what others referred to as "inner strength." God knows how many times she had to rely on that in the years to come.

Chapter 10

June had turned into July, which was notable for only two things: the heat and the Independence Day celebration. Early on the morning of "the Fourth," Mama was up and boiling new red potatoes, frying and dicing bacon, crying over the onions she was slicing, washing and dicing celery stalks, and measuring out flour, salt, celery salt, vinegar, and water; the ingredients for her delicious German potato salad. Vi and Maggie were put to work boiling eggs and "deviling" them while Daddy, in the coolness of the basement's wood-floored former servants'- kitchen- turned- laundry-room, grated cabbage for the slaw.

Mrs. Malenka, who had come for the day, this time as a visitor instead of housekeeper-cook, hummed as she beat to a light, fluffiness the dozen egg yolks, and sugar that would be added to the other ingredients making up her "mile high" lemon sponge cake. She gave in to my pleading to "please, please, let me grate the lemon peel" and tsk tsked when I soon gave up and ran to the sink to wash the blood from my grated knuckles.

On the top shelf in the wooden icebox reposed a couple dozen of Usinger's best wieners. The blue and white speckled roasting pan of baked beans stood in readiness on the pantry shelf along with the fragrant loaves of bread, each wrapped in waxed paper and a towel, that Mama had baked the night before. It would be a day of "good eating" for both the family, guests and the roomers, who had been invited to share in the festivities. Too bad we wouldn't be eating on the large screened porch of the cottage at Pike Lake instead of in our dining room here at the mansion.

At dusk we would all be going to Juneau Park to enjoy the fireworks display. All, that is, except Mrs. Malenka, who had generously offered to remain behind and "watch the place." Those 'oversized firecrackers' held no interest whatever for her, bringing back too many memories of the war in which her husband had been so badly injured that he had finally died. I remember that she had covered her ears and squeezed her eyes shut the previous Fourth, refusing to come out onto the mosquito-free cottage porch while the rest of us "oohed" and "aahed" over each of the spectacular bursts of the rockets shooting up into the night sky from somewhere across the lake.

She would be staying the night, sleeping in Vi's and Maggie's bed. We four girls would be sleeping crosswise across Laura's and my bed. It was what kids did when adults came to visit for the night.

Meanwhile, we had front row seats for the Parade, which was to pass by along Wisconsin Avenue. Our porch was crowded with family, roomers, and anyone else who could squeeze onto it. Pitcher after pitcher of lemonade was poured into waiting glasses. Some of the men had brought homebrewed beer offered in coffee mugs, "just in case anybody was "nosey." It was *gemutlichkeit*, that aura of fun and friendliness which seemed to have been lost during the past months. One of the men stated that "things were going to be better soon; this 'Market Crash thing' couldn't last forever" and glasses and mugs were raised in agreement.

Row after row of men, proud in their World War uniforms, marched behind the bands playing sprightly military tunes, receiving the applause of grateful citizens who stood with hands on breasts as the colors passed by. Several cars and a bus, loaded with those wounded who were still in treatment at the Soldiers' Home were viewed with respectful silence. They had returned home from the war but would always bear its scars.

Floats decorated with paper roses carried red, white, and blue clad Uncle Sams and living Statues of Liberty of various sizes and ages, the young ones receiving no more acclaim than those well-built matrons who represented all the waiting mothers of boys who had been "over there." Seated in a place of honor on our porch was a man I had never met before, a cousin of Uncle Max. He had arrived by yellow cab an hour before parade time, used a cane with a silver lion's head to assist him up the stairs and was greeted with deference by both Mama and Daddy.

Vi and Maggie shook his hand and pushed Laura and me up to him. He was tall, well over six feet, and had such piercing dark eyes beneath a thatch of bristly gray eyebrows that I was both fascinated and repelled. Something about him reminded me of the stuffed American eagle that had guarded the bookcase in Principal William's office back in Silver Spring Elementary.

"This is Jessie, Mr. Steinmann," Vi introduced me.

"And I'm Laura," she introduced herself.

"How do you do?"

"Just fine, thank you." I supplied. My eyes were fastened on his left leg which, Maggie had informed us earlier, was made of wood. I had the most terrible urge to kick it to see if she were making that up. Such a strange man. He was purported to have been in the Secret Service, whatever that was. It sounded wonderfully 'mysterious,' a word that I enjoyed pronouncing; it so aptly described what it meant.

We each accepted the stick of gum he handed to us in turn before he asked Daddy in a low voice if there were a bathroom he could use "to wash up a bit." I noted that he grimaced in what must have been pain as he laboriously mounted the stairs to the second floor. I especially noted that he had to hand-lift the left leg as he neared the top. Evidently Maggie had been speaking the truth.

Within minutes, he had an audience of curious children spying on him from between the posts of the porch rail. Each wanted to see the man who had not only been in the Secret Service but who had actually served in the Spanish American War, whatever *that* was. I had played that part up to the hilt when I collected a penny from each of the curiosity seekers. Evidently he met all their criteria, for they came away with pleased smiles and shining eyes. A REAL HERO! Laura's and my status went way up that day on the graph kids use in social casting.

Al Steinmann became an infrequent visitor from that day on, showing up at odd times of the year, always supplied with sticks of gum for the children and gifts for Mama, whom he obviously adored. He was a divorced man, which set him as apart as did his left leg. Somewhere there was an ex-wife and several now grown children. His home was up north but he came down to stay at Soldier's Home from time to time.

He declined Daddy's invitation to "join the family for supper and the fireworks" but lingered long enough to take from a silvery case two fragrant

Havanas and offer one to Daddy. In manly fashion, each rolled his cigar between thumb and forefinger, passed it beneath his nostrils in preview of anticipated pleasure, bit off the end and puffed as Mr. Steinmann lit first Daddy's and then his own from a silver lighter bearing the White House seal, a gift from President Coolidge, no less. Then the two of them sat there, one in the Morris chair, the other on the davenport, smoking their fragrant tobacco and from crystal wine glasses sipping the excellent Madeira that had been Mr. Steinmann's gift to his host and hostess.

The Volstead Act had many citizens ignoring that law concerning the partaking of alcohol. Home brew and homemade wine was imbibed with pleasure, looked upon in much the same manner as a box of fine chocolates, perhaps. The Victorian Age was still present in the minds of many of the older generation. In their eyes, one glass was not considered "drinking.

Mama, seated at her Steinway, played with a lightness of fingers that had been missing since "the Crash." We four girls and Mrs. Malenka listened from Vi's and Maggie's bedroom and all of us except Laura were moved to tears. It was almost like being back in the brick house when Mama and Daddy would entertain friends and business acquaintances.

All day there had been the sound of firecrackers of various sizes going off in the neighborhood but by the time Daddy had returned Mr. Steinmann to Soldiers' Home most of the shooters had run out of ammunition. We had been allowed only lady crackers, which popped off when you spun on them with a shoe heel, but we still had a supply of sparklers. We were saving those along with the "punk sticks" used to light them in case there were swarms of mosquitoes at the Lake Front.

Supper over, sunset having brought darkness, we piled into the Essex and followed the Parade Route to Juneau Park, Laura and I captivated by all the lights along the way. Wisconsin Avenue was completely different at night from its daytime appearance. Crowds of people thronged the sidewalks, autos were letting people off in front of various theaters; the streetcars, now lighted, clanged their starting and stopping warnings and we, the RENZES, were a part of it! All so exciting!

Daddy even went back to transport a carload of roomers who wished to share our blankets and there we were, an island of laughing and joking spectators among hundreds of similar groups who crowded the sands and grassy areas along the shore of Lake Michigan.

The first of the rockets filled the air with the resonant KABOOM! and beauty accompanied by the wailing of several frightened little kids and babies who could not tolerate the noise. To my chagrin, I learned that I had reacted in such manner for several years! Well, that time was past! I sat enrapt during the entire display.

Vi and Maggie had caught the eyes of several young men on a blanket a bit further over. Mama and Daddy did not seem to notice the distance between our blanket and the boys' was growing smaller until they were right up close. Then looks passed between Mama and our sisters and, although they were allowed to acknowledge their admirers, that was it!

By the time we were halfway home once more, both Laura and I were sound asleep. We were carried into the house, a couple of limp rag dolls who were undressed and slipped into nightgowns, too lost in slumber to even be aware of our older sisters when they pushed us over to make room for themselves in our bed.

What a wonderful Fourth of July it had been!

Chapter 11

Summer was ending; school was about to begin. We were taken downtown to Brower's shoe store to be fitted via their x-ray machine, which showed us our foot bones when we peered through the viewer. Mama had been busily cutting and sewing blouses and jumpers for each of us. As usual, Laura and I had matching outfits and as usual, she looked better in hers. I hated being so darned skinny.

Vi had sat in bed one night, knees up, head down on them, tears falling on the hand-pieced coverlet. She had been attending Shorewood High, which she loved, having been an A student and active in a number of extra-curricular activities. Now she and Maggie were enrolled in West Division, which was an older school and offered no such amenities as fencing and tennis.

Mama had phoned the School Board and learned that there was no way Vi could still attend Shorewood High. It was West Division or nothing and even that was not an option for by the law she must attend school until reaching age eighteen or upon receiving her diploma.

Maggie, a freshman and excited to be entering high school, could not understand Vi's feelings. Now they wouldn't be stuck with bed-making and dusting and all those other chores they had been doing all summer. Wasn't that enough to make them glad that school was starting? Besides, she had graduated from Silver Spring Elementary and as much as she loved going there, she was having to attend a different school, too, wasn't she? You had to be ready for new adventures, not wail about your old ones! Her cornflower blue eyes sparkled in anticipation.

I understood how Vi felt. I had loved everything about Silver Springs School. What if I didn't like our new school? I put my head down on hers for a moment and her arm reached out and held me tightly. I guess at that moment she didn't mind having a bratty kid sister.

Daddy was supposed to enroll us in our new school but he had been called to serve some papers. Mama had to remain home because someone was coming to possibly rent a vacant room so it was Vi who volunteered. We sang songs as we marched up Wisconsin Avenue and turned the corner onto Eighteenth Street. Another block to Wells and there it was –our New School- larger and more impressive than Silver Spring Elementary but somehow rather forbidding. Both Laura and I were suddenly uncertain about going there.

Fearfully we followed Vi inside and into the office where a lady with a skinny neck and a pencil in her brown hair leaned over the counter to peer at us over half lenses with silvery chains attached to the ear pieces. Vi told her that we wanted to enroll. That is, Laura and I did; she would be attending West Division. Smiling, the lady said she realized that was probably the way it was. When she looked over our report cards she frowned.

"For their ages they seem to be behind a grade. Hmm… their marks are good, passing and better."

"Well, the year before last…"

"1928…"

"Yes. Jessie started school that September. Two weeks later she brought home the chicken pox and Laura caught them from her and then our sister, Maggie, caught them, too. When the quarantine sign came off, Maggie and Jessie went back to school. Laura was still only four, so she hadn't started yet, though she would have in February. Anyways, Maggie and Jessie were barely back in school when Jessie came down with red measles: the bad kind. Naturally, Laura caught them and so did Maggie. Umm- she starts as a freshman this year at West Division, so she won't be enrolling here."

"I see."

"Well, to make matters worse, they were all barely over the measles without complications, thank goodness, and returned to school when Maggie came down with scarlet fever! Of course, so did Jessie and Laura. Not altogether; one after the other. Our poor mother was quarantined in that house with only our housekeeper, Mrs. Malenka, for company from October until April when all three of my sisters ended up in Deaconess Hospital to have their tonsils out!

"My father and I had to sleep in Mrs. Malenka's quarters over his tin shop and eat meals in restaurants and then we both stayed with relatives until our house was finally fumigated and declared free of germs so we could return home." She took a deep breath.

"Why how terrible! But you didn't catch any of those diseases yourself?"

"No. Mama thinks it's because I was so sick with smallpox when I was only three and that somehow the other germs didn't get through to me."

"You poor children!" peering down at Laura and me, "And did the scarlet fever leave any health problems?"

Vi shook her thick honey blonde hair. "I don't believe so, but our little friend next door, Betty, who was eleven and had scarlet fever at the same time my sisters did, well, she never got better. She died right at Easter time."

"Oh, mercy!"

"We got to see her in her casket!" I supplied. "It was right there, in their front parlor, her casket. She just laid there with her eyes closed and didn't open them or anything when we told her how sorry we were that she'd died."

"And she had on a white dress and her mother's bedroom slippers 'cause her feet were too fat to get into her shoes," contributed Laura.

"She had heart dropsy," explained Vi. "Now, about school...." The lady left us and returned with the principal, a jolly man in a brown suit who had a reddish face and a gold tooth. Studying our report cards, he came to some decisions.

"The younger child, uh, Laura, is it? Yes, hmmm, well she's about to enter first grade and that is very important. As for, aah, Jessica, is it? We could probably put her into third, since she *will* be eight in October. Skip her ahead a grade. She seems to have good enough marks for that...." He was looking at me over *his* spectacles.

I nodded agreement and was enrolled in the third grade.

That afternoon I sat on the porch steps and thought about the year we were so sick, especially those long weeks when the three of us were so ill with scarlet fever that Mama knelt beside each of our beds and prayed. Vi had not been entirely correct when she said that only Mrs. Malenka was there for company and assistance. Great Aunt Alice had arrived and bathed each of us and fed us delicious chicken broth. No germs of any sort would have dared to invade *her* lanky body! It meant, of course, that she, too, was quarantined with us for the duration but she never complained. Then, suddenly, it seemed, both Laura and I were very hungry. Together we had devoured an entire loaf of Mama's freshly baked bread topped with both butter and jelly.

What a joyful day it was for all of us when the health officer came to inspect us for rash and peeling and found us free of both. Down came that horrid quarantine sign and a reunion of the family was finally a reality. I remembered how readily Mama smiled at us in spite of being so thin and tired and how Mrs. Malenka grabbed up a long wooden spoon and one of the kettles from the hanging rack in the pantry in lieu of a drum and led Maggie and Laura and me into parading happily around and around the kitchen table.

Aunt Alice soon gathered up her possessions and, with a sigh of relief and a peck on the cheek and hugs around her tall neck from we three recovered patients, had marched out of the house into Clyde's cab. Afterwards, making sure she had departed, Daddy arrived with Vi and hugs and tears were exchanged all around.

I recalled, too, how we were driven to Deaconess Hospital to undergo tonsilectomies. Somehow, Maggie was given the same size hospital gown as mine and went off to surgery trying to protest in red-faced embarrassment that her posterior was showing. But who listens to kids? Back in our rooms, after surgery, we had each received large dishes of vanilla ice cream by kindly nurses to ease our painfully sore throats. After one or two spoonfuls even that cold treat had not helped.

Maggie and I had missed a great deal of classroom work but our teachers had worked with us, helping us to catch up, so that Maggie was able to graduate and I was going to be passed on to the third grade "on probation." It made me happy to know the principal of the new school was giving me the same chance. I did have some reservations, however, for although I read at a high-grade level, arithmetic was not my forte, which worried me.

Joining me on the porch, Mama sat in the ratten rocking chair, tatting, her shuttle darting in and out, the formed loops of lace edging growing longer and longer as we discussed my future.

"Ordinarily I would be against your skipping a grade, Jessie, but the principal is right; you should be with children you own age. If things don't work out, you can always go back to second grade."

"I'm not real good in arithmetic, Mama."

"No problem, Jessie. I kept Daddy's books when we..." Her eyes looked tearful but she smiled. "If you have problems, we'll solve them together."

We both laughed at her play on words. How I loved her! Rushing to hug her, my shoelace caught on her tatting thread. Down went the shuttle, sending it skittering across the porch floor and under the lower rail to disappear into the bushes.

My sisters would have yelled at me and called me a clumsy ox but not Mama. Together we located the errant shuttle with its tail of looped edging, rescuing it from the rain and mud streaked leaves. The lace was soiled but Mama did not announce this; instead, she hugged me and said it was time to start supper.

Running to Laura's and my room, I threw myself across the bed to let my tears of woe spill out onto the coverlet Mama had made for us, my fingernail tracing an outline around the appliquéd figure of a little sun bonneted girl whose sprinkling can watered, with blue embroidery floss stitches, a row of appliquéd tulips. I had only wanted to let Mama know I loved her and now she probably would have to undo a whole batch of tatting! Not only was I not cute and cuddly like Laura but I seemed to always be doing the wrong thing when I didn't want to. How come Laura never seemed to get into trouble, even when she planned naughty things? It just wasn't fair!

School turned out to be not so bad after all. One morning our teacher led us into a large yellow bus and we were transported to the Library. There we were indoctrinated into the correct use of the card files and each of us received our very own library card. For a glorious half hour we could browse through the books lining the shelves and select some to check out. Instructed by the lady in the half-glasses who said she was our "librarian," we understood that we must return them in good condition and by the due date stamped on the special page inside the front cover.

When I approached the checkout desk I was loaded down with six Andrew Lang fairy tale books, each one a different color. They were so heavy that I was bending backwards to compensate.

The librarian gently took them from me and softly promised that "if I were to take only one of them at a time, there would always be enough on the shelves that I need never to return home disappointed." I selected the blue one. All of them contained a large menu of stories that included ogres, fairies, princes, and princesses, ugly witches and crones and beasts of every form. I knew I would find them deliciously exciting. By the bus returned us to school I had already finished reading the first story.

The headquarters of the Knights of Columbus, directly across Wisconsin Avenue from our mansion, had never held much interest for me. It was just another big old building set back from the street and surrounded by a black wrought iron fence with gates that opened to admit large black cars that traveled up the long driveway. One day, however, as I sat on the front porch with my second of the fairy tale series, I looked up and was startled by its resemblance to the castle in the picture, in my lap, of the imprisoned princess who awaited deliverance by a handsome price.

Things suddenly fell into place. There, in that building directly across the street, hidden somewhere behind its white lannon stone façade, probably in the tower, there had to be a princess, perhaps, or, at the very least, a "*dasmsel* (damsel; my pronunciation of some words was not always correct) in distress." Often we would see limousines traveling up that driveway and letting out male passengers in long dresses. One particular passenger wore a red cap and a sash of the same scarlet about his middle. One of the princes, perhaps, or maybe the Head Knight.

I waited endless hours to see if any horse men in shining armor might appear to rescue that distressed maiden but so far none had arrived. It was very frustrating, for I was sure that they probably came and went in large numbers while we were attending school. I finally approached Maggie on the subject and was greeted with a scornful "Oh, silly, that's where the Knights of Columbus meet."

Well, I knew that. Vi was no more enlightening. She, too, stated that the building belonged to the Knights of Columbus. I consulted with my teacher who sat me down at my desk and explained that there would probably never be any maidens in distress at that building, since no females belonged to the Knights of Columbus.

"It's a religious society, you see, dear. All the members are men and they are all Catholics."

"But the knights…"

"Catholic men, dear."

In my heart I knew she did not know the real story. Where there were knights there were maidens in distress, *dasmels*, some with long hair they let down to have the princes climb up, like rope ladders. It was all there in my fairy storybook. Evidently she had never read one. Despite my constant spying on that castle-like edifice across the street, I was never able to spot an armored horse man but I had proof they existed, for in one of the rooms of the Milwaukee Public Museum there were several suits of armor complete with hooded helmets and mailed gloves grasping long lances. I questioned the blue uniformed guard, a gray haired man with a mustache and ruddy cheeks who stood with his hands clasped behind him, asking him if he knew if any of those suits had belonged to Catholics. He did not know.

" I'm not exactly sure what religion those Crusaders were; some kind of Christian, of course. You can tell by the Red Cross they wore over their armor so the enemy would know them. Some coulda been catholic, I guess. Some were Normans and they were French Catholics, if I recall right. Couldn't swear by it."

More than once Mama's sisters declared that I had too much imagination for my own good. I did not understand why they felt so. It felt good to lie in bed and think of things I could do someday and pretend I was someone beautiful and loved by everyone. I just wished I could sneak over to that building across the street and climb the ivy and let that poor *dasmel* know that there was a girl across the street who cared. I was too scared of heights to give it a try.

It was my hope that I would be on hand to witness her rescue but with having to attend school each day and do chores on Saturday, attend church on Sundays and go to bed each night at eight o'clock, chances were I would miss that wonderful event, should it occur during daylight hours. More than likely it would happen at night, since there was too much traffic going by on Wisconsin Avenue and there were all those men in long dresses and others dressed in black suits visiting there constantly for much rescuing to be done.

Once in awhile I would sneak into the front parlor, when everyone was asleep, and keep watch from one of the long windows facing Wisconsin Avenue but too often I dozed off and awakened to see the milkman and his horse making their first early rounds. My bed always felt wonderfully soft upon my return but I would have to move Laura over to her own side and she weighed as much as I. If that dasmel was ever rescued, I probably was asleep at the time.

Meanwhile, I read about other rescues of maidens in distress and wondered if somewhere in the world there might not be a prince in my future. Perhaps, if I desired it strongly enough, a fairy godmother would wave a wand and make me beautiful, like Cinderella. Someday, too, I decided, I would have read every book on the library shelves and examined every display in the Museum. Right now, I had to get through the third grade.

Chapter 12

The start of the new school year had brought more problems to Mama and Daddy. Roomers are not like boarders; they are more transient. Always there were rooms vacant which needed to be filled and for some reason September found us with five empty rooms which, because of the "bad-money-situation," would not be filled with Marquette students. The university must have felt the pinch, too, with fewer students signing up for courses.

Daddy conceived the brilliant idea of meeting the trains and buses and informing alighting passengers that on Fifteenth and Wisconsin was a rooming house with clean sheets and transportation to any place in Milwaukee. Wonder of wonders, he filled every room and some in the rooming house next door.

He got into conversation with a man in a business suit who, it turned out, was the manager of the Riverside theater. That gentleman was waiting for an entire vaudeville troupe arriving from New York via every vaudeville stage in between there and Milwaukee.

"Wonderful acts, wonderful! Now I have to round up places for them to stay during the four weeks they'll grace our stage."

So it was that Daddy made four or five trips delivering vaudeville people to our door. We ended up with a skinny contortionist and his very tall wife, who "sang;" a bird whistler; a scarred-faced knife thrower, and his pretty blonde wife, both of whom had foreign accents which Mama thought might possibly be Russian or maybe Romanian; a pair of comedians billed as "the Joking Jakes," and a juggler.

The theater manager had given Daddy enough free passes so we could attend at least one performance as a family. That turned out to be a Saturday matinee, with Mrs. Malenka again pressed into service "to watch the place." Daddy had two extra passes, one for her and the other for her "boyfriend." It seemed strange to us that someone so old should have one of those. It was even stranger when we learned he was at least twenty years her junior. But that is another story. It was fun seeing our very own roomers performing on stage. We had heard some of them rehearsing as they went about their morning toilettes in the bathrooms, the lady singer, especially, for her contralto voice carried.

The bird whistler had kept us entertained the night before. We kept poking each other when we recognized the calls of birds he had named, identifying them aloud until someone behind us admonished, "you kids shut up!" We did, hunching down in our seats and looking fearfully at Mama and Daddy. All we received, however, were oblique glances that warned us "that will be the last of that!" the "behave yourselves" message which we knew could bring on spankings when we returned home.

The singing lady had a gorgeous voice with which she belted out songs that had the audience clapping and cheering, for her repertoire included many of those by Irving Berlin and George Cohen.

The female half of the Joking Jakes came onstage wearing a long flowing glittery gown and fur neckpiece. Gliding over to her tuxedo-clad husband, who was seated at the Steinway, she proceeded to sing but seemed unable to keep time to his piano playing. Her rendition of some operatic aria was so off key that someone in the audience yelled out, "toss her some tomatoes." It was then that her "neckpiece" leapt to the floor and ran off-stage on its four doggy paws! She then proceeded to not only glide about the stage but do figure eights and other tricks on the roller skates her long skirt had been concealing. No wonder she seemed so much taller on stage.

Her husband kept up a running comment about her performance and things that had happened "back in Tuscaloosa." By the time the couple took their final bows, everyone was wiping away tears of laughter and holding their stomachs to ease their "stitches." We were so proud of those two "roomers of ours!"

I could not watch the knife thrower hurl those sharp blades at his poor wife, who stood so bravely against a board, her body outlined in balloons which he was breaking, one at a time, almost nicking her in the process.

The juggler not only "juggled" but rode a unicycle as he did so. Amazing! There were other acts: a dog and his trainer, even a live seal that clapped and barked to music, blew horns, and waddled across stage in imitation of his owner. The two halves of a horse kept coming apart and had an awful time trying to get themselves back together correctly, the "rear end" continually sitting down on things and the "head" section getting stuck in objects such as the lid of the Steinway and rungs of a chair.

One couple did soft shoe steps in unison, twirling canes, and strutting about the stage like a pair of Siamese twins. In fact, they *were* Siamese twins. We spent long moments afterwards discussing how they slept, dressed, went to the bathroom when they were hitched together like that at the hip. Daddy, grinning and remarking that they would probably feel very comfortable using the "two-holer" like the one we had at the lake cottage and receiving a pursed lip frown of condemnation for his boorishness from Mama.

Satisfied, Laura and I went to bed pretending we were Siamese twins, something that lasted only until we drifted off to sleep and curled up on our own pillows with the usual half-foot distance between us.
It was late when the vaudvillers finally arrived back at the rooming house. They assured us they would let each other in and would be sure to lock up behind themselves, so Mama and Daddy turned in for the night, but I doubt that either slept until everyone else was snoring into his or her pillows.
It was fun having out "special guests." The place was never livelier, for they would gather in the second floor hall and even take up half the staircase, discussing things that had occurred in the past or were happening currently. The Joking Jakes rehearsed new routines, even borrowing Mama's piano a time or two to see if something or other fit into their allotted stage time.

One morning Mr. Burke, the bird-whistler, accompanied Laura and me to school and entertained our classmates, helping them to identify calls of birds they would never see except in zoos and, I suspect, never at all since who ever heard of a suede-coated terminal bird? The other kids were jealous, which made Laura and me feel triumphant, because some of them seemed to think that those whose parents ran a rooming house were somehow not as good as other people's children.

Mama's family were horrified to think that she was surrounded by "circus type people." She had thought they would find the idea entertaining and learned otherwise. It had been Cousin Sedelia, of course, who went to Grandma with the news.

Grandma lived in a very large house. She had a cook-housekeeper who looked after her like a mother hen and oversaw us children on the rare times when we went to visit there. Grandma had suffered a stroke a few years before and needed a cane to help her walk, so she never came to the rooming house; she would not have been able to climb the stairs to the bathroom. Instead, she visited Mama via the telephone, which was a regular phone at her end of the line but ours was the coin-operated one out in the hall.

Mama listened with the receiver away from her ear because Grandma was not mincing words. Had Mama no pride at all? If she and Paul were in such financial straits that they needed to take in people of that "ilk," she 'should have been notified' for she had not lost a penny when the banks closed their doors.

"We're doing just fine, Mama. The theater manager promised that they were decent folks who worked on stage instead of in other places of employment and so far they have been faithful in paying their rent and… no, they have not brought in bedbugs! Certainly, I've checked. I don't believe vermin remain where it's nice and clean, like this place. Paul vacuums every other day and the sheets are changed twice-weekly. "No, Mama, it's not too hard for me. I've become very adapt at washing and changing them, and of course, the girls help. I wish you could see this place; it was once someone's lovely mansion. Why, there's a butler's pantry complete with dumb waiter… oh, you heard about the dumb waiter…well, Paul has it in good working order and it does a nice job of taking things to the basement. Of course, we keep it locked at the basement end so nobody can use it but us…"

Others called as well: Mama's sister and Daddy's sisters, Tante Kate and Aunt Elise, neither of whom had visited us in out new surroundings, as yet. Daddy had dropped by Aunt Elise's and told her about our unusual roomers. She wanted to know if there were any free passes for her and Uncle Otto, maybe four, even, so our cousins, Rudy and Bernice, could attend as well. Daddy said "I'll see."

Tante Kate asked if any of them might be from New Yawk, She had been born there and always wanted to know what was going on "down East" even though she had not lived there for over forty years. The opposite of Mama, who was fifteen years older than Aunt Mimsy, Tante Kate was fifteen years older than Daddy and was actually his half-sister, since their mother had been widowed when Tante Kate was only five and had subsequently married Daddy's father. Aunt Elise was a child of that second marriage and was almost ten years older than Daddy.

He was the baby of the family. His father died when Daddy was only three years old; at age eighteen he was orphaned. He boarded with Tante Kate until he married Mama.

Life continued on a smooth course in spite of Mama's family's fears, at least until the last night of the vaudeville troupe's stay. It started with the knife thrower and his wife.

Something must have gone wrong on the stage, because he came home in a fury. For over an hour he hurled invectives at his mate in their mother tongue. Then someone came running in from the street to inform us in excited tones "there's a man up there trying to kill a woman!"

A parade of Daddy, Mama, we kids in spite of being told to remain where we were, the stranger who had alerted us, and a few others, summoned from their rooms by the ruckus, all hastily trooped up to the third floor.

The door to the knife thrower's room was locked but Daddy had a key. When he dashed inside the room he found the poor wife face-up, the lower half of her struggling body lying across a streamer trunk, feet kicking wildly, her neck on the window sill, her head outside in the rain, and her husband trying to jam the window sash down onto her throat! Daddy was not as tall as the knife-thrower but he had been juggling heavy furnace parts for years and had muscles galore. The would-be murderer was grabbed from behind, hurled across the room and the victim rescued. On the dresser lay a set of knives that could have done Daddy in but the fellow who could have used them was now cowering on the bed in tears of remorse.

"It is my temper," he wailed. "I do not wish to *murx* her but she make me so mad I lose my senses."

The police were not called because the wife now sat beside her husband to console him! Evidently she was ready to remain with the fellow in spite of everything. Mama did make a report to Officer Jim later that week, however, as required by law if anything so bizarre occurred. By then the troupe was no doubt performing in Minneapolis or some place similar.

The next morning we were all awakened by a woman's screams. Wondering if it might be the knife thrower's wife, Mama hurried upstairs to the third floor to find the distraught roomer from number seven pointing hysterically to the bathroom.

When daddy and we kids trooped in there, we found Mama standing with hands on hips demanding in German that the trained seal barking at her form the water-filled bathtub "*gehen sie heim, gehen sie heim.*" Apparently the animal did not understand German because he made no effort at all to go home or elsewhere but instead splashed Mama from head to toe with seal-flavored bathtub water.

Drenched and dripping, Mama looked at Daddy with blazing eyes and let him know in a stream of German exactly how she viewed the situation. The darned rooming house and this "*ferschtinken, Gott in Himmel*, get me a towel," life we were leading there!

Sheepishly, the juggler came into the bathroom mouthing string of apologies. His friend, the seal's trainer, who was staying in the rooming house next door, had done too much celebrating after their final performance. He was at present taking up space in a cell in the city jail. The policemen would not allow the seal into the paddy wagon, so…"

Daddy, who was drying Mama off and helping her into the robe Vi had hurried up to her, told the fellow that the seal could not stay. People had to use the room and some were probably already late for work. "You folks get the money to bail your friend out and do something with this animal or it will find itself in Washington Park Zoo, for God's sake Willie! And you can clean out this tub! The whole room smells like fish!" Which was due to the bucket of them standing in the corner!

Afterwards, when the second floor bathroom was free and she had bathed and washed her hair, Mama's sense of humor returned. The seal was taken next door and ensconced in their third floor tub, which arrangement had been made for a fee by its trainer. We had received the unwanted guest because nobody in our group had a key to the other place nor had they dared approach the owner, a man purported to have a very bad temper when roused from his bed.

During the ensuing months, we had a series of roomers who somehow did not fit the usual category, men and women who, it seemed, were used to the services of nice hotels. Their demands had Mama and Daddy so tired by the end of the day that they went to bed crabby.

It was Cousin Sedelia who finally let the cat out of the bag. Mama's family were recommending our place to their friends, who passed the word on to business acquaintances, etc. Evidently these were led to expect personal maid service. A phone call to one of the aunts put a stop to that.

They had only been trying to help; " if she and Paul weren't so proud and would let them do something more substantial…; it certainly did not seem right that they had everything and poor Lydia was in such a terrible situation there in that rooming house; if she had listened to Mama and married Jack Murray…"

Mama had pinched her lips together and quietly hung up the receiver, cutting off any more of her sister's admonitions. She returned to our quarters talking out loud to herself. They had married *their* spouses for love, just as she had married hers. What the future might hold for them, God in his mercy only knew and, if it were not good, she would not make them feel less because of it, so why couldn't they do the same for her? When she came out of her bedroom her eyes were red-rimmed from crying. I wanted so much to let her know I agreed with her but then she would know that I had overheard her phone conversation from the window seat behind the piano, where I had been reading, so I merely leaned my head against her when she sat down and let her arm hold me tight. Perhaps she needed that from me at the moment. It eased my conscience to believe so.

Chapter 13

Vaudeville troupes were not the only different sort of persons in our lives during that period. As times got harder, people started behaving in bizarre fashion. It was not unusual to see some going through garbage cans and waste bins for things they could salvage to eat or to sell. In our neighborhood there appeared an elderly woman who met all my expectations of how an old crone should appear. Gray hair straggling from beneath a man's floppy brown felt fedora with brim turned down, long brown coat with scrungy fur at the collar wrapped about her skinny figure, torn shoes too big for her feet; she begged dimes "for bus fare" or "a cuppa coffee, please, and a donut to fill my poor empty stomach" from passing pedestrians.

I followed her on several occasions, hiding behind trees and bushes, watching as she put the coins she received into a man's sock fastened to something beneath her coat. Once in awhile someone actually put her aboard the bus and she would emerge a block or two later, angry at not having received the money instead.

One afternoon, Laura and I called out to her, "Oh beggar lady, we know what you do with all that money!" She came up to us so swiftly we couldn't even turn to run away and out flew her hand to slap each of us across the mouth!

Ordinarily we would not have let Mama know of our activity but we were frightened so we ran home to her, bawling and snuffling with every step, especially Laura who emoted all over the place. Officer Jim was soon there to question us.

The beggar woman no longer graced our neighborhood. Mama and Daddy had to go to court on our behalf. They reported afterwards that she was an eccentric who had money in several banks. She was sentenced to spend thirty days in jail for pandering and fined five hundred dollars and a year's probation for striking helpless children. Those thirty days did not seem long enough and it was several months before we felt safe. My imagination had her jumping out at us from doorways or from behind bushes, her eyes ablaze and her claw-like fingers with dirty, long sharp nails all set to scratch out our eyes. Maybe I also felt guilty for baiting her. Somehow Laura and I had not confessed to that part of it, though she probably told the judge about us. We were not the wonderfully good children we later purported to be when telling our children and theirs about our childhoods.

There were other unusual personages in the area, two of whom lived in the house that we had trespassed. Elderly sisters who wore only black, the two seldom left their home, but when they did it was to ride in their black electric automobile. An elderly gentleman in formal attire would assist them up the two steps, having first placed a fresh rose in each of the pair of crystal vases gracing the sidewalls of the interior, and off they would go, silently gliding along Wisconsin Avenue to some unknown destination.

One afternoon their butler dropped off an invitation to Mama, asking her to tea. It seems that they had learned that she was Grandmother's daughter. Their father and mother and our great grandfather and grandmother had come to America from Germany on the same ship. Both had relatives on Jones Island, out in Milwaukee Harbor, at that time a small fishing village whose inhabitants were a mixture of Germans and Kashubians. (Later the Illinois Steel Company claimed the island and won a court battle to oust the fisher folk, who settled in Milwaukee or other parts of Wisconsin.)

The two couples had become good friends over the years, though their lives had taken different directions, and their daughters had kept in touch. Possibly our Grandmother had revealed her concern over her daughter's living quarters and the two sisters offered to look into the matter.

Neither of the sisters married. Mama had known them only slightly, as Grandmother's callers who might inquire as to her health and how she was progressing in her lessons at the Music Conservatory in those long ago days before she had married Daddy. Now Mama became their occasional guest and Laura and I quaked in our shoes a bit until we felt certain that the two ladies had really not known that we, too, had once visited their house.

They would always coax Mama into playing their piano and bemoan the fact that she had chosen marriage over the concert stage. One had taught music and recognized talent in that field; the other had taught school. Both had spent years in Europe and had acquired a taste for excellent wine. Mama always returned home with the benign smile of one who had sipped a glass or two of one of their intoxicating offerings.

I often wondered why women like them did not have husbands. They had truly lovely faces, though body-wise one was almost too slender, and the other was "a bit wide at the beam" as one of our roomer's described her, he having witnessed her entering the electric auto. Both wore rimless prince-nez glasses. The skinny one had dark circles under her eyes and was given to fainting at times. Mama thought that maybe she was anemic and suggested to her that she might try whipping a raw egg into a glass of beer as a tonic, one which our Great Grandmother would offer to her family members when she thought they were a bit 'peaked.'

Whether this was done I could not say. Perhaps not, for she passed away the following spring. The funeral procession from the church to the cemetery was exceedingly long, Mama told us upon her return.

We all felt sorry for the remaining sister. It seems our pity was misplaced. Less than six months later she married the tall, distinguished man who had been seen visiting several times each week; their doctor! I guess he liked women who were a bit "wide in the beam."

Chapter 14

Saturday mornings were spent making the place shine, from bathrooms to the laundry. Laura and I were assigned the tasks of sweeping the laundry room floor and cleaning out the sink and toilet of the "commode room," which had once been set aside for the exclusive use of the servants, especially the cook, as this had been her domain.

There had once been a cook stove with pipes connected to the chimney next to the dumb waiter; now Mama's two- burner gas stove stood in its place, her oval copper wash kettle atop that. Mama wanted "nice hot water" when she washed clothes, so hot that she had to use a three foot wash stick to lift them from the copper tub of the machine and gingerly feed each item into the hand-operated wringer. With a plop, they would come out the other side and land in the cold rinse water of the first tub to soak while another pile of soiled items was put into the machine along with a pail or two of hot water.

Repositioning the wringer, Mama would lift the clothes from the first rinse water and send them through the wringer to make their flattened way into the final rinse water. Their third trip through the wringer dropped them into one of two oval wicker baskets. Daddy or one of our sisters had the task of taking the clothes out to the small yard I had seen that first day from the fire escape where they would be hung on wash lines to dry in the "nice fresh air" as Mama termed it.

White things received a special treatment with drops from the Little Boy Blue bluing bottle, probably in the first rinse tub. Shirt collars and cuffs were dipped into the kettle of Argo starch water. These washing aids, along with Climalene water softener and the paring knife used to shave slivers from the bars of Fels Naphtha soap, as well as the bottle of Bo Peep Ammonia, were kept on a shelf above the hooks from which the round galvanized washtubs hung, on the wooden wall of the coal bin, when not in use.

Daddy always had the task of emptying the tubs and folding the metal rack on which they rested when in use. This was leaned against the side of the chimney and kept from falling by the washing machine, which was quite different from any other I have ever seen. When it was plugged in and the motor started up via a toggle switch, the tub would gently rock back and forth, like a cradle. It was filled from each side through metal drop-down doors that were then securely locked with metal catches.

When Mama went upstairs for something and we thought she would not see it happen, Laura and I would each grasp the handle of a door and let ourselves be alternately lifted from the floor and back down again, she going up as I went down, our bodies turning rosy from the heat of the water inside. Footsteps on the stairway sent us each into letting- go and busying ourselves once again with cutting out the Betsy McCall dolls from magazines procure from the stacks in the store room, perhaps. Daddy had already had to re-bolt the handles a time or two because Mrs. Malenka had allowed us to "hang on and ride," just as she had allowed Vi and Maggie to do so when they were small, like us. Now it was "conserve, conserve; we can't afford to replace things, you know."

Daddy's bar of Lava soap had its own place in the once-shining-brass-now-turned-green soap dish above the commode room sink. We were given Dutch Cleanser Powder with which to hopefully make that dish shine but it was truly "too far gone."

Like the ones on the second and third floors, the old-fashioned toilet was operated by a pull chain that released water from a wooden box up high on the varnished, wainscoted wall. Such a drab little room from which we were glad to escape but where Daddy often reposed to read the evening paper in peace without having to listen to the chattering of his five female family members. We females used it only in an emergency, when the other bathrooms were in use.

We were not allowed to linger long at our laundry room chores because of Mr. Brewster, the man who resided in the former servants' dining room, which was a large room off the laundry. Its two barred windows, half-underground, faced Wisconsin Avenue. There was a door with a vestibule leading onto Fifteenth

Street: Mr. Brewster's own private entrance. He was also given extra courteous treatment, for he had the air of a gentleman about him and articulately presented his words in a voice that was both resonant and deep. I loved to hear him when he chose to speak to Mama and Daddy but this was seldom because he was not very sociable. In fact, we were told 'that he enjoyed privacy and we were not to disturb him in any way.' He, too, had the use of the commode room but we never found any of his personal items about when we cleaned there.

Mr. Brewster worked nights somewhere, at a job where he dressed in a tuxedo. Mama said he was a musician. A rather handsome man with just a hint of gray at is temples, he was over six feet tall, his black hair almost scraping the pipes in the boiler room the time he and Daddy chatted a bit while Daddy insulated, from the large roll of sheet asbestos, the huge 'iron monster of a boiler' that would heat the building when cold weather arrived.

Eyes as dark and deep set as his were usually sharply penetrating but not Mr. Brewster's. There was an air of sadness about him as if he were merely walking through life instead of living it. I wondered what kind of music would emanate from someone so unemotional and what had happened in his life to make him a loner? It even came to my mind to ask him if he would help 'the poor *dasmel* in distress' in that castle across the street, a deed which would surely make a man feel better about himself but I was afraid to disobey Mama and rap at his door.

Also, he was a Catholic; one day his door had been opened and I had noted the crucifix on the wall above his bed. He probably would not want to go against his fellow Catholics. Besides, rescuing *dasmels* required a horse and he certainly did not have one of those.

He was our mystery man, one we four girls discussed from time to time. He cleaned his own room, placing his neatly folded bed linens atop the wash pile. Since he had already lived there for several years when we moved in, Mama had no wish to disturb his routine. He always paid his rent on time and on Mama's birthday had even presented her with a lovely fresh American Beauty rose.

Maggie had read the book by Bram Stroker about the vampire, Dracula, and sent shivers down our spines by suggesting that Mr. Brewster turned into a bat at night.

Mama told us to stop our foolish conjectures and made Maggie peel a mess of potatoes to keep her thoughts on more prosaic matters so she wouldn't be giving her sisters nightmares. Mr. Brewster, she admonished was a perfectly respectable gentleman who had previously lived in Marshfield, Wisconsin and certainly did not hail from Transylvania. She also declared with finality that there was no coffin filled with earth in his room nor in any other place, ending that discussion. It was the following February that we learned the tragic truth about our mysterious guest.

Meanwhile, our Saturday chores went on, as usual and then we were free to play or visit the library or museum. Sometimes we four girls and Mama walked downtown and shopped while Daddy remained in attendance at home.

I loved those long walks with Mama. She had so much to tell us: about her life as a girl in Bay View and about her father, who had died of a stroke when she was only nineteen, just the age he had been when he arrived in New York from Germany.

An apprentice carpenter by age twelve, he was a noted architect and builder when he departed this world at age forty-six. The houses and business places he had built were large and imposing structures, including the one in which Mama had grown up and the two-flat several lots over. Grandmother sold the family home and lived in the downstairs flat after suffering her stroke, as all of the bedrooms in the family home were on the second floor. Like in the old family home, her living quarters were more than twice as big as our present ones.

It was much different walking those long blocks to downtown with Mama than when Daddy had us running along side him. We strolled, taking time to study the university buildings and resting a bit on a bench or two at Red Arrow Park from which the wading pool water had now been drained. At the Boston Store, we would admire the items in the display windows. Sometimes we crossed Wisconsin Avenue to examine something that had caught our attention in Espenhains or J.C.Penney's display windows and we always studied the latest fashions in the windows of the smaller shops.

Lunchtime might find us at Charley Toy's Chinese Restaurant, upstairs from the shops on the north side of Wisconsin Avenue, where we would sip tea from small cups without handles. We all enjoyed the beef chow mein and I especially liked egg foo yung. The owner would come to our table and with many bows, one hand curled inside of the other, welcome us to his establishment and inquire as to how things were going "at the looming house". It made us feel important to know that he respected Mama as a business woman.

Mostly we ate at Woolworth's second floor lunch counter where there too, we could order chop suey, passably good but not as tasty as at Toy's. The menu offered an excellent variety of meals that were nourishing, well prepared and most of all inexpensive. While we ate we would study the hanging displays and observe customers.

We did not receive a weekly allowance merely "because we were kids" but we were paid for chores well done, maybe a nickel or a dime. The roomers paid us for running errands, maybe a penny or a nickel, once or twice even a dime, so we usually had a quarter or so to spend on those shopping trips.

One Saturday my delighted eyes caught the sight of and my ears the tinkling sound of Chinese wind chimes on display across from the lunch counter. They consisted of varied shaped bits of hand painted glass suspended from colored strings attached to a circle of thin bamboo. The boxes in which they were sold were of the cheapest gray cardboard, almost paper thin, but my eyes saw only the red and white oval label bearing the words "Made in China".

My imagination presented me with a vision of people in long embroidered silk gowns with wide, wide sleeves and soft-soled shoes that curled upwards at the toes. All had their hands together in attitude of respect and were bowing low in obeisance to me, their beloved empress. I suddenly knew that I wanted to own a set of the chimes, As usual, my money had another place to go and nobody, not even Vi, would lend me enough for the purchase of "those silly things," as she put it. "They won't work inside, Jessie, and will surely break if you hang them on the porch this time of year. It's October, you've heard the wind howling." An exaggeration: most days a sweater was all that was required for warmth on the way to school.

I mentally kept those chimes on my wish list and hoped to earn enough to purchase them for future use. As Aunt Alice would say, "One always needs an extravagance or two to remind one that life is not all scour and scrub." Maybe the next time we went shopping I would be able to take them home with me. I sure wished that darned old "Depression" hadn't come along!

Chapter 15

Marquette's homecoming parade down Wisconsin Avenue, followed by a huge bonfire on their athletic field, brought contagious excitement to the mansion because of our college student roomers who sang "ta-rah! Rah! Boom de-ay" and other college type things as they bathed and shaved in the bathrooms and donned their long raccoon coats and fedoras. There was two-way traffic up and down the stairway as their friends arrived to pick them up. Two girls even made it into the third floor room of a pair of freshman males who were newcomers. Hip flasks were hurriedly tucked into purses when Daddy arrived to inform the young ladies that they were going against house rules and must wait in the downstairs vestibule for their dates.

Halloween arrived. We all dressed in costumes, roomers included, and feasted on homemade donuts, hot cocoa and apple cider and bobbed for apples down in the laundry room, which had been decorated with black and orange crepe paper streamers. A huge lighted pumpkin carved by Daddy, who had driven out to a farm to purchase it, stood on the two-burner gas stove. Mr. Brewster was at work and, therefore, was not disturbed by our partying.

To me the best of all was my birthday that first week of November…I felt so special inside, even if the outside of me was still pale and skinny and my teeth were so large, like Daddy's, that I would have to weigh two hundred pounds before they would fit well in my face!

Nobody else seemed to have that problem, especially Maggie, who was already attracting so many boys that Mama and Daddy were constantly counseling her about being vain. Not allowed yet to date, she had several admirers who vied for the opportunity to carry her books home for her at least as far as the White Tower hamburger stand catty-corner across from our place.

Vi, almost sixteen, had only one admirer, a tall, round shouldered fellow with red hair who stammered when he spoke. It was not that Vi was unattractive, for she had her own brand of beauty, but there was an air of seriousness about her that kept her from flirting and making "goo-goo eyes" the way Maggie did.

Peering at myself in the mirror, I was certain no boy would ever walk me home from school, not even one with round shoulders and a stammer. Things would have to change mightily in the next eight years before I turned sixteen.

Meanwhile, there was the matter of the banana spice cake with chocolate frosting and custard filling between the layers that reposed on the pedestaled cake plate awaiting eight candles. Mama's best china with a real gold band decorating each individual piece was stacked and ready to be placed on the damask covered dining table which, for the occasion, held two extra boards.

Tante Kate had been invited as well as Mrs. Malenka and her brand new husband. My heart almost hurt, I loved Mama so much. She knew just how to make an ugly duckling feel like a princess.

For my birthday meal entrée I had selected roast beef, mashed potatoes and gravy, creamed kohlrabi, creamed peas for those who did not like kohlrabi, with Mama's wonderful freshly baked bread as accompaniment.

The mouth-watering aromas emanating from the oven were wafting through the entire house. Several of the roomers had come downstairs to hand me small gifts and went back up declaring the place smelled "just like home." I wished we had room enough at the table to invite each and every one of them to share our meal. Later Mama would send me upstairs with roast beef sandwiches and a slice of cake for those who had given me gifts. If she could have, Mama would have fed all of the roomers so they would not have to take their meals out but I suppose, looking back, that she had already stretched her food budget to the limit.

Tante Kate arrived in the Essex, all two hundred fifty pounds of her, and she was pushed and pulled up the front porch stairs and escorted into the house by Daddy and we four girls. We accepted her warm hugs with pleasure and escorted her to the Morris chair where she plopped and remained until mealtime. No way would she have fit in the small kitchen, a fact that she bemoaned because she loved to assist in preparing delicious foods.

With her gray hair piled atop her head and caught into a pug held in place with large celluloid hairpins; her large features, ebony eyes framed with equally black brows and the full lips that alternately revealed and hid her still intact strong teeth, she needed only to have had brown skin to be the epitome of the benign "black Mammy" portrayed in the movies by such stars as Ethel Waters and Hattie McDaniels.

Her homemade dresses reached the tops of her high black shoes, these no longer the button type but were laced. In her carpet bag she carried whatever it was she was "working" at the time: crochet hooks, wool and a partially completed afghan or maybe the pastel silk anklets; cotton batting; contrasting embroidery thread strands; case of hand needles and small scissors with which she made her "honey-boy dolls" that she gave away to sick children so they would have something to hug.

Mrs. Malenka was all smiles when she and her bridegroom arrived. They wore matching wedding bands and she told us she must now be addressed as Mrs. Turner, Mrs. Alfred Turner. The Alfred half of their union was very shy behind his somewhat thick glasses but had kindly ways.

The new Mrs. Turner had previously explained to Mama that he had decided to marry a woman who was past forty because he had suffered from mumps as a child and would never be able to beget any children. This I had learned from listening in on their conversation held shortly before the marriage, when Mama and Mrs. Malenka had assumed they were alone and out of earshot.

As usual, when I overheard things, I had not meant to do so; it was merely that I was reading at the window seat behind Mama's piano and they were not aware of my presence. Fortunately for me, they went into my parent's bedroom so Mama could show our former housekeeper-turned-friend the lovely tablecloth she was crocheting, this to be later presented to the happy couple as a wedding present, and I was able to take shelter in Laura's and my room where I could mull over what they had said.

How mumps as a child could stop someone from begetting children? Daddy had said we came from "the lily pond." Maybe someone who had the mumps as a child must not go near pond- water? I wrote this question down in my notebook that contained many such ponderable thoughts.

My wish as I blew out the candles that year was for the times to change so that we would no longer be so "money short." It was a difficult decision to make, that wish, because I also wanted to wish for beauty but after weighing matters I decided that beauty could wait.The Essex was giving Daddy problems and he really did not have the money needed for repairs; not unless more people decided to get divorces or something so he could serve more papers. Still, there were a few calls for him to repair furnaces because he was still listed in the phone book yellow pages and for twenty five cents per month the phone company was transferring his calls to this line.

I had finally decided to put my beauty problem into God's hands as He was the one who had deprived me of it in the first place. Maybe He would reconsider. It did not occur to me to give Him the more pressing problem of money-need and let my petty problem be handled by the birthday wish. Eight years was not enough time for a child to be able to stand back and view the larger picture. There were all those tomorrows to learn to do that. Or were there? The accident almost took them away.

.

Chapter 16

The following Saturday Mama discovered that she needed two cans of tomato soup and a loaf of bread. Daddy was out on a furnace cleaning job, Vi and Maggie were cleaning bathrooms and wearing their "scrub clothes" so *they* could not be sent off to the A&P Store on Fourteenth and Wells without taking an hour or so to be 'presentable.' Elated at being eight years old, I offered to run the errand.

Placing the two quarters into my hand along with the red reed basket, Mama handed me the list and sent me off with the usual instructions regarding the crossing of Wisconsin Avenue.

"Now remember to look both ways, go to the safety island in the middle and then look both ways and cross to the opposite curb."
Happy, feeling like Little Red Riding Hood off on an errand with her basket, I skipped past the other sections of the rooming house, the house where the sisters abided, the dark red stone house surrounded by wrought iron fencing where the "old couple" lived and, looking both ways, crossed Fourteenth Street.

Traffic was light on Wisconsin Avenue. Making it to the safety island was no problem. There were several cars coming from the east, so I patiently waited. One of then stopped and waved for me to cross. Hesitating, I finally followed his hand signals and crossed in front of him. He was already extending his arm to indicate a left turn. Evidently the motorist who came up on his right from somewhere saw that and not the little girl who was suddenly in his path.

Everything happened so fast! There was a squealing of bakes as the car bore down on me, then the feeling of being tossed and a recollection of a metal bumper, some wheels and pain before I sank into oblivion.

I came to aware of people around me and struggled against whoever was picking me up and placing me onto a stretcher. My basket lay on its side, my two quarters catching the sunlight and sending it back to me from where they lay on the pavement. I tried to tell somebody that I needed to go to the store for soup and bread but nobody would listen. I doubt that my words were spoken expect in my aching head.

Inside the ambulance, I was strapped down because I was struggling to be free. Somebody kept wiping my forehead. I turned my head as we were starting up and saw Mama and several others coming out the front door of the rooming house.

"Mama!" I cried. Then we were past and the next moment, it seemed, I was lying on a table of some sort with bright lights shining down and a nurse telling me how brave I had been while they stitched my forehead!

I tried to reach up to feel but hands held me back and a man in white began to ask me questions.

"Sweetie, are you awake? Can you see my fingers? Do you know where you are, honey? You're in the Emergency Hospital. Nice men brought you here so we can fix you up. You tangled with a great big car! Did you know that? Can you tell me your name? What's your name, honey? Do you know your name?"

"Dolly. I want my Mama!" My tears were running down my cheeks and onto the hard pillow. I didn't like all those questions. My head ached.

"She seems to have come around. Says her name is Dolly."

"I call all my girls by that pet name when they're sad or hurting. I think she's telling us she needs me. Oh, I'm so glad she's going to be all right! I never dreamed when I sent her to the store that she'd end up here. It was only a week ago that we celebrated her eighth birthday…"

It was Mama! I knew her voice and suddenly, looking into both pairs of her wonderful green eyes, I saw her two beautiful smiles. Her faces were wet when she bent to kiss me.

"I'm sorry, Mama, I didn't get the soup!"

"Soup! Oh, Jessie, we don't care about the soup! All we want is to have you get better. That big car almost took you away from us! They're going to put you in a nice bed and I'll stay right with you."

"I'm awfully tired, Mama. Is it all right if I sleep?"

"I don't think just yet, Dolly. This is another adventure and you want to be awake so you can tell your sisters all about it. And Daddy, too. They want me to keep you talking."

"I don't like this adventure, Mama, and how come I see two of you?"

"Do you, Dolly?"

She seemed to be talking to somebody about this. Then I was wheeled into a room and placed in bed where I was finally allowed to sleep. Daddy's voice called me back to consciousness. His face, too, was wet when he bent to kiss me.

Not as wet as Vi's and Maggie's when I arrived home several days later to be placed in Laura's and my bed for another ten days. Laura slept with her sisters during that time but curled up with me whenever possible. It was Vi who had run down to the corner to the accident scene just as the ambulance pulled away. There, in a pool of blood on the street lay the red basket, a gaping hole in its side. It was probably that basket that saved my life, for I remember later that I flung it up as a shield against the impact of that shining bumper.

It was also Vi who admitted to being the one who had dashed down to Woolworth's and returned with the lovely Chinese wind chimes that now hung from the ceiling above my bed. She had even gone down to the basement storeroom for the electric fan that made them tinkle. I knew I would love them in the future but now I found that the tinkling gave me a headache.

I could not bring myself to let her know this because I loved her so much for being such a nice older sister. It was Mama who turned off the fan and whispered, "She needs a great deal of sleep. Let's just make it as quiet as possible for her at the moment." I drifted off to dreamland admiring my lovely wind chimes.

Dr. Becker had seen us through all our illnesses since he had delivered me and now came each day to check on my recovery status, "harrumph"-ing and "don't-you-knowing" as he and my parents discussed matters concerning me and others, such as "that fool, Hoover, who should have continued being an engineer instead of going into politics. "Look what he's got us into!"

My classmates sent hand-made cards with pictures of ambulances and girls with bandaged heads. My teacher came to visit several times; the roomers dropped by to whisper to Mama and wave to me through the bedroom doorway, Mama had endless phone calls from relatives and friends. Cousin Sedelia sent a basket of lovely fruit and Aunt Alice arrived with a pretty new dress which only needed hemming, "when your mother can stand you up on a chair and set the pins."

A most important visitor was the insurance adjuster representing the man who had run me down. Our family bore the driver no ill will but were glad to receive compensation. Laura happened to be curled up against me the day he arrived. He mentally compared her healthy tan with my normally pale complexion and, shaking his head in consternation, added two hundred more dollars to the amount of the check. When he left he sighed and said that he realized what a terrible ordeal this had been for the family and "hoped the little girl would get better fast and never be hit by an auto again," advice I followed diligently.

My teacher came each day, when I was allowed to sit in a chair and eat at the table, dropping off materials to help me to catch up with the rest of the class. Gradually my headaches disappeared and by Christmas I had almost forgotten that I had been so badly injured. I have no recollection of that Thanksgiving.

When I was able to be up and about, Daddy took us for a ride in our new car. The Essex had been pronounced on its "last legs," and he had gotten a "really good deal" on an "almost new" Hupmobile which we promptly named "Phyllis," in honor of the "gentle old lady" who had previously owned it and "hardly took it out of her garage except for Sunday drives." She must have taken very long and tortuous drives because one-by-one the tires got flat and the engine constantly needed some repair or other.

That was the first of many "Phyllises" Daddy would purchase over the years, each one probably previously owned by that same "gentle" old biddy who madly tore down the worst highways she could find and never changed the oil, rotated the tires or checked out anything else that made the car shimmy, grind, or groan.

I later learned that he had paid for the Hupmobile with part of the insurance money. In a way, my birthday wish had been granted.

Chapter 17

Vi's birthday arrived on schedule the sixth of December. Aunt Alice was taking her Godchild to dinner at a fancy restaurant and then off to the opera house to enjoy the ballet "Nutcracker Suite."

Nobody had use of the second floor bathroom while Vi soaked in water rose-scented with bath salts; Mama heated the curling iron on the two burner gas stove in the laundry room and curled Vi's hair into something a Southern Belle would have appreciated. Finally, it was time for her to slip into the lovely rose silk dress held in readiness for the occasion.

Aunt Alice showed up just as Mama was clasping Vi's birthday present about her slender young neck. The heart-shaped gold locket had a small diamond imbedded in its center and opened to reveal frames for two pictures. Vi had danced about the room displaying it and kept her hand over it to keep it from the flames of her birthday cake's sixteen candles that she wished over and blew out while Mama accompanied us on the piano as we sang "Happy Birthday to you!" in unison.

"This must have cost a great deal of money, Mama," Vi had half-whispered, her fingers fondling the lovely locket. "You and Daddy can't afford this. I feel guilty taking it."

"Hush, now. It's your sixteenth birthday. As of today, you're officially on your way to the world of womanhood. Besides, we received quite a check from the insurance company, remember? We all want you to have this, especially Jessie."

Our sister seemed rather quiet when Aunt Alice led her down the steps to Clyde, who bowed as he opened the cab door for the two of them. It was hours later that Aunt Alice and Clyde brought her back in such a state that Mama sent for Dr. Becker.

"She claims she can't see! In the middle of the last act of the ballet she suddenly lost her sight! What has happened to my daughter, doctor?" Mama was wringing her hands and neither Aunt Alice, Clyde nor Daddy could manage to stand quietly by. They all finally downed some hot coffee laced with whiskey, at Dr. Becker's suggestion, to "calm their nerves." Maggie, Laura and I, in our nightgowns and robes, huddled together in misery, unable to comprehend a sister who was sightless.

Dr. Becker administered some powders washed down with water to put Vi to sleep. "I can't find anything in her eyes to have caused this but it is late and perhaps in the morning things will have cleared up. It sometimes happens that excitement in a young girl can bring such things about, don't-you-know. You can reach me at the hospital to let me know how things are with her. If nothing has changed, it would be advisable to take her to an eye specialist. We'll talk about it then."

Patting both Mama and Vi's hands and Daddy's shoulder, he nodded to Aunt Alice and Clyde, picked up his leather bag, bid us good-night and drove off in his Pierce Arrow.

Morning revealed a still-sightless Vi. Tearfully she accepted all of our kisses. Aunt Alice, with Clyde, had finally departed but she had promised to return if needed.

Dr. Becker came to examine Vi's eyes once more and again declared that he could see nothing wrong and that the next step was to see the eye specialist, "harrumph." He was a tall, almost gangly man, with reddish hair and prince-nez glasses perched on his Romanesque nose. He wore an air of confidence, like a Prince Albert coat, that seemed to make him invulnerable to either germs or mistakes. His word was accepted along with the Ten Commandments and we did our best to dutifully obey.

Aunt Alice accompanied Vi and Mama to the eye specialist on Monday.

His opinion was the same as Dr. Becker's. "Nothing amiss in the eyes themselves. I've seen this several times in the course of my practice. I would say she is a victim of some sort of hysteria, which can happen in the case of girls her age. There may be something a colleague of mine can do. He's been using

Mesmerism in special cases. Puts the patient into a state of trance and speaks to the inner mind."

Since Dr. Becker had recommended the man, nobody pooh-poohed his suggestion and a day or so later we hopefully kissed Vi adieu and watched her being led out to Phyllis for the ride to the office of the 'man who was going to make her see again.'

Her return home was less than joyful. Vi had not responded. Mama said that the Mesmerist had explained that our sister was fighting the entire idea of being cured and was in some way punishing herself for something. Self-blame, he had called it. Unconsciously she was feeling such a sense of guilt that she could not allow herself to be relieved of the burden.

Vi, crying tears from her unseeing eyes, declared this was not so but evidently Aunt Alice decided otherwise. She was a great one for reaching out for the newest and the mot startling. On Wednesday evening we found ourselves in the Baptist Tabernacle on Wells Street. They were holding something called a "REVIVAL."

Songs were sung, people got up on the stage and spoke in quiet tones and loud ones, urging everyone to "give themselves up to the Lord" but none of this helped. Vi's eyes still refused to cooperate. We returned again the next night and the next, even taking our supper along in a paper sack to get seats closer to the stage.

On Sunday evening, a new evangelist came on stage and he was like nobody else we had ever seen. J.C. Kellogg was his name and he wore the trappings of a movie cowboy. Leather vest over plaid flannel shirt, furry chaps, boots with spurs and a pistol in a holster at each hip. His first action was to take both pistols and shoot into the ceiling.

We all jumped a foot but everybody whispered that he was shooting blanks, which would not hurt us. We did not calm down, however, for he spoke in fiery tones, telling of his pathetic life as a "sodden drunk," a life which deprived him of the love of his wife and children, kept him from earning a living and finally 'tossed him into the gutter.' "It was the Devil, Satan himself, who had me in his grips, just as he has YOU, my friends. We are CRAVEN SINNERS, black as coal in our sinfulness, but WAIT, there is HOPE, just as I found it, in our gracious and FORGIVING Lord, our blessed SAVIOR, JESUS CHRIST! There is no NEED to live under the yoke of our sins. Just as I was lifted from the gutter by a loving Samaritan who counseled me and showed me that I could have a BRAND NEW START, my friends, so is there a Samaritan in each of your lives! Just open your hearts to Him, come forward and receive HIM into your hearts and be CURED of your ILLS and your GUILT!!!" His voice dropped to almost a whisper, now, as he promised joy and eternal happiness.

Our row was filled by not only our family and Aunt Alice but friends who had joined us, people we had not seen in years but who wanted to help. Suddenly, Vi stood up and began to grope her way past knees and out into the aisle.

Tender hands reached out to lead her down the sloped aisle to the stage and up onto it. Mr. Kellogg took her in his arms and prayed with her, pushed her down onto her knees and prayed for her and at last, sobbing out her grief and fears and yes, her terrible GUILT in tones meant only for the ears of God, she stayed there, kneeling, while others joined her to form a circle of those held in the clutches of SATAN himself, whose bonds were about to be broken.

BANG!! Went those pistol blanks accompanied by a roll on the drums from the band situated in front of the stage. BANG!!BANG!! A trumpet played triumphant notes and suddenly Vi stood up and began to sob out, "I can SEE! I can SEE! Dear Lord Jesus, I CAN SEE!"

Mama and Daddy and Aunt Alice, who had been held back during the prayer session, now rushed onto the stage to clasp Vi in their arms and make sure she actually could see. It was the truth, all right! She told each one what he or she was wearing and rushed over to be embraced once more by the wonderful cowboy evangelist who had helped to cause this miracle.

He advised that we take Vi home to rest and to place a Bible under her pillow so she could touch it and continue to believe that it was no longer necessary for her to be blind. It was not until much later that we finally learned that she had been blaming herself for my injuries. Mama had requested that either she or Maggie go for soup and bread but both had begged off because of "how they looked." When she accepted the broken basket from the spectators who learned it was her little sister who had been injured, she found my blood on her hands. Like Lady Macbeth, she could not seem to cleanse herself of a feeling of terrible guilt.

Not so Maggie. She, too, had declined but then, she had not been the one to witness that pitiful broken basket laying there in the street. Poor Vi! I kept assuring her that I had been delighted to go to the store and would go again, if Mama wanted me to do so. After all, I was eight years old and crossed Wisconsin Avenue to go to school and home again, didn't I? So what if on Saturdays there was no safety patrol to see kids across? Like Maggie said, "accidents happen."

Of course they did but from that day on Vi contended that it was God's way of showing her that He needed her services. She became a choir member and later taught Sunday School, doing both faithfully well into her years of maturity…

Sometimes I pondered about that fateful trip to the store. Because of me Daddy had been able to purchase that Hupmobile and Vi's life had changed but first I had suffered a double concussion and had my forehead stitched. Did that make me a Good Samaritan and if so, why did helping others have to be so painful? I sure hoped life wasn't going to be full of such occurrences. If so, I hoped I had a guardian angel or a fairy godmother or something hovering about in the background, somewhere, just in case. Meanwhile, I didn't feel one bit different except that I jumped when I heard brakes squeal.

Because of Vi's miraculous return to the world of sight did we become Baptist? No, we remained Lutherans. Still, we were learning that people of other faiths, be they Catholics, Baptists, or whatever title they bore in the name of our Creator, had good things going for them, too. Our world was expanding.

Chapter 18

In previous years, the time between Thanksgiving and Christmas had been filled with preparation. For weeks the aroma of spices and other good things had filled the kitchen and drifted into the other rooms in the red brick house. Mama and Mrs. Malenka had busied themselves with wiping down walls, washing and ironing special table linens, placing decorations about, all contributing to the aura of expectancy that seemed to permeate our every waking moments and often our dreams. Our nightly prayers included pleas for Santa to see us as good children and not leave behind lumps of coal in lieu of toys. Tante Kate had a long list of boys and girls who had received the black hard lump in the toes of their stockings because they had sassed their parents or done some other naughty act.

This year, because of Vi's unexpected blindness and ultimate cure, Christmas came almost too soon. In school, Laura and I had each made small presents for our parents: baked clay ash trays for Daddy, who occasionally smoked a cigar, and tiny calendars for Mama pasted onto a drawing of a decorated Christmas tree. Children in grades 1 through 3 used the same materials.

Twice Vi and Maggie took us to admire the shop windows downtown. None of us had money to purchase anything but it was fun anyway and we stopped at the Karmel Korn Shop for free samples.

It had been the custom, through the years, that on the day of Christmas Eve we would have dinner either at our house or at that of Daddy's sister, Aunt Elsie, and her husband, Uncle Otto. Tante Kate, who lived there, too, spent most of her time during the afternoon playing board games with Laura and me. She loved children and was loved in return.

Afterward, we would all bundle up except Uncle Otto, who was Catholic, and ride off to Incarnation Lutheran Church for an hour of recitations by those of us in Sunday school and the singing of Christmas hymns. Rev. Moerke would read the story of the birth of Jesus from the pulpit Bible and we would leave, with his blessing, to return to the home of the host family for the opening of gifts.

Magically, a decorated tree had been set up in our absence. Ours was always a freshly cut spruce; Aunt Elsie's and Uncle Otto's was artificial, a fact of which I became aware only when I was much older, nearly in my teens. I often wondered how it was that Aunt Elise was able to keep their tree fresh enough to last until Easter when it was then hung with beautifully decorated eggshells that had been brought from "the old country;" in this case Hungary, by Uncle Otto's parents.

I presume that Uncle Otto attended an early morning mass at Holy Angels. No mention was ever made of this. Evidently, he and Aunt Elise had come to terms with their disparity regarding religion. Our cousins, Rudy and Bernice, who were close in age to Vi and Maggie, were being raised Lutheran. Aunt Elise was a strong-willed woman.

From pictures of her as a young woman, she had been the epitome of high fashion personified, with high pompadour, gorgeous large hats sporting plumes and bows and yards of veiling; beautiful laces encircling her swan-like neck. The toes of her shoes were so pointed that once she had to be forced to sit in one position during an entire theater-matinee performance because she had inadvertently placed her foot on the back of the seat ahead and a stout man, upon sitting down in it, had imprisoned her shoe toe in the process. Not only her foot but her entire leg had gone to sleep so that she could not rise after the final curtain.

A kind gentleman, who offered his arm, as she limped up the aisle, insisted upon escorting her to the streetcar stop as well. It was the beginning of a friendship that ended in a marriage. Uncle Otto was a kind, gentle person, who loved her with all his heart. The two of them adored their children.

After her marriage and motherhood Aunt Elise was guilty of "letting herself go," as our other aunts described her appearance. Gone was the high pompadour. Her beautiful chestnut hair, which, when let loose from the pins, hung down to the back of her knees, should have been her crowning glory but instead was parted in the middle and drawn tightly back into an unbecoming "pug." It never showed any gray, even in her later years, possibly because she always added baking soda to the rinsing water. Perhaps she reserved its beauty for her husband behind their closed bedroom door.

The dresses she wore were usually sewn by Tante Kate and never varied in pattern or style; frumpy things that went with her dumpy figure, all covered over with generously cut pinafore-type aprons. Her shoes had rounded toes, for comfort.

Life in that household was in many ways casual, though never downright sloppy. They bathed, faithfully, once a week, as we all did in those days, and hair was washed. So were hands, always with nicely scented soaps. Aunt Elise's ivory-skinned hands had long tapered fingers that would have looked wonderful adorned with beautiful rings. Her only hand jewelry was the wide gold wedding band that matched Uncle Otto's. "Old country" custom was the placing of it on the third finger of the right hand, instead of the left, and this is where they wore theirs.

The entrée at Christmas Eve dinner at Aunt Elise's was never ham nor turkey but might be goose, roast lamb or hasenpfeffer. The latter consisted of roast rabbit marinated in a sweet sour vinegar sauce that included gingersnaps, so the gravy was brown and spicy. For those who did not enjoy rabbit prepared in this manner there was always a platter of sliced roast beef surrounded by spiced crab apples from the tree in their backyard.

This was the first year that our families would not be spending the holiday together. We could not leave the rooming house unattended. Most of the roomers were gone to visit their various friends and relatives. Also, we had been attending the Church of the Redeemer, a few blocks away, and were in that Sunday school's evening recitation program. Bernice and Rudy were in the one at Incarnation. It was obligatory that Aunt Elise and Tante Kate attend that one.

Feeling gypped, somehow, because this Christmas Eve was not to be one of familiar festivity, Laura and I played "Stone Teacher," the stone-in-the-closed-hand guessing game, up and down the stairway to the second floor. I had reached the top step, with Laura trying to guess me down to the second, when suddenly, through the beleved glass transom above the front hall door, I saw the bus pull up and discharge five familiar figures: Uncle Otto, Aunt Elise, Tante Kate and cousins Rudy and Bernice, each bearing baskets and shopping bags.

It was a wonderful get-together. They had brought roast goose, pies, all the fixings for a holiday meal. In the shopping bags were gifts for everyone, nothing spectacular, a small game or nice handkerchief; the usual.

For the first time, Daddy did not attend our recitations but instead, drove his sisters and theirs back to the north side so they could hear Rudy and Bernice do their recitations, then stayed home to "take care of the place" while we five females walked through crisp winter air to the church service.

As usual, our tree had magically appeared. One special ornament was a small porcelain cherub with blond curls made of real hair. It had gossamer wings and appeared to be flying as it hung suspended from the branch. We girls had named it Baby Ralph, in remembrance of the child who would have been our big brother, had he lived. I think Mama and Daddy held it in special regard, as well. It had been a gift for their first Christmas tree from Mama's handsome, adoring brother, Erwin, who died during World War I from spinal meningitis and was buried in his uniform the very day his unit went overseas.

As with birthday candles, all lights were turned off except those in the tree. Mama sat at her piano and we sang carols in honor of Jesus' birth, drank hot cocoa topped with marshmallows, placed a plate of oatmeal cookies on a side table for Santa along with an enameled pie tin of oats for his reindeer, then tiptoed off to bed.

In the morning, waking up to the smell of brewing coffee, we donned slippers and robes and hurried to see what Santa had left for us under the tree.

The cookie plate and oat dish were empty! Santa had been there! Quickly, Laura and I reached for the packages bearing our names. Both were alike on the outside, each done up in red tissue paper with our names printed by Santa himself on small tags.

"Oh, look, Jessie, a doll just like the one in Gimbel's window! Oh, I love her! Thank you, dear Santa, thank you! I'm going to name her-umm-oh; I'm going to show her to Mama. She'll help me choose a name!" Excited, my sister was off to the kitchen where Mama and Daddy were sipping coffee and eating *stollen,* the long loaves of yeasty Christmas bread generously interspersed with candied pineapple, hazel nuts and raisins, iced with Mama's special blend of vanilla, milk and confectioner's sugar and decorated with halves of red and green candied cherries.

Our dolls were alike except for the color of the hair and eyes, which matched our own. Mine's blue eyes stared at me and lowered their lids when I laid her down. Like Laura, for me it was instant mother-love. I immediately decided upon Elizabeth Anne, the name I secretly wished Mama had given me.

At age twelve or thirteen, Lutheran children confirm their commitment to "God the Father, God the Son and God the Holy Ghost: the Triune God." Girls and boys are no longer looked upon as children but stand on the threshold of manhood and womanhood. Santa Claus was evidently aware of this, for he had stopped leaving things under the tree for Vi and Maggie for several years. Instead, Mama and Daddy gave them gifts, a pretty dress for Maggie, who had be complaining that her dresses were becoming tight across the chest area, and a crocheted tam and scarf for Vi.

Mama had lengthened both their winter coats. She had cut an old one of Maggie's down for me and passed my old one down to Laura. We, too, were given warm knit mittens, caps and scarves.

Vi and Maggie presented Mama with sheet music, several songs that she had looked over at the music department at Espanhain's and wistfully replaced because her money had other places to go that were more demanding.

It was a pleasure to watch her sit at her piano to study the music for a moment or two and suddenly fill the rooms with lovely sound, the keys responding to her fingers as her eyes read the notes on the pages. How lucky we were to have such a talented mother! She had taught Vi to play, also, and soon mother and daughter were bent over the music as Mama explained about this passage or another. Before long we were joined by the few roomers who had remained in residence during the holidays; the Englishwoman from the third floor whom Cousin Lawrence had scared out of her wits; the two elderly twin sisters on the second floor who arose at dawn each morning and did their breathing exercises in front of open windows and then hurried off together down the street to eat breakfast at the drugstore lunch counter, and, amazingly, Mr. Brewster, who shyly entered the central hall via the door, to the basement, that was located under the stairs leading to the second floor.

The day of my birthday, Tante Kate had mistaken it for a closet door and almost ended up in the basement.

Each person was offered *stollen* and coffee sipped from Mama's best china cups. Mr. Brewster presented Daddy with a fine Havana cigar and Mama with a box of Fanny Farmer chocolates. He stayed long enough to admire our dolls and listen to one more song, this one something from Mozart, which evidently reached into his memory and made him blow his nose and pretend that something was in his eye that needed wiping. I suppose that I was the only one who noticed, since he turned toward the window. I wanted to ask him if he had any children but decided against doing that. Mama always warned us that children must not be too forward.

Laura and I retired to our bedroom where we laid a damask cloth on our little drop-leaf table and set out the beautiful hand painted china tea set that Great Aunt Beatrice had brought back for us from Japan the year before. We introduced our new dolls to all of our old ones and held a tea party for them.

Chapter 19

At three o'clock, leaving the mansion in voluntary care of Mrs. Wentworth, in room 3, we piled into the Hupmobile, Phyllis, and set off for our Grandmother's house in Bay View located on Milwaukee's south shore of Lake Michigan.

A gray, cloudy day, cold with the promise of snow, it was not one of gloom, however, for in many of the houses along the way the Christmas trees were already aglow with lights enhanced by long streamers of tinsel icicles. We oohed and aahed and demanded that our sisters and parents "look over there! Oh, see that one! That house has red wreaths with candles in every window!"

The closer we got to the lake, the louder came the OOH AH warning of the fog horn, a sound that had lulled three generations of Mama's family to sleep each night since 1867, when our Great Grandparents reached their fisherfolk relatives after their long journey from Germany via horse cart, train, ship, train, and horse cart.

The Hupmobile had one feature that we truly enjoyed: heaters in both back and front seat areas. We four girls were cozy as bunnies when we finally reached Rusk Avenue.

Grandmother's porch had tall, Doric pillars. Her front door, of heavy oak, boasted a heavy oval beveled glass window. Opening the inner door for us her housekeeper took our wraps, whereupon we sought out Grandmother, placed a dutiful kiss upon her slightly wrinkled cheek, avoided her gold-headed cane and hurried off to the playroom to greet our cousins and the ever-present uncle who acted as chaperone.

We had the use of books, games, a chest filled with toys and an upright piano and round stool that rested upon glass balls held in lion's paws. It was fun to lie across the stool and spin around until the seat reached its full height, then reverse the spin and bring it back down to its lowest height. This activity was usually curtailed when the uncle, seated in the wicker rocking chair in Grandmother's huge kitchen, looked up from the newspaper or magazine he was scanning and cleared his throat.

Sometimes we would line chairs along the four sides of the kitchen table and play "Goldfish." Small magnets suspended by fine string from thin dowel fish poles attracted the paper clips attached to the brightly painted cardboard fish lying inside the octagonal cardboard "pool". Each fish was numbered and the uncle was designated scorekeeper. The winner might receive a chocolate candy or an xxx mint.

House rules demanded that you remained in the nursery until dinner was announced. Those who were not yet thirteen but who could behave themselves were seated at card tables set at one end of the huge dining room. Anyone misbehaving at mealtime was relegated to the kitchen with the housekeeper. Grandmother's house rules were not to be taken lightly.

Vi and Maggie ate at the large table, with the adults and our older cousins. Mama had drilled each of us in which fork and spoon to use from the time we were old enough to handle cutlery, so the move to the large table was more one of honor than one of learning. We, at the card tables, ate the same food as the adults, but in smaller portions, and did not dare to speak with food in our mouths nor accidentally spill milk that might damage Grandmother's oriental carpet.

Did we enjoy our meal? Absolutely! Everything tasted wonderful because everything was delicious, from the steaming soup to the fresh fruit cup. In between were the entrees and vegetable courses along with golden rolls hot from the oven. Gravies, condiments, jellies, butter pats with pretty designs on them, all were prepared under Grandmother's supervision. A very tall woman, she bore her extra fifty or so pounds with regal mein, whether in her best silk with pearls at her throat or in a housedress covered with an ample apron.

The females in Mama's family, of various girths and heights, had one similarity: slim ankles. It was due to this that Grandmother used a cane, for she had tripped on an icy step one Sunday morning and suffered a compound fracture of her left leg. Somehow, it had never healed properly, and, after suffering a light stroke, a bit later, she was unable to do her own housework. On this holiday, she sat, enthroned in her red velvet upholstered wood-armed chair, directing conversation, the serving of food by the temporary maid and enjoying her role as hostess.

Grandmother, like Great Aunt Alice, was somewhat forbidding. I have no recollection of ever sitting on her lap and having her arms enfold me as I have of Tante Kate, who would clasp a child to her huge soft bosom and fill one with the knowledge that here was all-encompassing love. Still, like Aunt Alice, our Grandmother commanded admiration and respect that made one want to do better, not only in behavior but in all phases of being; our role models for excellence.

Great Aunt Beatrice, on the other hand, while beautiful and queenly in her bearing, was so gentle and kind that, although she never held a child on her lap, made one feel warm and important, bestowing upon each small individual her sole attention. There was something about her hazel eyes that reminded me of a doe.

Her hands were always adorned with gorgeous rings and about her throat were pearls or other gemstones, all worn with such gracefulness that it would not have seemed out of place to find a tiara nestled among her abundant white waves and curls. Her adoring husband, Uncle George, took great pleasure in showering her with lovely things. A retired manufacturer, he was a tall, handsome man, dignified and courteous but apt to hold children off at arm's length. In his presence, one never was able to forget that he was "someone of importance," though nothing he did or said implied even a hint of snobbery. It was probably his air of complete self-assurance that held others in awe of him. He had traveled throughout much of the world and spoke several languages fluently.

Cousin Sedelia, actually our deceased grandfather's cousin, was quite unlike either of the other women at the table. Her nose, like her tongue, was very sharp. Always modishly garbed, having all the money she wanted to purchase a wardrobe, she lacked that aura of her three contemporaries that gave them "presence."

Cousin Jasper had a commanding "summer kitchen" front that required double breasted suits beneath which was usually an expansive vest complete with watch fob and chain. He was a demanding person, expecting his meals to be at the precise time of seven, noon and seven. Since today's meal was being served at six o'clock, he let everyone know that his digestive system was not yet ready for such sumptuousness. He was given a glass of wine to "prepare his palate" and, I suppose, to stop his complaining. I watched to see if his white mustache would dip into the glass but he was very adept at keeping it free of things .He had a habit of wiping his fingers across it to smooth it down.

I observed that Aunt Mimsey's fiancé kept clearing his throat and sipping water. He and Aunt Mimsey were seated at the far end of the table. From time to time, he and Grandmother exchanged glances, hers with narrowed eyes and his holding a look of expectancy.

It was not until dessert dishes had been cleared away, which usually meant that the men would rise and go to the parlor "for a smoke" that Grandmother tapped on her water glass with a spoon and announced, "It appears that the family is about to be enlarged by one, come June. I have been informed that Mimsey and Edmond have settled upon the first week in June for their wedding, and I have given both my blessing."

Wine was poured into all of our glasses and we now toasted the blushing couple. The glasses of the children held only about a tablespoon of the intoxicating beverage but we felt "grownup" at being included in this very important ritual. I studied Edmond. In June he would become our uncle. According to the whispers I overheard between Aunts Rose and Arlene, he would be taking "instructions" from their pastor so he could join the Lutheran Church. I would have to ask Mama or somebody if he would have to be "confirmed" and wear a dark suit with a flower in his lapel and have a party afterwards and have his picture taken at some photographer's studio? I also had another question but knew I would not discuss this one with anyone. Why did Grandmother approved of him so heartily and disapproved of Daddy?

I liked Edmond but felt a tinge of jealousy and wondered what Daddy was thinking? His lowered eyelids were protective shields as he studied the tablecloth in front of him but I noted the little muscle jumping in front of his jaw and knew he was upset inside. Mama's lips were smiling but her eyes kept moving to the head of the table, to Grandmother, who either did not note their plea or was deliberately avoiding it. I wished at that moment that a good fairy would wave her wand and make Grandmother love Daddy but in vain. I felt a big lump in my throat as I watched Daddy follow the rest of the men, enter the parlor and close the sliding doors behind him…

With dinner over and the dining room cleared of dishes and table linens, it was now time for the exchange of gifts. We women and children entered the parlor to "ooh" and "aah" over the tree that, as usual, reached clear to the eleven foot ceiling. The aroma of cigar smoke still hung in the air. The men's faces were flushed from their heated discussion concerning which of their favorite football teams had performed up to expectations and whether or not Mr. Hoover should be re-elected President.

Now Grandmother clapped her hands and requested that the men fetch the boxes from her bedroom.

The adults did not exchange gifts, so we grandchildren were the ones to look with expectation at each of the tall boxes we knew contained presents for us.

Mama had been sewing for weeks in preparation for this night; flannel nightgowns for the girl cousins, flannel pajamas for the boys. Her packages, wrapped in red or green tissue paper, were brought in from the car to be placed in the wicker wash basket provided by the housekeeper. That was soon heaped with many gaily- wrapped packages and boxes.

Now came the distributing of gifts and the "thank yous" to the givers. Vi and Maggie were delighted with their real silk hose from Aunt Beatrice. We smaller kids were not quite as excited, for ours were also stockings but of beige lisle for the girls and plaid knit knee-highs for the boys. As usual, Grandmother presented each of us with a storybook. Mine, to my great delight, was a copy of Aesop's Fables, beautifully illustrated. However Grandmother might feel toward Daddy, she did not show favoritism toward any of her grandchildren and seemed to know instinctively what each child wanted or needed.

Aunt Arlene had sewn dresses for each of the girls and knickers for the boys. From Aunt Rose came boxes of her delicious homemade fudge. Cousin Sedelia and Uncle Bertie gave each one a crisp five dollar bill.

Aunt Alice had provided lovely decanters and spray bottles of cologne for the older girls and wood handled jump ropes and sets of jacks and balls for the younger children. We immediately headed for the kitchen table where a merry game of jacks was started.

The temporary maid was just leaving. The housekeeper said she lived "just across the ally on the next street." Her son was waiting; cap in hand, to walk her home. I studied him as he helped her on with her galoshes and gallantly buckled them, liking his nice even features and dark blond curly hair. He was at least twelve, a tall boy who was already wearing long pants. He offered his mother his arm and she was suddenly no longer "the temporary maid" but somebody's well loved mother. Their departure down the back stairs and out through the side door was accompanied by soft laughter over their own plans for this Christmas night at their house.

Tiptoeing out to the back hall, I peered out into the darkness to watch them traverse Grandmother's back yard, open her gate, cut across the alley and open their own gate. How I wished baby Ralph had not died but had, instead, lived to be our big brother.

"Hey, Jessie, it's your turn!" my cousins called me back to the kitchen to toss my own little rubber ball into the air and pick up as many jacks as each turn required. Meanwhile the housekeeper, whose name I now knew was Mrs Wellington, having put the stacks of freshly washed dishes into the tall china cabinets lining the hall to the dining room, sat down in the wicker rocking chair to rest her feet and nibble on Christmas cookies washed down with coffee from her favorite cup.

Amid good-byes and promises to drive safely from Daddy and "see you soon" from Mama to her sisters and Grandmother, we drove off in Phyllis, grateful when the back seat heater began to warm up the frigid air inside the car. By the time we reached home Laura and I had stopped oohing and aahing over other people's tree lights and fallen asleep leaning against our sisters, who eventually cradled us against them to keep us upright and, hopefully, because it was Christmas, felt that little sisters "weren't all that much pain when it really came down to it."

Chapter 20

1932 arrived with the usual partying and hopes that this would be a better year financially, though many did not feel that this would happen. President Hoover's name was becoming synonymous with all that was wrong in the country.

Living in lavish style in the White House, he did not seem to understand the true plight of the citizenry living in the depths of poverty. Storms were brewing among the population but, according to what was filtering down to those who kept an eye on Washington, he had both a blind eye and a deaf ear.

Mama and Daddy were beginning to feel the pinch. Several of the roomers informed Mama that in paying the weekly rent they were having to skip a meal. She set up a table in the lower hall and each morning provided homemade *schnecken* and loaves of her wonderful homemade bread along with coffee, canned milk and homemade jam.

We girls were not allowed to set foot in the hall and watch while the hungry partook of the food "lest you embarrass them," Mama explained.

Laura turned seven that January. I noted that she had lost some of her baby fat and was growing taller. The thinner face was no less pretty; in fact, now her eyes appeared to be larger than ever. She had changed in other ways, too. No longer a burden for me to watch over, she was more of a companion, though I still felt duty bound to keep her out of harm's way.

February brought Valentine's Day. Maggie and Vi had helped Laura and me to cut paper lace dollies into heart shapes, paste paper 'legs' onto them and fasten the legs to inexpensive valentines purchased at Woolworth's. They were now things of beauty, the lacy hearts standing away from the Valentines to give them a Victorian look.

It was Maggie who had thought of this. She had a real eye for things artistic.

She also drew dolls for us, copying movie star's faces so well that we recognized Jean Harlow, Delores Del Rio, and others immediately. Laura and I had fun drawing dresses for the dolls, clothing them in the ultra-fashionable garments movie stars might wear.

We made valentines for each of our classmates and our teachers. Then, at school, we watched as classmates dropped valentines into individual shoeboxes each of us had decorated with crepe paper as a classroom art project. At the end of the school day, Laura's box was stuffed with valentines. Mine had exactly two; one from my teacher and another, anonymous, from someone who thought I "stank." It was a terrible blow to realize someone held me in such low esteem,

Mama, Daddy and each of my sisters assured me that I truly did not smell bad, that "you stink" was certainly not a nice thing for someone to say, especially on a valentine, but then, as Maggie suggested, it could have been sent by a boy who really liked me but was afraid someone, including himself, might find out. Not much of a consolation in view of all the pretty valentines Laura had standing on her side of our dresser top but at least it dried my tears of humiliation.

Although Vi had regained her sight, she had been forced to return to the eye specialist because her vision was not as good as it should be. He prescribed glasses. There were no such things as glamour lenses back then. Glasses were glasses, utilitarian and ugly, with black frames and round lenses that made Vi appear as if she had been hatched by an owl. Maggie still had boys taking turns walking her home, at least to the White Tower hamburger stand, but even the lanky redheaded boy had now deserted Vi. She and I commiserated together over the fact, sigh, sigh, that we were probably destined to be 'old maids.'

All thoughts of Valentines Day woes were driven from our minds when the next morning, just after dawn, we were roused by Officer Jim and a plain clothes detective, who asked if they could come in and discuss something with Mama and Daddy. We girls were sent back to our rooms, but listened from the bedroom hallway.

"I'm afraid there's been a terrible accident down at the railroad tracks under the Thirty Fifth street viaduct," Officer Jim told our parents. "A man was run over by a train. When I saw his instrument case and the name in his wallet, I immediately surmised that it was your basement roomer, Mr. Joseph Brewster."

We were all sent into a state of shock. Our Mr. Brewster struck down by a train! He had always seemed so invincible!

"How bad is he?" Daddy asked.

"Dead, I'm afraid. We're going to need positive identification by someone who knew him. Do you think you could do that, Mr. Renz? We can take you down to the morgue whenever you'd be ready."

"Ja, of course. You'll have to give me time to get dressed." Daddy was in his bath robe, and Mama in hers.

"Certainly. This is good coffee, Mrs. Renz. Why, thank you, those sweet rolls look mighty good." It was the other man who was speaking. "And, now, I'm here because we need to look over Mr. Brewster's room, if you don't mind."

"His room! Oh, he doesn't like…" Mama stopped, realizing, suddenly, that whatever poor Mr. Brewster liked or did not like no longer mattered, that is, if he were truly the victim of the train. "What I don't understand is why he would be on the train tracks under the Thirty Fifth street viaduct in the middle of the night. He worked at a dance club downtown. Thirty Fifth street is twenty blocks from here, in the opposite direction west and Lord knows how many blocks south! Unless, maybe, he was playing for some private party. Even so, under the viaduct!"

"Exactly!" agreed Officer Jim. "The engineer said it looked like a deliberate thing…"

We could hear Mama gasp. "Suicide! Oh, dear."

"Which is why we must look over his room. A note, possibly."

They were correct in their surmises. Inside the front cover of a huge book having to do with the precepts of the Catholic Church were two envelopes, one addressed to Mama, the other to an Evelyn Brewster, who turned out to be his sister, the only one in his family to not completely turn her back on him.

Mama's envelope contained a note of apology and a full month's rent "to tide you over until another occupant can be found, dear woman. You have been most considerate and gracious."

The sister in Marshfield was contacted. Unable to come to Milwaukee, due to poor physical health and certainly in no position financially to make the trip, she suggested that whatever estate there might be could probably be turned over to the city in exchange for a decent burial. "Not that any priest would bury her brother, under the circumstances..."

The circumstances had to do with the picture of the rather pretty woman and a small boy that stood on the late Mr. Brewster's nightstand. A priest in the Catholic Church, he had left his calling and married. The child was their son. The marriage ended in divorce. Seven years previous, on Valentines Day, Mr. Brewster had been excommunicated, condemned to the fires of Hell.

We often discussed what the poor man must have gone through, alone in the basement room, able to stare out at the Knights of Columbus from his barred windows. The church may have ousted him but he still said his rosary and on the wall was that crucifix. His priestly robes neatly hung on a hanger in his closet. A small leather case, velvet lined, contained a small glass for wine, a vial of oil and a small covered jar to hold communion wafers. He had given himself communion and the last rites, his letter informed.

Daddy duly went to view "the remains." Upon his return, he declared that, because Mr. Brewster had been disconnected in various places by that train, the best thing to do, probably, was to have the poor fellow cremated. Since, due to the divorce and his suicide, his soul has already been consigned to the flames down below; "a few more minutes of heat certainly could not make much difference."

Our minister at the Redeemer Church consented to handle the ceremony at the cemetery where the urn would be interred. The day of the funeral, some of the roomers stood quietly along side us in the chilly mausoleum with its rows and rows of brass markers and stared at the urn that held what had once been a tall man with deep set eyes. After all, he had been one of them, even if few knew him. There were also two other persons present, the pretty woman in the picture and a handsome boy of about thirteen with deep-set dark eyes. The woman came over to Mama and Daddy and thanked them for their kindness. Mama offered to give her whatever she wanted from Mr. Brewster's possessions but she declined.

I'm not sure what happened to any of his things, probably they were given to the Salvation Army. We ended up with that large book about the Catholic Church. I don't know why, but it was among our books for years and years and sometimes someone would take it out and study the picture of Pope Pius XI.

Wherever Mr. Brewster's soul ended up, we felt that, even though the words had come from the lips of a Protestant minister, God might have pitied the poor man and let him escape those flames. One thing we girls decided; none of us would ever fall in love with a Catholic priest. We also decided that, even though he had died, and in such a sinful manner, it being a suicide and all, Mr. Brewster still lived because he had begotten a son. A living memorial to one who had transgressed.

Chapter 21

March stole in on a lamb's feet but the days were not gentle. More and more Daddy had to depend upon money he earned as a process server. February had been bitterly cold. He had been called upon to repair furnaces, many that were of inferior quality installed by a well-known unscrupulous company that had recently declared bankruptcy rather than pay off claims for shoddy workmanship. It should have brought in quite a few dollars but instead Daddy had to settle for items such as a pretty necklace and bracelet or the hand-crocheted bedspread wrapped in blue tissue paper that an elderly lady had lovingly patted before handing it to him; obviously a treasured possession.

A farmer out in Waukesha had swapped him two chickens and a couple dozen fresh eggs as well as smoked ham in lieu of cash. People were hard up and Daddy did not have the heart to turn them down nor let them know that he, too, was in financial straits. Which he and Mama were. Some of the roomers had left, causing Daddy to meet more trains and buses. Among those who ended up at our place were several who gave excuses instead of rent for a couple weeks, then let their luggage down via bed sheets, walked out the front door and were never heard from again. This left Mama short on rent money and the rental agent let her know that he would not allow her to be late another time. There came a day when it was only bread instead of *schnecken* on the hall table, though she still provided canned milk, coffee and jam.

I had started to read the paper. I came to Mama and Daddy with questions they could not always answer. "What's the B.E.F., Mama?"
"B.E.F? Why, I don't know, Jessie. Where did you hear that term?"
"In the Journal. The men who fought in the war are 'up in arms' and have started something called the B.E.F. What do they do when they're up in arms, anyways?"

"It means that they're very disturbed about something. Show me where you read that and let's see if we can figure things out."

Her eyes scanned the column and she let out a sigh. "It stands for Bonus Expeditionary Force, Jessie. Daddy wasn't in the war, you see, because he had a wife and children and he had injured his back but many men were and, if I understand this correctly, they were promised that they would receive a bonus for their service to their country, but not until 1945. That's quite a few years from now and many are out of work and unable to support their families, so they want that money now. They're talking about marching to Washington, thousands of men who served, and demanding that money from Mr. Hoover."

"What's a bonus, anyways?"

"Well, its extra money paid for services and many of the men came home injured. They feel that they deserve that extra money now, when it's so badly needed, not in the years ahead. They say they answered their country's call without hesitation and now it's their country's duty to answer theirs."

We heard more about the Bonus Force in the months to come when thousands of men did march to Washington D.C. with their families and lived in tents and houses made of orange crates and other stuff. The newspapers nicknamed the temporary village "Hooverville" and made President Hoover and someone named General Douglas MacArthur mad as could be.

Mr. Steinmann came to call one afternoon, bringing with him raw oysters and tomato juice which he and Mama downed with enjoyment while the rest of us squeamishly fled to our rooms because we could not bear the sight of the slippery things disappearing into their mouths. He had brought some for her to fry for our supper that night and we did enjoy those, along with his conversation.

He knew all about the plans to march on Washington, D.C., he living at the Veteran's Home and in close contact with many of the men who wanted to participate. His disapproval of the entire affair was spoken in hearty tones.

"Those poor fools think they can reach the pea brains sitting in Washington, especially that ignoramus, Hoover? Hah! It will never work." His predictions were correct. There was no bonus paid. Later that summer, some men were shot and killed when MacArthur set his soldiers, under the command of Major George Patton and Dwight Eisenhower, on the poor hapless men and their families, driving them out of and burning their temporary shelters. Many bystanders were injured as well.

It was probably that, more than anything, that ended Mr. Hoover's presidency and opened the door to Mr. Franklin Delano Roosevelt, who came to the rescue of the citizenry and eventually gave men like Daddy dignity and hope once more. First, however we all had to go through more rigors and, for me, a very scary incident.

It was shortly after Easter that someone had given us jawbreakers and I had tried to bite mine in half. Out came part of a molar. Toothache drops did nothing to help and Mama decided that I must see a dentist. Her pocketbook told her we must wait for that, since she barely met the rent and had nothing left over for medical expenses. This did not displease me. A toothache was one thing but having a broken tooth pulled was not an enchanting enticement leading me to demand that we go to the dentist's office.

Evidently Daddy took it upon himself to remedy that situation. Someone told him about the Marquette Dental Clinic where students practiced on volunteer patients.

It was a Saturday morning in late April. Laura and I had finished our chores and were playing hopscotch across Fifteenth Street with some neighbor kids. Daddy appeared out of nowhere and, taking my hand, informed me that we were going "somewhere." Not Laura and I; just he and I.

My mind held two thoughts. I needed to use a bathroom; like all kids, I would put the call of nature in the background rather than miss a turn at whatever game we were playing. The other thought was rather scary. In my fairy tale book I had read about Hansel and Gretel and how the parents, too poor to feed their darling children, had taken them into the forest to die. As much as I loved Daddy, the memory of that day when he almost drowned us was firmly embedded in a far corner of my brain.

As usual, his strides were longer than mine and I kept pulling back, trying to let him know that I truly needed to use the bathroom. He, however, had heard too many protests about dentists and had closed his ears to this one. We reached Clybourne Street, turned the corner and headed for Sixteenth. I did not worry about the Clybourne Street Gang; at least not with Daddy there for protection. Besides, they were the other way, to the left.

Against my will, we entered a building where a nurse greeted us with a smile. Almost before I knew it, I was ensconced in a dentist's chair and a young man with a nice smile asked me to "Open wide, Jessie." "Well," he promised, "this presents no problem at all and you won't feel a thing. Just relax."

Despite my hands trying to push it away, a rubber thing was placed over my nose and mouth. I breathed in a few whiffs of something I could not identify and awoke to the unpleasant sensation that I was sitting in a puddle of something. I was. My bloomers were soaking wet! In a moment, so were my eyes. Never in my life had I been more embarrassed. I barely noticed that the molar that had broken off was no longer there.

The nurse helped me out of the chair. Groggily, I accompanied her to a bathroom where she fashioned diapers of a sort from a towel, all the while trying to calm me with assurances that nobody would know. I knew, she knew and so did the nice dentist as well as Daddy and…my sobs were louder than ever. Heading for the door, tears of mortification and anger streaming down my face, I ran ahead of Daddy up the hill of Fifteenth Street on our side, my soggy under pants in a paper bag.

Laura saw me and called out for me to come and join her and the other kids but I paid no attention. When she saw Daddy worriedly striding after me, she followed. Once inside the hall of the Mansion, I dashed to our bedroom and threw myself across the bed to sob out my unhappiness. My jaw ached but I didn't care! I hated Daddy! I never wanted to speak to him again! I wished he *had* left me in the forest where I could have been eaten by a bear or something. All he had done by way of consolation was his usual statement that I would have forgotten all about this by the time I was twenty one! He had given no thought to my *feelings* at all!

Laura kept asking me what was wrong but I refused to answer her. She went to search for Mama, who was probably on the third floor changing linens or something.

I suddenly could not face anyone else, even Mama, certainly not Vi or Maggie! Unpinning the offending diaper, I donned fresh bloomers, took my library card and the fifteen cents I had saved and headed for the front hallway. Daddy was in the kitchen, pouring himself some coffee. I heard him call out after me but shut my ears and hid in the vestibule until I heard him go upstairs.

In one moment I was out of the house and heading down Wisconsin Avenue toward downtown.

When I reached the library I changed my mind and crossed over to the Museum side of the shared building. Here I moved from room to room, upstairs, downstairs, wherever my feet led me, only half-seeing the various displays. Deciding to check out a book after all, I returned to the Library and selected the orange book of fairy tales, which I proceeded to read. The pain in my jaw interfered with my concentration so I recrossed to the Museum. I wished I could lean my head against Mama's soft breast and feel her comforting hands on my hair.

That gas I had been given at the dental clinic was still affecting me. My eyes felt very heavy. Finding an empty chair, I sat there, half-dozing. People eyeing me could see the open book on my lap and probably assumed I was reading. After a time I needed to use the bathroom and slipped into the ladies' washroom. A bell was ringing somewhere. Whomever was in the next booth hurried out but I was so sleepy. Washing my hands, I spied a padded bench, curled up on it and entered dreamland.

Back home, Mama, Daddy, and the rest of the family were searching for me, calling out my name all over the neighborhood; Vi, Daddy, and Maggie even ventured down Clybourne Street, all to no avail. When Officer Jim came along on his beat walk, he joined them, first suggesting that every inch of the house, from basement to closets, be investigated.

Hours passed. I awoke to silence and a terrible thirst. Cupping my hands, I drank from the water in the sink. My jaw had stopped aching and my tongue found the space where my tooth had been.

Leaving the washroom, I stepped out into gloom and silence. The lights overhead were no longer lit: the display cases were unusually dark. Also, where were the people? Was I asleep and dreaming? My pinch told me otherwise. Deciding that I had better leave and return to the Library, it suddenly dawned on me that I had left my book somewhere.

Returning to the washroom, I couldn't find it and realized it must still be on the chair in one of the rooms. Somewhat apprehensively, I made my way through various exhibit rooms, trying to remember where the chair was located.

Passing the suit of armor that stood by itself against a wall; I had the eeriest feeling that it was not empty! My imagination inhabited it with someone whose eyes were following me; I was sure that the mailed fist holding the long lance had moved just a bit. The tip of that lance was very sharp; I could almost feel it entering my body. My feet grew wings; I sped from room to room only to be confronted with exhibits of Indians who all seemed to be staring at me.

Fear left me mute, unable to utter a croak, much less let out a scream. Deciding that I had to remove my shoes and hide somewhere, I quickly pulled them off and held them close to my thin chest. Oh, if only there were a guard about, even the mean one who disliked it when kids without adults to keep them from touching exhibits were loose in the place and needed to be watched with narrowed eyes lest they steal or destroy something. I hoped, if there were a guard nearby, that it was the nice one with the fluffy mustache.

Blindly running from room to room, I finally reached the main hall where the skeleton of the mastodon loomed menacing, his huge tusks and teeth ready to turn me into prey. Forgetting the library book, I ran to the front door only to discover that it and the entrance to the Library were both locked. In complete panic, I fled upstairs. Now the displays, so interesting and friendly at other times, seemed to be waiting to do me harm. Too tired, finally to continue on, I entered a room, moved to the tall windows and, pulling the shade aside, peered out. The street lamp admitted enough light to help me to identify my location. Oh, no! This was the room filled with mummies!

There, in that one case, was the one from Peru that was not bound up in cloth but laid on its side, its eyes mere slits and its ancient yellow teeth exposed through parchment skin. Ordinarily, that mummy fascinated me but now, dropping the shade back into place, I slid down against the wall, too frightened to move, certain that the mummy was aware of me and was stealthily lifting the lid of the case. Shutting my eyes, I scrunched into a ball of woe, silent tears and equally silent sobs taking over.

When the night watchman found me, I was still huddled there, eyes tightly shut, bloomers wet. It took him a few moments to get me to understand that he was going to help me, not harm me.

He had received a call from the police enquiring if there was a little girl locked in the place somewhere. When he discovered my bright orange library book and read my name on the card inside, he phoned back to let them know it was possible that the missing child was somewhere on the premises.

It was Daddy who lifted me up and carried me home, clutching me tightly to him despite my wet bloomers. It was Mama who fed me and, while I ate, softly instructed me in the ways of fathers, especially Daddy. "Daddy has never been a little girl and he had no little sisters so he sometimes forgets that they are not the same as little boys, which is what he was once, Jessie. It was not right, the way he grabbed you up and marched you to the dentist. I had no idea he was going to do that. He had decided it was the best for you and that was that. It's his way. He was trying to take care of you and instead he made you unhappy."

"I know," I sniffled. "He never once thought about how I felt!"

"You're probably right," Mama agreed. "But Jessie, did you give any thought to how he or I or your sisters might feel about your running away without a word and going to the library and the museum, places where I allow you to go *with* someone but never by yourself? You see, Jessie, we must agree that Daddy was inconsiderate; even he acknowledges that. However, when it comes right down to it, I believe that Jessica Renz has some thinking to do about how considerate she was during all this. We were worried sick, Jessie. I'm sure you were terribly frightened there in the museum, enough so I won't punish you for running off like that, but I also think you owe everyone an apology and when that's done, it's over. We're just so glad you're back home safe and sound." Her arms were a nurturing haven when she hugged me to her.

Consideration for others. A lesson that was imprinted in me for the rest of my life. Daddy and I both made our apologies and the entire matter was dropped. None of Mama's sisters were told about it nor was anyone on Daddy's side. Laura and I hugged each other especially hard after saying our goodnight prayers. It was good to be home, safe and sound, among people who loved me and who, I realized for the first time, how much I loved in return.

I had to admit, also, that having a vivid imagination was not always a blessing. Exploring the museum was still one of my favorite pastimes but I never again went alone and was one of the first ones out when the closing bell sounded.

Chapter 22

As times grew financially worse, people seemed to draw closer together. We began to have a constant stream of visitors from our 'past life.' Gilly wanted Mama and Daddy to meet his girlfriend, Tess, who stood almost a head taller than he did. They both worked in the same restaurant, he as a dishwasher and she as a waitress. Nobody, it turned out, wanted an apprentice helper in the sheet metal and furnace trade these days. He was no longer living with Otto and his family but had found a cheap room just a block from Tess and her girlfriend.

Tess was like nobody we girls had ever met. Her frizzed red hair, parted in the middle and drawn back behind her ears, was held in place with bobby pins decorated with rhinestone stars. She wore the brightest of red lipsticks, Tangee brand from Woolworth, she informed Vi and Maggie as she proceeded to 're-do' her lips.

"That Gilly, he likes the taste of it, I guess, the way he's always causing me to repair myself," she told them, all while keeping time to the tempo in her mind with the sideways shakes of her head and the rolling of her large gray eyes that were enhanced with lush lashes, also from Woolworth's.

Her stockings, held up with round elastic garters, were rolled down to just below her knees and she would dab a bit of the lipstick on each kneecap and rub it in, then lift her printed voile sleeveless dress a bit and examine her handiwork to see if both knees "matched." The wad of gum she chewed kept her busy when she was not "informing us" of something or telling Gilly he was simply "the very *most*! Don't you just love this boy?"

It was evident that he thought that she was "the very *most*" herself and never raised a thick dark eyebrow when she sat on his lap, almost hiding him from view, and stretched like Meetzer before springing up and sitting demurely on the davenport beside him.

Mama said, later, that Tess seemed like a nice, wholesome girl who had probably seen a few too many 'flapper' movies. "Basically, she's very sweet. It's certainly evident that he adores her. They're both orphans, so they do have that in common, anyway."

This was said to offset Vi's and Maggie's comments that she seemed rather "trashy."

One morning, Aunt Alice arrived via Clyde's taxi along with Aunts Rose and Arlene and our cousins Nancy and Lawrence. Aunt Mimsy would be getting married in June and preparations were being made. Aunt Arlene had learned the art of millinery and was going to be making the bridal veil and the bridesmaid's garden hats.

"I only hope that I don't end up in the hospital a bit early," Aunt Arlene told Mama in the kitchen over coffee and some of her delicious schaum torte that she had brought with her.

Since neither Laura nor I had any idea where babies really came from, we were unaware that quite soon Lawrence would have a baby brother or sister. He told us that he was sure going to be glad when that wedding was over. He was tossing a part of somebody's chalk 'impressions' across a hopscotch as he complained that his mother made him stand still in the middle of their dining room table to 'model' the veil and hats so she could pin things here and there on them.

"I have to take a bath first and stand there, in my underwear, so that I don't get anything *on* anything and I can't even rub my nose if it itches. I'll sure be glad when the doctor brings my baby sister so she can do that, instead."

"A baby sister? For real?"

"It's what Papa and Mama ordered."

Secretly I hoped the doctor brought a boy cousin. There were enough girls in the relation already.

Studying Laura, I wondered why neither of us were boys, since Daddy had wanted one so badly. Maybe we were all they had on hand at the time in the 'lily pad', which is where Daddy said doctors got babies. Possibly this was so, since, whenever I looked in the mirror, reflected back, in my estimation, was someone ugly as a toad. I could probably ask Aunt Arlene about it.

When I brought up the subject, however, I was stared down and told to "go play and don't be so involved in what we grownups say and do." I felt a hard lump inside my chest when Aunt Rose remarked to Mama, "That one is so *different* from your other three," as if to be *different* was shameful or odd, like, maybe, Old Man Steiger and his wife washing their money and hanging it on the wash line to dry.

"She's a very bright child," I heard Mama say. "Each of you has only one, at least for now. When you have more; you'll realize that they're sometimes as different as night and day." Somehow *her* "different" did not sound critical. I was glad that *she* was my mother and not either of her sisters.

Grandmother was going "all out" for Aunt Mimsy's wedding, according to Aunt Alice. Her wedding reception was to be held in the ballroom of the Hotel Pfister. There were to be six bridesmaids and an equal number of ushers. The supper menu was to include breast of squab and smoked oysters. A fountain of French champagne would fill the guest's glasses.

After they had left, Mama stood in the doorway for a long time, lost in thought: When she turned, her eyes held tears.

"What's the matter, Mama?" inquired Maggie.

"Oh, I was just thinking how unequal things are in this world. My sister will sit down to her first meal as a married woman to an elaborate feast and in this same city there are people whose stomachs are aching from hunger." It was the first time I had ever heard Mama sound so dispirited. She was always the one to bolster everyone else's morale. "I don't suppose, however," she continued, "that if Mimsy's wedding supper were comprised of hard boiled eggs and toast served in Mama's backyard, any of those poor people would be any the less hungry. At least, this way, the waiters and the members of the orchestra, as well as everyone else concerned, will have more money to spend afterwards."

Having settled that problem to her satisfaction, she propped open the lid of the piano and began to play some of her favorite tunes. As usual, we girls moved toward her to watch her fingers dance over the keys.

"Play *Falling Waters*, Mama."

"And then *II Trovatore*."

"Something by Chopin, please, Mama. I love Chopin."

"*Moonlight Sonata*."

"Some Strauss waltzes." It was Daddy, just returning home from having ducked out to avoid Aunt Alice. He danced Vi and the rest of us around the room while Mama filled his request first. An hour later, having satisfied all of our pleas, she rose to start supper but the magic of her music remained with us.

Later, looking back, I was grateful for those special moments because that unbending villain, later labeled as *The Great Depression*, would steal even that joy from us.

Chapter 23

The day of the school outing was filled with sunshine, laughter and large yellow school buses that transported us to the Washington Park Zoo. Laura and I felt rich. Rather than bring along a brown paper sack lunch, like most of the other kids, we had each saved fifteen cents of the quarter apiece that Aunt Alice had given us before she left, so we both had enough for a hot dog, a box of cracker Jack and an ice cream cone. Our teachers were treating us to soda pop.

Because I was older and we had been to the zoo before, Laura's teacher allowed her to stay with me and even ride back to school on my bus. Our orders were to be at the pavilion for lunch, otherwise we were "free to roam to our heart's content," as Tante Kate would say.

We were never really alone because other children were always with us as we traipsed through the aviary, lion, tiger and reptile houses and at last arrived at the main attraction, Mary Lou. She was a chimpanzee who lived in a glassed-in cage, wore a baby bonnet and a dress, had her own toys, such as a wooden kiddie-car, three wheeled and similar to a tricycle but without pedals; a large rubber-ball; a teddy bear and a small table and chair set where she would sit to eat her bananas and other food. She also had a tree from which to swing by her long arms.

Laura almost pulled a tantrum when I told her it was time to purchase our hotdogs and join our classmates at the pavilion but I finally succeeded in dragging her away. She was appeased by the smell of the food, admitting that she was hungry, and ordered two hotdogs for herself. Her remaining nickel would go for Cracker Jack, she declared through mouthfuls of hotdog and bun downed on the way to the lunch tables.

How she could eat so much and never become too fat was beyond me. I knew why I was skinny. I was a "picky eater," as Aunt Rose termed it. Like Jack Sprat, I "could eat no fat."

Later, the two of us, nibbling at our caramel coated popcorn confections, circled the fenced around Monkey Island, watching with delight as one particular gray monkey gave a clown's performance, turning somersaults, jumping onto other monkeys and was finally hauled off to his own group by his mother.

I wanted to see the elephants and giraffes but Laura had decided that she would rather keep on watching the monkeys. Making her promise that she would remain right there, I joined the group of kids who were heading for Jumbo, the elephant's cage. The rhinos taking underwater swims were also intriguing and I fed a giraffe a leaf, screaming in glee when his soft lips swept over my hand and arm seeking more food.

When I returned to Monkey Island, Laura was nowhere in sight. At first I was not too disturbed but as I went along, asking kids we knew if they had seen her, I became somewhat alarmed. We had promised Mama that we would stay together and I had left her alone. Maybe she had returned to see more of Mary Lou, I decided, since she had been so reluctant to leave there before lunch. With fingers hopefully crossed, I assured myself that she would be enjoying the chimp's antics.

I pushed my way through the throng of people around Mary Lou's cage but Laura was not among them. Darn it! I thought, as I headed back to the monkeys, she promised to wait here! She'd better be there or else!

She was not. Maybe she had tried to follow me to the elephant cage or to the giraffes. My return trip in that direction was a vain one. The park was so big and she and I were so small. My eyes filled with tears of frustration and worry. I had to *find* her before the buses were due to leave.

Asking a grownup for the correct time, I learned that I had only ten more minutes in which to locate her. Frantic now, I decided I had to notify my teacher. Let's see, now, which way was it to the pavilion? No, wait a minute, we had been told to meet at the entrance to the park. I headed that way.

Suddenly, I heard Laura calling my name. It took a moment or two to locate her and then I stood with hands on hips, shaking my head. She was actually standing behind George Washington on his statue horse! How in the world had she gotten way up there?

"Laura, for Pete's sake, what are you doing up there?"

"Looking to see you. You were gone a long time, Jessie, and I got worried about you, so some big boys helped me up here so I could try to see you, and I did, only they went away and now I can't get down!"

"Stay right here!" I warned, as if she could fly, "I'll get some help."

Our classmates and teachers were coming toward me, heading for the buses. Intercepting them, I pointed to where Laura was perched.

"Oh, dear!" Laura's teacher exclaimed, "We have to get back to school. Why in the world would she go up there?" She was both angry and concerned.

"Laura's adventurous!" I defended, using a new word I had recently added to my vocabulary, repeating my statement to anyone willing to listen.

"Well, she certainly is and it seems to have gotten her into a heap of trouble," the policeman who had been summoned declared as he studied the situation. Taking the teachers aside, he told them to depart without Laura and me. "We'll see to the girls," he promised.

It took awhile to retrieve Laura. A couple of men armed with a ladder got Laura down from behind George Washington. Instead of arresting her and taking her to jail, as I had feared, the policeman bought each of us an ice cream cone, took us into an office in the main building and phoned Mama.

Daddy was off somewhere, serving a summons or something. Mama did not drive. How were we to get home? She wanted to know.

"We'll deliver them, Mrs. Renz, don't you worry," the officer promised. Laura and I licked our cones and thoroughly enjoyed our ride in the police motorcycle sidecar. We would really have something to tell the kids at school! Mama was on the porch, awaiting our arrival. We did not enjoy the spanking she administered before sending us to our room to "think about how naughty you two have been. First the museum, now the zoo! I'll have no more of this, do you understand?"

We understood.

Our teachers evidently did not hold anything against us because the last day of school we students poured out of school crying, "School's out! School's out! Teacher let the monkeys out!" and waved report cards that showed that most of us had passed into the next grade. Mine had only one merit and two special merits, of which Mama and Daddy would be very proud. Laura's, too, was top grade.

Rushing home to show them off, we dashed into the foyer to find Mama on the phone.

"You have a new little cousin," she exclaimed, beaming, when she hung up. "Lawrence has a lovely little baby brother." Then she frowned. "Oh, dear, now Arlene will miss the wedding."

I might have had three special grades on my report card but I sure did not know why doctors could not bring the baby the parents ordered.

Chapter 24

Vi and Maggie, lucky girls, attended Aunt Mimsy's wedding but Laura and I were taken to Grandmother's house and left in charge of the lady across the alley who had helped serve the meal at Christmas, so the housekeeper could attend the marriage service.

Lawrence was there, too. We spent the afternoon playing fishpond and "Old Maid." In spite of the fact that Grandmother was not there in her special chair to preside, we still felt obligated to tiptoe through the hall to the bathroom and only peer through the swinging door from the butler's pantry into the dining room. Lawrence wanted to trespass but we would not let him. Somehow, I suspected, Grandmother would know; she had that sort of aura about her, as if her eyes could reach out from the church and see what we were doing.

I asked Lawrence how he liked having a baby brother and he said, "I don't know; he isn't home yet. Mama's in the hospital taking care of him."

He was wrong. The baby was still in the hospital but Aunt Arlene had signed herself out, temporarily, against everyone's warning that a new mother positively had to remain in bed for ten days lest she have blood clots or worse. She was going to be at Aunt Mimsy's wedding or else! Having made the veil and the bridesmaid's hats, she was therefore in charge of how her sister was going to look as she walked unescorted down the aisle in her bridal finery.

Fatherless, brotherless, Aunt Mimsy had elected to have the "who giveth this woman away in marriage" to be answered from the pew by her mother.

The minister almost had a stroke of apoplexy over his inability to sway her from her argument that "I do not feel that I should ask Uncle George or Cousin Jasper, since they don't own me and never have, so I'll do this my own way. I'm a grown woman, after all."

So now there was Aunt Arlene showing defiance to the tradition as well and using the argument that a few days less on her back reading magazines would not hurt anything. Hadn't her Grandmother gotten up the next morning to prepare breakfast for her Grandfather when her mother was born in that log cabin and didn't Indian women of those days have their babies in the bushes somewhere, if they were on the march, and then hurry up to join the rest of the tribe in a day or so? Evidently Indian babies came from the bushes instead of lily pads; I was surprised to learn. Hmmm. Daddy and Mama had collected us from Grandmother's house in Phyllis so we could return home and he and Mama could get dressed in their evening clothes to attend the wedding dinner and reception at the Hotel Pfister, downtown. The minute we entered the car both Vi and Maggie warned us to "Watch out for our dresses; we have to wear these to church tomorrow." Once we were on the way I began to listen to what Mama was saying to Daddy in soft tones.

"Once Arlene puts her mind to something, nothing and nobody will change it. Now that poor baby will have to be taken from the nursery and probably sent home early so she can feed it. After only a week, mind you. She's certainly inviting disaster!" Mama was so incensed that she forgot to speak German. "She could even lose her milk!"

"Ja, well, it's not just Arlene," Daddy was saying, "all of you Hohenfeldt women are like brick walls."

"Why, Paul Renz, whatever do you mean!" Mama sputtered. I saw Daddy's grin as he quickly replied, "You married me against all their protests, didn't you?"

What had been said about Aunt Arlene was quite perplexing. How did having the doctor bring a baby from the lily pad cause a woman to have blood clots, ugh, if she didn't remain in the hospital to take care of it and to even lose her milk? The milkman brought milk, didn't he? Couldn't she just place another order? Or was it like in school where we had to drink all of our milk along with our graham crackers at rest time or not have more until our parents signed a note? I tried asking Vi about this but she wanted to hear what was being said in the front seat, so she merely shushed me with her finger on her lips and a warning frown.

When I turned to Maggie for answer, she merely shrugged her shoulders and shook her head. If she knew the answers, she was certainly being her own darned stubborn self and not sharing the information with a "mere child." After all, she was now in high school! On her way to womanhood. I felt like kicking her shin but she was on the other side of Laura, who was now fast asleep.

Being eight years old was a real strain at times. I was expected to be a' big sister' and keep Laura from going astray, like at the zoo, but I was considered too young to be included in lots of other things. Just when did things even up, anyways? Maybe Maggie didn't know the answers, either, and was acting big so I wouldn't guess.

Home once more, Mama changed into her pretty peach flowered voile dress that Aunt Alice had helped to "take in here and there" because Mama had lost weight since we moved into the mansion. It was the dress with the peach taffeta slip that made interesting crinkly rustles when she moved; the one she would have worn aboard the ship when she and Daddy went to Paris if the stock market had not crashed and changed everything. Mama had kept it in the cedar chest in her bedroom, beneath the window where Meetzer now sunned himself these days because the butler pantry-turned kitchen had no windows like in the red brick house. Mama's black patent leather shoes with French heels and the buckles set with marquisettes had also been stored in that chest. She could have taken the dress and shoes back to Chapman's store but somehow never did, and now she had them for the wedding festivities.

Laura and I sat on the davenport with our knees up and our dresses covering them to our ankles, like little tents, as we watched our parents wind up the Victrola and put a Strauss waltz record on the turntable. Vi and Maggie quickly rolled up the rug to expose the waxed hardwood flooring.

Daddy was handsome in the rented tuxedo that he really could not afford but was *darned* if he would let Mama's family know that and was going to pay for it by calling former customers to see if he could drum up some extra furnace cleaning jobs.

With a grin that told us he thought Mama looked lovely, he waltzed her around and around, her strand of long pearls, knotted on the bottom in the fashion of the day, swaying back and forth, her green eyes sparkling like emeralds.

Then it was time for them to leave for the dinner and reception and for us to eat hamburgers Vi was bringing back from the White Tower place across the street so we would not feel cheated because we could not accompany Mama and Daddy to the Hotel Pfister.

We put other records on and danced together, pretending we, too, were at the ball. Vi made us swear to secrecy the fact that two of the university summer students who were rooming together in number 4 came down to dance with her and Maggie and stayed for about an hour.

When our parents returned, after eleven, they were giggling and acting like kids Vi's and Maggie's ages. They woke us up to present us with napkin-wrapped slices of wedding cake with white icing and beautiful pink icing roses for each of us to "tuck under your pillow to dream on. We've extra for all of us to eat tomorrow."

I could never remember my dreams so I don't know if my piece of cake did anything or not. Sometime during the night, Laura sneaked the cake from beneath both our pillows and devoured both her piece and mine.

Now Aunt Mimsy and our new uncle, Edmond, were on their way to the Bahamas on their honeymoon, Mama informed us the next morning. We later learned that Aunt Arlene had attended the wedding supper and the reception long enough for everyone there to "wag their tongues." Laura and I went up to the second floor bathroom to stand in front of the mirror and wag ours and try to imagine what it must have looked like to have a whole roomful of people doing that! Grown-ups sure lead funny lives, sometimes.

Aunt Arlene survived her rash behavior and we eventually got to meet our new baby cousin, Jimmy. I realized at once that he would have to do some real growing to be able to take cousin Lawrence's place on the dining room table and model wedding veils and garden hats in his underwear while his boyfriends got tired of waiting and went to the sand lot to play baseball without him.

Chapter 25

Maybe times were bad but the Fourth of July Parade brought out a crowd anyway. If you can't find work and there is nothing to do but sit around and grouse, you might as well enjoy a parade. At least for a little while you are not worrying about tomorrow and the next day. Besides, Milwaukeeans love parades.

The people on our porch that year did include some from the year before but there were new roomers in place of the old ones and Mrs. Malenka-now Mrs. Turner had brought her husband, Alfred. Upon studying her, I noted that our former housekeeper had a very funny shape. Her stomach was as big as her behind, maybe even bigger. What seemed strange was that all the men were kidding Mr. Turner about it and slapping him on the back and telling him, "all it takes is a good woman."

Blushing clear down to his collar, he smoothed out his cookie-duster mustache, adjusted his glasses with the round black frames, like Vi's, and changed the subject to his new job as a Florsheim shoe salesman in a store someplace on Vliet Street. He stood stoop shouldered, as if his six feet of height needed to apologize to shorter men, which made him seem ineffective, somehow, yet he had a resonant voice when he spoke.

"You have to believe in the product to be a good salesman," he explained. "One thing I tell people is how important it is to make a good first impression, especially if you're going for a job interview. Nothing speaks for a man like a pair of well-made, well-shined shoes."

Those on the porch wearing shoes with scuff marks and in need of polish began to shuffle their feet, trying to hide them behind legs of their chair and surreptitiously giving them a shine of sorts by rubbing them along their trouser bottoms or by hand. From my vantage point on the top step, I found this very interesting. Evidently this well dressed fellow who held a good job was looked upon as someone to respect, even if he was twelve years younger than his wife, who Mama's sisters said had "robbed the cradle."

Conversation in the kitchen, when I went to see if the lemonade was ready, had to do with Mrs. Turner's age. Forty one was "old for the first time." What had the doctor said? At this point I was noticed and told to have Vi and Maggie come in for the refreshments. Doggone it, a first time for what? Now, I'd never find out!

Mr. Steinmann came, of course, but this time nobody in the neighborhood wanted to pay to see him. His value as an attraction was gone and pennies were hard to come by. He was enthused about how things were going to be in Washington when that "idiot, Hoover," was replaced by "the man from New York." Shaking his forefinger, he predicted, "and it's bound to happen; you mark my word. Every man who ever wore a uniform will be at the polls, come November, to vote him out! The way he treated his nation's heroes--- IDIOTIC!!"

"And even those who never held a gun will vote with them," Daddy said.

The parade started and we all rose to place our hands over our hearts to honor the passing colors. Mr. Steinmann, tall and erect in his uniform, kept his hand at his forehead in salute. We were terribly proud to have him there with us, wooden leg and all.

He had brought small flags with him, which he doled out for us to wave. Someone had slipped Laura and me a bag of lady crackers to pop on the sidewalk with our heels "when the parade is over." Our saved-up pennies had purchased sparklers to light when night fell. Like last year, we would all end up at the lakefront to watch the fireworks.

As Fourths of July went, to Laura and me, this one was no different from the last but we were kids; we were not privy to much that was going on, even if I was a good listener. Somehow, I had not learned that several of the roomers had walked away without paying their back rent and Mama had been short in the amount that she owed for the rent of the building. The agent had given her until the 5th to make up the difference.

Daddy had decided he would approach Attorney Kaufman for an advance. He would do it first thing the next morning. The lawyer had always been satisfied with Daddy's work and was basically, very kind. Things would work out; they always did. Confident that he was right in his assumption, Daddy and Mama put their worries aside for the day and enjoyed their company.

Whether Mr. Kaufman would have done this turned out to be a matter of conjecture, no longer important. When Daddy did not return home with money to pay the agent, who was alternately drumming his thumb on the kitchen table and sipping coffee while he and Mama checked the clock on the wall every few moments, Mama finally took Vi and Maggie aside and asked them to "run down the block and see if he's coming."

He was, but with dragging footsteps. The elevator operator in Mr. Kaufman's office building had given Daddy the news. "Terrible thing about Mr. Kaufman dying like that, ain'a? According to his secretary, he went in his sleep, just like that…"

From habit, Daddy had walked down the hall to Mr. Kaufman's office. The door was open and his secretary was inside, eyes red-rimmed from crying. Whether for poor Mr. Kaufman or because now she was without a job herself, probably a combination of both, was not determined. That Mama was now short of necessary money was a certainty.

Mama listened to his news with sinking heart but with a smile requested another few days, telling the agent that there would be money for July and August when he returned or her husband could even deliver it to the management office. She gave him a nickel to make a phone call to his superior.

An extension was not granted. Instead, in the mail came a notice that the Renz family had thirty days in which to vacate the premises. A lease had already been granted to someone else.

We cried. We moped. We felt like outcasts. We did not personally know the people who were in charge of making such decisions but they were sending us packing to someplace, any place, and that was demeaning! Now we faced another problem; how to secure enough money to rent another place and move our furniture there. Mama spoke of going to Aunt Alice or Grandmother but Daddy would not hear of it.

"I'll ask Elsie and Frantz. They might be able to help."

They were. Ever thrifty, they owned several properties. The third floor apartment in a house on Atkinson Avenue, up on the 'North Side,' was going to be vacant by the end of July. We could move into it for only nineteen dollars per month rent, without utilities. It was small, of course, but it was a roof over our heads, at least.

Mama wanted to see if something else might be available, something larger, but Daddy said he had already paid the first's months rent with money borrowed from Tante Kate. He and Mama had words in German that sent us kids scurrying but eventually we all sat down to a well- prepared meal and they spoke to each other in English.

I suppose it hurt Mama that he would take money from his family but not allow her to approach her own. He called it pride but she called it being a German "blockhead." After all, Cousin Jasper wasn't the entire Hohenfeldt family.

Perhaps not, but he would not let her family know that he had once again failed her and give them something more to "cluck about."

"They don't 'cluck,' Paul."

"Don't they?"

Somehow, this struck Mama funny and she began to laugh. We all felt better.

Nobody was laughing, however, when the moving truck pulled up in front of the mansion and three men covered Mama's piano with thick pads and carefully carried it out through the double front doors.

There was absolutely no room in the third floor apartment for a Steinway grand piano. Besides, it was going to cost money for us to move and we would need funds to live on until "something turned up."

So, Mama had reasoned when she walked over to the Conservatory of Music and approached one of the professors. That same day he had arrived, old fashioned formal attire and all, his white hair and mustache perfectly groomed, his fingernails well manicured, his coat tails flipped out as he sat down at the piano to play something undeniably wonderful.

"Ach, such tone. You have a beautiful instrument here, Mrs. Renz. It should bring a good price and I have just the young man in mind who will be most interested. Mind you, his is a fine musician and well able to pay. I shall contact him this very day."

The young man arrived the next afternoon, sat at the piano in shirt sleeves, and no tie, tossed his hair out of his eyes and, closing them, began to play. The professor was correct; the young man had talent. Mama's eyes were filled with tears as she listened.

Very quiet when he paid her in cash—she had explained that she would not accept a check due to the banks being in such a shaky state—she waited until he had left and sat down to play only to end up in tears that dripped down over her folded arms where she laid her head. We four girls ended up crying with her. Daddy, as usual lately, was out 'job hunting.' Without success.

When they came for the piano, he was down in the basement, working on something he was inventing. I found him there, his soldering iron seaming two pieces of metal together, the rivulet of melted solder and the odor of the muriatic acid bringing back to my mind the tin shop on Green Bay Road. I laid my head against his shoulder for a moment and asked what he was making.

"Something to keep the danged flies out," he replied, the muscle in his jaw working like it had in Mr. Jack Murray's office so I knew he was upset.

"What kind of something?"

"A window. See, in the winter it holds glass but in the summer it has this pull-down screen to take the place of the glass and…" he demonstrated how one would pull the screen down from a metal shield at the top of the window.

"That's a good idea, Daddy. What happens to the glass part when you aren't using it?"

"You put it in the basement or garage or something. Now that's enough questions. I need to concentrate."

I was dismissed, and returned back upstairs to contemplate the empty space where the piano had been. Soon all of the furniture would be gone and we Renzes with it. I was attached to this place, this mansion-turned rooming house; maybe I was like those cornflowers that grow along side the road, putting roots down and quickly wilting and dying when somebody pulls them up. I had wilted inside when we had left the red brick house and I felt the same now. We had spent more than a year here. The feel of it was stored, someplace deep inside of me, never to be forgotten.

Wondering what the next place would be like, I headed for the window seat. Without Mama's piano, to hide it from view, there was no privacy for me now when I curled up on it. Covering my drawn up knees with my dress skirt, I stared out at Fifteenth Street, taking in the view of the Conservatory, a bit of Wisconsin Avenue, people playing miniature golf behind the hamburger place and sullenly contemplated Mama's instructions to look upon this next move as another new adventure. I just wished her eyes had been smiling when she said those words. To me, they had looked like a pair of green pools that had no sparkle because the sun had gone behind a great big cloud.

Sometime during the year, I had put all thoughts of the 'dasmel in distress' behind me. I thought about her now and wondered who would care about her. Maybe I should march across Wisconsin Avenue and confront those men in that castle, letting them know I cared.
Just as I was about to cross Wisconsin Avenue to carry out my decision, Maggie called to tell me, "We're going to the library. Want to come along?"

Mama accompanied us, each of us carrying the books we had borrowed. At each corner, we exchanged places, with first Vi and Maggie walking beside her and then Laura and I and so on. Her talk was light, about the cars that passed and how good the nice fresh air felt but her eyes were troubled. I could tell because her brows were pinched together like upside down commas instead of dancing up and down to add interest to her face as she spoke. Vivacious is how people often described her. Today she was not vivacious. I guess, like me, she was wilted inside.

I never did confront those men in the Knights of Columbus castle. For a long time I felt guilty about that, feeling that the poor *damsel* now had nobody to care about her. Then it came to my mind that perhaps, unknown to me, she had already been rescued. There were men on horseback, like that policeman who chased Daddy's truck the day we moved in. I had seen few policemen on horseback since then but they *were* around, weren't they? Why, of course! They rescued people, didn't they? It made me feel better about the whole matter.

PART TWO
Chapter 26
1933

It was February. Mr. Franklin Delano Roosevelt had been elected
President, as Mr. Steinmann had predicted, though he would not take office
until March 4th. We all felt bad, however, because Mr. Steinmann had died
and would not be able to listen to the inauguration speech on the radio.

There was a discussion about that. Nobody could see radio waves
wandering about through the air, ready to be captured and sent through
receivers; maybe our souls were the same way, able to travel here and
there, and maybe, somehow, Mr. Steinmann knew about Mr. Roosevelt.
Who could say he did not?

Back in November, when the election returns were being
broadcast, Uncle Edmond had fastened the radio aerial to the metal springs
of the rollaway bed where Laura and I lay, half asleep, to bring in better
reception. He and the other two uncles were there because their wives were
not interested in the election and Mama was, so it was to our humble
apartment that they had come.

Uncle Frantz, too, had joined us and had brought along some of his
home brew "to toast the new president, and toast that guy Hoover out of
office." Nobody ever got drunk on Uncle Frantz's libations because he
never proffered more than a glass or two apiece. For we kids there was his
delicious home brewed root beer. The men had left after midnight but we
were fast asleep by then.

At night, in our beds, we were cold. Mama piled blankets on us but
the heat from the round-bellied coal stove, the fire inside "banked" for the
night with just enough coal so the fire did not go out, did not reach clear
across the living room

to Laura's and my rollaway bed. Often Vi and Maggie left their too-cold bedroom to join us. This was a severe winter, even by Wisconsin's standards, and our combined body heat left us just this side of shivering.

Mornings were better because Daddy would get up at dawn and shake down the ashes and add coal from the bucket with a small coal shovel. At least we dressed in warmth, each of us taking a turn in front of the stove that toasted one side while the other was goose-pimpled.

It had proved to be traumatic, the move from the mansion to this third floor flat where Daddy now had to carry coal up in buckets from the basement. During the hot late summer and warm Fall, it was block ice clamped in heavy black iron tongs that he toted to our icebox (which now had a water pan beneath like other people's), dripping water that we had to hurriedly wipe up from the stairs and landings so the tenants below would not complain.

They had learned that Daddy's sister and brother-in-law were the owners so it was to him that they now brought all their petty complaints. He should DO something when a faucet washer needed replacing or the neighbor's dog howled at the moon. Usually he obliged, though he came home with a pant leg chewed by the dog and cusswords under his breath because the neighbor threatened him with a bloody nose for "sticking his into places it did not belong."

To keep our perishables fresh, Daddy had built an insulated box that he fastened to the outside kitchen windowsill. Sometimes the cream on top of the milk bottle was frozen and stuck up from the bottle, its thin cardboard lid resting atop that like a little cap.

Mama had to lug wash baskets and soaps down three flights of stairs to the basement. There was a water heater, like in the mansion, but it was match-lit and heated only for baths or washing and she still filled the copper boiler resting on the two burner gas plate because the first few loads, which were sheets and pillow cases and long johns, required water that was HOT.

Our portion of the basement was not large. Her washer and galvanized rinsing tubs took up so much space that there was no room for "helpers." Daddy was the one who hung the washing on the line, most times, if he was not out job hunting, and that meant carrying heavy baskets of wet clothes into the yard in good weather or, on bad days, up to our apartment, to wash lines strung through the rooms and fastened to the top hinges of doors. No wonder Mama was always tired and Daddy 'down in the mouth' and Mama's sisters were not encouraged to visit.

Mama's "piano money" had run out. We reached the day when there was nothing to eat in the house but flour, oatmeal and canned milk. The fifth day of oatmeal for breakfast, oatmeal mush for lunch, and oatmeal pancakes for supper, our parents decided that there was no more saying, "We don't accept charity."

"When we were first married we had more than this, Paul. We lost little Ralphie; I'm not letting the rest of them get sick."

"I know, Lyd. I'll go today."

Phyllis' gas tank was empty. Daddy borrowed a coaster wagon and, with we kids at his side to "prove we existed," walked the mile and a half to the "relief place." Luckily, most of the sidewalks were cleared of snow.

The lady who handed Daddy the forms to fill out either had a bad cold or was sniffing to see if we "stank." It took him the better part of an hour, with Vi leaning over him to help him pencil in the necessary information; he frowning and licking the pencil point each time before he wrote.

He had finished the eighth grade and then gone to work, like so many children in those days, his widowed mother needing money. He spoke well but had never been able to make the transition from writing in German to spelling in English. In Milwaukee, up until World War I, many of the schoolchildren, were taught in German. Many of the Protestant church services were also in German. When the U.S. entered the war, good people of German descent or who had fled Germany to become American citizens were forced to suddenly learn English or be in danger of being strung up on the nearest lamp pole if the conversed in public in their mother tongue.

"Shut up that Kraut language and speak United States!" one woman admonished an old grandmother who was telling the butcher that she wanted *zwei hahnchen* and pointing to the two nice fat hens she desired. He usually joked with her in German, his own mother tongue, too, but in the presence of the hostile woman, silently, eyes downcast, wrapped up two hens and patted the grandmother's hand in apology. We had heard that story several times from Daddy. Vi did not want that lady with the sniffles to look down her pointed nose at him and us.

Both the woman and a man checked over the papers, asked several questions and finally started to place packages of this and bags of that on the counter. When we left the place, we had the coaster wagon heaped with food and Daddy had the assurance that our rent, lights, and coal would be "taken care of."

We had gone possibly two blocks when Daddy's eyes began to stream tears. He blamed it on "the danged cold weather" and brought out his navy blue bandanna to wipe them away but that muscle in his jaw was dancing a jig. I slipped my mittened hand into his large mittened one and leaned my head against his arm. He reached over to bring me close to him and reached for Laura as well. Vi and Maggie were also crying. It had been an ordeal for them as well.

When we reached home, Aunt Alice was there. Daddy had heard her voice as he carried packages upstairs, and, turning around, stashed them, instead, in the washer, indicating for us to do the same. "She doesn't need to know about this," he stage whispered.

She had come laden with food, as usual, and wonderful food it was after all that oatmeal. Mama had placed the last scoop of coffee in the percolator. Her eyes questioned Daddy's and he nodded ever so slightly. Yes, he had gone to the relief station and yes, he had food. He mentioned something about having to fix her washer, took his cup of coffee and headed down to the basement.

Aunt Alice might have verbally deplored Mama's present situation "in no uncertain terms" while we were gone but did nothing to offend our ears during the balance of her visit. When Clyde came for her, she allowed each of us to kiss her cheek and her fingers placed a silver dollar into a hand of each of her four grandnieces, then, gave us gimlet looks that said we should make no special remarks about that in front of Mama. A woman to be feared at times but also to be loved. We might now be "on relief" but we were still rich in other ways…

Chapter 27

Unknown to Mama and Daddy, Vi had not returned to school when the mid-term classes began. She had no desire to continue on at North Division High with Maggie, and swore her sister to secrecy. Instead, she filled out employment applications at several shops and at the Nunn-Bush Shoe Company, where she was hired. On her application she had written 18 in the age space. Her glasses did make her appear older. Hoping to get office work, she was, instead, placed at one of the shoe shining machines.

Many of the employees were Polish, most recently arrived from that country. As in most factories, the jokes and stories were far earthier than those of the white collar people and her ears turned red at the connotations, even if she did not understand them. She was also the butt of sly tricks, such as the time one of the men taught her a Polish phrase that she proudly used in conversation with another female worker. The slap she received almost sent her reeling.

That afternoon I found her sobbing on the stairway and tried to comfort her. She did not tell me what was wrong and made me promise to say nothing of her tears to Mama and Daddy or anybody else in the family. Her head seemed very warm and her eyes were strangely glassy.

At supper time she did not feel like eating. By the next morning she was burning with fever. Mama hated to run up a doctor bill but she used the phone in the first floor apartment and phoned Dr. Becker. His examination of our very ill sister brought out several "Hrumphs" and quite a few "Don't you knows" when he took Mama and Daddy aside to tell them Vi had pneumonia; in those days before penicillin often a pronouncement of doom.

A day or so later, as Mama was sponging Vi's forehead, there was a knock on the door. Standing there with head slightly bowed, due to his tallness and the slant of the hall ceiling, was a man who introduced himself as Mr. Nunn, from the shoe factory. Daddy told him we were not interested in buying any shoes and besides, we had a sick girl here.

"Does her name happen to be Violet?" the shoe salesman asked.

"Why, yes. How do you know my daughter?"

"She works for me and I consider her one of my better employees."

Frowning, Daddy waved him inside with a sideways movement of his head. "What do you mean, she works for you? She just turned seventeen; she goes to high school. You must have the wrong person in mind. Renz is the last name here. R-E-N-..."

"Z," finished the visitor. "Are you telling me that Vi isn't eighteen, as she put down on her application? Now that puts me and my company in trouble, Mr. Renz. I would never have believed that she would lie like that."

Mama had come to see who was calling and heard the story Mr. Nunn iterated. "Oh, dear! We thought she was attending North Division High. I knew how much she missed Shorewood High when we moved to Wisconsin Avenue and how she disliked West Division, probably because of her loyalty to her former school but—oh, dear, and she's down with pneumonia and burning with fever!" Sitting down at the table, she stared out the window at the roof next door.

"Well, perhaps she felt that she was contributing to the family welfare by working. I can't keep her on, under the circumstances, but I'd certainly take her back when she's of age."

"And who did you say you were?" Mama inquired, then almost fell off her chair when he answered, "Charles Nunn. My fellow workers call me Charlie. My Dad owns the place."

"Owns the place...are you speaking of the Nunn-Bush Shoe Company?"

"That's the one. I'm learning the ropes. Dad wants me to know every phase of the operations and I've been working along sideViolet, polishing the finished product. She's a bright and interesting person behind those glasses. She belongs in school no matter how much she dislikes that particular institution. Why don't I tell her that?"

"She wouldn't know you, Mr. Nunn. We're praying that she recovers at this point. I hope you aren't interested in her—well, romantically...?"

"Of course not, Mrs. Renz. Absolutely not! I take an interest in all our workers. When she didn't show up at work I thought I'd see what was wrong. Didn't want to see her get fired. Jobs being at a premium, it's not too likely that someone just walks away from one. You know, if she—when she gets well, if she doesn't want to return to school full time, she could attend vocational school one day a week and work for us the other five, if you need the money. We could find something for her where she wouldn't be running a machine."

"We thought she was attending North Division every day," Mama repeated wearily. "Thank you for your concern. It was nice of you to come. I have to get back to her, Mr. Nunn, if you'll excuse me."

Instead of leaving, he followed her into the living room where Vi was temporarily installed on the rollaway so she could be closer to the heat of the stove there.

He stayed only a moment, his eyes filled with compassion. A nice man, as Mama later described him to her sisters; even nicer when Vi, finally recuperating after days of prayers by all of us that she "pull through," received a huge bouquet of flowers. Attached was a card wishing her good health and advising her to enroll in Vocational School one day a week. In it was a promise that her employer would find work for her the other four or five at a task that did not require running machines.

Another visitor was the truant officer, who would have pressed some sort of charges if Vi had not been so ill. Instead, he, too, advised that, since she did not desire to attend regular high school, she could enroll at the Vocational School for the one day per week required by law.

What a pity! Vi had been an A student at Shorewood and the same at West Division. Now she was forfeiting her schooling to "help out." It was probably this more than anything, that determined Mama to find a job. Men were not being hired but women were, it seemed. "And as soon as this year is over, Violet Renz, you go back to high school. Times are bound to pick up," she remonstrated, hugging her eldest daughter to her.

In a cigar box in her dresser drawer Vi had stashed her payday money, enough to purchase a warm coat and galoshes for her; the rest she donated to 'the family fund.' Daddy used some of it to have a phone installed and place a small ad in both the Journal and the Sentinel. From those he began to get what he termed 'small jobs': cleaning and repairing furnaces and replacing gutters, etc. Mama got down on her knees and asked God to please help her to secure employment and Daddy to earn enough so they could get off the relief rolls.

Mama found a job, in the bundling room of Schuster's Department Store warehouse, wrapping packages for delivery. For her forty eight hours of work she brought home the amazing sum of twelve dollars per week! At the end of six months, Daddy was able to go down to the relief place and have his name removed from their list.

We were with him that proud day. A roomful of people were ahead of us, so we waited. One old lady was handed a dozen eggs. In turning to place them into her cart, she was jostled by someone and the eggs fell to the floor, creating a mess of shells and raw egg . Silence prevailed as the man at the counter stared at her, muttered something about "clumsy" and called out, "Next!"

The woman began to cry. Moving up to the counter, Daddy stared at the fellow, eye level with him and a good twenty pounds heavier in muscle.

"That was an accident, mister. She needs those eggs."

"We go by quotas. Those were hers and she's the one dropped them." The fellow hissed. "Now get back in line or get out of here."

Taking hold of him by his white shirt front, not caring if he rumpled the expensive silk tie, Daddy replied, "Look, you little weasel, a dozen eggs might not mean anything to you but to her it means the difference between being able to make pancakes or other stuff with that weevily flour we have to sift the bugs from before we can use and add it to the rancid butter you hand out so gallantly before you go home to your own good meals. Give her another dozen to replace those!"

"What's your name?" inquired the man, venom of scorn dripping with every word.

"Paul Renz, mister, and you can give her the eggs I would have had because we don't need your type of charity anymore. Every one of these people would gladly work if they could and some do, I imagine, at jobs that don't pay enough to keep them in groceries. I appreciate the help we had but THANK GOD, I no longer need it!"

"Give the woman another dozen." The fellow ordered his helper, closing his own against his antagonist's eyes. Daddy released him and we left the place but not before we had used some newspaper to clean up the eggy mess and patted the old lady on the shoulder as she gratefully thanked us. Everyone clapped.

For the first time in months, Daddy was grinning.

That night, at the supper table, when we were eating our desserts, we had our usual "family discussion time." Anyone with a problem could discuss it and have the family try to solve it; those with "beefs" could vent their spleen politely and those with stories could relate them.

Daddy had not mentioned his actions of the morning so Maggie told Mama what he had done. Mama smiled and asked, "Paul, would you have been that brave if we were still on relief?"

He scratched his head and smoothed back his now graying hair. "That's a good question. I don't know. Maybe we'd have had a dozen less eggs in our wagon."

Mama's eyes were filled with love. Maybe her family did not see him as she did but in her regard he was quite a man.

Chapter 28

During the next few months we moved from Atkinson Avenue to another larger upper flat on Tenth Street and from there to a lower flat on Twelfth, near Burleigh. All were located within our school district, which pleased Laura and me. We liked Robert M. La Follette School; both of us had many friends there.

One of Daddy's money making plans, back on Atkinson Avenue, had to do with fifty one-gallon cans of aluminum paint. He had read an ad on one of the back pages of True Detective, which Uncle Edmond would purchase, read and pass on to him. The paint could be sent on assignment, the consignee had only to sell it door-to-door, keep half the profits for himself and send the rest to the consignor within sixty days. This promised to be a never-ending money making arrangement, with all persons scheduled to live happily ever after.

From the very first, it was doomed to failure; considering the small amount of room in the laundry, the addition of fifty gallons of paint made Mama very unhappy.

Daddy's promise to get rid of it and make money besides was not to be fulfilled. Nobody, it seemed, was interested in purchasing aluminum paint. The cans remained for Mama to detour around every washday. When the sixty days were up, Daddy wrote to the consignor that he did not have the necessary funds and wished to return the entire shipment. His letter was returned unopened, bearing the news that there was no longer such an addressee.

This was probably what prompted our move to Tenth Street, where our section of the basement was larger and had central heating. However, the landlord's kids, were such bullies that there was no dealing with them and in their parent's eyes they wore both halos and wings. We were their third tenants in a year.

The house on Twelfth was much better, offering a large basement, good size yard and even a two story former stable-turned-two-car garage behind it where

Daddy could put all his tools as well as Phyllis and all those cans of aluminum paint. All forty eight of them. He and Mama took one look at the dark brown grease-and-dirt-soiled walls of the lower flat and were given permission to repaint in colors of their choice and with a five dollar reduction in rent the first month to cover the cost of paint.

Our Metropolitan Insurance Agent, Mr. Jossi, who came around each month to collect our small premiums, was now our landlord and a nicer one could not be found. It was he who had suggested that we become his tenants when the present ones proved to be very destructive. Before we moved in, he fumigated the building "just in case." The young couple upstairs stayed with relatives for the night.

Clever people, Mama and Daddy. By first applying aluminum paint to every visible painted wall surface, leaving the lovely varnished woodwork as it was, they brightened up the place considerably. When that was dry, they took sponges, dipped them in another color paint, each room a different hue, and "tiffanied" the walls, using only about three quarts of enamel purchased "on sale" at the hardware store on the corner.

They left the dining room silver, since it was wood paneled from floor mid-wall. Above that the wall was covered with some sort of textured reed matting that, soaked up the aluminum paint like a thirsty desert traveler. A soft gloss varnish on the wood areas gave the entire room a lovely appearance. When we sat down to our Sunday dinners it was in the "Silver Room of the Renzshire House."

Mr. Jossi liked it so much that he brought his wife to see it and purchased another two gallons of aluminum paint from Daddy so the upstairs tenants could tiffany their apartment. That left only forty six cans, some of which were still around well into the Sixties.
Aside from those two cans that the landlord purchased, the rest never brought one cent, but at least Daddy had received enough to cover the original shipping costs, though belatedly...

The kids in the neighborhood were a microcosm of the United Nations. None was black, since Milwaukee was unkind and short-sighted enough to keep the majority of its black citizens confined to a small area until they later burst from the seams and took over large sections of the city sometime during the late fifties.

Many in the neighborhood, like us, were second generation Americans but some were children of immigrants, either born across the waters themselves or born shortly after their parents' arrival. Post war babies: Polish; Irish; German; Dutch; etc, though no Italians since they tended to congregate in another section of the city; kids with accents and funny clothes but not as strange as their parents. Mothers in babushkas who looked as old as grandmothers, careworn from hunger and suffering back in "the old country" and fathers who dressed in homemade shirts and trousers and wore long beards or mustaches spoke little or no English, as a rule. The children interpreted for them when English was necessary. Laura and I adjusted to hearing the letter 'j' pronounced as a 'y'. The men "ruled the roost" with iron fists and leather belts applied to tender bottoms when penetrating stares were not enough to curb unruly behavior. Nobody teased anybody about haircuts, accents or ethnic ways. When it came to religion, however, that was another matter. Each thought his was the only one recognized by God and each was proud to proclaim church affiliation.

Four houses away, on our side of the street, was the Steinberg family, who resided in the lower flat because they owned the place. The Steinbergs were Jewish. Solomon and Irving, nicknamed Sol and Itzy, were the two big brothers of our new girlfriend, Rebecca, whose nickname, Becky, was one I wished I had. Mr. Steinberg owned a wholesale grocery firm. By the neighborhood standards, they were "rich".

Beside their front door, the Steinberg's had something they called a *mezuzah*, a little box containing a small piece of parchment. Becky said it had sacred writing on it from something called SHEMA.

"I learned about parchment in Sunday School," I told her. "Could I just look at it?"

"No! Only Jewish people can. We have some on the doors of the rooms inside our house, too. They're very special."

"Well, what's a Shema?"

Her shrug said she didn't know. Itzy would know, since he had attended

Yeshiva, a special school Jewish boys attended in preparation for their Bar Mitzvah but Laura and I would never dare to ask him because he stared at us through eyes of disdain and referred to us as "*goy*".

Becky had explained that the term meant Gentile, which we knew we were from our Sunday School classes. Back then, there was no Bat Mitzvah for girls so she was not educated in Hebrew readings.

Sol, handsome, dark-haired, slender, much kinder than blond, stodgy Itzy, might have explained things to us but he was always in a hurry, either returning home with a briefcase filled with papers or on his way out with a briefcase filled with papers. A junior partner in a law firm, he carried with him, along with that briefcase, an aura of importance, though he was not a snob. Nor did he ever refer to us as *goy*. We admired him, from a distance that involved more than inches or space.

We were afraid of Becky's mother, a tall chicken breasted woman with a pointed nose, square jaw, heavy graying hair and a mink coat. She, too, looked upon us with disdain but did not prevent Becky from playing with us, though we were not allowed to knock politely on the door. Instead, we had to stand outside the side door and call out, "OH, Becky!" Since the houses were no more than four or five feet apart, if we called too loudly or too many times, someone next door might rap on a window or raise a sash and tell us to "shut up or beat it!"

If Becky were free, she would come out to play, if not, up went the kitchen window sash and her mother or someone would inform us, "She can't play right now." Finis. You did not question why nor ask if she could play at a later time. If so, chances were that she would stand on our front sidewalk and call out, "OH, Jessie, OH, Laura." It's the way it was in that neighborhood.

Mr. Steinberg was always home on Friday night. A little man in both stature and build, he would arrive before sunset, he and his sons would place black skullcaps on their heads, he would formally bow to us and tell us it was "candle lighting time" which was a signal for Laura and me to leave the premises.

Little he might be but everyone obeyed him, including us. He had an air of quiet authority about him that demanded respect. He also always had candy mints with him that he dispensed to us as we took ourselves off to our own home.

Upstairs from the Steinberg's were the Familie Roubar, from Bohemia. Their rooms were as large as the ones downstairs and they had a front stairway with a heavy bevleled- glass windowed door that opened onto the Steinberg's front porch. In deference to their landlord, however, the Roubars never used that porch for other than to traverse it from their door to the sidewalk, and then only on Sunday. The rest of the time they used the back stairway, being careful to not make too much noise and possibly disturb the Steinbergs.

Mrs. Roubar, wrinkled and bent, spoke very little English. When she smiled, revealing some missing upper teeth, her faded blue eyes would come alive. Most of the time she sat silently at her tasks, listening to the conversation of others. When Laura and I first met her we thought she was the grandmother. She loved her children and enjoyed watching the three of them: raven haired Dodie, Vi's age, who worked in an office, brown haired ten year old Evelyn, our girlfriend, and their big brother, Reinie, too slender for his height, whose bright red hair and eyes as blue as a summer sky were only outshone by his beautiful smile. A door-to-door salesman, he attended night school so he could become a teacher. Unlike Itzy, he never treated Laura and me with anything but big brother kindness. We both adored him. More than once, looking at him, I tried to picture what Baby Ralphie would have been like had he lived to be our big brother. Hopefully, like Reinie.

Mr. Roubar, the father, was bald as a balloon on top but with a heavy drooping black mustache and a chestful of hair that resembled the horsehair in Daddy's leather Morris chair where one of the tacks had let loose to reveal the inner stuffing until Daddy repaired it. He was "hot blooded" and tended to wear only a sleeveless knit undershirt, trousers and bare feet while in the house. His upper arm had knots of bulging muscles, firmer than Daddy's.

When he spoke, his English was interspersed with words and phrases in his mother tongue but his voice and deep-set dark brown eyes overhung with thick black frowning eyebrows were laden with authority. Back in Bohemia he had been a butcher. Probably that was his occupation here in America, as well.

He had a portable grindstone that he turned with a foot lever. He would sit in front of it, knees spread wide, big feet planted firmly on the linoleum of the kitchen floor, and sharpen his fearsome array of knives. When a blade could cleanly sever one of the wire-like black hairs pulled from his mustache, he would let out a sigh of satisfaction, oil the blade with a piece of knit undershirt and place it in its sheath. It was fascinating to watch him, but from a distance. He had the look of a fairy story villain about him. I was glad he was not my father.

The Roubars were strict Catholics. When any of them left their upper flat, they dipped a finger in a hand painted porcelain container of Holy Water, blessed by their priest, which was fastened to the wall beside the door leading from their kitchen to the back stairway.

To reach Evelyn we also had to call out, but from the back yard, looking up…"OH, Evy. OH, Evy!" It usually took both Laura and me awhile of calling in unison to make her hear us. Meanwhile, if they were ripe, we picked grapes from the arched wood-slat arbor protecting the two-seated wooden swing, one grape at a time, savored for a long moment and twice as tasty because they were purloined.

At the supper table one night, Laura and I bemoaned the fact that we had no holy water nor a little box called a *mezuzah* containing words from the sixth chapter of Deuteronomy, as we had recently learned. My Sunday School teacher had taken the trouble to find out what a *mezuzah* contained and I had read the words in Mama's Bible. Beautiful words, I decided. I wished Lutherans had little boxes like that.

The next day we found Daddy standing at his wooden workbench out in the stable-turned-garage-turned-Daddy's tinshop, hammer and awl in hand, punching holes in a piece of metal shaped like a fish. Lying in the workbench were the tin snips, ice pick and the galvanized sheet scrap from which he had cut the fish.

"Whatcha doing, Daddy?"

"Making a Lutheran fish for our door post. We can't let our Jewish and Catholic neighbors think that we don't respect God, now, can we?" he asked as he punched an eye into the head of the metal Pisces. "Now you'll have something special, too, right?"

"Right!" Our noses were almost nailed to the yellow clapboard of the porch wall along with that fish when he fastened it beside the front door. We wanted to make certain that it was nailed at the correct angle, straight across:not mouth or tail up, and almost made it impossible, by our concentration, for him to do the job right.

Thereafter, we were proud owners of "a Lutheran Fish" quite possibly being the only Lutheran family or any family in Milwaukee or elsewhere whose kids kissed their fingers and touched a metal fish and uttered the word "Amen" when they left the house. It began as a way to impress Evy and Becky but became a habit we never broke as long as we lived there, which was until I was in the eighth grade.

Chapter 29

That was the year of the Chicago's Century of Progress Fair which, although almost a hundred miles away and far too expensive for any of us Renzes to attend, caused me a painful experience and set me on a path that would last for the rest of my life.

It was the first day of the fall semester. Everyone, it seemed to me, had been somewhere during the summer, especially George Daus and his pal, Billy White, both of whom had been to the Chicago Fair and wore shirts bearing the picture and logo of Fort Dearborn.

Perhaps this was what prompted our teacher to ask each of us in turn to come forward to the front of the class and tell "what exciting thing we had done during the summer."

What had I done? Laura and I had played house, with and without Evy and Becky, each of whom disliked the other so we had to play with only one at a time. Mama still made me keep watch over Laura, so we were always a threesome when either one joined us.

Once we had ridden the streetcar with Vi and Maggie to visit our Aunt Arlene and Cousins Lawrence and the little one, Jimmy. Actually, Vi and Maggie were to take care of Jimmy while Aunt Arlene attended a wedding for which she had designed and made the bride's veil and bridesmaid's headpieces. Laura and I played "cars" with Lawrence and read some of his Big Little Books, which he collected.

Aside from that, the furthest we had been was a trip to the country one Sunday, after church, for a picnic and to swim at the public beach at Lake La Belle. On the way, Phyllis had two flat tires that we girls had to help Daddy pump up and "shut our ears to his German phrases that may or may not have been cuss words but sounded bad enough to help ease his frustration." I even got a chance to scrape the patch and the inner tube where it was to be attached and enjoyed the smell of the rubber cement that he applied to stick the two together. Somehow, compared to those trips by the boys to Chicago, nothing I had done seemed to add up to anything exciting.

As chance would have it, I was called immediately after Billy. I stood silent for a moment and then, from somewhere, I don't know where, came the words that did me in. "I went to Mexico this summer, with my rich uncle, John, who lives on a huge ranch in Texas."

"You did!! Oh, Jessie, how exciting!" my teacher, Miss Harrison, exclaimed. The dismissal bell rang just then, for which I was extremely grateful; now I would not have to make up any more lies to enhance the large one I had already told. But no, that was not to be!

What I thought had ended had actually only begun, for Miss Harrison took me aside after class and said, "Jessie, tomorrow is auditorium day when all the classes meet together. I want you to tell the entire school all about your wonderful vacation. We'll be meeting together right after attendance is taken and if you have any souvenirs of your trip, why, feel free to bring them along. It will make your speech all the more exciting!"

Right then and there I should have confessed that I had made up the entire story about the trip. Mama had always said that to tell the truth was the best way.

How I wished I had followed her advice! Miss Harrison was nice but she could be mean, sometimes and had even used a ruler across a few palms when a student broke a rule. It had never happened to me but I could imagine the pain of it and the shame when she would make me confess to the entire class that I had told a lie. Possibly, she would phone Mama and Lifebuoy soap would be used to wash out my mouth for something like that. While I was debating the error of my ways, she left the room and disappeared down the hall.

What was I to do? How could I get up on front of the entire school in the morning and lie my head off about a trip I had never taken with an uncle who did not exist? And what about Laura?

Heart pounding, tail dragging, I headed home to search out the Book of

Knowledge to see what it had to say about Mexico.

That night, armed with a flashlight and the M and T volumes of the encyclopedia, I huddled in the bathroom with the door locked and read every word about Mexico and Texas, taking notes on things that were of interest.

In the morning, I sneaked into the living room to remove the beautiful embroidered shawl with the gold fringe that covered our "library table." Brought back from Spain as a gift by Great Aunt Beatrice, it was Mama's pride and joy, now that her lovely peacock lampshade had been destroyed by Meetzer.

The library table held an honored place in the center of the Aubusson carpet in "the front room. It was rectangular, of dark wood, with a shelf below which we rested our stocking clad feet as we did our homework by the light of the amber Tiffany lamp in its center.The lamp was a wedding gift from Cousin Sedelia and Cousin Jasper to Mama and Daddy. Hanging from the shade was four-inch-long fringe of tiny amber beads that, over the years, had become sparser and sparser as childish fingers surreptitiously slid bead after bead from the threads to which they were attached.

Having purloined the Spanish shawl and slipped it into my school bag along with my notes, I herded Laura off to school. No matter how I tried, I could not seem to get the words out to warn her of what I was about to do. All I could do was hope she would be loyal enough to stand by me. I did promise to buy her an ice cream cone after school with money from my piggy bank.

"How come, Jessie?"

"Because I saw how much you wanted a lick from Becky's cone when she stood in front of us using that long tongue of hers to make us jealous. I'll buy us each one. We're sisters and sisters have to stick together, right? We can stand in front of *her* and lick *our* ice cream cones." Laura was enthused with the prospect. Poor trusting child, little did she know that her big sister was spinning a web of deceit around her. Armed now with a bit of confidence, I entered the school and raised my hand when attendance was taken.

Anxious but determined, I followed the others into the school auditorium, actually the size of two classrooms but to me tremendously large, and with shaky legs, stood for the pledge of allegiance to the flag. The principal welcomed all of the students to the new school year, each of the teachers was introduced and then Miss Harrison introduced me.

"One of our students had a wonderful adventure this summer. She traveled to Texas, with an uncle and aunt who took her sight-seeing in Mexico. "Are there any students who do not know where Mexico is located? Well, it is directly south of our Texas border and is not part of the United States but is its own country. But Jessie will tell you about that."

"Jessie" stood up, mounted the steps to the stage and prayed that she would not be struck down dead for lying her head off. On occasion during the lecture on Texas and Mexico, taken straight from the Book of Knowledge but interpreted in my own way, I met the wide with-amazement large green eyes of Laura, who was probably wondering how I could have achieved this wonderful adventure and still manage to sleep in our bed with her each night.

My talk took up most of the period as I waxed enthused, enjoying more and more of each moment, telling how my Uncle and Aunt, in Loredo, Texas, owned a huge cattle ranch and taught me how to ride a horse. In their large motorcar, we went to Mexico, visited Mexico City and some Mayan pyramids. We rode donkeys up and down steep winding trails and in the little markets purchased items of gold and beautiful handmade things such as "this Spanish shawl," and I ended my travelogue by reaching down, withdrawing the shawl from my school bag and, with dramatic arm movement, flung it about my shoulders to wrap it around my skinny body.

Had the audience been any but *ignorant* children, I would undoubtedly have received a standing ovation but the bell rang and everyone hustled off to their various rooms.

The kids who knew us questioned Laura. Did Jessie really go to Texas and Mexico? Evy and Becky thought they recognized that shawl. Laura, poor child, told them that the trip had actually been taken earlier in the summer, before we moved to Twelfth Street, which was quick thinking on her part, so none of the kids in our neighborhood could know that the farthest we had been from Tenth Street was the corner grocery store. Her reason for not going with me was that our aunt and uncle wanted to take only one child at a time and that she would go next summer.

Laura had her revenge, however. After licking her cone free of ice cream and chewing the cone bit by bit to the very tip, she turned to me and said, "I really don't like drying dishes. It would be nice if you dried them on my nights, too."

How could I protest to that or any other task she imposed on me when all she had to do was say, quietly, "Mexico?" Someday, I decided, I would travel to Mexico for real and make an honest person of myself. I still intend to do that.

A few days later, Miss Harrison asked me to remain for a few moments after school. When everyone else had left the room, she seated me at a chair beside her desk and looked at me for a long time. Her eyes were serious but the faintest smile played at the corners of her lips.

"Jessie, you have a gift for words. Your speech about your trip was wonderful and you also recognize the drama of enhancing your words with movement. Have you ever thought of becoming an actress?"

"Oh, no! I'm not in the least pretty."

"There's no need for prettiness on the stage. Being able to make the audience believe that you are the one you are portraying is the real magic. Some of the most wonderful actresses in the world are not in the least pretty. They have stage presence, which outlasts beauty every time. I believe that you have stage presence."

Unknown to me, another teacher had entered the room and now stood quietly beside me. "Jessie, I'm Mrs. Beyer. I was listening to your presentation yesterday and some of the children seemed to think that that you made up your trip to Mexico."

I felt my heart drop into my shoes and tears began to slide down my cheeks.

"Oh, Jessie, there's no need to cry," Miss Harrison said, dabbing at my face with a pretty lace hanky. "What we're both saying is, we recognize that you have been given the gift of creativity. Not everyone has that. The words you chose were excellent. You have a wonderful imagination. Mrs. Beyer has a request for you, if you don't mind."

"A large one," the other teacher said. "We need someone to write a Christmas play for us. If I give you a book on how plays are written, do you think you could write one? It need not be long and I'll work with you on it."

My tears flowed again, but this time with happiness. My feet danced all the way home. My imagination was not something to be ashamed of but instead was a gift! I could be an actress! I could write plays! A door was opening for me that I had never even dreamed was there! And the first person with whom I wanted to share this news was Mama.

Chapter 30

It was not to Mama that I blurted out the news but to Vi, who arrived home an hour earlier than Mama each day and scolded Maggie into helping to prepare the evening meal. Lately, Maggie had seemed to be sleepwalking. We would talk to her and ask her questions and she seemed to have a hearing problem. Mama attributed it to her being tired from too much homework but her eyes never seemed sleepy. Poor Mama was so tired, herself, that she probably felt that everyone else was the same.

Each night Laura and I traded off setting the supper table. This was Laura's night but I quickly volunteered when she whispered, "Mexico." I really didn't mind because it gave me the chance to tell Vi about being asked to write a Christmas play.

Her hug was quick in coming and she looked into my eyes through her own blue ones from behind her new rim-less panes and said, very seriously, "I've always known you had the gift of words Jessie. Now you must make a promise to me and to God that you'll never use them to hurt anyone. Being able to put words on paper brings a big responsibility. Look what Mr. Roosevelt's gift of words did for him; it won him the presidency!"

I had never thought of that when I listened to his speeches over the radio.

"And William Shakespeare! He wrote so beautifully that people have been presenting his plays for hundreds of years."

Maybe so, but I had never heard of him. The idea of having words you wrote being repeated for hundreds of years was amazing.

"Or Hans Christian Anderson. Some of those fairy stories you read are about a hundred years old. No, not the books, silly, but the words in them. The pictures in them certainly don't show people dressed as we do, if you recall.

"For Pete's sake, Maggie, look what you're doing to that bread! The slices are thick on one side and too thin on the other. The jelly'll run right through! What's the matter with you, lately?"

"Nothing's the matter with me. I-I was just thinking of something. Jessie, how come you're setting he table tonight? I thought it was Laura's turn."

"Oh, I decided I love setting the table, so I told her I'd do it for awhile." The looks I received from both Maggie and Vi held wonderment. Laura and I always groaned when our lazy bodies were put to work at something useful.

To change the subject, I said, "I was thinking something. I'm not going to tell Mama about the play. When it's all written, I'll let her read it. Okay?"

"Well. She does like surprises and this is a very nice one. I'm sure she'll be proud but are you sure you'll be able to write an entire play?" Vi knew that I hardly ever finished a project, like the "horseline" carpet that never took shape.

Back on Tenth Street the neighbor kids, both boys and girls, Laura and I, included, sat on porches together and looped wool strands around four brads set into the tops of empty wooden thread spools. Using straightened out bobby pins or, in our case, Tante Kate's celluloid hair pins, we wove long 'tails' which were pulled through the hole of the spool. Old sweaters were raveled to retrieve the wool or, if parents had extra money, some kids had new wool skeins. The tails were supposedly destined to eventually be coiled and stitched into oval rag-type floor rugs. Ours had no such destiny. Untouched since our move to Twelfth Street, the horselines were too long for dollhouse rugs and too short for anything else. Like other unfinished projects, they had been "put aside for some other day."

"Oh, I'll finish it," I declared and knew that I would. Mama would be so proud of me. That is, if Laura didn't get mad at me and tell her about my 'trip to Mexico.'

That big lie of mine really had me in checkmate. We had a pair of roller skates between us and could either each wear one skate or be generous and let one or the other of us use both. These were screwed onto the soles of our shoes with a key, which Mama kept and doled out. Now, Laura had full use of both until she tired of skating and then would "allow" me, her lowly slave, to take a turn. How I wished I had never let those Century of Progress sweatshirts turn me into a liar.

I suppose I should have hated Laura but, she being the little sister and always under my command, I understood how much she was enjoying her new role. I only hoped that eventually we could go back to being just plain sisters and the best of friends.

This did eventually happen. One night when I was about to take her turn at drying dishes, she took the towel from me and with a kiss on my cheek, released me from bondage. I'm not sure, looking back, if it was through sisterly love or because Christmas was lurking on the horizon but by the time that holiday arrived, Laura's halo was shining so bright that Santa *had* to be good to her.

I could have confessed to Mama that I had lied. Each Sunday in Sunday School I asked God to help me to tell her but He had His own way of doing things and I would return home still guilty. Tante Kate would have termed this "stewing in your own juices." Her descriptions were very apt.

For several weeks, having studied the book of scripts that Mrs. Beyer had lent me, I tried to think of a plot for my play. Eventually, I found one, "right at my own back door," as Tante Kate would have put it. My own situation, shown under different circumstances by characters I made up. The story of a little boy who never told the truth and how a wonderful Christmas angel showed him how to tell the truth and live a better life.

Mrs. Beyer was very pleased with the play, which had three acts. So much so that she asked Miss Harrison if she could borrow me for an hour each afternoon so I could help her to select a cast of characters and even direct it!

At a bit less than ten years of age, I was being accorded an amazing amount of encouragement and was learning so much from those two women, wonderful teachers who knew how to recognize talent and channel it in the right direction.

The weeks sped by quickly. Before I knew it, Halloween and my tenth birthday had come and gone, along with Thanksgiving, and Vi's birthday. She was now eighteen and able to work full time at the shoe factory. We all wished that she had not left high school though, as Daddy said, there was no money for any of us to go on to college and besides, speaking from the era in which he had been raised, educating girls was not as important as educating boys, who had to support families.

Mama and Vi were supporting ours along with whatever extra money Daddy was able to bring in but, because they were females, their rate of pay was far lower than for men doing the same work. I guess nobody reasoned out that the more money people spend the more money other people earn. Nobody, perhaps, but Mr. Roosevelt. He was doing his best to get things started so the economy could perk up.

Each night I read the Journal from front to back. At the dinner table, I was able to discuss things that Laura and Maggie found boring. Often Vi and I would find a corner somewhere and finish the table time discussion. She, too, was an avid reader. She bemoaned the fact that her fellow workers seldom read the paper except for the sports pages and the comics. I was finding problems with the kids at school because I not only had written a play but my teachers spoke to me almost as if I were an adult. With them I could discuss what Mr. Roosevelt was doing. I still enjoyed playground games, like every other kid, but sometimes they would shut me out with, "Here comes the BRAIN! Here comes teacher's PET!"

To make matters worse, in spite of my being a picky -eater, I had begun to grow. Now I was not only the skinniest girl in my class but the tallest, as well. Darn old Karl Klemm nicknamed me "skin-a-ma-rink the boneyard dancer." I hated Karl. I hated all boys. I really could not see how Maggie and Vi could be so *gaga* over them.

The play rehearsals could have gone much smoother if the darned boys would only cooperate but they had to always play tricks on the girls and mumble their lines. What good were words if nobody understood them? Most afternoons it was a relief to go back to my classroom and when the bell rang, collect Laura and race home with her, remembering to slow down a bit because now she was so much shorter than I.

When the week of the play finally arrived, I was devastated to learn that Mama could not get off work to see it. I tried to talk Mrs. Beyer into having the performance in the evening but she said that was not possible.

Daddy promised to come to the performance and said that he would bring Tante Kate. Mama was disappointed and sad that she could not be there. It seemed, lately, that Mama was never there when I needed her the most. It was not her fault but just the same, I really missed her.

We had become latchkey kids, Laura and I, and at noontime often came home to wonder what to eat and sometimes ended up frying bread or pouring out a box of gelatin into two glasses and drinking the concoction. Sometimes Tante Kate would be there to serve us delicious soup. She worried about us and would take the streetcar to our house and stay through the supper hour and have Daddy return her to her boarding house room afterwards.

For her, getting on and off a streetcar was some sort of victory, accomplished only with the aid of the motorman and some of the other passengers. The steps were high, her legs were short and her abdomen, as round as that of Santa Claus, jiggled like a bowlful of jelly when she laughed.

One day, while being helped down the streetcar steps, the elastic of her huge bloomers gave way. Down around her ankles they fell. Probably mortified but still capable of taking things in stride, she bent down, there in the street, lifted each foot from a leg, scooped up the offending undergarment and tucked it into her basket. With head held high, she crossed the curb and continued on her way to wherever.

The day of the play, even Daddy had to offer apologies. He had been called to repair a furnace and simply could not turn down the extra money it would bring in. Aunt Kate could take the streetcar to our house because it stopped on the corner of Twelfth and Burleigh but our school was five blocks from the nearest streetcar stop and her poor legs would not carry her two hundred fifty pounds that far, especially in the snow.

My feet dragged to school. Laura kept consoling me but to no avail. This was to be my special day and now nobody except strangers would be there to see the play. Mama had packed lunches for us so we would not have to come home at noon. Nothing tasted good. Even my favorite peanut butter and banana sandwich had no flavor. I was too steeped in disappointment and self- pity to enjoy anything.

At 2 p.m. all the kids except kindergartners trooped into the auditorium. Backstage, we were busy making certain everyone was in their correct places and hushed up each other in loud whispers that were silenced by Mrs. Beyer's raised forefinger.

Miss Harrison hugged me and led me through the curtain to face the audience. I saw a sea of faces of children and parents and then, suddenly, my heartache was gone, for there, smiling encouragement, were Aunt Alice and Tante Kate, sitting together as if they were friends instead of antagonists, and with them Clyde in his taxi-driver's uniform but without his usual cap. He was almost bald on top!

Grinning, now, from ear to ear, I made a deep curtsy when Miss Harrison introduced me as the person who had both written and helped to direct the play.

As plays go, it would probably never have made it to Broadway, but to the parents of those acting in it, the portrayals were magnificent. Mrs. Beyer had to cue a few of the actors and actresses to remind them when to utter their lines but all told, everyone did well, even the boys. Proudly, I introduced my beloved aunts and Clyde to both teachers. Then Laura and I had our first ride in a taxicab. When the family began to arrive home, Aunt Alice had each change into a "best dress" so we could go to the Schwabenhof, a nice German restaurant, for supper.

Daddy had to take time out to bathe. He was black with furnace soot when he came through the side door. Standing on newspapers, he removed his coveralls and shoes and took them down to the basement. Not once, in the years when we were growing up, did he ever come to the table with dirty fingernails or without being shaved. He would have bathed with a washcloth and water in a saucepan if that were all that was available. First came the gritty bar of Lava soap, then the bar of Lifebuoy and finally the aftershave lotion. He always smelled nice and fresh.

At the restaurant, the grownups each had a now legal glass of beer with their meal but we four girls had hot chocolate.

The repeal of Prohibition had officially been ratified by the Twenty First Amendment that December 3rd, according to the Journal. Nobody in our family did any special celebrating, though the restaurant on the corner of Twelfth and Burleigh reopened its doors as a tavern, with a free beer for everybody the first night. It had been serving fish fries and family meals during the interim, with soda pop and coffee as libations. Now it was a place of singing and drinking for a night or two and then settled down to being the "neighborhood tavern" once more, as it had been since first opening its doors back around the "turn of the century."

Milwaukeeans enjoyed their Friday Night Family-style fish fries, which were the main attraction in taverns, and now they could wash them down with nickel steins of beer, the fish being served with American fries or potato pancakes. It was not our custom to eat out, especially in taverns, but this caused no suffering on our parts, since Mama could fry a fish so it practically melted in your mouth and her potato pancakes and her golden American fries were really something special. She was such a good cook!

Now that the breweries had again reopened, on nights when we were having hodge-podge, the Great Depression dish consisting of macaroni, tomatoes of some form or another, onion, ground beef, and kidney beans, Daddy, carrying a cut glass pitcher, would mount the steps of the corner tavern, purchase a pitcher of Pabst, Schlitz, or Blatz and sip one glass by himself as he waited for the bartender to 'fill it up,' the cost for both being a quarter.

Sometimes Laura and I would accompany him but only as far as the cement stoop. No minors were allowed in the barroom. Families ate in the dining room, entered by a side door. Those times we would sit on the tavern steps and, by leaning back, we could peer under the swinging half-doors to catch sight of whatever evils were taking place there. All we ever saw, however, were men's trousers and shoes hooked around tall stools rungs or resting on a brass rail.

We spotted a brass cuspidor and once saw a man lean down and spit into it, which caused us to screw up our faces and with hands grasping our throats, gasp out, "Yeuch!" and discuss how terrible it would be for whomever had to clean the filthy thing at night's end. Daddy said it was probably the bartender's job. We decided we would never marry a bartender.

But the Schwabenhof was not the corner tavern and had never been one. Aunt Alice would never have set foot in one of those. "Tonight," she announced, "we are celebrating two important occasions: Jessie made her debut as a playwright and director and my dear Godchild, Violet, has turned eighteen. May God bless you both. I hope He allows me to stay on this earth long enough to see each of you as grownups and long enough for me to make Vi's wedding gown."

I stared at her and suddenly realized that she was quite old. Almost as old as Grandmother. People died when they were old, although I had never known anyone who did. Jumping from my chair, I hurried to hers and slipped my arms about her neck. "I hope you live a long, long time, Aunt Alice. I don't expect you'll ever have to make a wedding gown for me because I'm never going to get married but just the same, I wish you a long, long life."

"Thank you, child. I wouldn't speak so lightly of marriage. If I had my druthers, I expect I would reconsider some of my proposals. But that's water over the dam." Her words were softly spoken and she patted my hand, dismissing me. People referred to her as a spinster. For the first time I wondered whether spinsters were happy being tall and thin and unmarried and, yes, old. I was tall and thin. Would I, too, be called a spinster someday? But I hated boys and even the thought of marrying one someday made me screw up my face. Oh, well.

Still and all, it was a merry group that piled into Phyllis and waved goodbye to Aunt Alice and Tante Kate when Clyde picked them up. We sang all the way home.

As she was tucking Laura and me into bed, Mama's eyes filled with tears. "I wish with all my heart I could have been at school today, Jessie. You'll have to write another play so I can see that one."

"I know, Mama. Having Aunt Alice and Tante Kate and Clyde there was almost as nice. I'll hurry and write one just for you."
She bent down and looked deep into my eyes. "Jessie, why Mexico?"
For a long moment I was silent. Then, "I don't know. Maybe because it was far away and sounded intriguing. Who told you, Mama?" I was staring at Laura who was busily shaking her head "No."

"Mrs. Beyer dropped by on Saturday when you and Laura were at your friends' house."

"Are you mad at me, Mama?"

"No, not really. Disappointed that you felt you had to lie, but I suppose, as Mrs. Beyer said, your gift of creativity had grown enough to let you know it was there. My music took hold of me like that. The first time I sat at the piano I felt at home there. I understood, then, why music always filled me with wonderment."

Her sigh was wistful. She missed her piano. We all did. In my prayers that night I asked God to help her to get another one. I also told Him I was sorry I had lied and thanked Him for Mama not being mad at me and for the wonderful day He had given us to put away in our memories. I fell asleep before I could think up another plot for a new play.

Chapter 31

1934

In spite of Mama's admonition that she do so, Vi had not returned to high school but had decided to remain at the shoe factory because she knew how much her income was needed at home. Now, at eighteen, she was working full time.

Even though they shared a room, she and Maggie continued to grow farther apart in interests. They no longer shared secrets, opting, instead, to do so with their girlfriends. Still without a beau, Vi spent much of her free time in church activities, singing in the choir, teaching Sunday school and taking part in plays and other activities put on by the Luther League, a group of young persons in our church.

Vi did share her day experiences with us, whenever there was something to share. She had made friends with the girls at the trade school and had one or two at the factory but so far no beaus. Most of the men at the factory had what she termed "nasty mouths." They smoked, chewed tobacco and cussed and were not hesitant about touching a girl in more than friendly ways. Her ideal, I knew, was Mr. Nunn, who had treated her with respect. He was already happily married but there had to be other men like him about somewhere, she hoped.

I wished she had not quit school. She would have been a wonderful teacher. Like me, she was interested in the world about her and in what was happening outside of Milwaukee.

Sometimes we read the newspaper together and discussed what we had read with Mama, who, lately, was almost too tired to read more than the headlines. Mama was going through menopause, which gave her headaches, hot flashes, and "nervous irritability." Stuck in a sitting, job at work, she had put on weight that she tried to eliminate through something called "Kruschen Salts." From there she went to other diet remedies and finally, after reading a book by a person named

Lindner, decided he was right; you were what you ate, and nibbled on lettuce and cabbage leaves, skimmed the cream off the top of the milk bottles and drank only the watery liquid that was left. Cottage cheese found its way from the Luick Dairy to our table, via the milkman and his horse, Bob, who pulled the milk wagon. We ate the curds with jelly, chives and various fruits in season.

Maggie, who was receiving the benefits of a high school education, did not actually appreciate school. She was taking stenographic courses so she could get a job once she graduated but her mind was not on things educational. Her reading material ran to movie magazines that her girlfriend, Lillian, gave to her when she was finished with them. Many had pictures of Lillian's favorite actors and actresses already cut out so sometimes the magazines resembled home made "snowflakes."

It was not that Maggie was lazy, for she kept her half of hers and Vi's room immaculate and helped Mama with the washing, hanging it out in the backyard because she was taller than any of us and could reach the lines better. No, it was more as if she were "living on a cloud somewhere," as Tante Kate declared one day, the third time she asked Maggie to do something.

"I do declare, that child is in love, or something."

"Maybe so," Mama declared, "but she isn't dating anyone so it's probably just a crush on some boy or maybe even one of her teachers. She'll undoubtedly grow out of it. My goodness, it is strange that a pretty girl like her has not yet dated, and she's almost seventeen."

Mama was right; Maggie was probably the prettiest girl at North Division High but Laura and I could have told them that their assumptions were all wrong. However, Maggie had sworn us to secrecy on the promise that she would do us bodily harm if we tattled on her. We knew she would keep that promise, too, because on Sunday mornings she was the one who curled our hair with the curling iron heated in the flames of the gas stove. When she was irritated or angry, chances are we would end up with blisters on our ear tops.

One Spring afternoon, dismissed from school early, we had decided to visit the playground on Eleventh and Chambers, a few blocks away. There, on the swings, sitting and talking and holding hands were Maggie and a handsome dark haired boy. Tall, with dark brown eyes, he was staring into her blue ones with the look of a movie star about to kiss the leading lady.

"Hello, Maggie," Laura and I called together.

Blushing clear up to her eyebrows, she quickly withdrew her hand and began to swing until her toes touched a small tree branch. The boy waved goodbye and hurried off. Age-wise, he was at least a high school senior.

"Maggie has a boyfriend, Maggie has a boyfriend," we teased in sing song voices until she stopped swinging and angrily ran up to us with hands raised and a determined look on her face that meant trouble if she caught hold of us. "You darned brats! If you tell Mama or anybody you'll be sorry! I mean it."

"We won't," we hurriedly promised as she grabbed each of our dress backs.

"I want you to swear to God you won't tell. Cross your hearts right now!"

"Mama says we aren't supposed to swear to God and you know it!" I parried.

"Then just cross your heart. I mean it. Liam is a really nice boy and I wish I could bring him home but I can't."

"Why not?"

"Because he's Catholic, that's why."

"Evy's Catholic and we bring her home."

"That's different."

"Why is it different?"

"When I was sixteen Mama said I should never date anyone I couldn't marry and in our family people don't marry Catholics. His family is the same; they don't marry Lutherans. *Protestants*, they call us. Like it's some sort of dirty name. We can't help what religion we are; it came with being born into the family."

"Well, Catholics are Christians. Evy said so. And it isn't true that they worship the Pope Pius the Eleventh, like Cousin Sedelia said; he's the head bishop of the Catholic Church. I just don't understand why all Christians don't love each other, like Jesus said."

Not too demonstrative a person, Maggie drew me to her and hugged me. "Thanks Jessie. It's what I believe too. It's just that Mama's family is so darned set on things. Look how nice Uncle Edmond is and he was a Baptist. Only-well, remember, he had to join Aunt Mimsy's church so they could get married."

"What's a bishop, Maggie?" asked Laura.

Maggie shrugged. "Somebody high up in the church, I guess."

"We could find out in that big Catholic book we got when Mr. Brewster got chopped into pieces by that train," I supplied.

"Jessie, don't you ever let Mama hear you say that! Mr. Brewster was a nice man. We should remember him like that and not like- well, like you said!" admonished Laura.

"Well, I'm sorry. It's just that- how many people do we know who got chopped up…"

"Let's change the subject right now," Maggie advised.

I put my hand into hers and told her I hoped that somehow Mama and Daddy could meet "what did you say his name is?"

"Liam. It's Irish."

"Are you going to marry him?" Laura grinned and batted her lashes.

"I'm only sixteen, silly. There's years yet before I can think of things like that!" Her sigh was heavy with pathos.

"Do you love him, Maggie?" Laura persisted.

Our sister's eyes were dripping tears. "Yes, I do. And he loves me. I met him the first day of school and we've been friends ever since. I just wish Mama and Daddy could at least meet him."

Now we were consoling her. We three walked home together. I wished there were some way Mama could meet him, too. Sneaking around was certainly not the best way. It was like lying and I knew the result of doing that. It just seemed so strange to have a sister who loved someone outside the family. A boy, at that!

A few weeks later, Mama opened the door to find Liam on our front porch. "Excuse me, but is this where Maggie Renz lives?"

"Yes it is."

"Uh, I'm Liam McCall. She dropped one of her school books on the way home." He presented it to Mama. "Are you her mother? Is Maggie home?"

"Yes she is. It's good of you to return this. Won't you come in?"

"I-uh, I have to get to work…at Walgreen's. I, uh, work there."

"I see. Well, thank you for bringing this by. McCall, did you say? You're Scottish then?"

He shook his head. "Irish. My dad was. My mother was German. They both died in the flu epidemic when I was little. My aunt and uncle took their places."

"I see. That had to be hard. You're sure you can't come in?" Maggie had heard voices; recognized Liam's and came up behind Mama. Mama might have been tired but she was, first of all, our mother and observed how Maggie and Liam looked at each other.

"Your friend brought your shorthand book, Maggie. I've asked him in. He's on his way to work but maybe you would like to introduce him to the rest of the family?"

Both Maggie and Liam were blushing as she introduced him all around, to Daddy, Tante Kate, Vi, and Laura and me as if we had never seen him before. He winked at us, which made us giggle.

From then on, Liam came to the house on Sunday afternoons, his day off. Tante Kate liked him and it was she who let it slip that Mama and Daddy had decided, during their German conversation, that it was best to welcome him rather than have Maggie meeting him on the sly. This way, if she saw enough of him with their approval, she might eventually tire of him. Meanwhile, the two of them were under family supervision and neither had any reason to do things out of rebellion. Personally, they, too, liked him; it was just that he was Catholic…

Well, so was Uncle Otto, and he and Aunt Elise got along fine, didn't they?

Cousin Sedelia saw things in another light. Aunt Rose and Uncle Max had dropped by unannounced one Sunday afternoon on their way back from an outing and had stopped at a roadside stand to purchase honey, still in the comb.

"We thought you might like some to put on your nice home baked bread," Aunt Rose said.

Uncle Max smacked his lips over the fresh slices Mama cut and put out for them along with a fresh pot of coffee. "How come you never learned to bake bread like Lydia's," he asked his wife.

"I was more interested in sewing."

"Mama sews," I announced and was sent from the room for daring to intrude on grownups' conversation.

"That girl! I declare!" said Aunt Rose.

Anyway, they were introduced to Liam. The very next day, Cousin Sedelia phoned to let Mama know that she was playing with fire, letting that "Catholic fellow" put his foot inside the front door. "You'll end up with a Catholic son-in-law, mark my word!" she predicted. "Maggie McCall! Can't you see it now, Lydia? Shanty Irish with a whole slew of Catholic babies on her hip while she hangs washing out on the line."

Tante Kate and we girls tried to picture Maggie with six or seven babies clinging to her while she hung up sheets and pillow cases and ended up laughing so hard that Tante Kate's coffee went down the wrong throat and we had to pound her on the back to stop her coughing so she could breathe again.

Cousin Sedalia's call was soon followed by ones from Mama's sisters and another from Grandmother.

Mama and Daddy stood their ground, especially Daddy. He liked Liam, too. However, they let Maggie know how much the family was putting pressure on Mama over the entire thing.

"If you realize what's happening to us, think of poor Liam. I'm sure his family is doing the same."

They were, but Liam and Maggie continued to date. She turned seventeen in July and she and Lee, as we now called him, were still going on hikes with their friends, having picnics in one of Milwaukee's many parks, sometimes going to the movies, in which case, Vi and one of her dates accompanied them as unofficial chaperons. Like mine, Vi's task, as older sister, had always been to watch out for Maggie.

Sometimes, when Daddy had enough gas for Phyllis, we would go to one of the city beaches to swim. Vi, Laura and Lee would return home with nice tans but Maggie and I would suffer for the rest of the week with painful sunburns treated with Unguentine ointment. Maggie, blonde and blue-eyed, would become white again but I would acquire another batch of freckles. It was because I had inherited some of Daddy's mother's skin, he would tell me. Our paternal grandmother had beautiful chestnut hair, like Aunt Elise's and even when she died; it was still not even gray, though she was in her sixties. I kept studying my hair, seeking some sign of red in it but it remained rather dishwater color, as if it could not make up its mind what hue it favored.

One day, sighing over my looks, I told Mama that I would probably have to be an old maid and be a missionary somewhere in Africa.

"Oh, dear, Jessie, what in the world did those poor Africans do to deserve that?" she teased.

Unknown to Maggie, I also had a crush on Liam, even if he was a boy. Only he always treated me as if I were just a little kid, which of course, to him, at almost nineteen, I was. I hoped that someday a fairy would touch me with her wand and let me become beautiful so a handsome boy like Liam might see me and forget that I came from a lily pad, as ugly as a toad. Did boys come from lily pads, too? I would have to ask someone about that. Maybe Tante Kate. She never talked down to kids or made fun of their questions even when she did not know the answers.

Chapter 32
1935

Times under Mr. Roosevelt's term in office were not much better than under Mr. Hoover's. At least not in 1935 for us. We struggled to live on the combined wages of Mama and Vi and whatever Daddy could earn at his sporadic jobs. Because of his back he could not secure work in his own field. There were too many men younger than he was and without back troubles who could lift furnaces and carry heavy loads up and down ladders and nobody hired bosses when they could do their own bossing. He tried to be a door-to-door salesman and ended up with tired feet and few orders. People were interested but they simply had no money for more than essentials.

In the Journal, I kept reading the name Harry Hopkins. He was Mr. Roosevelt's right hand man. He got bills passed and got the Government to start something called the CCC. My teacher said it stood for Civilian Conservation Corps. Boys from the slums in big cities were sent to camps and taught to plant trees and do other tasks to keep them off the streets and out of mischief. They received room and board and a small amount of money to spend. The rest of the money they earned was sent home to their families.

At first the camps were only "down South, somewhere," but gradually boys from the Milwaukee area became CCCs. By then we were hearing about other initials, TVA, the Tennessee Valley Authority and WPA, the Works Progress Administration.

Cartoons were appearing in the paper with Mr. Roosevelt making speeches consisting of nothing but strings of letters. Songs were coming into our homes via radio about some of his projects. The one about "brother can you spare a dime" disappeared along with Mr. Hoover's name though housewives still wore

Hoover aprons, wrap-around housedresses made up of flour and feed sacks or other cheap cotton material.

We were told that we were no longer on the 'gold standard." Anybody with gold certificates were supposed to turn them in to the banks and receive silver certificates in their place. For awhile people would examine their paper money to see if the word gold was on them anywhere.

One day Daddy received a notice from the bank that had kept his money that he might receive some of it back. We crossed our fingers and hoped.

Lee had graduated from high school but Maggie still had a year to go. His aunt and uncle did not accept Maggie's invitation to the cake and hot chocolate party we gave him. They wanted nothing to do with *Protestants*. It seemed strange to be looked down on for loving and worshiping the same God they did. I wondered if God and Jesus felt sad or maybe angry at the way people down here on earth treated each other. Mama had always told us to make our Creator glad that He had created us. Maybe, if people did not come from lily pads they could do better. I did wonder when reading in our geography books how there could be lily pads in places like the Sahara Desert.

One Sunday we had unexpected company in the form of Gilly and Tess. They had gotten married! Not only that, but they were going to have a baby! It was from Tess that I learned that babies did not come from the lily pad at all but from the mother's abdomen! She showed us how much she had "grown" there, and the sight of her great belly with its turned-inside-out-belly-button was quite interesting.

Later, I thought back to how Aunt Arlene had looked before little Jimmy was born and Mrs. Malenka after she married her husband. Mama had told us that Mrs. Malenka-turned Turner had twins, a boy and a girl!

Well, I was almost eleven years old and finally some of my questions were being answered. Laura and I lay in our bed and wondered about Mama having each of us inside of her. How did we get there? So many questions, so many answers yet to be learned. We wanted to ask Mama but were shy about that. Maybe some day she would tell us, "when the right time came."

A few Sunday afternoons later, Evelyn and I were lying on our stomachs across her bed, our stockinged toes touching the backs of our heads as we studied a movie magazine she had filched from the pile in her sister's room. Suddenly Evy's sister, Dodie, was grabbing it away and telling us we had no right to borrow her things without permission. "You're too young to be having your silly noses in movie magazines."

"Why?" I asked.

"You're really a mouthy little brat, aren't you?" she declared.

"Why do you have to know everything before it's time?"

"Is there a book somewhere that tells people when kids are old enough for this and old enough for that?" I demanded. "I hate not knowing the answers to things."

"Like what?"

"Like how do babies get inside the mother's stomach and what has all that to do with lily pads?"

Relenting, she laughed and sat on the bed with us. "Sometimes, most times, it's best to find out things gradually. I don't know anything about lily pads. It seems to me we were told we came from cabbage patches. Actually, it all has to do with boys being different, you know, down there, from girls."

"They are? In what way?"

"That's right, you don't have a brother. Of course, I've never personally seen Renie, either, but I have seen little boy babies. Jessie, you're only eleven…In a year or two you'll be ready for more information but right now stay a child as long as you can. Growing up comes far too soon. Once you know the answers to some things, you're no longer innocent and innocence has it's own beauty."

I liked Dodie. She reminded me of Vi; you could talk to her. I wasn't quite sure she was right about boys being different, however, so when Lawrence came to visit I asked him and he was surprised to learn that this might be so. He and I went into the bathroom and he was kind enough to open his pants and let me see.

Dodie was right; boys were built different. Very. I was just about to let him see how I was built when his mother rapped on the door and we hurriedly ran water over our hands and smiled angelically as she frowned and asked what we had been doing.

"Just washing our hands." Somehow the opportunity for Lawrence to expand his knowledge of my anatomy never arose.

One Saturday afternoon, I overheard Maggie and Mama discussing some girl who had to leave school because she had gotten "too close to one of those CCC boys." Instinctively I knew that it had something to do with how boys and girls were built differently from each other. The girl had been sneaking out to meet the boy.

"You and Lee keep your heads about you," I heard Mama warn. "In the end, everything depends upon a girl respecting herself enough to hold a man at arm's length until after marriage. You keep on the right path, Maggie, and you'll find yourself in white walking down a church aisle. That poor girl from your school has lost her innocence and she'll pay the price for the rest of her life. You just wonder what kind of parents she has that they didn't instruct her in the ways of right and wrong. Always remember that you're a Renz and that what you do affects the entire family. For every action there's a reaction. That's the truth of the matter."

Placing a kiss on Maggie's hair, she went into the kitchen to prepare the evening meal. I stopped her long enough to slip my arms about her waist and lay my head against her. My hair, too, felt the pressure of her lips. Mama, the protector of our innocence.

Chapter 33

At school the teachers announced that we could take music lessons. I knew that we could never get the money to rent an instrument but there was one class in piano that seemed appealing to Laura. That one was free once you purchased the music kit, which cost three dollars and included a cardboard keyboard and printed sheets of beginner's music.

She did not have three dollars but we sisters pooled our money. We collected tinfoil from the inside of cigarette packages that we sold to the rag man when he called out his arrival from atop his horse drawn wagon as he rode down the alley. We took our soda pop bottle collection to the drugstore for the penny return on each. At last we had a grand total of three dollars and four cents. Laura's ability to play piano was to be a surprise for Mama.

One of the requirements for taking the class was the availability of a piano on which to practice. We had none but Becky did and offered the use of it, so there was no problem. For awhile.

Very mercurial, Becky's mother allowed Laura to practice for a few days and then told her she could no longer use the instrument as it gave her headaches to listen to "all that climpering." Apologetically, Becky explained that she no longer took lessons for the same reason.

Aunt Elise and Uncle Franz had a piano, grossly out of tune, and once a week Laura and I would walk the mile and a half to their house to practice. They promised not to tell Mama and even accepted Laura's invitation to attend the "recital" when it eventually occurred.

The cardboard keyboard was bulky, even when folded in half, the entire thing as long as a piano keyboard, the printed black and white keys standard size. It took ingenuity to keep Mama from catching sight of it but we managed.

When I started catechism classes at church on Saturday mornings, Laura began to accompany me. There she would practice her piano lessons on the upright piano in the basement Sunday school room.

She began to feel more and more at ease with the notes, playing each one industriously, often with tongue between teeth for emphasis. What she could not seem to master was the tempo, even when our minister placed a metronome on top of the piano to help her keep time.

A slip of paper announcing the date of the recital had everybody clued in to November 18th, 7 p.m. in the school auditorium. There was to be no charge for admission.

It would be up to Daddy to somehow get Mama to school without a clue as to why she was to be there. The big day arrived and in the audience were Aunt Elise, Uncle Franz, our cousins, Bernice and Rudy, Tante Kate, we three sisters, girlfriends Evy and Becky and both of our parents as well as all the guests of each of the other students.

Mama had been told that Laura was taking part in a performance. She thought she was about to see a play. When students began to sit at the piano and play their pitiful renditions of Twinkle, Twinkle, Little Star and some song about a cobbler tapping into a shoe sole, her eyebrows rose into twin caret marks and her large eyes held both amusement and pity as well as apprehension. Laura had never displayed musical talent. What was her child up to?

Eventually it was Laura's turn. Clad in her best taffeta dress, handed down from Cousin Nancy to me to her, she sat confidently at the piano and rendered the most hideous sounds one can imagine. She had not begun on the correct note, so everything was off key. Halfway through Twinkle, Twinkle, it dawned on her that something was wrong.

Looking expectantly at the teacher, she sat there, waiting for assistance that never came. He was not a man with kindness in his heart, evidently. To him she was ruining his reputation. It was Mama who finally moved to the piano, set Laura's fingers on the correct keys and whispered, "Its fine. Now play."

Laura did, each note falling onto our ears like so many dropped rivets. Those stars did not twinkle, they rattled. The cobbler in the second song hit those nails so hard and fast that he must have used an air drill rather than a hammer. When her ordeal was over, Laura stood up, bowed correctly, and dashed out of the room to hide in the cloakroom and drip tears over everyone's coats and hats.

In spite of everything, we all trooped back to our house for hot cocoa and toast sprinkled with cinnamon and sugar. Laura received a great many hugs and words of praise for her "wanting to surprise her dear mother." Nobody mentioned the music she had so innocently but deftly betrayed.

As far as I know, it was the last time Laura ever approached a piano. Once cousin Rudy unkindly remarked, when we were visiting, "They laughed when she walked over to the piano and they were right; she couldn't pick it up." Like a little wildcat, she tore into him, beating at him with her fists and kicking his long legs with her shoes until Daddy dragged her off into another room and she ended up on a dining room chair for the balance of the evening. So much for musical talent being passed on to the children.

Chapter 34

Maybe Milwaukee was not one of the truly important cities in the country, back in the thirties, but it had a great deal to offer. Situated on the shore of Lake Michigan, it was the largest city in Wisconsin, bigger than Madison, the state capitol, 80 some miles to the west. Relatives of Great Grandmother still lived on Jones Island, a small fishing village out in the harbor that was eventually, by hook and by crook, preempted by the U.S. Steel Company.

Our Grandfather had met Grandmother out on Jones Island when he first arrived from Germany in the late eighties, and married her in 1886. The next year they had a son and a year later Mama was born to them. In the family plot in Forest Home Cemetery is an empty grave with a stone commemorating the deaths of two of Grandmother's cousins who were swept overboard two years apart during raging storms on Lake Michigan while fishing for perch and whitefish that people came in droves to purchase, either raw or smoked.

Culturally, Milwaukee was a bright spot in the lives of artists, actors and actresses, musicians and others in the "arts." Like the vaudeville troupe that had stayed at the mansion, opera stars, ballet companies, dance teams and such made the city an important part of their itinerary.

The Museum and Library offered travelogues. Sometimes Daddy took us there. From our brown paper sacks we would nibble on sandwiches downed with soda pop as we sat in the Museum lunch room, then go to whatever room where the travelogue was being shown. Usually, we were the only young persons there. We learned to sit quietly so the oldsters around us would not bend over and "Shush" us.

The lectures included slides and sometimes black and white movies about New Guinea, Samoa, Australia, Alaska, Africa, India and other interesting and exotic places. During "intermission" we would join in the sing-a-longs, reading the words from the handouts received at the door. "Moonlight and Roses" and "Grandfather's Clock" which "stopped when the old man died," were two of the regular standbys. We "row, row, rowed our boats gently down the stream," and always ended up with "Good night ladies." even when there was another half of the program yet to see.

Some famous people gave those lectures. Osa Johnson, Margaret Mead, and Admiral Richard Byrd, to name a few.

On Saturday's, the Milwaukee Art Museum held classes where, for a quarter, you could learn to charcoal sketch. For several years Laura and I attended classes. One day Mama studied our drawings and ascertained that we were doing nudes. Nude statues, not nude persons. She decided we had taken enough art lessons. It was not until I was married that I learned that what I thought had been a masculine "down there" was actually a fig leaf. I did not confess until many years later that I thought, for a time, that my bridegroom was possibly deformed.

Kids, today, know far too much. We knew far too little. Somewhere there must be a happy medium.

Playgrounds were well supervised. Under Mr. Roosevelt's programs, there were instructors who taught us to play horseshoes, chess, and to toss beanbags into triangular slanted wooden score boards with numbered holes. We formed beanbag teams, the winner receiving a tootsie roll or maybe a fish-shaped lollipop.

Backless park benches narrow enough to straddle offered painted checkerboards, two to a bench. Four could play at once. The checkers were usually pop bottle caps. Championship marble games offering bags of marbles as prizes were enjoyed. I won, once, and became very adept at "marbles."

Most of the larger parks had pavilions. Here ballroom dancing was taught and couples could attend the dances held on Saturday nights where they waltzed and two-stepped to real three to six piece orchestras. Sometimes it was Polka Nite and then the music came from accordions. Maggie and Lee and sometimes Vi and her date attended the dances. Several times Mama and Daddy attended, gliding together on the waxed floor while Laura and I watched. Daddy had earned medals and silver cups for his waltzing at the Turnverein when he was courting

Mama. From eating too much "depression food," both had become somewhat roly-poly but they still "cut a mean rug" and people clapped when they became aware of our parents terpsichordian ability, giving them floor room with a real spotlight to follow their moves. Not exactly Ginger Rogers and Fred Astaire but satisfactory, nonetheless.

The city also offered sports. The natatorium had an indoor pool, where Daddy swam. Our uncles and Cousin Rudy golfed on the city "links," Rudy caddying to pay for his golf balls and tees.

Laura and I jumped rope and did the usual girl-things but we also became interested in baseball and soon had our girlfriends interested as well. Borchert Field, on Eighth and Burleigh, was were the Brewers, then a farm league, played their games. Today Milwaukee has its major league team called the Brewers but, as with ponies who never grow up to be horses, the first team of Brewers did not evolve into that one. Kenny Keltner, of the early Brewer team, went on to the majors and made quite a name for himself, sports wise.

Becky was too chicken to follow our procedure in gaining entrance to the ballpark. Having spending money, she paid her way in but Evy, Laura and I would stop along the fence at Eighth Street, one of us would stand guard while the others pulled aside a certain green-painted board and presto, we were under the bleachers.

We had early selected Kenny Keltner as our favorite. He had that certain something that draws fans. Neither of the four of us knew him personally but we selected him as "ours" and were a four-girl fan club. Edging our way from beneath the bleachers under the pretext that whatever it was we had dropped was nowhere to be found, Evy, Laura and I would find Becky and join her and whoop and shout for our hero. Had it been the fashion of the day, as with the Beatles in later years, we would probably have swooned for that idol who never knew we existed except as voices in the crowd.

Becky did have him sign a baseball for her brother, Itzy, which made us jealous all the way home but that was the extent of it. Kenny went on to play in the American League for the Cleveland Indians but we grew up without ever seeing him play for them. Our range of interest was strictly local. I am sure he was an excellent "major leaguer."

As many times as we crawled through that fence, we were never caught. Strangely enough, none of those in the bleachers ever told on us, even when they spied us entering in this fashion. Maybe it was because we were girls. Back then, being a girl had some advantages. Or, perhaps we were not the only ones to secure admission via that loose board.

Politically, Milwaukee was pristine clean compared to Chicago, a hundred miles away. In fact, the entire state was cleaner politically than its southern neighbor. Crime was not a problem. There was no Al Capone and his rivals to hold shoot-outs in restaurants or garages. We kids could borrow a streetcar pass, usually from someone who paid the dollar a week it cost to reach a place of employment, and ride all over the city without fear of harm. Sightseeing via streetcar was one of our favorite pastimes. Those passes helped us to visit our cousins, Nancy and Lawrence. We had to transfer downtown to take the Bay View line but that was no problem. The streetcars were well marked and you could always ask the motorman if it was the right car for where you were going. As Mama would instruct, "You have a mouth; use it."

Aunt Rose always welcomed us because Nancy, an only child, was often lonely. We loved to play with her things: bikes, dolls, dollhouses, etc. At home Laura and I had our shared pair of roller skates but even Nancy's Shirley Temple doll had a complete pair of her own and Nancy had several extra pairs of clamp-ons, shoe skates not yet being in mode. A special key worn on a string around the neck was put to use in case a skate came loose. Our skating rink was the Burdick schoolyard, a few blocks from her house. My favorite pastime during my visit was to read from some of her lovely story books, especially the one with over five hundred pages. She called me a 'stick in the mud' sometimes but she had no idea how much I enjoyed those books.

It was completely different visiting Lawrence. Everything there was "boy stuff." In his room he had his collection of Big Little Books, now worth a fortune to collectors; his model cars sat on shelves; model airplanes were suspended from the ceiling; bats, balls and other sports equipment filled his second closet.

Often, Laura and I would split up, she continuing on to Nancy's while I got off on Kinnickinnic and Logan to hike the four blocks to Aunt Arlene's; Laura, once a tomboy, now preferred things feminine.

Lawrence and his boyfriends were 'movie mad': When Gunga Din arrived at the neighborhood theater they attended every showing possible. Paying my way with money from "the penny jar" on his dresser, Lawrence would let me accompany them to the matinee. Afterwards we would go to "the gravel pit" to play our version of Gunga Din.

Pinning men's handkerchiefs to the backs of painter's caps, we would race up and down the hills of that pit, shooting off cap pistols and riding imaginary horses. One boy had an old beaten-up bugle from somebody who had once been a Boy Scout and he would play sour notes to let us know that off in the distance somewhere "help was on the way." Somehow, I was always elected to be Gunga Din and either Lawrence or one of his boyfriends would bend over my dying body to exclaim, "You're a better man than I am, Gunga Din." while my face, darkened with charcoal, did its best to not smile.

Usually my visit began on Saturday and lasted until Sunday afternoon when Daddy would "collect us." Aunt Arlene often went away on Saturday's, in the morning, if the wedding was a Catholic one, or in the afternoon for one in a Protestant church. Her fame as a milliner and designer of wedding veils and "head pieces" had spread and for each bride she was there to see that all went well. An early version of the "wedding counselor," it was probably her way of handling her frustration at not having a daughter.

If the wedding was in the afternoon, she would sometimes recruit me to "come and baby-sit" with Lawrence and baby Jimmy. This ended disastrously one Saturday.

It was a rainy day and the house felt damp and cold. Baby Jimmy had a "cough," so we were to keep him in bed.

Her father-in-law, Opa, a dear sweet man with white hair and gold-frame glasses with small lenses, had been recently widowed. A sad, bent little wraith, he had come downstairs from his lonely "bachelor quarters" upstairs to wander through the house in his maroon bathrobe and leather bedroom slippers. If we spoke to him he would look at us as if we were not connected to anything pertaining to him and roam from window to window to peer out at something beyond our ken.

When baby Jimmy began to cough, deep, racking sounds that frightened Lawrence and me, we tried to enlist Opa's aid but he was absolutely of no avail.

"What do you think we should do?" I asked Lawrence.

"Well, when we get colds, often Mama gives us a little wine. I think there's some in the pantry."

There was: a full gallon of elderberry wine that Opa had made before his wife died. "I'll get a baby bottle," offered Lawrence. It was one with a very large tough-to-put-on- the-bottle rubber nipple. We lifted the wine bottle to the pantry ledge and poured. Much more entered the baby bottle than we had planned on but Lawrence spilled some trying to pour it back, so we merely replaced the cork in the wine bottle, set it back down on the floor and, all thumbs, replaced the nipple on the baby bottle. "That looks awfully full. Maybe we should pour some out." I said.

"Naw, it's okay. It'd be too much work getting the nipple back on. He'll just drink some and fall asleep."

He did. In fact, he was still sleeping when Aunt Arlene and Uncle Bill finally arrived home. He slept through supper and far into the evening. At last, worried, Aunt Arlene tried to waken him and he did not respond. It was ascertained that he was still breathing; in fact, he was snoring like an old man with asthma.

"We gave him some wine," confessed Lawrence.

"Where did you get the wine?" asked Uncle Bill.

"From that jug in the pantry."

"Opa's elderberry stuff? Ye gods, how much did you give him; a teaspoon or a tablespoon or what?"

"We half filled his bottle." I informed them.

"You WHAT?"

The bottle was empty.

When Dr. Becker arrived, he checked over little Jimmy, declared that "this child is dead drunk!" and immediately had them dip Jimmy into first cold and then hot water, slapped his face, rubbed his body, made his two year old feet walk back and forth around the dining room table until we were all dizzy and at last, several hours later, declared that he "would make it."

I was eleven and a half. I should have "known better." I was sent home in disgrace, picked up at the door by Mama and Daddy early in the morning and told to "be sure to thank God when you get to Sunday school that you and Lawrence didn't kill little Jimmy." It was a long time before I was welcomed back into that household.

Mama and Daddy consoled me on the way home and somehow Mama's relationship with her sister remained stable, as usual.

I can still see Dr. Becker, a glass of elderberry wine in his hand, sipping it with appreciation as I cowered forlornly on the living room sofa. "Excellent flavor, don't you know! Harrumph! No wonder the child downed it all."

He left with the balance of the wine, two of his long, expressive fingers curled about the handle of the glass jug, a gift of gratitude from Aunt Arlene and Uncle Bill, who vowed there would never be another bottle of the stuff in the house.

It was the last time I saw Opa. He more or less evaporated, too spent by grief to remain here on earth without his beloved "Emma."

Chapter 35

Ethnic mixture that our neighborhood was, we kids got along quite well. During school days we stayed in the house until our parents came home, doing our homework and helping to prepare supper. After the dishes were washed and dried, we might go out to play, if it was still light out. Usually, however, we stayed in to listen to our favorite radio programs or pass the time in some quiet activity.

With the arrival of summer, it was as if the children sprang up from the cracks in the sidewalk. Always, there was the sound of shouts, laughter, unleashed dogs barking out their joy of freedom as they watched or tried to enter games with their owners and the sound of wheels from roller skates; orange crate 'scooters;' tricycles and two wheelers.

Sometimes it was the sound of entreprenuers calling out their wares that echoed through the area.

"Rags, bottles, iron!" came the plaintive cry from the Jewish rag picker. I conversed with him one day. He had come from Russia and was sending his two sons to college. "Education, it is the secret to success," he told me. "Me, I do not have that opportunity to attend much school and learn, only what the Rabbi teaches, but my sons, they will one day be good businessmen, maybe even rich."

Most of the kids made fun of him with his hooknose and raggedy clothes. His old horse was draped with intricately woven string netting to help keep off bothersome flies. Its back sagged. Perhaps the wagon he pulled might be too heavy but his felt hat was jauntily tilted, held in place on his head by holes through which his ears protruded.

I saw that man in another light. He wanted more for his sons and was willing to collect other peoples'junky stuff to make sure that they had a chance for success "Here in America," the name of his adopted country spoken with loving, hopeful tones in spite of the Great Depression "is freedom and a future." For him, what we had lost to the market crash had never been in his possession, so what he had was deeply appreciated.

It was an Italian, who sang, "Bananas, bananas, three pounds for a quarter, bananas," in a rich baritone from atop his wagon, a scale making little clinking sounds as it rocked back and forth, awaiting its owner's use of it to weigh out the various fruits housewives purchased along his route. Different from the rag picker's, which had a square platform, this boasted a shiny brass curved dish suspended from equally shiny chains attached to a piece of metal with numbers, and a sliding indicator that went up or down depending upon the weight placed in the dish.

The iceman did not have a horse. He drove a truck and let out streams of blue exhaust from his tailpipe. His eyes searched windows for the display sign that told him the household needed 25, 50, 75 or 100 pounds today. Spotting one, he would stop the truck, walk to the back, take out a leather carrier, chip off the correct amount of ice from the scored blocks with his ice pick and, grasping the ice block with black iron tongs, place it in the carrier and go around to the back door and pound to let the homemaker know he had arrived.

We kids, meanwhile, were all over that truck, grabbing up the cooling chips of ice that had landed her and there in the truck bed. The tallest kids always came away with the biggest chunks. Upon spotting the iceman's return, we would disperse, with him shaking his fist at us and telling us to "stay off my truck." He never seemed truly menacing, however, probably because we were the kids of his customers, so we disregarded his instruction and repeated our raid the next time he came around.

Sometimes we ran out of ice before his scheduled visit. Then Mama would send us to the icehouse, located on our side of Burleigh, midway between Twelfth and Eleventh streets. Inside the small but well insulated little house were blocks of ice packed in sawdust. The iceman would take our order, go inside; bring out the correct size block;; drop it onto the heavy towel lining of our old coaster wagon and wipe off most of the sawdust. Accepting our money, he would present us each with a penny sucker and we would be off, having carefully wrapped the towel about the ice to keep it from melting in the hot sun.

It was a struggle getting the coaster wagon up the five steps to the level of the narrow sidewalk running between our house and the one next door but we would somehow manage, then pull it even with the side door and announce our arrival. Our next door neighbor took pride in his small front lawn. To pull that wagon up green hill beside the steps would have brought the police, no less.

Hopefully, Daddy would be there to lift the ice from the wagon with his very own set of tongs. Otherwise Mama would take hold of the ends of the towel, grunt and strain and, with our help, carry the ice into the house and let it slide into the ice section at the top of the wooden refrigerator, carefully dropping the door back down on it and securely latching it to keep it contents from melting too fast.

Probably the most interesting character was the scissors grinder man. Set into a wheeled wooden frame that he pushed along the sidewalks was a large grindstone. . An Italian, he had deep-set dark eyes, graying black curls, full, loose fitting sleeves in his shirt, baggy gray trousers held up with red suspenders and a very thick black mustachio, under his nose, that curled up at either end. His sing-song voice called out to the housewives that here was a man who could sharpen a blade to a fine edge.

"The scissors man is here," we kids would run shouting into our houses. Lucky ones returned with a mother or grandmother in need of his services and the privilege of standing close by to watch as the foot pedal was used to keep the wheel spinning. His conversation was sparkling as he worked, his brownish thumb, its nail curled up like the toes of an Arabian prince's shoes, from time to time tested the keenness of the blade.

Those of us who had nothing to offer him by way of business were relegated to standing back and peering through people's arms, or if there were a lawn sloping upward, watching from that vantage point.

Sometimes an organ grinder wandered into our territory. Attached to fine-link chain was his monkey, who wore a red cap and matching jacket. In its hand was a tin cup, which the little animal held out to each of us in turn, enticing us to place a penny or more into it by turning somersaults and chirping at us while his master turned the crank on the box organ.

Best of all was the photographer who led a pretty pony that stood still while a child was placed upon its back to have his or her picture snapped. Laura and I were never fortunate enough to pose on pony-back because, we would explain to our friends, Mama was not home when the pony clip-clopped along our street.

The photograph would arrive in the mail and was set atop a piano or on a table for everyone to view. We envied those kids who had this experience but never complained to Mama or Daddy, knowing they did not have the necessary dollar fifty per photo to dish out for such an extravagance.

The streets were paved with tar that bubbled up in the summer heat and if you had a reason to walk upon it with bare feet, you found yourself dancing from one foot to the other. It was fun to break bubbles and scoop out some of the tar, chewed in place of gum. It was purported to "whiten the teeth."

Bare feet also meant stubbed toes and running games played on sidewalks often brought on skinned knees. We would go home to secure first aid for such bloody injuries. Daddy had something called "Sabine's plaster" which he would heat on the gas flames and apply after we had thoroughly washed the injury with soap and water, preferably using Lifebuoy soap, this purported to contain carbolic acid and therefore hygienic. That Sabine stuff was hot when applied. I can't remember ever getting third degree burns from it but we did an Indian dance until it cooled off. We much preferred Mama's soothing kiss and Vaseline covered with a strip of clean white torn sheet or pillowcase.

Evenings found we "older kids" playing sidewalk games such as "Simon Says," "Captain May I?" or hopscotch, or tag games. Young voices called out the rules and such chants as "olly, olly oxen free, who don't come will be I-T" echoed through the buzz of mosquitoes. Then there was the chatter of adult voices of neighbors sitting on front porches to get a breath of coolth. Porches were to use, not to look at.

"Chase the Rabbit," popular back in the mansion neighborhood, was also played here; one team, the rabbits, starting out ahead and leaving clues for the foxes to follow and give chase. It was okay to go clear around the block or even cut through the alley but to cross a street and enter another block or alley was forbidden. We tended to stay in our own neighborhood.

One evening, Laura, Evy and I decided we would explore the alley between thirteenth and fourteenth streets. It was not 'our territory' and you never knew who might challenge you, through not in the way we had been challenged by the Clybourne Street Gang.

As in our alley, this one had garages on either side; wooden ash boxes with covers where coal ash and clinkers were dumped for pickup; garbage cans and gates opening onto back yards. One back yard offered a fully loaded plum tree, the fruit just ripe for picking. A branch hung down over the fence and into the alley just out of our reach. Evy bent over and I lifted Laura onto her back.

"Pick three nice ones." We instructed her.

Reaching up into the tree, her hand came into contact with another hand, this one attached to a very angry man.

"I got you now, you little thieves. Take my plums, will you? Strip my tree every night! It's the cops for you!"

"We've never been here before, mister. Let her go. It's just that our alley doesn't have plum trees and..." The branch hanging over the fence had been a decoy. Laura's teeth sank into his hand and he dropped it. We ran lickety-split to the end of the alley and hid behind a car. After a time, when no police sirens or whistles blew, we felt safe enough to dash home. It was just another incidence that Mama and Daddy knew nothing about. We stayed in our own territory from then on.

Looking back, I'm surprised that so many kids survived childhood. One of the games we played was "Dare." It demanded that we do all sorts of things that we should not be doing. One of them was "Beat the cars." We had to wait until a car was within an eighth of a block away and then dash across the street in front of it. Brakes squealed, people dabbed their foreheads with handkerchiefs and shook their fists. Great fun to watch. Fortunately none of us tripped and fell in front of the car on our way across to the other side of the street.

One motorist decided to teach us a lesson. He was at least six feet tall, in his early twenties. He hit the brakes so hard the car rocked. No fist shaking for him! He was out of that car and had the back of my dress in his fist before I knew what had happened.

"You want to get hurt, huh, you danged little brat! Well, how does this feel? It's what your Pa shoulda done way before this!" Up went my skirt! Exposed were my bloomers! In front of all the other kids, he landed five or six hard blows to my bottom! Then it was back into his car and off he went.

I could hardly sit but Mama and Daddy were not informed. Laura knew better than to blab. I had given her my narrow-eyed stare and let her knew there would be results if she did. After all, she had been playing the game, too. It was the last time any of us did that again.

Kids love secret clubs and we were no different. We had tried to have one under our front porch but there were spiders there and it was too cramped, so Becky talked her mother into letting us use their fruit cellar, a small room in their basement. There we held our secret meetings with Evy as our fourth member of the club. We made up special club colors, had a motto and hand signals that meant absolutely nothing to either us or other kids but we pretended they did.

Our club activity ended the afternoon the bulb hanging from the fruit cellar ceiling burned out. Evy got a votive candle and lit it. Laura, pinning a picture to the wall above it, was suddenly afire. Her skirt had dipped down over the flame and it had grabbed at it hungrily.

Her scream had me at her side immediately, beating out the flames with my hands and yelling to Evy and Becky to "get water."
It was over in moments. Laura's dress had no skirt, I had burned hands and Becky's mother was drying Laura off with a towel and yelling at all of us in Yiddish. She applied chicken fat to my hands, lent Laura a dress and said there would be no more clubhouse!

Strangely enough, Laura suffered no burns. We sneaked into the house, hid Laura's dress in the ragbag, she donned something else and I treated my hands with Vaseline. It was weeks before Mama found the burnt garment. By then my hands had healed. I don't remember what I gave as an excuse for the burns but I can still feel them. I thanked God that night that I had been there to save my little sister. It was a night of tossing and turning. She could have died or been horribly burned. I, too, could have caught on fire. Kids must have guardian angels, for sure.

Another form of danger presented itself, one that could have had a sadder ending. Laura and I wore the hairstyle named "the Shingle," in vogue at the time and very popular with many of the movie actresses, such as Claudette Colbert. Up in the back, down to the ear lobes at the sides, with short bangs, it took a skilled barber to do the cut and most of us went to one seven or eight blocks away. He charged fifty cents a head but he first shampooed you and then cut it when wet. To children he presented each with a lollipop.

A tall man, he sat shorter kids on a board placed across the arms of the barber chair. He would lift each child up and set him or her down, fasten the length of paper about one's neck, cloak garments with his over-large barber cape and start snipping away.

I had grown to almost five feet tall and my body had begun to sprout small 'chest bumps,' which I hated and tried to hide by holding my arms against them. The last time I had been to the barbershop, the man had picked me up under my arms to assist me into the chair and his fingers had groped for, found and explored those bumps. I sat through that haircut both embarrassed, ashamed and angry, aware that his hands had somehow behaved indecently. When the haircut was completed, I pushed his hands away and left the chair without his help. He presented me with two lollipops, both of which I refused. Laura, however, had reached out for them and queried me all the way home as to why I would turn down such a treat. I refused to answer.

Now it was "trip to the barbershop day" and I gave all sorts of excuses for not going but Mama had not been informed of the man's actions; I was too embarrassed to discuss it even with her. She placed the dollar into my hand and admonished me, as usual, to "not let Laura bite the barber's hand," and took off for the streetcar and her job.

We had decided to ask Evy and Becky if they would accompany us and were on our way to their house when a man who lived across the street in an upper apartment came along. and stopped to ask, "and where are you fair maidens off to on such a lovely day?"

"To the barbershop," Laura replied.

"Barbershop? And how much does he charge you?"

"Fifty cents apiece," she revealed.

"Fifty cents! And you have to walk all the way to the shop! Not a bargain at all. Why, I'm a barber too, and I never charge more than a quarter."

"Do you do shingles?"

"I do everything. A jack of all trades, you might call me."

Laura and I conferred. "Do you have a barber's chair?" I asked.

"Don't need one. You two young ladies are tall enough. Besides, I do my work in my house. No room for a barber's chair, now, is there?" Hmmm. Twenty five cents was a bargain. We would have a quarter apiece for ourselves or we could even give the change back to Mama after we deducted a penny each for a lollipop or a licorice stick or something.

We followed the man to his apartment. He sat Laura down on a kitchen chair set on spread out newspapers, covered her dress with a large towel, and proceeded to give her a haircut.

When it was suppertime, Laura unwillingly came to the table. She wore a babushka.

"Why do you have a kerchief on your head," Mama wanted to know. "Let me see your haircut."

Laura's large eyes filled with tears. Her fingers tightened on the knot under her chin and she shook her head. Mama gently removed them and untied the flowered material, then exclaimed, "Oh, Mein Gott in Himmel!"

She turned to me. I had not had a haircut.

"What IS THIS, Jessie?" she demanded while the others at the table sat with bated breaths.

It was my turn to weep. Between sobs and gulps of air, I explained about the man offering us a bargain and reached into my pocket for the extra change. Laura had been too upset to even think of a treat. Her hair was only an inch short all over her head and none of it cut evenly. She looked incredibly terrible.

Tossing the quarter onto the kitchen table, we had both dashed from the man's apartment and run home, grateful that none of our friends were in sight at the time. Laura had taken shelter in our bed until Mama had called out, "Supper, girls. Come eat!"

We were hurried back into our room where Mama demanded an explanation. "WHY WOULD YOU LET SOMEONE DO THIS TO YOU? JESSIE, WHY DID YOU LET THIS HAPPEN?"

Between sobs I explained about the man in the barbershop lifting me and feeling my "bumps." I never wanted to return there and here was another barber offering his service and for half the price.

When Mama heard me out she exclaimed, "Why, that old sot! All he wanted was the money for more booze! I think we must inform the police of this. Oh, Jessie, you and Laura are fortunate that all he did was cut her hair. It could have been your throats. You certainly must know better than to ever accompany a stranger into his or her house! Oh, Lord in Heaven, I have to work but my poor children! Oh, Laura, I'm so sorry this happened." She was holding Laura in her arms and rocking her back and forth, her own tears wetting the shorn head.

A note was sent to the school and Laura was allowed to wear the babushka until her hair grew to a decent length. No more barbershop for us. Once a month we were sent to the beauty shop for our haircuts. Vi kept us trimmed in the meantime. At the trade school she had taken one course in beauty culture and grooming.

Mama had not mentioned my chest problem but one day, in the mail, a small booklet arrived addressed to "Miss Jessica Renz." It was published for the Kotex Company and explained in flowery terms that I was a rosebud and would one day soon become a "full-bloom rose." Those 'bumps' as I called them, were developing because I was maturing. One day, I would be required to wear a brassiere to protect them so I could nurse a child, eventually. I would also be required to wear a "sanitary pad" as well, at a certain time of the month and it explained about this as well.

Now I understood about the pans of water hidden beneath the skirt Mama had placed around our claw foot bathtub. Sanitary napkins cost money. My sisters and Mama used folded cloths that they soaked and later washed with the towels in the hottest water. Someday my pan would be there, too. I did not look forward to that time.

Studying myself in the mirror, my shoulders sagged. I was still the homeliest girl in the entire world. Oh, dear, the time when I would become a missionary and sail off to Africa was drawing closer. I would never need worry about nursing a child. It was highly unlikely that I would ever have any.

Chapter 36

Mama's birthday was in September. We four girls pooled our money to purchase a nice gift but Daddy had a gift of his own, one that he had worked for, donating the materials and labor and saving up to rent a truck to haul it home.

He took us into his confidence and instructed us to "keep her busy in the kitchen" while he brought her present into the living room with the help of Gilly, whom he had recruited via phone.

Boards were placed on the steps and the well-covered behemoth was rolled up onto the porch. A strong neighbor volunteered his strength as well and soon, against the south wall of the living room, stood a beautiful upright player piano; its highly polished mahogany case gleaming softly in the light from the amber shaded Tiffany lamp in the center of the library table.

We had blindfolded Mama and led her through the dining room and into the living room where we seated her on the long wooden piano bench. Daddy uncovered her eyes.

For a long moment, she stared at the keys of the piano, then her fingers lovingly traced each key. At last they fell into position and she began to play, only to discover that three years of wrapping packages and tying string at Schuster's bundling room had taken their toll. Tears formed and rolled down her now chubby cheeks and dripped onto her ample bosom. Silently she rose and indicated that Vi should take her place.

She turned to Daddy and went into his arms and the two of them stood there, listening to Vi play "Minuet in G" without the éclat of Mama's talent.

Each evening, after that, Mama sat at the piano practicing finger stretching exercises that eventually brought back her ability to play with almost the same brilliance as before.

Daddy promised her, that birthday night, that he would eventually replace for her all that they had lost. That piano was not a Steinway baby grand but it gave us all enjoyment. Along with it came music rolls that we threaded onto the rollers inside the sliding doors above the keyboard. We would pedal our way through "In a Little Spanish Town" and other songs, sometimes using the harp attachment by pushing a little lever beside the keyboard. It was a lovely instrument.

The old lady who had owned it had needed a furnace; Mama needed a piano. Daddy had provided both. An excellent deal all around.

Now I begged Vi to teach me to play. She showed me how to find the key of C on both the piano and in the simple instruction book she purchased. I would never match Mama's skill on the keyboard but it was fun learning, even with my atrocious fingering. It seemed strange that Mama could play so well but not be able to impart her musical knowledge to her children, yet that was how it was.

Vi and I began to play duets together and our sisters would join in singing songs as she played. Their boyfriends joined in sometimes, too, and there were merry evenings of singing, sipping cocoa and enjoying each other's company.

Lee had become an accepted member of the group. Vi's boyfriends varied. Somehow she had not yet found the one to share her life. I wondered if she would end up a spinster, like Great Aunt Alice. Only, Aunt Alice had "means" and it would probably be Vi's destiny to become the 'genteel poor' that I read about in books; so sad, dressed in dull clothing and gloves with holes in the fingers as they purchased their pitiful small amounts of food and counted out their pennies from purses with squeaky hinges. Maybe she could accompany me to Africa and we could be missionaries together. She could play the piano and we could sing to the poor unbaptized natives.

I never approached her with the idea, not wanting to make her feel that she was not as attractive to men as Maggie. Maybe if she did not have to wear glasses… She had very pretty hair and a nice smile but her younger sister, like mine, certainly outshone her. It was so unfair! But then, what about life was fair? We were still merely existing, living off of Mama's and Vi's earnings and whatever Daddy could bring in from his furnace jobs. I could barely remember what life had been like in the red brick house. Sometimes, it seemed, that had never been a part of my life at all.

Meetzer was still with us but he was getting old and stiff in the joints. He had mellowed and allowed us to cuddle him these days. Sometimes he even allowed Laura to give him rides in our old doll buggy. He did hate it when we sang, however, and set up such a mewing that we had to send him from the room. Lee thought that maybe he was singing along but not with his tail switching back and forth so angrily. Perverse old cat! I loved him dearly.

Chapter 37

Evy's father, Mr. Roubar, was master of his household. His wizened little wife meekly did his bidding. He also did all of the grocery shopping and was very fussy about things being fresh.

On a summer afternoon, probably a Saturday, since he was home, Laura and I stood in the backyard of their house and called up to them, "Oh, Evy! Oh, Evy." She appeared at the side door and motioned for us to come in.

Halfway up the stairs we were met by her father, who held out a dollar bill. "You run over to Linz's Meat Market and bring home a nice fresh soup hen, the fresher the better."

"Yes, Papa. Can Laura and Jessie go with me?"

"It takes three to carry a chicken? Hah, why not? Just hurry back!"

We skipped off to Linz's. It was on the corner, across Twelfth from the hardware store and where Mama sent us to purchase freshly ground meat and other items in the meat line. It was fun to go there, because the butchers were jolly fellows who wore white aprons blood-stained from wiping their hands on them, and whacked off hunks of ring baloney to "eat while you wait" or sometimes offered a wiener from the coiled strings of them in the white enameled meat pans kept cool in the refrigerated display case.

On the floor was a generous sprinkling of sawdust in which we made designs with the toes of our shoes while our orders were being filled.

"So, your Papa wants a fresh hen. Just how fresh does he want it?" teased the butcher.

"As fresh as possible, he said," Evy instructed.

"Hmmm. Would you say this is fresh enough?" With a twinkle in his eye, the man brought out a live hen.

"Oh, can we pet him?" Laura begged.

"Her."

"Her then. Can we? Please?"

He let us touch her feathers. Suddenly, Evy decided that this was what she should take home to her father. He knew all about killing chickens. He had raised them in "the old country."

"I'll take her." She declared.

"Oh, I don't know! We wouldn't want to get you in trouble." The man was hesitant. "Your Pa might come back here and wring OUR necks." Adamant, Evy handed him the dollar, accepted the hen which the butcher fastened to her wrist with a string attached to its one leg, put the change in her pocket and off we went, the envy of the neighborhood as we stopped to let each child who came running "to see" take a turn at petting the bird.

Eventually we reached Evy's side door and together we three and the cackling hen began to ascend the steps to the upper flat. We were met at the top by Mr. Roubar who stood with arms folded across his red-underwear clad chest, his black pant legs tucked into laced up boots that were spread apart to bar our way. His fierce dark eyes glared down at us and in his hand were the sharpest set of knives I had ever seen, each blade gleaming in the sunlight pouring through the upper hall window.

"SO! YOU MAKE FUN FOR YOURSELVES, YES? I send you on a small errand and you come back with a live hen! It's funny, YES?"

"No, Papa, you told me the fresher the better..." Evy's voice trailed away as he moved a step down toward us. Laura and I began to back down the stairs, our intent to escape from the scene, but he roared out at us, "NO! YOU STAY!"

I was into Bluebeard, the man who cut off the heads of his wives, in my reading of fairy stories that summer. Suddenly, here he was, in the person of Evy's father, knives all ready to do us in.

My heart was pounding in my chest and I eyed the side door as he marched us down stairs to the basement. As usually happened when I was frightened or in pain, I lost my voice. Laura was sniffling.

Into the dark cavern of the basement he herded us, lit the bare bulb hanging from the ceiling, pointed to three chairs upon which we were to sit and tied the hen to one of the laundry sink faucets. As we sat cowering, he filled a huge kettle he had placed on the laundry stove with pail after pail of water.

In silence we waited while it heated up. He, meanwhile, played with the largest of the knives, testing it against the skin of his thumb, pulling a hair from his mustache and neatly severing it into two halves, all the while humming some song from his boyhood memory.

Suddenly, with a swift motion of his hand, he grabbed the neck of the hen, held her in the air and, with a flash of steel; her head lay on the floor. He let her down and she ran, headless, bleeding, back and forth until at last she fell over, her feet kicking back and forth a time or two before lapsing into inertia.

We had all screamed, albeit my scream was silent, and covered our eyes. Now I knew what our fate would be; our heads, too, would soon be lying there beside the poor hapless fowl's! I began to silently pray for someone to rescue us.

Testing the water with his finger and grunting in satisfaction, Bluebeard plunged the lifeless body into the scalding water, lifted it out and, tossing it at our feet, commanded, "PLUCK!!!"

Tears of fear running down our cheeks, we plucked, our trembling fingers removing each and every feather while he emptied the kettle and rinsed it out and mopped up the blood from the floor.

When not a pin feather remained, Bluebeard inspected the little carcass and grunted with satisfaction. Reaching into his pocket. he placed into each of Laura's and my hands a small silver coin bearing the head of Mercury. Ten cents apiece to spend any way we wished! Never were two girls so flooded with relief!

"SO! Next time it is not a live chicken, yes?" His grin was wide.

Nodding, we made our escape. How beautiful that warm afternoon sunshine felt on our living faces! How swiftly our legs took us back to the front sidewalk and homeward! How wonderful it was that Mama was not preparing chicken for supper.

Chapter 38

1937

It came so swiftly, that transition from childhood to the onset of adulthood, that the years seemed to have run together. After two years of catechism study, I was confirmed, promising to be a Lutheran for the rest of my life before a full congregation of people, wearing a dress I hated but told Mama I liked because the one I actually wanted was a dollar more.

The day before I had suffered the agony of the permanent wave machine, each curler attached to my wound-up hair on one end and by cord to the metal stand sending out intolerable heat. The Beauty operator did her best to cool me off with a paper fan advertising somebody's funeral parlor.

I was supposed to have become a raving beauty but that frizzy hairstyle only enhanced every freckle, the thinness of my face, the tallness of my neck and the hugeness of my teeth. It did nothing to enlarge my eyes. Alas, I was to be photographed-for-posterity in that condition!

My white shoes and the large shoulder corsage merely emphasized what I knew to be the truth; I was absolutely unbearably homely. My silent tears in the bathroom only made my eyes and nose red. Somehow, I got through the church ceremony, the dinner and relatives who spent the afternoon and evening presenting me with gifts and exclaiming over Mama's delicious food.

Soon after I became a' full blown rose' and was grateful for the babysitting job that paid me the quarter it cost to purchase sanitary napkins. No pans of water for me! It was not the right to vote that freed womanhood but the invention of cotton and gauze held in place by an elastic belt complete with two tabs and two safety pins.

Nothing did much to help those danged monthly cramps that Evy never had when "her red haired cousin came to call." Childbirth pains were not so excruciating. An unmarried girl was not to be examined by a physician, at least not by Dr. Becker, so I suffered. It was the expected thing to do. You were cursed because Eve had picked an apple from a tree. Even the Bible reported that. A woman's lot! Nobody knew about PMS back then. Nor did you discuss things so personal. Daddy probably never knew about those pans of water under the tub or why his daughters resorted to tears if he 'looked at them funny'. Men were not expected to understand women's ways. That was the way it was. Even in the movies they emphasized this. That Christmas I received a pair of real silk hose from Great Aunt Beatrice and sat with the grownups at Grandmother's table.

Grade school graduation came the following June and before I knew it, I was looking to high school. Maggie had already graduated from North Division and we had moved once more, this time to Eighth and Keefe. If was just around the corner from Aunt Elsie and Uncle Franz. Cousins Lawrence and Jimmy now had a baby brother, Michael, and Aunt Mimsey had given birth to a pretty little girl she named Shirley. Mama's side of the family was growing in number. Daddy's remained the same. Evy and Becky were left behind and we acquired new friends, especially the girl next door, Lisa, who was athletic and belonged to the Girl Scouts. She had even been to camp the previous summer. She also was enrolled in a new high school that had just been built as a WPA project, another of Mr. Roosevelt's programs.

When he had learned of the Program, Daddy had applied. One day he received a letter telling him to appear at an office somewhere downtown. He came home with a wide grin on his face. They had said they needed men to dig ditches and do all sorts of work. He had a job!
Mama's face had fallen at the news. "Oh, Paul, how can you dig ditches all day with your back? You'll be crippled for life!"

"But I won't be digging ditches, Lyd! Roosevelt's given the green light for a whole new town to be started out near Hales Corners. Another WPA Project. They're talking about putting up over three hundred homes and they want me to supervise. I'll be in charge of installing the heating systems! They had my name down as a former contractor and knew I had helped install the heating system in the State Capitol!"

Just south of Milwaukee and a few miles west, the government was about to put up a "garden city." When completed, each of the homes was destined to be sold to deserving families who would be able to secure low interest mortgages from the government. The name of the new community was to be Greendale. It would be one of three such communities in the country, the others located in New York State and in Ohio. Each to be surrounded by a greenbelt of trees and grass, the houses would be large enough to accommodate families of four or more.

There would also be some multiple family dwellings, according to the Journal. Each house was to have 5,000 square feet of lawn space so the families could have a yard and a garden n which to grow their own vegetables. In charge of everything was the Resettlement Administration and thousands of unemployed men would now have jobs. Mr. Roosevelt's plans had finally filtered down to us.

Lisa took me along to show me her new school. For some reason she was in Rufus King High district but our house was not. The cut-off ran between our yards! I would have to attend North Division High. One look at the cream brick and glass of King High, the stadium, the greenhouse, the tennis courts and I was in love. I HAD to go to school there; I just HAD to! But how?

As a graduation present, I had received the very gift I wanted. The Milwaukee Journal was offering a twenty- four volume set of the complete works of Mark Twain, each volume to be purchased, one a week, for 39 cents if accompanied by a coupon clipped from their paper. With covers of green and black leatherette and titles in gold lettering, it was a true bargain. It would be my task to clip the coupon and purchase the book. Mama provided the money.

The Journal Building was almost downtown. Every Saturday that I could not borrow a streetcar pass, which seemed to be most of the time, I walked several miles through all the various neighborhoods to purchase a volume.

I became acquainted with the owner of a Karmel Korn shop on Third Street who let me rest my feet and gave me a sample to munch, he admiring me because I was so determined to acquire a library of my own. Along the way I had to pass through the "Negro District." People with dark skin and ready smiles nodded to me and eventually a few of the women came to know that I was from the North Side and that I was on my way to purchase my grade school graduation present. On the return trip I would open the volume and show them the pictures and read a page or two. A few of them decided that their children, too, should own such nice books and I found myself with company for the six or seven blocks from their district to the Journal Building and back again

Having purchased our volumes, we studied them as we walked. Hopefully, one or more of their lives were changed because I had come their way. I liked those dark people whose ancestors had once been slaves. If they represented the people in Africa, maybe my future as a missionary there would not be so bad.

My seventh grade teacher was a robust woman in her mid fifties who was a member of the Polar Bear Club. During the coldest days, if there were some open water in Lake Michigan, she and her fellow club members took a dip in the icy waters. She also had a heart as big as her enormous bosom. It was she who told our class, with anger, that the Negro population of the city was being cruelly contained within an area that someday would not hold them.

"You listen carefully, class; Mr. Lincoln gave the Negroes Emancipation from slavery but it is up to us to give them true freedom. Right now, not a one can buy a house anywhere in this city. Rent, yes, if any landlord will put himself on the block and fight his neighbors. Why, my cleaning lady and her family of eight are living in three rooms and using a bath, at the end of a dark hall, which they must share with six other families!"

They had been merely words until I actually met my brown-skinned counterparts. They were people, like me, with feelings for their children and each other. Why, we even shared the same interests, at least some of us. Owning books. Learning about the world. Maybe I would someday make enough money to purchase a whole block of homes which I would gladly rent out to them or even allow them to purchase. That word *allow* bothered me. Who was I to *allow* anyone what was automatically their right? No, I would *assist* them. There, that was a better way of putting it. The walk home was jauntily traveled.

One day I was lucky enough to discover that the man standing at the water cooler in the Journal Building was a reporter. I confessed that I would some day like to work for a paper but that, at present, I was only writing plays.

"Oh, yeah? Well, if you can write plays you can write other things, too, honey. Best tools in the world for a writer are words; the more you know, the better you can write, but you have to know when to use the long ones and when to stick to prose. And then there's spelling. And punctuations, of course. Get yourself a degree in Journalism and come around to my office; I intend to be top editor by then."

"Well, first I have to go to high school. I sure wish I knew how to get to go to the new one, Rufus King. I'm stuck in North Division District."

"Oh, yeah? Well, why don't you try the School Board? Maybe they'll let you switch. No promises, mind you, but it's worth a try. A good reporter never gives up without trying."

Elated, I walked on air all the way home and the next morning dropped a nickel in the slot of the coin telephone that had somehow followed us from the rooming house to each of our abodes and was still with us, attached to our kitchen wall. Once a month a man from the phone company used a special key to open a little metal square and empty out the coins that we and the neighbors without phones had deposited there. The lady who answered put me through to someone on the school board and presto, I had an appointment to meet with the board members the following week.

It was raining hard the morning I started out. By the time I reached the Karmel Korn shop I was wet and cold in spite of my umbrella. The owner treated me to a cup of coffee laced with cream and I explained my mission. He said I had "gumption." I confessed that I was scared stiff. "Nah, they're only people, Jessie. You tell them how much you want to go to that school. Promise them the world."

Entering the building, I climbed stairs, walked down a long corridor, entered the room pointed out to me by a nice young woman and found myself staring at a table surrounded by at least a dozen men and women. They offered me a chair and began to ask questions. Why did I select Rufus King High? How many blocks would I have to walk to school? Only ten to North Division but almost eighteen to King? Did I have transportation? Had I any idea how long eighteen blocks were? Etc,etc,etc,

I stood up and, calling upon my best ability to act, as I had on the stage the day I told of my trip to Mexico, I told them that for seven long years we had done without. We had sunk to the depths of poverty, even landing on the relief rolls for a time, but we were trying very hard to pull ourselves up by our bootstraps. "Why, my father is even in charge of installing the heating systems out in Greendale!"

"To me, North Division is probably a fine school, in fact, my sister Maggie graduated from there and is presently working in an office, but Rufus King High is so beautiful! Like a fairy palace! I just know that if I am allowed to attend classes there, I'll be an honor student when I graduate! I don't mind walking eighteen blocks. I walked all the way here from my house. I walk to the Journal Building to get a volume of Mark Twain every Saturday, too. It's my graduation gift from my parents, you see. They're very education minded.

There were gasps. "Child you walk? Why, that's several miles. And today, in this rain?"

"Oh, yes. I had no money for carfare and I had to come, to plead my case."

"My dear, why don't you go out into that waiting room and let us discuss this among ourselves," one board member advised.

Shortly I was readmitted to the boardroom and heard the words, "With such determination, Jessica Renz, we feel that you would be a great asset to Rufus King High. However, we will be keeping track of your progress and you must keep your grades high enough to not make us change our minds."

"We also wish to commend your parents for instilling such a love of education in their children."

The sun had come out and the walk home seemed incredibly short. I wanted to tell everyone I met how happy I was. The owner of the Karmel Korn shop presented me with a ten cent bag of his freshly made confection.

"Someday you'll see your name in print, Miss Renz. Maybe I should have your autograph right now."

I might have been the homeliest girl in the world but at that moment I was also the happiest.

Chapter 39

That summer I played chess almost every day with Everett, the boy next door on the other side of our house from Lisa's. He had broken his leg and had to be in a cast for three months. The year before his left leg had been crippled by infantile paralysis. The leg he broke was his good one; the lame one was too weak to bear his weight, even with a brace, so Laura and I took him under our wings and kept him amused. She pushed his wheel chair all around the block and even down Green Bay Avenue so he could 'window shop'. Our favorite store was a gift shop with pretty items on display in the window. His was a store filled with sports equipment. None of us had enough money to purchase anything but we could gaze.

Everett was a good sport. He did his best to keep his own spirits up but there were times when nothing we did helped much; an only child, he was just too lonely. One afternoon Daddy strode over to his house and stepped inside to chat with Everett's parents. The next day Daddy again entered their house, this time with a box containing a lively shepherd puppy that he had found sitting forlornly beside the road on his way home from Greendale... It wore neither collar nor identification. We girls fell in love with it immediately but he had already decided that this was to be Everett's dog.

No boy was ever so happy as that one. The puppy's tongue licked Everett's face, sniffed him from head to toe and settled in his lap. By the time school started once more, Everett was out of his cast and walking his now large dog, his weak leg growing stronger from the exercise. Daddy would have done well with a son. I wished more than anything we had a brother.

Maggie's birthday was in July. She and Lee had taken their tennis rackets when they left the house but first, Lee had stepped into the kitchen where Mama was putting the finishing touches on Maggie's cake.

"Ahhh, Mrs. Renz, I wonder if you and Mr. Renz would mind if I spoke to you privately for a minute or two…"

"Oh? Well, of course, Lee." Mama put down the spatula and called down to the basement for Daddy to come up. He had been working on a new invention of some sort for the past week. We were seldom told about those inventions of his, because he always had "a few knots to wrinkle out first."

"What gives, Lyd?" he asked, passing his oily rag across his face to wipe away the perspiration. The oven had heated up the already too warm kitchen. Even the portable fan did not help much. Summer was summer and you expected it to be sweltering in July.

"Maybe you'd better stop in the bathroom and wash your face and hands, Paul. That rag is only making you face dirty," Suggested Mama. "Lee wants to speak with us privately about something."

"Oh, yeah?" He stared at Maggie's beau, and then went to clean up.

Mama shooed us out of the house and led Lee into the living room where Maggie was waiting.

He and Maggie had been "keeping company" for almost five years. They were in love and wanted permission to marry.

"And what about your aunt and uncle, Lee?" enquired Mama. Daddy was already protesting. "No, no, no! She's too young."

"Daddy," Maggie reminded him, "This is my twentieth birthday. Lee is already twenty three. There's nothing to stop us from going down to City Hall and having a judge marry us-only I would rather be married with my family there and with everyone's blessing."

"You won't get that, Maggie. Not from everyone, but you have mine. Paul? They're in love, just as we were. I do not want her feeling about her family the way I did when I married you. Mama wouldn't even announce our wedding and my sisters weren't there; only your sisters, remember?"

"But we were both Lutheran, Lydia. Lee, here is Catholic."

"I'll marry her in your church," Lee said, putting his arms about Maggie. "I love and respect my aunt and uncle; they've devoted their lives to raising me but

Maggie's right; we're old enough to make our own decisions. And, I promise, your daughter will not have to turn Catholic. We've already talked this through."

"Well, Paul, you always wanted a son. Now it appears you're about to have one." Mama stared at her husband, her eyes swimming with tears. "God isn't Lutheran and He isn't Catholic and He certainly didn't care what part of Germany your folks or mine came from or whether you were an orphan or not, even though Mama did. In my estimation, we've done just fine, and so will they."

"Daddy?" Maggie's eyes were pleading with him.

"Mr. Renz?"

"Okay, but none of the "Daddy" stuff, Lee. You're a grown man and Lydia's right; I've wanted a son for a long time. Guess this is the only way I'll ever get one."

"Four, Paul. You have three more daughters to marry off," reminded Mama.

We three daughters had sneaked back into the kitchen and were listening in on their "private" conversation. Now we gave whoops of welcome. We were finally going to have a brother.

"Not until November, though. I want a fall wedding. I've always wanted a fall wedding."

"Thank you." Lee was shaking Mama's and Daddy's hands.

That night, after supper, he placed a gold ring with a solitaire diamond on Maggie's third finger. It had been his mother's engagement ring.

Our sister was engaged to be married!

Chapter 40

The long walk to King High was one filled with enjoyment. Lisa and I became fast friends. She was not in my homeroom, since her name began with a D and mine with an R. We had English together as well as typing, a subject I selected because a writer had to be able to type. I had also selected German as a foreign language but kept it a secret until report card time. Mama and Daddy looked at me out of the corners of their eyes when they discovered that I might be able to understand some of their private conversations. I pretended to know much more than I actually did, since the first semester consisted of only the basics, such as the alphabet and its pronunciation, the numbers one through a hundred and such phrases as *ent schuldegen sie, bitte*- pardon me, please.

King High had a little theater, so I enrolled in the drama group. It was my desire to become a stagehand, thinking it might help me in writing my plays to know exactly how long it took to set up a scene. Here, in this most modern of settings, with teachers young enough to be flexible, I met with a brick wall. A girl was not considered strong enough to be a stagehand. It was not lady-like. No amount of begging changed anyone's mind. In disgust, I dropped out of that group and signed up for fencing.

Armed with a foil, chest protector and mask, I emulated Errol Flynn in his roles of swashbuckler. Next came tennis. Maggie lent me her racquet. She and Lee were so beautiful on the tennis court, she with her bright blond hair and he so darkly handsome, his skin a lovely olive shade by summer's end. Both dressed in white, he with his sweater sleeves over his shoulder and tied in front, his long legs neatly clearing the net to hug her or console her, depending on their game. I envied them completely and wished I could have somebody to care for me that way but a gangly thirteen year old is lucky to have a girl partner.

Field hockey, working on the school paper and acceptance into the acapella choir, all served to make attending my chosen school both interesting and exciting. The school- work came easily, as usual, so my grades hovered in the A's and B's, insuring my continuation as a student there.

Because Daddy now had an income, Mama finally gave up her job at Schuster's and her sewing machine kept her busy as she "ran up" the seams on Maggie's wedding and Vi's maid of honor gowns.

It was to be a quiet wedding, the ceremony private because Lee's relatives had refused to attend. Maggie had no intention of filling the bride's side of the church with her relatives and letting him stand there, alone, with the pews on the groom's side mockingly empty.

Invitations were sent out for the reception, to be held at our house. It meant a lot of cooking and cleaning but Aunt Elsie, Cousin Bernice, Tante Kate and Great Aunt Alice had all volunteered to help.

Between school work, extra curricular activities and trying to keep Laura's spirits up, this being the first time she and I had not attended the same school together, and preparations for the wedding, the weeks sped by. Halloween had been just another night. Daddy did carve a pumpkin to set in the window but there was no costume party this year. Instead, we went to the movie house.

Once a week the theater offered "dish night." You not only saw a double feature, cartoon and newsreel but, for your fifteen cents, received a free piece of what was later termed "Depression glass."

Pink, with a design of flowers imprinted into it, each piece was well made and would look nice on Maggie's and Lee's table. With six of us attending faithfully, we would have a full set to offer as a wedding present. Maggie and Lee sat in seats apart from ours but that was okay; we understood that for them it was "a date."

Luckily, none of us dropped our dishes because Mama brought along a shopping bag and newspapers to wrap the dish in but inevitably, especially when the movie was a mystery thriller, someone in the theater accidentally sent one crashing in a splash of glass and had to purchase another ticket to receive a replacement. The larger serving pieces took two weeks to receive; the first week we were given only a coupon to be turned in the following week in exchange for a vegetable dish or gravy boat, etc.

Daddy seldom attended because he was usually too tired from working the long hours he put in at Greendale. Not content to merely supervise, he figured out ways to make the heating systems better and the installations easier. He even made some of the special pipes at home, in our basement, and tied and wired them to the top of his square old second hand Hupmobile, our present Phyllis, to carry to "the job."

Sometimes, in the newsreels, we had glimpses of what was happening over in Europe. It had nothing to do with us, of course, but the name Adolph Hitler kept cropping up. Back in eighth grade, my history teacher had told us about Hitler's book, *Mein Kampf,* (My Struggle) in which he had stated over and over again that he would one day conquer most or all of Europe. His followers, according to my teacher, were called Naz-eyes. In the newsreels, they were called Nazis. We watched him speak and laughed; he reminded us of Charlie Chaplin, with his little cookie duster mustache and his goose-stepping henchmen. Our concern was what would be happening in November.

I would be turning fourteen in November. Nobody seemed to remember that. The morning of my birthday, I asked if I would be having a birthday cake.

"Oh, my goodness, it's your birthday!" Mama remarked and worried about how she would have time to bake anything.

"I know, I'll ask Tante Kate to do the honors." Tante Kate was presently living with Aunt Elsie and Uncle Franz. The little cottage she had owned when she and her late husband lived there had been rented out because his insurance money had finally run out.

"You don't have to; I guess I can get along without a cake. After all, Maggie is the important one right now." Fine words spoken with a heavy, jealous heart.

"Oh, Jessie, that's not the way it is. We love you and want you to have a nice birthday, it's just that, with the wedding so close …" Mama's hug sent me off to school feeling martyred.

My favorite cake was not on the table. Instead, Tante Kate had made an angel food cake with a hole in the center, which she had filled with the last of the daisies growing in the yard. She had also rummaged up fourteen candles, most of which, having barely made it through the hot summer, resembled bent oldsters.

Supper was eaten in a hurry and the birthday song sung at a fast clip. The family was heading to Sears Roebuck where Daddy was to be fitted for a suit.

Nobody had thought to buy or make me a birthday present, so Mama said, "For your birthday, now that you're fourteen, Jessie, I'm going to let you select you own dress. How will that be?"

Well, at least she was acknowledging that I was no longer a child, even if it would be two full years before I was to be allowed to date.

While Daddy was looking over the men's suits, insisting on navy blue serge. Laura and I headed for the dress department.

"Girls dresses are over here," Laura reminded me.

"I'm not interested in girls' dresses. Mama said I could pick out my very own and I'm no longer a child." I entered the ladies dress section. Keeping in mind that we were not rich, I searched until I found the clearance rack. Most of the dresses were way too big but I finally spotted one of maroon taffeta with wide lapels and a dickey of flowered satin. Down the entire front of the dress were flowered satin buttons.

When I tried it on I saw myself as "older." Of course, my too thin frame did not exactly fill out the top but the lapels hid that problem.

"Do you like it?" I asked Laura.

"We-ll, it makes you look rather old. Maybe you should look in the girls' department."

"No! This suits me just fine." Handing the saleslady the five dollars, I said, "I'll take it."

Not one person seemed to like the dress but I did. To me it showed that I was a year older. Sure, Maggie's wedding was in two weeks but my birthday was now! I was important, too, wasn't I?

The dress was too long. With a sigh, knowing she had to stick to her bargain and not make me exchange the dress, Mama cut it two inches shorter and hemmed it.

Chapter 41

The day of the wedding arrived, finally. Maggie was going to be a beautiful bride. Aunt Arlene, in spite of Lee's being a Catholic, had made the veil and headpiece as a wedding gift and also Vi's headpiece. Both dresses were of moiré, Vi's in a deep rose.

I wondered how Vi felt, being the oldest and having Maggie get married before her but I saw no tears nor frowns. My two sisters were not truly close, as they had once been, but they loved each other. Vi's generous heart bore no grudges.

Aunt Arlene had not asked if she could come to the wedding. She made that decision herself so she could make certain her nieces looked perfect and, of course, Uncle Bill was there to transport her. In fact, after checking out the Hupmobile, he offered to take the bride to the church in his new Cadillac.

Somehow, Aunt Rose and Uncle Max arrived "ahead of time," as well. Then Aunt Elsie and Uncle Franz made their appearance. Tante Kate had wandered over before breakfast, "to make sure the bridegroom did not show up to see the bride before the wedding, since that was bad luck."
Our house had an attic. I had sneaked upstairs with some purloined objects and proceeded to dress before the old pier glass mirror that had once been Grandmother Renz's, about the only thing Daddy had to remind him that he had once had a mother.

Hitching my silk hose to the garter belt, I fastened each button of the dress, stepped into my new patent leather shoes and tiptoed downstairs.

Aunt Rose spotted me and gave a gasp. "Oh, good heavens, Jessie, hurry out of that awful dress and get on your wedding finery. It's almost time to head for the church!" Whereupon she reached for the dress and in her haste to unbutton it, accidentally tore off one of the buttons. I, meanwhile, had tried to escape her hands and discovered, to our horror, that the buttons had all been attached with loose basting stitches.

The dress fell open and there I stood, in full view of my uncles and all the others in the room, without a slip, wearing Vi's size 36 bra stuffed with cotton and tissues, her garter belt pinned at the sides to help hold up my hosiery!

I let out a shriek, headed for the bathroom and locked myself in, my sobs loud enough to cause a contrite aunt to apologize and insist that she would do her best to correct everything if I would only open the door.

Doing so, at last, when Mama told me to "either come out or Daddy would remove the hinges," I was wrapped in her bathrobe while she and my aunts busied themselves sewing the buttons back in place.

An embarrassed and angry Vi relieved me of her undergarments and I donned my own small bra and a slip and obediently held my hose in place with round elastic garters.

"I just wanted to look my age" I tearfully explained, carefully avoiding my uncles' grins.

"What age is that, Jessie, thirty five?" was Aunt Rose's exasperated inquiry.

Subdued, red-eyed and red-nosed, I sat through the wedding ceremony, uncertain whether my tears were for my sister or myself. Everyone else looked so lovely and here I was, in that ugly dress I had selected myself, with only myself to blame for how I appeared!

The reception was held at home. Our relatives had each contributed food. Tante Kate had made the three tiered wedding cake topped with a small bride and groom beneath a flowery arch.

Uncle Franz had brought along his concertina, which he played sporadically throughout the evening. Vi's current boyfriend had brought along an 8mm movie camera and took pictures of the receiving line that included our Grandmother. It was the first time she had ever visited our house. Two of the uncles had assisted her up the stairs and ensconced her in one of the two wing-back chairs that Mama had purchased on sale at Schuster's, she receiving her employee discount as well, so she could afford both.

There would be no honeymoon. At the end of the evening, Lee and Maggie were driven to their small rented apartment in Uncle Bill's Cadillac.

A few days later our blushing sister related that someone had visited their apartment the day of the wedding and hidden alarm clocks about, each one set an hour apart.

"Uncle Bill had handed Lee a bottle of champagne for us to drink together. We finally polished off the whole bottle and let the darn clocks run down!"

Nobody ever confessed to the dastardly deed.

Chapter 42

It was during the wedding reception that I became acquainted with Grandmother. She motioned for me to sit in the matching wingback chair and informed me that she had heard about my embarrassing experience of the morning.

"There is only one way to counteract embarrassment, Jessica, and that is to hold your head high, chin up. You are now in high school and will one day be a young woman. I once fell into the pigpen at a neighbor's farm, down the road from our house. There were boys in that place, a number of them, all laughing their heads off at my predicament. There I was, covered from head to toe in the vilest smelling stuff and they were laughing! I looked each of them in the eye and put my chin up as if I were a princess dressed in the most beautiful silks and jewels."

Looking at her, this majestic woman seated in that wingback, sale-priced and discounted chair as if it were a royal throne, it was almost impossible to picture her as ever being a young girl, especially one decorated with pig manure.

"What happened then, Grandma?"

"Why, a few days later the oldest boy, Juneau, came calling, wanting to be my best beau!"

"And was he?"

"Oh, goodness, no! I was barely fifteen. My father ran him off. A good thing, too, because a year later he eloped with another girl and they ended up with thirteen children! Besides, three years later I met your grandfather."

The tone of her voice told me she still missed him. For the first time I saw her as someone with feelings.

The next time I headed for Bay View I called on Grandmother, having phoned her ahead of time to make certain I would be welcome. It was the first of many visits to her lovely lower Flat on Rusk Avenue and Linebarger Terrace.

From her I learned what it was like to grow up in a log cabin with Indians still around. Friendly Indians squaws, who visited with her mother. She and her sisters rode a large, swayback horse to school, all three of them perched on his uncomplaining back, with only a blanket for a saddle.

From her, also, I learned to eat cottage cheese with a dab of grape jelly as a garnish, and to sip coffee from a saucer, "like in the old days." There was a sparkle of impishness in her eyes when we did this as her housekeeper frowned and shook her head. I learned the reason why there were teaspoon holders on the table, special glasses holding bouquets of teaspoons. They were a throwback from the days when, during threshing season or, in her parent's case, apple gathering time, workers would stop in for coffee and it was handy to have spoons available for them to individually sugar their drinks and stir, taking a clean spoon each time so they would not get the sugar wet.

One afternoon, when she was feeling spry, Grandmother asked me to accompany her to the footbridge that crossed railroad tracks located in a deep ravine running parallel to Linebarger Terrace. The walk was about a half block of level ground but the footbridge arched upward and she would have had to use both her cane and pull herself up the incline with her good arm. I took her cane and gave her my youthful strength as assistance and together we reached to top of the arch.

"Now we wait," she said.

"For what, Grandma?"

"You'll see."

Meanwhile, we studied the layout of the drop forge at the other end of the footbridge. Every so often the entire earth would shake, something felt even inside of Grandmother's well-constructed abode, the cause being the huge drop forge machinery in motion

"Doesn't that bother you, Grandma?"

"It took some getting used to but after all these years, no, anymore than that fog horn calling out to ships and boaters on the lake. Now *that* I heard from my cradle back in the log house. We were only about two city blocks from the water back then, but up on a high bluff."

Suddenly, we heard a train whistle and down the tracks below came the barreling steam engine and cars. Closer and closer they came and, as if in greeting to us, the engineer let out a heavy blast of steam and she and I were enveloped in a cloud of it.

We clapped our hands and laughed in glee, my forebear and I, two kindred souls wrapped in a blanket of vapor that soon dispersed as the train sped along to its destination.

Leaning heavily on me, as we descended back to the earth leading to Rusk Avenue, Grandmother said, "That was really fun. I haven't done that since your mother was a child."

It was she, too, who had me drop the "s" from anyways, making me look up the word in the dictionary. "If you are to be a good writer, you must use the best grammar. Read, read, read and use that dictionary until you know your language by heart!" she advised.

Those were special moments that I still treasure. I stand at her grave and remember that day on the footbridge when I learned that deep in my heart I loved not only her but all those who had come before us. Our heritage, reaching how far back we shall never know, but each one contributing a small piece of us, some of which we shared together, some of which she had passed on down to me....

Chapter 43
1938

One day my homeroom teacher introduced us to a tall, heavy-boned girl named Rutta, a new student who had dark circles under her eyes, as if she never slept well and who spoke with a heavy Germanic accent. She was not very friendly, fending off all who attempted to speak to her. She was from Czechoslovakia, we learned, and was here, in America, because her family had been murdered by the Nazi soldiers. How horrible! Here we were, safe in America, and that poor girl had lost her entire family!

It was whispered that Rutta had been raped by those murdering soldiers, then shot and left to die. One of the girls in our class who knew the family that had taken her in, some relative or other, had told us about her.

I had never heard the word "rape" before and discovered that it meant "to be forcibly, sexually ravaged." No wonder she was so silent! She must have hurt so much! One day I reached out and took her hand. Her brown eyes filled with tears and she turned her face away.

"Its okay, Rutta. I see you as a very brave person. I just wish nothing had ever happened to you. We all feel like that. We want to be your friends."

"I feel dirty!" She whispered. "I'll never feel clean again."

"Yes you will. My mother says time and God heals all our wounds."

"I hate God."

"It's okay. I'm sure He understands why. Only, I'm sure He still loves you anyway."

A few weeks later she was found hanging in the basement of her relatives' home. Poor Rutta. I had never read *Mein Kampf* but I hated that Adolph Hitler and his gang of Nazis. Now he and his little cookie duster mustache no longer made us laugh. He was no Charlie Chaplin at all but some sort of monster. I prayed that somehow he would be stopped dead in his tracks and the people in Europe would be free of him. Little did I know that his ambitions would reach out to touch my life. In a way, because of Rutta, they already had but that was only the preliminary.

Laura was now a freshman and I a sophomore. Back in LaFollette School they had moved her up a grade. It was nice having her as my companion again. We both liked Lisa, who graciously included Laura's friends in our walks to and from school.

There had been no problem in enrolling Laura at King High. Just a call to the school board and she, too, was accepted there. Like me, she was required to keep up her grades and together we helped each other with homework.

I was still baby-sitting on weekends. One Friday night Aunt Elsie phoned to ask if I would be willing to spend a few hours sitting for her new neighbors who did not know anyone yet.

"I don't really know them, Jessie, but they're new here in America. They have heavy German accents. So do their two children."

Remembering Rutta, I felt sorry for them. They, too, had probably come here to escape that monster, Hitler. Of course I would help them out. Their house was not centrally heated; the warmth coming from coal stoves in the kitchen and living room. The door to the children's room was kept open so they, too, could obtain some warmth.

The Meyers proved to be in their mid-thirties. Both were scrawny with fierce, piercing eyes, as if they were seeing right into your very brain. I really did not like them but their two children were darling little ones, with rosy cheeks and cute German accents. Due to my courses in German, I was able to understand them when they lapsed into that language.

"Ve return at eleven, ja?" Mrs. Meyer told me. "Ve visit friends." It was a scanty bit of information and they had no phone. I would be on my own in caring for the children. Hopefully, there would be no problem but Aunt Elsie and Uncle Franz were just next door. So were Bernice and Rudy.

Bernice never baby-sat. She was a nice friendly girl, a few years old than

Laura and me, but painfully shy with strangers. A very poor reader, she had barely made it through the fifth grade and was finally allowed to remain home, supposedly to be tutored by her mother. Aunt Elsie was not neglectful but she knew that her daughter was unable to learn more from books. Perhaps Bernice was dyslexic but in those days that was not a recognized problem. She was considered to be mentally "slow." Once labeled as such, that was the end of it.

Rudy, on the other hand, was a brilliant student and a tall and handsome fellow, who golfed, played the trombone in a band and teased his cousins and Bernice unmercifully. Of the two of them, I preferred Bernice.

Having tucked the Meyer children into their beds and telling them, *Gute Nacht*, I took my homework into the small living room and did my lessons.

I wished I had thought to bring along a book to read. I was also feeling chilly, even after adding coal to both stoves. Perhaps, somewhere, there was an extra blanket or an afghan.

There was nothing on the shelf of the front hall closet. Possibly the Meyer's bedroom closet contained a blanket or something. Tiptoeing in, I opened the closet door, feeling guilty at trespassing but feeling the cold more. There was a blanket but there was something else and I felt a cold chill down my back as I turned on the lamp on the dresser to closely examine the uniform hanging there.

It was identical to those I had seen in the newsreels. There in that closet was a Nazi officer's uniform! Hurriedly, I closed the door against it and sought warmth from my coat. How dare the Meyers come here to America with their Nazi ideas! Had it not been for those two sleeping children, I would have fled their house immediately and rushed home to tell Mama and Daddy.

They returned at exactly eleven, paid me the fifty cents they owed me and I left, hurrying out into the darkness of Eighth Street and around the corner, past the church, past Lisa's house and into ours. Mama was waiting up for me, as usual, and listened to my story about that closet and what it held.

"You're sure it was a Nazi uniform, Jessie?"

"Oh, yes, Mama. And they were the ones who made Rutta hang herself! We have to do something. Tell somebody!"

"I'm not sure who to tell, Jessie. Perhaps the police would be interested. We'll see. You get to bed now. No more baby-sitting for strangers. I'll have a talk with Aunt Elsie in the morning. She can keep an eye on them. I'm sure that would be right up Rudy's alley." Rudy had aspirations of becoming a detective.

Mama contacted the police, who were very non-committal, telling her that this was America and people had the right to whatever beliefs they wanted to hold. Still concerned, she phoned the local office of the Federal Bureau of Investigation. A few days later, a well-dressed man stood at our door and showed us a badge identifying himself as a Federal Bureau of Investigation agent. He gave his name as Joseph Johnson. Mama invited him in, gave him coffee and one of her freshly baked sweet rolls and called me into the kitchen to answer his questions.

"The uniform you saw, Jessie, could you identify it from pictures I will show you?" he asked.

"I-I think so."

Reaching into his briefcase, he withdrew several photos. They were black and white but I was able to select the one that seemed to match the uniform I had seen hanging in that closet. My eye for detail had served me well, evidently, for he let out his breath and nodded. "Now, Jessica, can you describe the man and woman who hired you to sit with their children?" I closed my eyes, summoned their faces from my memory store and described each as I recalled them, adding, "They have really thick German accents. So do the children."

"Good girl, Jessie. Mrs. Renz, thank you for contacting us. Most people would not have done that. I now ask both of you to not mention my visit nor make any special event of Jessie having spotted that uniform. In other words, don't do or say anything that might draw special attention to their house. Our agents will be keeping the couple under surveillance."

"Mr. Johnson, why would a Nazi officer be here in the United States?"

His eyes met mine and I saw the seriousness in them. "Milwaukee is made up of a large population of people who came here from Germany. Many of those are sympathetic to Mr. Hitler's cause."

"Whatever for? Germany is way over in Europe. We come from a German background, too, but I don't feel any loyalty to Germany and especially not to that Adolph Hitler. Look what he did to Rutta." I explained about my pitiful fellow student and her suicide.

Mama patted my hand and nodded. "My father came from Germany. So did my husband's parents. My husbandl and I and our children are Americans by birth. I feel no loyalty to Germany."

"There are those who came here because Germany was having so many problems due to the losing of the war. Now, with Hitler in charge and the United States in the throes of a financial depression, Germany looks good to them again. We believe that people like the Meyers are being sent here to contact them and secure funds and to find out exactly how much sympathy there is here in this country for Nazism."

He left with our promises of silence. We were both glad that Mama had said nothing, as yet, to Aunt Elsie.

Several months later, Gerda Neuhaus, one of the more athletic girls, a senior, made it her business to sit at Laura's and my lunch table.

"You both were in German classes. Do your parents speak German?"

"Only when they don't want us to know what they're saying," grinned Laura.

She laughed. "So they came over here from Germany?"

"No. They were both born here. So was our mother's mother. The other three grandparents came here, though."

"Haven't they ever been there to see where their parents came from? To Germany?"

"No. We're not rich. How could they afford to? Our Great Aunt Beatrice and Uncle George went there a few years ago. He was born there but he came here when he was fifteen. All by himself. He has a great deal of money. He calls himself a self-made man," I bragged. We were all proud of Uncle George and his ability to make money. Unlike Cousin Jasper, he never flaunted his wealth. He and Aunt Beatrice led quiet lives in a house that was beautiful inside but not spectacular like the houses in the movies.

"Aunt Alice went with them, supplied Laura.

"I can see that you come from good, solid backgrounds. I would like to know both of you better." She kept toying with the Indian bracelet made of woven beads that encircled her strong wrist. I studied it, deciding I could weave one like it on Lisa's bead loom that she had made at Girl Scout camp.

Several times a week Gerda ate lunch with us, each time learning more about us and finally she approached us with a proposition. "How would you two like to spend a couple of weeks at a youth camp?" Laura and I exchanged raised eyebrow looks. Lisa was always telling us about what fun she had at camp. We were both interested. "But what would it cost us?"

"Not a single penny. It's a special camp, paid for with special funds. You just have to know how to speak German and come from good, solid German backgrounds."

"Where is the camp?" I asked.

"Up north a ways. Near Sheboygan. It's loads of fun and there are many handsome boys there.

"Boys? At the same camp as the girls?"

"Well, they don't share tents, if that's what you're asking. There's boating and folk dancing and hiking and lots of activities. Talk your parents into letting you go. You'll really enjoy it, I promise. A bus will take you there and back again."

"Will you be there, too, Gerda?" Laura inquired.

"Of course. I'm one of the counselors."

Once more I studied her bracelet. Lisa had lent me her loom and even supplied me with a large jar of beads. I would need mostly blue beads, some yellow and red for the birds and a black one for the crossed Z in the center. I was certain I could copy it. "Write down the details and I'll ask them," I told her.

It took me two days to make the bracelet but when Lisa saw it, she said I had done it wrong. "The Indians make this in reverse. Or rather, this is in reverse from their sacred symbol."

"But, it's exactly like Gerda's."

"Oh, that Nazi! I can't stand her. That's not an Indian sign, silly, it's a Nazi swastika."

My heart gave a big leap. "A swastika! You mean, like on the Nazi flag?"

"Yes. We were studying that in civics just the other day. And now that I look at them, those birds represent the mythical Phoenix that rises up out of the ashes of a fire. It's more of Hitler's symbols of the Third Reich."

"Lisa, has Gerda ever approached you to go to a youth camp?"

Lisa laughed. "With my Dad an Italian and my mother French? Don't be silly. That camp is for good little Germans who worship Hitler. She's recruited quite a number of silly geese for that. I heard that some of those who went last year are signing up for a cruise to Germany on the S.S. Bremerhaven, all expenses paid. They'll live in youth camps over there." Feeling sick to my stomach, I told Mama what Lisa had revealed. She called Laura to her side and spoke to us very seriously. "We are Americans, through and through. When my grandfather and grandmother came to this country, it was to make a new start. Here they did just that. Yes, right now money is scarce. It was for them, too, at first, but there is nothing here to keep any of us from doing what we truly want do to, if we work for it.

"My grandfather knew back in Germany, that he would never be able to own his own land. His older brother inherited that. Here, he was able to purchase acre after acre and plant trees and became well known for his orchards.

"My father came here because he, too, wanted a future. He did well for himself, as you can see from how your grandmother lives. We don't need anything from Germany that you don't already have in your bloodstream and we certainly don't owe Mr. Hitler one single thing that I can think of.

"You tell that Gerda person that you will have nothing to do with her youth camp nor anything else connected with Germany. Do you hear me?"

We both nodded. I could see the disappointment in Laura's eyes because she wanted to go to the camp, if only for the activities. Mama saw it, too, and said, "This summer I'm enrolling both of you in our church's camp. There will be all the fun that other camp promised and neither of you will be falling into the wrong hands."

The next day, when Gerda sat down at our table, I studied her bracelet. Yes, I had copied it correctly and it *was* a swastika she wore. She began to tell us more about the camp offer and I told her that we were no longer interested.

"Why?"

"Because we're Americans and not GERMANS and nothing in the world will ever turn us into NAZIS!" I had half shouted it and heads turned our way.

Her hand shot out and grabbed my wrist, twisting it, and there was hatred in her eyes. "Just wait until Hitler takes over this country like he's doing in Europe and then tell me you won't be a Nazi. You'll all be," and her other hand came down sharply on my wrist. Luckily, it was my left hand that had to wear a sling for two weeks. Gerda was called to the office and told she could no longer attend King High. We did not learn more about that but she was out of our lives.

That summer a group of teen-agers of German heritage left for Germany on the S.S. Bremerhaven. Word came back that those who had been born there were kept there in youth camps "to make babies for Germany" and were not allowed to return to the United States. Perhaps it was only rumor but then again, perhaps it was not. I had no wish to find out.

Laura and I spent two glorious weeks at church camp where the theme was "love one another," not hate your enemy or Jews or anybody else in the world. I crossed my fingers when I said the words "I shall always love my neighbor as myself" because in my heart I despised everything the Nazis stood for. Rutta was gone but as long as I lived she would not be forgotten.

Looking back, I can make comparisons. While Hitler, in his part of the world, was destroying cities, my father had been helping to build one. Greendale was almost a complete community and Daddy had reason to be proud, for each of the homes was well- heated, due to his and his fellow workers' labors.

During the early stages of construction, First Lady Eleanor Roosevelt had visited Greendale accompanied by the regional director of federally sponsored women's programs, Florence Kerr, and both women had reached out to shake my father's hand and quietly ask intelligent questions about his phase of the project. That was a night to celebrate and we did, calling up my friends and relatives to tell them that our father had actually shaken the hand of the First Lady. Vi had even taken a chunk of clay and had Daddy press his hand into it so everyone could see the hand that had been shaken by such a celebrated person. I had carried that clay to school and in a spirit of patriotism and kindness, my seventh grade teacher had it baked in a kiln by an artist friend. The entire class had known that my father was some sort of celebrity, if only for the moment.

We were proud of our father's accomplishments. Like our forebears, he was a builder and not a destroyer. A creator of things. It had not been his fault that the Depression had come along and brought him to his knees but those same knees were bent in work.

When the first of the houses in Greendale was open to the public for inspection, we were there to see first hand what Government money and our father's abilities had wrought. Oh, of course, there were the carpenters and stone masons and all the others who helped to put that community on the map, from those who turned the first earth with their shovels to those who put the caps on the chimneys, but our own father had been the one in whom we felt the most pride, naturally.

Back in 1928, Martin Krieger had started the same sort of project but this one had become a reality and not a nightmare and had given new life and hope to those who built it and to those who moved in and became home owners for the first time. I suppose we, too, could have purchased one of the homes. Why we did not is a question no one is alive to answer.

Chapter 44

Throughout the years of the Depression, on nice Sunday afternoons, when my father had enough gas for whatever "Phyllis" he presently owned, we would go on short trips out to the country. Often we would stop at a certain farm where he and Mama would purchase and down fresh glasses of buttermilk. The barn was the usual red with the usual Wisconsin stone and cement base that housed the dairy herd. We girls hated buttermilk but we enjoyed the bovine sounds, if not the smell, and would walk along the cement walkway between the stanchions and pet the cows.

It was a beautiful Sunday afternoon in early June when, as usual, we heard a loud "pop" and yes, Phyllis had a flat tire. Up ahead was a farm though not the one that sold the buttermilk. We could see the farmer moving back and forth in his yard. He also noticed us and Dad had no sooner placed the jack under the axle and did his usual cussing as he unloosed the nuts on the bolts that held the wheel in place when the farmer strode our way.

Tante Kate was with us, which probably contributed to the flat tire, since it was on the right back wheel where she had, as usual, been pushed into the car and, turning, flopped into place, causing Vi, Laura and me to squeeze into whatever space was left. Once ensconced, Tante Kate could not maneuver her bulk to give us more room. Poor Vi often had either Laura or me on her lap during the trip.

"Looks like you folks could use some help." The man in the blue and white striped overalls was young, not much older than Vi. His reddish blond curls, ruddy complexion and wide shoulders exuded an aura of good health and his grin showed strong white teeth. He was speaking to Daddy but looking at Vi with evident approval.

In no time he had the tire off the rim and was patching and pumping up the inner tube. We women, meanwhile, accepted his invitation to "go on up to the house. My folks are home and they always enjoy company."

Upon reaching the sun porch of the house, Mama and the woman stared at each other and suddenly were giving exclamations of recognition and exchanging hugs.

"Lydia Hohenfeldt! I cant's believe it! Why, how many years has it been-twenty five? But it's no longer Hohenfeldt, is it?" reaching out to each of us and patting a shoulder here and a head there. She was assisting Tante Kate up the two wooden steps and onto a porch glider.

"Why, Ellen," Mama declared, "This is wonderful! I knew you had married a farmer but we had no idea where your farm was located. Girls, this is my best friend from back in grade school. Oh, dear, I don't know your last name, Ellen. And is that young man who's helping my Paul with the flat tire your son?"

"It's Klein. Mrs. Thomas Klein, and yes, that's my son, Tom Junior. I also have three daughters, all of them married and with families of their own."

We were treated to glasses of lemonade while our mother and Mrs. Klein caught up on twenty five years of events in their lives.

Soon Dad and Tom Junior drove into the yard and Daddy was introduced all around, as was Ellen's son.

"Why don't you show the girls the farm, Tom?" suggested his mother.

We were given the grand tour but it was to Vi that he spoke. There were pigs, geese, chickens of many types, several sheep and lambs, and a black and white long-haired dog that alternately licked our hands and dashed ahead and back again as if he were the one doing the guiding. Most of the cows were out in the field, munching on grass that would eventually turn into milk and cream. A huge bull was tethered inside the barn that, as usual, was made of fieldstone, cement and wood painted red.

Climbing the ladder to the hay mow, the four of us sat, sniffing the wonderful fresh-hay smell as Tom, chewing on the end of a stem of sweet grass, gave us a short history of himself. He had attended high school and had two years of agricultural school behind him. His father was too ill to work much so he would be taking over the farm. Money was scarce, as it was for everybody, but there was always plenty of food.

When we finally left, after a supper of fried chicken, mashed potatoes and gravy, yellow beans and dried apple pie, Tom had asked and been granted the privilege of "calling on Vi" the following Saturday. There was going to be a barn dance on a farm 'up the road." She could spend the night, since, with his sisters married off, there were plenty of extra bedrooms.

It was the beginning of a romance that, the following January, culminated in marriage. Vi was to be a farmer's wife and she loved the entire idea. She and Tom's mother had become the best of friends.

Great Aunt Alice made Vi's wedding gown. Her eyes glistened with tears as she measured and cut into flowered gingham. "I always prayed that I would last long enough to make your wedding gown," she declared.

"But, Aunt Alice, that looks more like a house dress," Laura told her.

"That's exactly what it is. It's an old custom and a good one. First I use the pattern to make this and *then* I do it up in the beautiful French silk that I have kept in my cedar chest just for this occasion. I purchased it in Paris. The lace is Alencon. Just you wait and see how beautiful a bride your sister will be. And no, this dress will not be floor length. It will be her first house dress as a married woman."

She was right. Wearing a headpiece and veil that Aunt Arlene had designed especially for her and with we, her sisters, dressed in aqua taffeta with feather headpieces, the wedding procession down that aisle was beautiful. In fact, her wedding was absolutely perfect.

My sixteenth birthday had come and gone without my having a boyfriend. It had been a nice party, with my favorite cake and many gifts, unlike the one preceding Maggie's wedding, but the magic number sixteen, when we were finally allowed to date, had produced not even a prince-turned-toad. My mirror still reflected a plain Jane but not quite so plain as before, because those "darned bumps" had turned into nicely rounded contours and my newer hairstyle formed a frame around my face that flattered rather than detracted.

Tom had male cousins who swung me around the dance floor of the rented hall. They stomped rather than danced but that was fine with me because most of them were so tall that I was able to avoid their large feet. In high school I had become a member of a jitterbug team but none of these fellows knew how to jitterbug. No matter. Perhaps I was not the best piano player but I had rhythm. I could follow their leads. We had no dance cards but if we had, mine would have been filled. A good time was had by all.

This time, Grandmother did not attend. She had fallen and was confined to bed. It was Aunt Alice who pulled me down beside her and questioned me about my future.

"All this nonsense about becoming a missionary in Africa is quite enough, Jessica Renz. I want to know what it is you really want for yourself."

"To be a good writer, I suppose, Aunt Alice. I've always loved words. Only, I don't believe I'll ever get to college. I'm taking secretarial subjects in school so I can get a job, like Maggie has. It's what is necessary so I can help out with family finances."

"Those include shorthand and typing?"

"And bookkeeping, which I hate."

"All good things to know, Jessie, but you have your entire future ahead of you, child. I would like to read something you've written."

"Really? Nobody else seems interested. Except Mama of course, but then, she's prejudiced in my favor, being my mother and all."

"Well, I believe I can do it justice without a jaundiced eye. You bring something along next time you're out my way."

Sadly, Aunt Alice never saw my writings. Two weeks after the wedding she was found dead in her bed, having quietly slept away during the night. It was as if a great mountain had sunk into the earth, leaving the landscape barren… She had been so strong, so much a part of our lives.

As we stood beside her casket, one after another declared, "She did have her wish, she sewed Vi's wedding gown with her own hands."

Clyde was given the honor of being one of the pallbearers. I believe he probably wished his taxicab was large enough to hold her coffin. He looked fine in his new black suit as he stood beside her bier during the visitation. It seemed fitting that this man, who had carried her so many places over the years, would assist in carrying her to her final resting place in the family plot in Forest Home

Cemetery where she would lie beside her parents.

Vi was devastated at the loss of her godmother but Tom was there to lean on and when their first child, a son, was born the following year, his christening gown was made from the balance of the bolt of French silk from which Aunt Alice had cut her wedding gown.

Chapter 45

With Vi and Maggie married, I was now the oldest daughter living at home. It seemed childish to keep on calling my parents "Mama and Daddy" and gradually they responded to "Mom and Dad." It was what my friends called their parents and this was, after all, 1940.

Hitler's war now had our country alerted to the fact that he needed to be stopped. Many of the boys in the June graduating class were enlisting in the Armed Services. Many were my friends and it was with both pride and sadness that I told them my "good-byes" but, as Mom pointed out, at least they would not be pounding the street looking or work.

We had slipped into preparation for a possible conflict overseas, although the contracts being issued to companies by the government were termed "defense contracts."

Great Uncle George had been quietly buying up foundries that had closed down during the Depression. Now, we heard, he was standing to earn a great deal more money because they were needed for defense work and he was in a position to supply them.

Aunt Beatrice, meanwhile, was also being discussed. With her own money she had been purchasing the deeds to houses that had been lost to people who could not keep up their mortgage payments and allowing them to live in them as renters. Now, she was helping those with defense jobs to re-purchase them for almost the same amount that they had owed as balances before they lost them.

Cousin Jasper declared she must have a loose nut somewhere but she merely smiled and said, "Jasper, there is more to life than money. We both sit in the same church on Sunday but evidently hear different sermons from the pulpit. I believe it is my duty to help the fallen and downtrodden. The good Lord, above, has been more than good to me. I owe Him."

Evidently, Aunt Alice had been her accomplice. In her will she left instructions for those whose house deeds she held to be able to purchase them back at low interest and no down payment.

Her will included all of her nieces and theirs. Laura and I suddenly had five hundred dollars apiece in a trust fund to use toward college expenses "upon our graduation from high school!"

Mom, too, received money, a thousand dollars, but Dad would not accept a penny of it. "You spend it whatever way you like, Lyd. It's you money."

Aunt Alice had stipulated that the money was to be used for something that Mom would not ordinarily have been able to purchase. This meant not for household bills or food. She thought about a fur coat and decided it would make her look too fat. A better car? Dad would not allow that, since she did not drive, had no intention of ever learning to drive and a car would be something that only he would use. No way!

On a bright Saturday morning in June, she served our breakfast with a tiny smile at the corners of her lips. Dad declared that she looked like the "cat that had swallowed the canary."

From her apron pocket she produced several items cut out of the Journal and placed them beside his plate. He studied them.

"These are ads for lake lots."

"That's right, and as soon as the dishes are done, we're going out to see each of them. I think I've missed the lake cottage more than anything except my Steinway, Paul. And so have you. I'm taking half of my money and purchasing a lot and you can build us another cottage."

"With what?"

"With your own hands and whatever material you can scrounge up. Since you won't accept help from my family, you'll have to be the one to supply the cottage."

With money available once more, people were not about to sell off land cheaply. Lake lots were expensive. Every available Saturday and on Sunday afternoons we "took a drive out to the country" to visit one lake after another. Wisconsin is dotted with them, most of them carved from the land when the glaciers melted, filling valleys with pristine clear waters.

Mom had set aside five hundred dollars; the other five hundred was put into a savings account "for a rainy day." The real estate people started off showing us beautiful lots with high price tags but she continued to hold her price at five hundred. At last we were down to one lot, on a lake loaded with lily pads. I now knew that was not where babies hailed from but if they had, the sky would have been filled with low flying storks. Somewhere among those lilies there was purported to be water.

"We could all get together, even Lee and Tom, and in no time those lilies would be out of there," Mom declared, her optimism taking the forefront, as usual. In my mind I wrote an article titled, "Renz Family Sets Off on New Adventure" and peopled it with swimsuit clad family members, each with beaver-sharp teeth chewing at the stems of the lilies while those unable to swim gathered up the loosened plants with bamboo rakes and cast them ashore. Was there a market for gathered lilies or would they have to dry and become bonfires over which to toast marshmallows?

Over our protests, Mom paid four hundred dollars for that lot, which had forty feet of shoreline but was two hundred feet deep, all uphill. "We'll use the extra hundred to furnish the cottage when it's built." She told us.

Perhaps she should have insisted upon Dad using the money toward materials. Inventor or innovator, he had his own ideas of what should go on that land. It took shape in the garage at the back of our city property and one day, in late summer, he hitched it behind his latest Phyllis to tow it out to Eagle Springs Lake. Lee and Maggie, Tom and Vi, and Laura and I rode behind in Tom's car. Our "cottage" drew stares along the way as the one room "eight-by-sixteen house on wheels" hitched to Dad's latest Phyllis,wended its way along the country roads.

Until that day, none of us had been allowed to see it. We girls were not in the car with Mom and Dad so I do not know if words were spoken in English or German. I do know that inside Tom's car were four embarrassed daughters. Dad did not trust wood, so most of the "cottage" was made of sheet steel with a corrugated metal roof, metal windows and a metal chimney complete with a funnel-type "Wizard of Oz" tin-man cap.

When we reached the lake property, Gilly and Tess and their two boys were there. Hugs were exchanged between females and Mom unloaded the picnic basket while the men were organized into a "winching team."

Nobody was injured; nobody believed it would be possible to winch that Rube Goldberg creation down that hill but, by mid-afternoon, there it stood, its front propped up with sturdy tree stumps, all leveled and ready for occupancy.

Tom, who knew about such things since that was their facility out on the farm, dug a pit and the following Saturday erected a wooden "two holer."

Among the trees on the property were tall oaks and hickories that dropped acorns and bur-clad nuts onto that roof. The squirrels played tag there, each trying to garner the most nuts. Hailstones and raindrops played their own orchestrations and we lily gatherers came inside to drink coffee or Kool-aid and munch on whatever goodies Mom had brought along that particular day. Ours was the only lot sold, to date. The owners having died; the deed was discovered to have been registered in the wrong county; it would be almost a year before we would have neighbors.

Eventually, Mom's sisters and our uncles and cousins got wind of the lake property and decided to drive out to see it. Heads were shaken and undoubtedly, Dad was the butt of jokes when they returned home. By this time, he had painted everything inside and out with some of the aluminum paint he had taken on consignment during those Depression years. That one room cottage on wheels and the hillside "facility" gleamed in both sunlight and moonlight.

Tante Kate and Aunt Elsie did not get along too well when they were together every day and after a nasty quarrel, Tante Kate had packed her things into two carpetbags and tearfully made her way to our front steps. Laura and I had helped her into the house and she became "our guest."

She began to accompany us to the lake, so Dad invented an elevator of sorts so she could be winched downhill and back up again. Because she took up a great deal of space, he built a screen addition so the rest of us could find shelter and relax in folding chairs without having to crowd inside for our meals or snacks.

He had secured enough old lumber and some railroad ties that there was a pier and a railroad tie bench near the shore for her and Mom to sit and watch how the "dredging" was going. By autumn, we had enough cleared to take a boat out and fish but the following spring there they were again, lily pad upon lily pad, each with its own frog tenant. We could probably have made a fortune in frog-legs had we caught them and sold them to restaurants. In spite of everything, we had to admit that we Renz's did own "lake property." Dad termed it, "getting back on our feet."

Both Laura and I came to realize that somehow the Depression had changed our father into a "character." A good-hearted one, whom we loved dearly, but a character all the same. Somewhere along the way in his fight with poverty, our father had lost his inner pride. How things looked no longer seemed to matter except when it came to anything connected with furnaces and sheet metal. Then he was not only precise but extremely proud of the finished results.

Perhaps it started with the winter after we moved from the rooming house. Too broke to purchase goulashes for himself or us, he had cut strips of inner-tube and wrapped them about this shoes, tying them on with strips of cloth, then, taking, turns, carried one or the other of us on his shoulder all the way to Schuster's where we could tell Santa what we wanted for Christmas. We were not embarrassed by his strange footgear; on the contrary, we loved him for thinking up the means to take us to talk to Santa Clause.

Now, in our mid-teens, we allowed others to shape our perspectives. Perhaps the most embarrassing moment, for Laura, was the day I left early to work on the school paper. By the time she was ready to leave it had begun to rain, large splattering drops that would have soaked her feet and legs by the time she walked eighteen blocks.

Dad was on his way to a furnace job but willingly offered to go out of his way to drive Laura to her destination. Upon the completion of Greendale he had once more turned to furnace repair work and seemed to be earning enough to get us by with that, even without Mom's and Vi's incomes.

That morning he had a stack of metal furnace pipe "doughnuts" tied on top of the current Phyllis, a square-top car of some sort. In the trunk were his tools but the trunk handle had somehow broken off and in its place was a white china doorknob!

Had she not been in danger of being tardy, Laura would not have accepted the ride, but accept it she did and two blocks from school told Dad "You don't have to take me the rest of the way. I won't be late now and it's almost stopped raining. I can walk with my friends up ahead there."

Always the caring father, he would not listen. "No sir! I'm not letting my daughter walk in the rain! I'll take you right to the front door!" Which he did and an embarrassed Laura crept from the car with head down so none of her "friends" would recognize her. That night she cried herself to sleep. "Nobody else has a white china doorknob for a trunk handle! A white china doorknob, for Pete's sake! And every car he gets is worse than the last. I went along the last time and tried to get him to buy a decent one but no, we came home with that old wreck! We aren't that poor any more. You and I both baby-sit for spending money and Vi and Maggie aren't here to feed and clothe and Tante Kate gives them money."

"Not that much! He's applied for a defense job so maybe he won't be doing furnace jobs if he gets that but Laura, he's our Dad. He's the way he is!"

She sat there, tears streaming from her large green eyes, sobs wracking her slender body. "Jessie, you, Vi and Maggie can remember the time before the Depression but I don't. All my life I've worn hand-me-downs and had to watch our cousins doing things I wanted to do but couldn't afford and listened to our aunts and Cousin Sedelia make fun of Dad and how we live. Well, I'm telling you right now, when I get married or maybe even before, I'm going to own only the BEST of everything. I AM NEVER-EVER-GOING TO LIVE WITH A WHITE CHINA DOORKNOB FOR A TRUNK HANDLE and-and- I'll have my own bed! And furthermore, I'm not riding in that car until he gets a different trunk handle!" And she did not.

Fortunately, it did not rain often and she made it her business to get to school early. The defense job finally became a reality and the car was traded in for another, still a second-hand junker but this one with a conventional trunk handle.

Chapter 46

1940 turned into 1941. From time to time I had dated boys from high school and even one from church but none of them really held my interest. I could not, like Laura, look up into their eyes and declare how strong and manly they were. Maybe what I was seeking was more of a brother than a boyfriend.

I did enjoy being kissed, but when one or another of them tried to progress further, that was it. Good-bye. Thanks for the movie or the dancing but I don't happen to be "for sale." Not that there were so many dates that I was turning them down. Compared to Laura, who even made the mistake of dating two boys on the same day, forcing Mom and Tante Kate to entertain one until the other brought her home from an afternoon of bowling, my dates were few and far between.

All thoughts of Africa had been relinquished and replaced by the dream of my becoming a journalist. First, I must graduate from high school and then ahead was college. Luckily, the University of Wisconsin had an extension division in Milwaukee that offered courses in journalism and there was that money in trust.

My visits to Grandmother had slackened off with her latest stroke but by spring, she was up and around again. Her speech was a trifle slurred and her left foot very weak but her spirit was undaunted. She phoned to ask when I was coming for a visit. I promised to come on Saturday.

I found her in her back yard giving instructions to a male type person kneeling in front of one of her flower beds. When he turned and rose, I recognized him as the boy across the alley whose mother "helped out" at Grandmother's Christmas dinners. A boy no more; he was tall, well built and very good looking.

"You remember Keith Mueller…" introduced Grandmother.

"Not really. I think I remember you walked your mother home, on Christmas."

We nodded to each other as Grandmother introduced me as her "granddaughter, Jessica."

"Oh, the writer," Keith Mueller exclaimed. "Your grandmother told me about your ambitions along that line." His dark brown eyes looked down into mine and moved to take in the rest of me.

Blushing, I looked toward Grandmother, who was suddenly busy selecting a packet of seeds from her lap. "Here," she said, extending one to Keith, "these will do nicely along the fence. Jessie, would you be kind enough to run into the house and ask Mrs. Wellington to make us some nice, cold lemonade? This young man has volunteered enough of his services without refreshment."

Together the three of us sat in lawn chairs, sipped lemonade and nibbled on ginger snaps. I learned that Keith was already attending classes at the University Extension Division. He would someday be a certified public accountant, he explained. That is, after he did his stint in the Army."

"I leave as soon as the semester is over. The draft board gave me an extension."

"Oh. Then you won't be there in the fall when I start classes." I felt a strange disappointment. He was so easy to talk to; it would have been nice to know he was there, at school, especially when he said he was also interested in journalism.

Grandmother looked at her watch and declared, "It's just about time for the four o'clock. Why don't we go up on the bridge and catch a bit of steam?"

"Do you think you can make it that far, Mrs. Hohenfeldt?" Keith asked.

"Let's find out."

Together we helped her to her feet and assisted her to the front of the house but there she signaled for us to go ahead. "I'll just rest here on the steps until you return. Hurry, now, or you'll miss it!"

Taking my hand, Keith raced us up the arched footbridge. When the train came into view, we both waved and were answered with a cloud of white steam. *De ja vu* but not quite, for it was not with grandmother that I shared the experience but with a young man who made my heart beat faster.

Now it was not I who made trips out to Bay View but Keith who traveled to the north side to take me to movies and on long walks during which we talked on just about every subject, getting to know each other's likes and dislikes, sharing our hopes and dreams of the future.

In June, he was there to see me graduate. It was a time of pride and one of sorrow, for he would be reporting for duty at Fort Sheridan in a few days.

"I'll put in my year of service and then go back to school," he promised.

It was not to be. On December 7th, the Japanese bombed Pearl Harbor, and Mr. Roosevelt declared war on both Japan and Germany. Within two weeks, Keith, was shipped overseas. When he left, I wore his diamond.

Neither of us believed in a wartime marriage so he promised to hurry up with the war and return home as soon as possible. Meanwhile, life went on.

Vi had been delivered of a son and a bit later Maggie announced that she was also going to be a mother. Neither Tom nor Lee would be going into military service. Tom had a farm to run and Lee was found to have a ruptured ear drum. He took a defense job at Allis-Chalmers, where Dad worked.

So did I. My training was in office work but by taking a second shift factory job, I could still attend school. Without Keith, I was not interested in attending either movies or dances so I patriotically did my stint at work and spent an hour each night writing to him.

Christmas came and went, as did Valentine's day and Easter and then it was time for Laura to graduate. Proudly, we all sat in the auditorium of King High and the last of the Renz girls marched up in cap and gown to receive her diploma.

Laura and I took our last look at King High. We had both graduated with honors. We had kept our solemn promise and not disappointed those school board members who had given us the chance to attend classes there. Like me, Laura wrote a letter of thanks to mail in the morning.

As usual, I said my nightly prayers and asked for Keith's safety. My sleep was deep and undisturbed. At least I had that much.

The next day was Laura's graduation party. Keith's parents had been invited, so when their car drove up at noon, all I could think was that they had arrived early. Then I saw their faces and their tears of anguish and with a broken heart I read the telegram that had arrived a few hours before, one announcing that we would never again see those dark eyes smile into ours, never again hear Keith's beloved voice. He had died in action!

Somehow, my family got through that party but I did not attend. In a state of shock, I boarded a streetcar, transferred to the Bay View line and walked down Rusk Avenue to the familiar footbridge. It seemed a long time before the train approached. When it did, in the midst of a cloud of steam I screamed out my sorrow and rage! "ADOLPH HITLER! I HOPE YOU ROT IN HELL!"

For the rest of the years of steam engines, I could never see one without remembering that footbridge and the first kiss I had received while enveloped in a cloud of steam. It was there that Keith Mueller had placed his ring on my finger and promised to return to marry me.

My feet carried me to Grandmother's house, where I rushed past Mrs. Wellington to bury my head in Grandmother's lap and sob out my grief. I felt her hand stroking my hair and, looking up, saw her own tears wetting her wrinkled cheeks. She had watched Keith grow from a tiny boy to the wonderful, handsome man who had kissed her goodbye on that last day, when, in uniform, he had to proudly shown her the PFC stripe on his sleeve. He was not the first uniformed young man to do that; she had lost a son to war herself, Mama's brother Erwin, and previously another son to typhoid fever and her husband to a stroke as well as Mama, in a way, to her stiff-necked pride about Daddy.

As she must always have done in the face of diversity, with determined practiced gesture, Grandmother straightened her shoulders and back, cleared her throat and forced a smile to her quivering lips. Her cupped hand lifted my chin. Her still nicely tapered fingers brushed away my tears and she smiled and nodded encouragement.

"While Mrs. Wellington is making us a nice pot of tea, Jessie, you and I shall go out into the yard. There is something I want to show you." The housekeeper had been standing in the dining room, ready to help if help ware needed. Now she preceded us into the kitchen and out into the hall to assist her employer and long-time friend down the steps to the side door.

Grandmother led me to the flowerbed where I had first seen Keith as he knelt there, preparing the soil for seeds. Now there was a blaze of perennials in their second summer of growth, flowers that he had planted.

Following Grandmother's instruction, I went into the garage and returned with a bucket of small garden tools. At her coaxing, I lifted a sturdy bleeding heart plant from the earth. It went with me on the streetcar, wrapped in wet newspaper covered with wax paper as I returned home. Tom and I planted it beside the steps of the lake cottage where it thrived, it's pink hearts, arow on their slender stems.

Life continued on, somehow. Laura was working at Allis-Chalmers, too, in the office. I would continue on at the university in the fall…. Meanwhile, I still worked the second shift as an inspector of electrical parts that helped control the guns on ships. Each one had to be perfect. I passed nothing that was even slightly, imperfect. Those guns needed dependable parts; our men had to bring our country's enemies, Keith's murderers, to their knees. It was what I could do to avenge him.

On Sundays after church we used up precious gas coupons to drive out to the lake to dredge lilies. Dad had fashioned a rowboat from sheet metal, some of that still on hand from when he was doing furnace work. Now he worked in the welding department, had become very skillful with an acetylene torch, each seam and juncture was carefully welded. Like everything else, the rowboat was given a coat of aluminum paint. Amazingly, it floated.

He should have purchased wooden oars, however, instead of nailing hollow metal paddles to wooden handles. They allowed water to seep in, filling the paddles so that, when Lee took the boat out to the middle of the lake, they filled with water and were too heavy to lift from the water. Finally, imbedding themselves upright in the mud of the lake bottom, they refused to be budged and remained where they were, resembling, a pair of goal posts.

Clowning, Lee stood erect in the boat, both arms folded across his bare chest like an Indian chief, lily pad stems and leaves adorning the handkerchief he had tied around his head to keep the perspiration from dripping into his eyes. Silently, the oar-less boat glided along in a spring-fed current until it hit a patch of lilies and came to a halt. Lee stepped into the shallow water and towed the unwieldy craft back to shore amid hails of appreciative laughter.

From my vantage point atop the hill where I had been gathering a pail of raspberries and fighting off mosquitoes, I looked down on the scene at my family. Their laughter and bantering was what I had heard all of my life. No matter what had happened, they had always managed to somehow grin their ways through it and face the future. Now, in my sorrow, they were my strength. How I loved them!

I studied the cottage on wheels. Dad had probably fashioned the first metal mobile home. It had interchangeable windows, also his creation. Years later, metal rowboats would be in the fashion, though of aluminum and not sheet steel.

My gaze moved across the expanse of lilies to the other side of the lake. Someone was building a cottage there. Someday, probably, Mom and Dad would be able to build another cottage, possibly on another lake. Meanwhile, this one served the family well.

In the autumn, Tom and Vi had used it as a hunting cabin while they brought down ducks and geese, some of which graced our table at home. Vi had become an excellent sportswomen under Tom's tutelage and felt comfortable moving through the fields with a shotgun in the crook of her arm, a bevy of hunting dogs at her side. She enjoyed being a farm wife. She adored being a mother.

Soon Maggie, too, would be a mother. Dad had winched both her and Tante Kate down the hill. The two of them sat together on the railroad tie bench. Mom was walking back and forth, cooing to and cuddling her first grandchild.

There were clouds in the sky, fluffy ones, like flocks of newborn lambs… Everything seemed so normal. There was the feeling of continuity, of people living, of children being born and yes, of people dying. I wished Keith and I had married and that I had his child under my heart but we had not.

Someday …. What?

Standing there, I could not see into the future; could not know that one day another as dear would stand in Keith's place as we pledged our troth.

There would be a career in journalism, travel, and children who would have their own talents and their own futures and who would, as I had done, wonder, about what had come before.

My parents and all of Grandmother's generation would die and I would become a grandmother. I would also know widowhood and learn to carve out a new life for myself. I would look back and realize that, in growing up, we had not had "egg in our beer" but we had enjoyed a rich life. As Mama had predicted, if you looked on life as a series of new adventures then that is what it became. For me this would be true. Taking up my pail full of berries and rubbing my mosquito bites, I marched down the hill to take my place in the group below.

*** *** *** ***

Dear Reader,

The world keeps turning on its axis every twenty-four hours, orbiting the sun, year after year. Only a few of its millions of population will ever have known the Renz family. Still, isn't a life worth recording? The writer in me felt that it was. And so it has been..

Sincerely,

Jessica

CPSIA information can be obtained at www.ICGtesting.com
Printed in the USA
238159LV00006B/144/P

9 781456 337087